countless families. The characters really come to life. . . . Much of *Sun-flower Sisters* is heartbreaking . . . but there is also much hope and joy in the courage, fortitude and victories of those courageous and determined to succeed and survive. . . . Quite a family, well worth getting to know."

—Fredericksburg *Free Lance–Star*

"A well-researched, realistic narrative . . . It's the women and their activism that tell the story of the struggle to end slavery. They become the real heroes of the war."

—*The Spokesman-Review*

"Vibrant . . . a vivid, impeccably researched saga . . . page-turning."

—*Publishers Weekly*

"Kelly weaves a far-ranging tale of interlocking destinies and moving displays of kindness and bravery. . . . emotionally satisfying."

—*Library Journal*

"Ambitious . . . historical verisimilitude worthy of a Ken Burns documentary but oh so much more lurid."

—*Kirkus Reviews*

PRAISE FOR

LOST ROSES

—

"In an era crumbling under the weight of war, hatred, and devastation, the bonds of women not only endure but offer sustenance and hope in Martha Hall Kelly's stunning depiction of the lives of Eliza Ferriday and the women she fought to save. *Lost Roses* is not only a brilliant historical tale, but a love song to all the ways our friendships carry us through the worst of times."

—LISA WINGATE, *New York Times* bestselling
author of *Before We Were Yours*

"Remarkable . . . I'm still having difficulty believing that it's Martha Hall Kelly's debut novel. . . . Very rewarding [because] it truly brings to light just what happened to these women, and many others like them."
—Fredericksburg *Free Lance-Star*

"A compelling, page-turning narrative . . . falls squarely into the ground-breaking category of fiction that re-examines history from a fresh, female point of view." —Fort Worth *Star-Telegram*

"*Lilac Girls* is *Gone With the Wind* for World War II. . . . [This] is a book you cannot put down." —*The Martha's Vineyard Times*

"Intimate and appalling, and will keep you transfixed."
—*Historical Novels Review*

"Martha Hall Kelly has recovered a great story about a warmhearted, generous woman who should never have been forgotten."
—*Cosmopolitan Review*

"A remarkable and compelling new novel . . . The author imbues all her women with souls we can recognize on some level; it is lyric but accessible writing of the highest quality. . . . One of the best reads of 2016."
—LIZ SMITH, *New York Social Diary*

"This is not a book one puts down easily. . . . Kelly's vivid descriptions and careful research will stun even the most informed reader. . . . *Lilac Girls* is truly an incredible novel. . . . Easily the most affecting book I have read about World War II and the Holocaust, and I recommend it to any reader." —*Bookreporter*

"Kelly's debut brings historical facts to startling life. . . . [A] gripping read that lingers well after the book ends. Offer this to WWII aficionados, biography fans, and book clubs." —*Booklist*

BY MARTHA HALL KELLY

Lilac Girls

Lost Roses

Sunflower Sisters

Sunflower Sisters

SUNFLOWER SISTERS

A Novel

MARTHA HALL KELLY

BALLANTINE BOOKS

NEW YORK

2021 Ballantine Books Trade Paperback Edition

Copyright © 2021 by Martha Hall Kelly
Reading group guide copyright © 2021 by
Penguin Random House LLC

Published in the United States by Ballantine Books,
an imprint of Random House, a division of
Penguin Random House LLC, New York.

BALLANTINE and the HOUSE colophon are registered
trademarks of Penguin Random House LLC.
RANDOM HOUSE READER'S CIRCLE & Design is a
registered trademark of Penguin Random House LLC.

Originally published in hardcover in the United States
by Ballantine Books, an imprint of Random House,
a division of Penguin Random House LLC, in 2021.

Images courtesy of the Bellamy-Ferriday House & Garden Archives,
Bethlehem, Connecticut, owned and operated by Connecticut Landmarks.

ISBN 978-1-524-79642-6
Ebook ISBN 978-1-524-79641-9

Printed in the United States of America on acid-free paper

randomhousebooks.com
randomhousereaderscircle.com

246897531

Title-page art from iStock

Book design by Barbara M. Bachman

Map by Holly Hollon Designs

To my son, Michael, who traveled with me to Gettysburg.
And to all the mothers whose sons never returned.

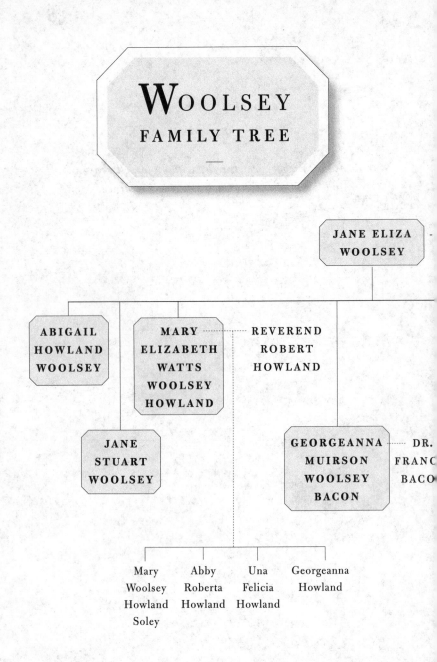

WOOLSEY FAMILY TREE

—

JANE ELIZA WOOLSEY

ABIGAIL HOWLAND WOOLSEY

MARY ELIZABETH WATTS WOOLSEY HOWLAND --- REVEREND ROBERT HOWLAND

JANE STUART WOOLSEY

GEORGEANNA MUIRSON WOOLSEY BACON --- DR. FRANC BACO

Mary Woolsey Howland Soley

Abby Roberta Howland

Una Felicia Howland

Georgeanna Howland

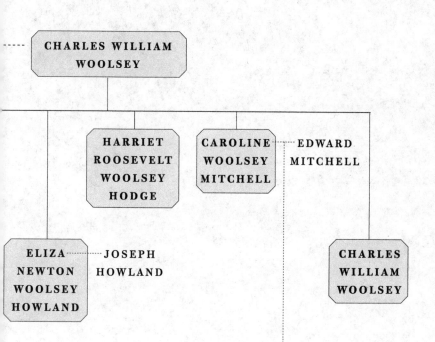

CHARLES WILLIAM
WOOLSEY

HARRIET
ROOSEVELT
WOOLSEY
HODGE

CAROLINE
WOOLSEY
MITCHELL

EDWARD
MITCHELL

ELIZA
NEWTON
WOOLSEY
HOWLAND

JOSEPH
HOWLAND

CHARLES
WILLIAM
WOOLSEY

Eliza Mitchell
Ferriday

Henry McKean
Ferriday

*Caroline Woolsey
Ferriday*

PART
ONE
..

Mary Woolsey

NO ONE SUSPECTED THE BLOND BOY'S CARGO AS HE DROVE his crude pony cart through the streets of Charleston.

Mother, my younger sister Georgy, and I had come to South Carolina by the invitation of Pastor Cox at the African Free Church for a two-day stay. We'd stepped out the previous morning past the mansion houses and palmetto trees, the atmosphere so gentle and refined, to make our daily calls and leave Mother's ecru cards on the silver trays.

Mrs. Charles Woolsey, 8 Brevoort Place, New York City.

Certainly nothing forced itself unpleasantly on our attention, but every black face in the street or greeting us so kindly at a front door reminded us of the system of slavery so robust there and strengthened our resolve to continue the fight.

Upon our walk home from Sunday services, the scent of crape myrtle in the air, a boy driving a pony cart drew up beside us dressed in a clean white shirt and homespun trousers. His rear wheel in disrepair, it bumped with every rotation, keeping his rate of speed not much greater than ours.

"We find ourselves a bit lost," Mother called to the boy. "Can you guide us to the Charleston Hotel?"

"I'm going that way, ma'am. Will point you there."

I warmed to his southern accent, a good-natured boy, milk-skinned, twelve years old or so, yellow hair shining in the sun. That brought to mind my own towheaded daughters, left back at the hotel with our friend Mrs. Wolcott, who no doubt stood near the door waiting for my return. Though we'd been gone less than two hours I missed them terribly as well.

"Where do you live?" Mother asked the boy.

"Here and there." He set his face toward the sun. "You? Sound like a Virginian."

Mother smiled, happy when someone recognized her accent from her former home. "Indeed I am. Left there when I was a girl but suppose I still speak with a trace of it. Live in New York City now. We are here as the guests of Pastor Cox at the African church. Do you know him?"

"No, ma'am."

We walked along, the only sound the thump of the broken wheel.

"It was a lovely celebration of the Eucharist," Mother said. "Over three hundred celebrants."

He turned and smiled. "Bet you was the only white folks there."

"Yes. But we were welcomed quite enthusiastically."

"Once, my ma had me in church every Sunday. She's dead now."

The boy pulled a piece of bread from a tin lunch bucket at his feet, took one bite, turned and slipped the rest under the tarp.

"Do you attend school?" Mother asked.

"No, ma'am. No school'd take the likes of me."

"I doubt that very much," Georgy said.

My attention was drawn to the back bed of the cart and the slightest movement beneath the tarp there.

"Where are you headed?" I asked.

He pointed to a white building up ahead. "The mart. Go every Sunday. Make my rounds on Saturday, come here the next day, so my stock's fresh."

"Rounds where?"

"All over, ma'am. Pa's regulars. Hardly ever come empty-handed."

The boy rode toward a white building with high black gates at the entrance and we followed. It was a hulking place, the word MART shining in gilt above the entrance, a crimson flag flapping in the breeze.

The boy pointed at a roof off in the distance. "Your hotel's up the road a piece and hang a right."

"You've been terribly helpful," Mother said.

The boy rode to the iron gates and a stout, red-bearded man, bamboo cane in hand, swung open the gate door.

"Hey, boy," he said, rapping his cane on the wood of the cart. "You're supposed to come round back with these, not to the front door, for pity's sake."

"Pa needs me home."

The boy turned in his seat up front and flung back the tarp. There within lay three colored children of varying ages, each dressed only in the crudest cloth diaper. The oldest, perhaps nine months old, held on to the cart edge and pulled herself up to standing.

"My God," I said.

The child reached her arms up to me in the universal baby language of love and goodness and I lifted her from the cart. I held her close and breathed in her heavenly baby scent, of milk and soap and innocence. Someone had taken loving care of her.

Upon the cart floor two infants lay upon the crude boards, one not more than a few days old.

The boy handed the gatekeeper a folded paper.

"Where are their mothers?" I asked, shaken through. "They've not a blanket among them. When did they last eat?"

The gatekeeper read the paper and then stepped to the cart. "All girls? Supposed to be one boy."

"Take it up with Pa," the boy said.

The gatekeeper bent over the cart and lifted out both infants. "One of 'em's runty."

The boy shrugged. "Just pick up what I'm told. That big one cried most the way here."

I held the girl closer and she settled her head upon my shoulder in a most tender way.

The gatekeeper handed the boy a folded stack of bills, which he tucked in his hip pocket, shook the reins, and started off.

The gatekeeper charged at me. "Don't have time to coddle the likes of you. Hand it over."

I stepped back. "I will not, sir."

"You northern women? What a pain in my ass. You got one hundred dollars to buy her?"

I reached for the purse at my wrist. "I can write you an IOU this minute."

As I reached aside, the man took his opportunity to wrench the child from my arms. She cried most piteously, reaching back, arms outstretched as the gatekeeper handed her to another filthy accomplice who carried her away at arm's length.

We tried to follow, but the gatekeeper clanged the gate shut, and through the bars said, "No ladies allowed at the sale. This is rough trade here, not for delicate sensibilities," and walked away into the crowd.

I wrapped one hand around an iron bar as I watched the children spirited back to a room beyond our view, one palm across my mouth to contain the horror of it all. What feeling human could hear those cries and not feel compassion to the quick? Three mothers sat somewhere in fresh agony without their precious girls.

I turned to Mother. "We spent all of yesterday calling on Charleston's best. We must appeal to someone."

Mother kept her gaze on the gathering crowd. "To *whom*? This is about money, Mary. These planters will never give up slavery willingly. We can only elect a president who will cut it off at its head."

All too familiar with the concept of slavery, we'd attended Dr. Cheever's lectures at the Cooper Institute, read *Uncle Tom's Cabin* many times over, and seen advertisements announcing slave sales in *The Charleston Courier* that morning. But nothing could have prepared us for seeing such a horrific spectacle in the flesh.

We examined the crowded market area with growing dread as the sale began, a low-ceilinged room, open to a rear yard where a brick building rose up, its barred windows crowded with dark faces. In the long room an auctioneer took his place upon a crude wooden platform, slapping his leather crop against his boot, the tense spirit of moneymaking in the air.

He seemed a ruffian, in his check trousers and shabby Panama hat, pulling at his tuft of yellow chin beard.

"Gentlemen, are you ready?" His voice echoed off the stone walls.

Groups of bidders clustered around the platform, gentlemanly looking men just such as we met every day at the hotel table, wearing their beaver top hats and beards of formal cut. Most held a cigar in one hand, the catalog printed with that day's human stock in the other.

The objects of the sale stood, in every shade of complexion, backs against the walls, being roughly examined. Groups of mothers and children stood near us, the women in good calico dresses and clean white pinafores and headscarves, children bareheaded.

We craned our necks to see into an anteroom off the main chamber, where men questioned the women, prying open their mouths, lifting their skirts, and exposing their most private parts.

"I saw such a sale in Richmond as a girl. Many masters sell their own colored children, and their own children begot of those daughters."

"And this is the nineteenth century," Georgy said.

"Tonight, not a steamer or row of train cars will leave this cruel city without its own sad burden of these unhappy ones."

Georgy linked arms with Mother. "We mustn't get complacent and accept it simply because it's the norm. Mrs. Wolcott knows the mayor. We must speak to him."

Mother moved her gaze to the auctioneer. "The mayor most likely buys and sells his slaves from here. It's all perfectly legal. Our urgings for freedom will fall on deaf ears and they will certainly have us carted off."

"We must also do something, now," I said. "Otherwise we condone it."

"I agree, Mary," Georgy said. "But it may take some stealth to do good here."

The gatekeeper prodded two young boys and a slightly older girl up onto the platform. The girl stood poised and well mannered as she watched the crowd with a guarded expression, an arm around each boy, her hair wrapped in the same white cloth the older women wore. The boys stared out into the crowd, too young to hide the terrible fear in their eyes.

The auctioneer presented them, arm extended, with an open palm.

"Boys—Scipio, age ten, Clarence, twelve—and girl, Sukey, fourteen. Girl, good housemaid, clean back. The boys bound to be prime field hands."

Just inside the gate stood a woman with an infant in her arms, another clinging to her skirts. She bowed her head and cried into one palm.

"Do you know those young ones?" Mother asked the woman, her voice low.

The woman wiped her eyes, cast a furtive glance toward the platform and then turned toward Mother. "My children, all," she said, barely above a whisper. "There, missis, that's mine on the stand now."

Mother pulled her shawl closer. "Dear God."

"That's my two boys and my girl, Sukey. She's not my blood, but I raised her. A good girl. Those boys love her fierce."

The woman clutched her infant closer and looked about.

"You can speak with us, madam, without fear," Mother said.

"I expect them to sell some off, but I just want to keep my two little ones here. They're too young to be without a ma."

"And your husband?" I asked.

"Sold. Months back."

"Where to?" Mother asked.

"Don't know, missis. It's hard having the old man drifted away. But what can I do? My heart's broke and that's all."

Buyers crowded the platform around Sukey and the boys.

"Take off her dress," one called out.

"Should've checked her earlier," the auctioneer said. "You know the rules."

The auctioneer yanked the girl's dress down off her shoulder and then grabbed her by the chin. "Smile, girl."

Sukey forced a smile.

"And look at those dimples. She could be a fancy girl one day."

The auctioneer lifted her hem to show her ankles and legs, but Sukey grabbed the skirt from his hand.

"What's the matter with her eyes?" one bidder called out.

"She's crying, that's all," the auctioneer said. "But she's fine."

"Sell the girl separate," one bidder said. "Six hundred for her."

"Sold—" the auctioneer called.

Sukey's brothers locked their arms around her waist. The auctioneer pulled them from her and the boys cried and fought him with fists.

Through the bars, Georgy passed the woman Mother's card, a twenty-dollar Liberty gold coin hidden beneath it. "Quickly. Take this."

"Oh, no, miss."

Georgy lowered the card down the iron rung of the gate, toward the woman's hand. "Here. No one will see. It isn't much, but it's all we have at the moment. If you can make it to New York City, come to the address here on the card for help."

The woman glanced about, then slipped both card and coin deep into her apron pocket. "Thank you, missis. Most kind. I'll keep it hid."

The gatekeeper approached and nudged the woman, babe in arms, and her young son toward the block.

She turned. "I'm called Alice," she said, as he prodded them more urgently up the platform steps.

"I don't know if she'll ever be free to find Brevoort Place," Mother said.

"It's something at least," I said.

Alice slowly mounted the steps with her two children and gathered them to her. The auctioneer gave his usual recitation, suggesting a separate price for Alice and her children, and the gavel quickly fell.

"Sold," called the auctioneer. "One hundred dollars for James and the infant, Anthony. Alice, nine hundred dollars."

Alice fell to her knees in front of the auctioneer, begging to keep her children.

Mother turned away in terrible temper, heading up Chalmers Street toward the hotel, and we followed, the misery of those sold still keen in our minds, Alice's frantic wails echoing around us, her agony beyond sympathy.

I'd seen that look before on Mother. After Father died, leaving her with eight children to raise. When we cried as she moved us all to strange New York City.

The look that said, *We will change this terrible situation. Or die trying.*

Georgy

BREVOORT PLACE, NEW YORK CITY

APRIL 1861

UNCLE EDWARD DROPPED ME AT THE NEW YORK HOSPITAL, A massive, stone wedding cake of a place, an oasis of calm after our carriage fought its way down Broadway, the street teeming with frantic citizens mobilized by the prospect of impending war.

Hours earlier, the day had started as any other. I stood during breakfast in the dining room at our home at 8 Brevoort Place, a four-story brownstone-fronted town house on the east side of Manhattan, as my sister Jane fixed the fallen hem of my new dress, a black silk simply relieved in white.

Mother sat at the table, closest to the fire, clothed in her morning dress, directing Margaret, one of our two day maids, in her white servant's cap and apron, where the hot dishes should go. Only three of my six sisters, Abby, Jane, and Carry, were gathered there that day, with Mary and Hatty off traveling and Eliza at her country home.

Abby, the eldest, sat next to Mother, bent over her correspondence.

Jane, her next in age, crouched at my feet, intent on my fallen hem, her black sewing box with the mother-of-pearl flowers splayed open beside her on the carpet, a surgical kit of needles and threads, ten shades of white alone.

I smoothed back her red-blond hair, which waved down past her shoulders and always brought to mind Botticelli's Venus. "Do hurry, Jane."

She pulled at my skirt. "Stay still, Georgy, or I'll draw blood."

Our youngest sister, Carry, sat on Mother's other side, feeding our little white mongrel dog, Pico, scraps of doughnut.

"Frank Bacon will like that dress," Carry said.

I brushed a phantom speck off my skirt. "I'm not interested in Frank Bacon in the least."

Abby looked up from her letter. "You shun a perfectly good beau when others go without."

"Marry him yourself, then."

Color rose in Abby's cheeks and I instantly regretted those words. At thirty-three years old, Abigail had long since stopped waiting for our dear cousin Theodore Winthrop to propose; and at thirty-one, Jane no longer had any prospects either—her suitors had all married others or joined the military in preparation for war or drifted off to Europe. So it was generally believed Abby and Jane would never marry.

"He won't come around forever," Abby muttered.

"With that little beard of his cut so short, he looks like an Italian king," I said.

The trill of the doorbell sounded from the front of the house, sending our devoted Margaret, cap ribbons fluttering, out to answer it, as we froze like startled elk at the idea of a morning visitor invading our sacred space.

"At this hour?" Mother asked.

In seconds Uncle Edward bounded in, folded *New York Tribune* in one hand. Uncle was always welcome, a fine man whose name was repeated with praise by all who knew him, his only two faults a touch of vanity and a bit of a loose tongue. His bright appearance was so like Father's had been, his honest blue eyes full of charity and love. He even dressed as Father had, in quality cutaway coats, his pant legs nicely tailored, accentuating his well-rounded calves.

Mother nodded to him. "Oh, Edward, it's you. Do sit."

"I'm on my way to the club—can't stay long. What *news*. It's pandemonium out there. How can you all be so calm?"

"Have a cup of tea. Jane found sugar harvested in Haiti without the cruelty of slavery."

"Certainly you've heard?" he asked, looking from one of us to the next.

Carry leaned in, her hair ribbon dangling close to the syrup on her griddle cakes. "Heard what, Uncle?"

"I know you've been following the events in South Carolina closely. . . ."

"Yes," Abby said.

"Word just in from Charleston gives the profound impression—"

"Uncle, *please*," Abby said.

"—that Fort Sumter has been fired upon."

Carry jumped up as if stung. "We're at war!"

"Confederates fired the first shot at four-thirty, before sunrise, upon the national flag. Major Anderson is withdrawing from the island. The citizens of Charleston stood on rooftops and cheered."

Jane tied off her thread and tossed the little scissors into her sewing box with a clatter. "So the South is indeed seceding. It's all so upsetting."

"Which states will stay with the Union?" Mother asked.

"All the Northern states have sent dispatches to President Lincoln offering money and men. Maryland and Kentucky have yet to declare."

Mother stood. "Margaret, bring the mahogany table down from my room. And the lint press. We will set up in the front parlor. There will be great need for bandages."

Uncle Edward walked toward the rear hallway to the bedroom stairs. "Where's your son? Still abed so late?"

Mother stepped into his path. "What do you need with Charley?"

"Well, he may want to enlist. There's already a center up on Broadway. The Winthrop brothers will join, I'm sure."

"His cousins are grown men, Edward. Charley is just twenty-one. You want to encourage your poor, dead brother's only son?"

Uncle Edward tossed the newspaper onto the table and Carry snatched it up. "They've been calling for nurses all week in case of war. Recruiting this morning at the hospital."

"Nurses? I've never heard—"

"We're at *war*, Mother," Abby said.

I stepped toward Uncle Edward. "I'm applying."

Abby dropped her pen. "Goodness me, Georgy. A *nurse*? They make female convicts do that work. Ten days in jail and then it's off to nurse at Bellevue."

"This is different," I said. "Dr. Elizabeth Blackwell is involved. I've read the notices in the paper all week. Preparing a brigade of trained nurses."

"All nonsense," Jane said.

I slid my gloves from the mantel and tried to avoid the sight of the ivory-handled fan, fanned out like a peacock's tail, displayed there in the glass box Mother had made for it. The thank-you to Father and me for our actions that day on the beach.

I turned to face Carry. "It is all very proper. Overseen by a committee of esteemed doctors. And who will stop me, with none of you yet dressed?"

Uncle Edward touched my forearm. "Georgy, it is not a pastime for a refined young woman. Assisting crude soldiers with their bedpans—"

"I couldn't care less about being refined, Uncle."

Abby looked to Mother. "She'll catch something dreadful."

"I'm twenty-eight. I can manage myself, thank you. Besides, Eliza serves as a nurse up in Fishkill."

Mother hurried to me and smoothed one hand down my back. "Eliza bandages the locals and hands out tonics. This is *war*, Georgy dear. Isn't it best we stay together through this?"

I tried not to look at Mother's careworn face or meet her steely gaze; she was always able to woo me with her kindness and platitudes. Jane Eliza Woolsey was a smart opponent, formidable in her tenderness and grace. "There are many other ways to contribute to the cause, here at home," she said.

I smoothed two fingers down her powdered cheek. How could I tell her I'd go mad here on the sidelines, in this dear old house filled with reminders of Father, as the whole world marched off to war?

"I will not just sit here, Mother."

Carry held up the newspaper. "There's a whole list of nursing qualifications in here and you have none of them."

I pulled on my bonnet with the pink rosebud face trimmings and tied the ribbons under my chin. "I've seen it."

Carry read from the paper. *"In order to earn the coveted blue ticket, candidates must possess the grace to submit to firm discipline—"*

Abby laughed. "May be challenging for someone Father called his wild child—"

"—and the willingness to wear very plain regulation nursing costume."

"Certainly wear that French bonnet for the committee," Jane said. "It marks you as a fly-away for sure."

"Stay, dear," Mother said. She caressed the golden locket she wore on a chain around her neck, mourning jewelry she'd worn for Father, a jeweled spider embedded in the cover. "Think how those who've gone before us would be pleased by our war work safe here at home."

"I'll be perfectly safe, Mother."

"You can't walk to the hospital alone," Abby said.

I stepped toward the door. "Since I am his favorite, Uncle Edward will surely drop me on his way to the club, won't you, Uncle?"

Uncle Edward studied the floor and barely nodded.

"Father wouldn't have wanted this," Carry said.

Father. I stopped and turned to her. "How would you know what Father would have wanted, Carry? You were an infant when he died."

Carry looked down at her plate, and I caught a glimmer of a tear. I'd gone too far again.

I hurried to the door.

Abby pushed back her chair and stood. "Every Florence Nightingale in New York will be there, competing. And they'll only take a small number."

"One hundred, actually. And I'm bound to be first in line, thanks to the early hour."

Uncle Edward and I stepped down the hall, past the front parlor to the door.

"You need to be over thirty years old," Carry called after me. "And quite plain. You're not anywhere near ugly enough!"

I STEPPED INTO THE marble-columned hospital hall and found it nearly full with my fellow early risers. Women from all walks of life packed the chilly room, a lucky few seated on the oak benches, most standing, some with a child or two in tow. A woman dressed in a long gray cape, her doughy, round face remarkably like Mary Todd Lincoln's, distributed applications and pencils.

"A line, please, ladies," she called out over the crowd, exhaling a little white cloud as she spoke.

"Why is there no fire lit in here?" I asked.

"If we had male applicants, there would be." She handed me a two-page application and a small pencil. "If you can complete this quickly, you may have a chance to get in right away—a candidate just dropped out, sick with fear about going before the doctors' panel, poor thing. Wait down that hall to be called into the committee room."

I glanced at the forms. "It says 'Complete in ink.'"

She shrugged. "The committee hasn't complained yet. And they've seen fifty applicants already today. Accepted twenty-three."

I penciled in my name and address: *8 Brevoort Place, New York City*. Surely that would please the examining board, an esteemed address, near the famous Brevoort hotel. I stopped, pencil in midair. *Age*. Of course, I was well underage, two years in fact. What if I stretched the truth and wrote *30*? I left it blank.

The woman leaned closer. "Don't say I told you, but they're looking for head nurses—matronly sorts who won't rouse the affections of the patients with fancy fashion and smiles." She sent a pointed look toward my necklace. "Last lady who went in there wore earbobs and they cast her out quick as she got in."

"This is a family piece I wear every day. I'll take my chances."

"And what about that bonnet? Not to overstep, but those flowers—"

I hurried toward the committee room as I ripped the tender French rosebuds off my bonnet and tucked them up my sleeve.

After waiting in the hallway for what felt like an eternity, I heard my name called and stepped in to stand before the board. There sat five men, most of them snow-haired and dressed in black suits, sitting broomstick straight behind two oak tables pushed together, a tented paper name tag before each.

I handed Dr. Harris the application.

"Good day, Miss . . . Woolsey, is it? Would you state your full name?"

"Georgeanna Muirson Woolsey."

"And why, Miss Woolsey, would you like to join the ranks of the Women's Central Association of Relief?"

"I wish to make an equal contribution to that of a soldier, sir."

Two doctors to my far right exchanged glances.

"That may be impossible, Miss Woolsey," Dr. Harris said. "Since you will not be on the battlefield."

"I don't know why I shouldn't be, sir. It seems unfair they will be dying while I sit home."

"Tell us your particulars, Miss Woolsey."

"If you can tell me what particulars you are interested in."

Two doctors examined what appeared to be a restaurant menu, while another cleaned out his pipe, tapping the bowl on his palm.

"Well, would you consider yourself a detail-oriented person?" Dr. Harris asked.

"Yes, Doctor."

"How so, Miss Woolsey?"

"I wouldn't, for example, ask an applicant to sign an application such as this in ink if only a pencil was provided." The doctors shifted in their seats. "Or leave the great hall out there unheated when women and children wait there, some for hours."

Dr. Compton laced his fingers and sat forward. He looked younger than the rest and wore a prominent brow, and a permanently pained expression. "An unheated hall will be nothing compared to some of the unpleasant conditions you would be expected to work in, Miss Woolsey."

"Only martyrs tolerate hardship when simple solutions can be found, Dr. Compton. I do my best to solve problems."

He leaned back and folded his arms across his chest. "It's just a matter of time before you and your fellow nurses will be switching things over with your hoops, giving unlimited oranges to the men with dysentery, and making the sure surgeons mad."

"I don't wear a hoop, Dr. Compton."

"And what of your education, Miss Woolsey?" Dr. Harris asked.

"As a child I attended Miss Murdock's School in Boston, and then the Rutgers Female Institute here in Manhattan, and finished at the Misses Anables' Young Ladies' Seminary in Philadelphia, whereupon I traveled to India and Egypt with my younger sister Eliza."

"Ah, a Grand Tour?" Dr. Harris asked.

"Men have done it for centuries. In my family women broaden our horizons as well."

"Your school marks?" Dr. Compton asked.

"Quite good, Dr. Compton. On my commencement day our teacher Mr. Holan joked to Mother that if she did not remove her daughters from the school the trustees would not be able to afford to give any more medals."

Several of the doctors twittered at that.

"Languages?" Dr. Harris asked.

"German, French, Latin, and Italian. I learn quickly and the thought of having a teacher like Dr. Elizabeth Blackwell is most stimulating, sir. The first woman to earn a medical degree in this country? It would be a tremendous honor to be in the same room with her. I've entertained the notion of opening a nursing school of my own some—"

Dr. Compton leaned in. "A school for female nurses?"

"Is that such a foreign concept?"

"And what of our dedicated male nurses? Should they go home and knit?"

"They can do as they like, Dr. Compton. Perhaps join their brothers in battle."

"Were you raised with servants in the home?" Dr. Harris asked.

"Kate, the cook; Margaret, a maid; faithful William in the pantry is—"

Dr. Compton straightened his cuffs. "Must we hear the entire household staff list?"

"Mother employs help, but I've always been expected to perform domestic tasks."

Dr. Harris sifted through his papers. "Nursing is hard work, especially for someone not used to adversity and so, well, *privileged*. Do you cry easily?"

"I don't cry, Doctor. *Ever*, in fact."

Dr. Benson raised an eyebrow.

"We are looking for women who are not averse to plainness of dress," Dr. Compton said. "You know nurses are not allowed to wear jewelry of any kind."

I glanced down at the bodice of my dress, to Father's brass watch fob I wore as a necklace. "I wear this so often it is a part of me."

Dr. Harris gathered the papers of my application and tapped them on the table. "I'm afraid we are done here, Miss Woolsey."

I touched the fob. "I will not wear this while tending patients, gentlemen. It is my father's watch fob. I've worn it every day since he died. I was very young when it happened. We lived in Boston at the time and he perished at sea commuting from New York to Boston on the steam packet *Lexington*."

Dr. Harris set down his pen.

"It was a terribly cold night, the mercury at ten degrees below zero, and floating ice filled Long Island Sound. The alarm of fire was given as flames spread through the cotton bales in the ship's cargo bay. Of the crew and one hundred forty-three passengers, only four survived. My father was not among them."

The doctor at the far end of the table leaned in. "You have our deepest sympathies, Miss Woolsey."

"The brass letters here on the fob represent the seven daughters he left behind—my sisters and me. My brother, Charles, was born soon after."

Dr. Harris removed his glasses. "Your father never knew he had a son."

"It's not something that leaves one with a sense of privilege, I assure you, Doctor. I've worked night and day since his death to help my mother, to shoulder the burdens of housekeeping and make her life easier."

Dr. Harris sat silent for a moment. "How does your family feel about you pursuing this line of work?"

"They vigorously oppose it, but their opinions have never stopped me before. In fact, nothing will stop me from dedicating everything to my country, sir, and if need be, giving my life to keep it united and free of the scourge of slavery. I think my father would applaud it."

The doctors sat silent until Dr. Harris came to life. "Miss Woolsey, I must ask you to give us a few moments of privacy while we deliberate."

I stepped out into the hallway and stood, my back against the cool stone wall, and reviewed my answers. Dr. Compton would certainly vote against me. I closed my eyes and could only see Abby's I-told-you-so face when I came home without my blue ticket.

After what felt like an age, Dr. Harris called me back into the examination room.

"Miss Woolsey, have you had the measles?"

"I have, Doctor."

He handed me my application. "In that case, Miss Georgeanna Muirson Woolsey, it is my honor, on behalf of Dr. Elizabeth Blackwell and this board, to award you a place in the first training program at the Women's Central Association of Relief for the purpose of providing the army with trained nurses. You have impressed us, almost unanimously, with your strong character and resolve, and it is our opinion you will be a credit to the association. May God protect you."

"Thank you, Doctors."

I took the application and left with haste, hoping they would not change their minds, and hurried out through the great hall, bumped and jostled as I stepped through the horde of women coming and going. I found a quiet place to unfold and read the application, signed with Dr. Harris's impressive signature and straight-pinned at the top with the famous blue ticket, upon which was written *student number 24*.

Before I refolded it, I noted the age space was still blank and, at long last, allowed myself a smile.

———

THEN BEGAN SERIOUS BUSINESS. I sprang out of bed each morning at five o'clock to report to the New York Hospital for fourteen days of classroom training and another ten of hospital rounds with Dr. Blackwell and others. I spent every minute of the doctor's classes rapt, taking in her stories of her own struggle to become a physician, and her painful details of how she lost her eyesight in one eye while treating an infant at a hospital in Paris.

"Learn from my mistake," she said. "Handle patient sanitary needs with the utmost vigilance."

I enjoyed memorizing bandaging technique, regimens of ward care, and vast classifications of medicines. Dr. Blackwell stood before all one hundred of us in a small amphitheater classroom, dark hair pulled back in a white snood, a passionate speaker. She had lost her father at a young age and was a staunch abolitionist, which made me feel even more connected to her.

Once the session adjourned, I stood with two of my fellow students outside the classroom.

"She is quite an engaging teacher," one said.

"I've never heard anyone so supportive of the female cause," I said. "Maybe she'd consider teaching one day at my nursing school."

"*Your* nursing school?" The two laughed and one pulled me closer. "It's one thing for Dr. Blackwell to teach us bandaging and bed making just for the war."

"Quite another to start a permanent school for female nurses," said the other. "Once the men return after the war, they won't appreciate you instructing ladies to take their jobs."

As the two hurried off to our next class, Dr. Blackwell emerged from the classroom and closed the door behind her. I tried, but could barely form a sentence in her presence.

"Don't listen to naysayers," she said as she locked the door. "You're head and shoulders above them, and those who discourage you do so to justify their own lack of imagination and will never accomplish anything extraordinary."

I tried to speak, but barely croaked, and the doctor continued.

She turned to face me. "When I first decided to pursue medicine, I was told that strong prejudice would exist, which I must either crush or be crushed by, and I offer the same advice to you, Miss Woolsey. Don't be afraid. Train your army of lady nurses."

She started off down the hall and called back over her shoulder, "And I would happily teach at that new school of yours someday."

NEARLY A MONTH LATER, Dr. Blackwell's words still ringing in my ears, I hurried toward the hospital for my last day of rounds that determined whether I received my graduation certificate. I quickened my step as thousands of flags suddenly came fluttering out of every window and door. The city was brilliant with excited crowds, the air full of the sound of incessant patriotic bands and the footfall of regiments.

I felt quite official in my new nurse's costume. My family had come around enough to the idea of me as a nurse to help fit me out for hospital duty in a gray skirt, cropped jacket, white apron, and washable petticoat, which swished as I walked.

My practical training thus far had been a baptism by fire—I'd been thrown into an enormous ward with one other nurse associate, and put in charge of it all—but I was finally comfortable commanding a shift. Several of my fellow students had dropped out of the course or had been dismissed due to excessive squeamishness or unpleasant temper. Those of us left were competent to any very small emergency or simple fracture. I said a silent prayer as I walked that nothing would happen to derail my course completion.

I found one of our instructors, young Dr. Prentiss, just in time, as he began his rounds. He stood at the bedside of a gray-faced male patient who wore an adhesive plaster applied to the side of his neck.

"For your last day of instruction, I've chosen a particularly interesting case. A gangrenous dog bite to the neck. The wound is suppurating and shows laudable pus, similar to those you may someday see on the battlefield. Let's begin." He glanced in my direction. "Nurse, basin."

I hurried to the sideboard, excited to prove myself capable of assisting with such a wound.

He called after me. "Never run, Nurse. Keep calm at all times. That will serve you well in the most chaotic of wards."

I walked back and handed the basin to the doctor. He held it to the man's neck and pulled back the plaster, releasing a putrid odor that caused my stomach to turn. I steadied myself against the bedpost.

"Would someone kindly provide Miss Woolsey a chair?" the doctor called out.

"I'm perfectly fine, Doctor," I said, though the room began to spin.

"Please yourself, Miss Woolsey," Dr. Prentiss said.

He turned back to the patient and began to probe deep into the wound, causing the patient to cry out in pain. I leaned toward the bedpost but could not reach it before my knees gave way and the world grew dark around me.

Jemma

I RAN ABOUT THE FRONT PARLOR THAT MORNING, POKING THE turkey-feather duster up the picture frames and down the ivory keys of the big old piano nobody played, hoping the dust would stay in the air long enough for the wedding to happen, and keep Miss Anne-May happy as she could be. It was bad enough six new slaves from South Carolina were marrying in her house. If she saw dust on her piano, in the fanciest room in the place, she'd use her leather on me, no matter it was the Lord's day.

Sunday was my favorite day, when I got to leave the house and visit my kin at the cabin down the bottom of the hill, when Ma combed out my hair, my head in her lap, and Pa saved a funny story to act out just for me, and Sally Smith fixed me an ashcake with her quince jelly on top.

I squeezed my eyes tight shut and asked Jesus, "Please let this wedding go fast so I have time with Ma and Pa back in the cabin. And please send another girl my age with this group."

Sweet Clementine, last girl my age, was gone before I got a chance to know her, whipped by Anne-May so bad she ran away to the swamp, where LeBaron and his pattyroller boys finally found her, dead for days. They left her out behind the hog pen as a lesson to us, poor girl all puffed up and bit all over by any swamp thing that flew or crawled, until Pa made one of his pine boxes and those that LeBaron let off work buried her.

But least she was free.

I waited for Anne-May, dressed by me that morning, but still putting on her finishing touches, meaning drinking a cordial glass of brandy she thought nobody knew about, while she stared at her new diamond ring.

I stood on my toes to fly the feathers along the gold mirror with the painting of ships and along the fireplace mantel to the flat-faced white china dogs that don't look like any dogs I've ever seen and the sky-blue flower vases painted with gold and half-naked ladies, so precious to Anne-May she never put any flowers in them.

I stood before Aunt Tandy Rose's portrait, her looking down on me, in her white bonnet and the usual sour face. I knew Tandy Rose best, since I was her eyes and especially her ears because toward the end she was deaf as a stump without the ear trumpet Pa made her.

Most folks had considered her a fine, churchgoing woman, who only reminded us slaves of our place every so often, under her strict rules. But she could be mean as any and sure took it to Carter before she sold him off. Took it to me now and then, too. Though she tired easy, being so old, she striped me once for reading her newspaper, which hurt like nothing I'd ever felt, since she could get up a proper crack with her little whip. My back felt on fire for days and I could only sleep on my belly, but it left me with the impression there must be something special in that paper to read.

We all prayed thanks she never let LeBaron whip any of us, except runaways, since when he came there when I was little, he was famous for miles around for his rough way of breaking in new slaves and she didn't want him "killin' her investments."

Tandy Rose especially looked out for Ma. She was the old lady's out-and-out favorite, Ma bein' so pretty, plus nobody got Tandy Rose ready each Sunday like Ma, powdered and primped, hair done just so, and got her showered with compliments from the other ladies at church. 'Course all that changed once Anne-May came, since she was full-on jealous of anyone a hair prettier than her.

I ran the feathers down each windowpane, the lazy Patuxent River in the distance, the water deep blue as the indigo dye squeezed from the tall plants that grew near the banks. We were well into spring, Aunt Tandy Rose's favorite time when she was alive. I got to sleep with Ma and Pa every night back when we belonged to Aunt Tandy Rose and thanked Jesus for that. Even after the bad thing happened to my little brother Toby, we still had each other.

Old Sally Smith the cook lived at Peeler her whole life and was cooking here already when Ma and Pa came to that house from Georgia, and Sally became like a mother to Ma. They even looked the same—heart-shaped face and wide-spaced pretty eyes, and Sally taught Ma all her remedy plants in her garden inside the high fence Pa made, nigh to the cabin.

Aunt Tandy Rose called Sally Smith her root doctor and loved Sally's garden where she grew herbs and fruit trees and a truck patch of yams and onions just for us. She had every remedy for what ailed anybody, like peach tree leaves for worms, stinky Devil's Dung for colds, and Everlasting Bone-set for her lung fevers and to ward off ghosts, even grew belladonna for Aunt Tandy Rose to rouge her cheeks with and poppies for her opium.

Sally was not so skinny as the rest of us, from years of standing at her iron stove, sinking her tasting spoon into crayfish bisque and turtle soup, but hers was a lap to soften even the worst day's ills and troubles, the clove and sugar baked right into her.

Both Ma and Pa were barely my age now when they married. Pa asked Aunt Tandy Rose's go-ahead and she got them married in the white people's church one Monday afternoon. Once I came along, with my twin sister, Patience, Aunt Tandy Rose taught us our letters, and did the same for little Toby when he arrived, so we could read to her from her favorite leather books and Bible once her eyes got bad.

I learned to write by taking down Sally Smith's grocery list, copying the names off tins and boxes in the pantry, since Sally had no use for learning her letters. *Preston and Merrill yeast powder* was first thing I wrote perfect. Then *Welch's Female Pills,* which Tandy Rose took with brandy. *Old Partner Kentucky Tobacco,* the leaf Fergus favored over his own. Seemed everything in that pantry claimed it was "Best in the world."

Tandy Rose turned a blind eye when she caught Patience and me reading books from her library, which led LeBaron to come over and raise his voice to her, him on his horse and her out on her sittin' porch.

"I'll get the sheriff over here, you keep lettin' your coloreds break the law that way, Miss Tandy Rose. You don't want to be the downfall of our peculiar institution, do you now?" Then he muttered something about her bein' a Negro-spoiler.

Aunt Tandy Rose set down her ear trumpet, drew all eighty pounds of herself up, and tossed her glass of milk at him, which hit him in the back and dripped all down in his saddle. "You work for me, Mister Caruthers. I will do things *my* way. And no sheriff will say boo to me about it."

Aunt Tandy Rose taught me what Ma called my "White People Manners" so I could make her feel at home in the house when she had me fetch things. Words like, "Why certainly, Miss Peeler." "Let me get that for you right away, ma'am." "That will be but a moment, miss." And always with a sugary smile at the end, and a tip of the head.

And she let Patience and me go to Sabbath school, where they taught us slaves about the good book, for a few days before they shut it down. Went with some of the boys from Ambrosia Plantation next door, where my sister's lent out now and with my almost-sweetheart Carter, who got sold off two years ago. Tandy Rose even promised Pa up and down to free us when she went to the great beyond, and showed him the letter saying so.

But somehow that letter got lost once they laid Aunt Tandy Rose out on a mahogany plank right there in that very room, and just like that we belonged to her about-to-be-married niece, Miss Anne-May Wilson, who inherited the house and us. Pa said, *God don't always work to plan and we'll just find another way out.* But it still stuck like a rock in my craw that Tandy Rose took so long to free us and we were still somebody's property.

First difference we saw with our new mistress, Miss Anne-May, is she pretended most times like she didn't even see us. Then she put an end to my White People Manners and had me only say, "Yes, missis," when she tasked me.

Soon after came the new rules. She locked up the library, saying colored folks have no business reading nothing. At first I didn't learn her rules fast enough and she'd get out her cowhide, long as your arm, or

Anne-May's other favorite, a fresh hickory switch. Soon the backs of my dresses got shredded, the cotton stuck to the blood, and I did my work all day feeling like a hundred bees got me. Seems I made ten new dresses that first month. Kept the old ones, though, in my ragbag. Never know what you can do with things.

Then she got smart and made me shimmy out of my dress before she got to work on me in the pantry. No matter what they say, no one ever gets used to the deep, hot sting of a whip. Especially with Anne-May so proud of her special way, so long and hard she took to her bed after, and with vinegar poured on the cuts for extra hurt. Especially having never felt it like that before she came. Especially seeing my ma on her knees get it first time ever.

That made me want to kill Anne-May right there. Could tell Pa wanted that, too.

But we all knew the penalty in Maryland for a slave murdering somebody. The state constitution said the one doing the deed would have their right hand cut off, would be hanged in the usual manner, have their head severed from their body and divided in four quarters, and set in the most public place in the county where the act was committed.

But some days it still felt worth killing Anne-May anyway.

At the sound of wheels on gravel, I threw down my duster, hustled next door to the study, and looked out the window just as the two-horse wagon pulled up, with the seven new folks sitting in the back, all brown of complexion, with the usual looks of people scared of a new place, the overseer Caruthers up driving.

He was something to be scared of, LeBaron Caruthers, sitting out in his foul little cabin butted up next to the tobacco barn. Medium fat and dirty all over, especially his mind. From his perch on the wagon seat, he spied me through the window with his pig eyes, but I looked away.

I got my notebook fast, since Miss Anne-May had me write an account of each of the new ones for her, and if it's not perfect that's trouble. She didn't want us reading, but she was no good with a pen, so I had to write things down for her. She had me list each of the new folks' old names, their new name she chose (one Miss Anne-May liked better), a guess at their age, who they'd be marrying, and "one characteristic feature to know them by." Three would live with us here at Peeler, the others over cross the county at Mister Watson's beet farm. It was nowhere near enough hands to get our usual tobacco crop in, but we prayed for more soon.

I'd already sewed their new name into the dress or shirt collar of the garment I made, what I'd guessed to be the right size, based on what I knew about each one. Though most of these were field hands and got the meanest, cheapest white homespun, I made each dress and loose shirt with care and put Canton felt inside the cuffs and collars, since it's a hard day, coming here to live with Anne-May. At least one part of it could be soft.

"Why can't they marry who they want?" I asked Sally one day as I stood sewing in the kitchen, since no colored folks were allowed to sit with the Watsons in the house. Sally Smith was making her cornbread kush, the onions sizzling in the lard making my belly grumble. More food Anne-May would not eat herself and just toss to the hogs.

Anne-May walked in as I asked, and for a second my blood raced when she started her hand toward the cowhide hooked at her waist, but I settled quick, knowing she'd never give it to me out in the open, in front of old Sally Smith. Sally's ancestors had lived at Peeler for over a century and she also had major sway with Mister Watson, since he liked her, you could tell, and no one could keep his belly full of his favorites like her.

But Anne-May just said, "Every time you open your mouth a stupid question comes out, Jemma. Not that I owe you an answer, but it's the way my mama did it in New Orleans. One weddin' upon arrival, so we can get it over with. Otherwise there's a party practically every *week,* for goodness' sake, and no work gets done and it costs good money to do these things, which is barely appreciated by you colored folks."

But of course the real reason she married everybody off first day was so they'd fasten up quick with each other and bring about a bunch of children she could work to the bone or sell off.

I reminded myself to tell the new ones there'd be hell to pay if they called themselves Wilson or Watson. "You are owned by me," Anne-May told me a hundred times, "but don't you dare take my name. You tell folks your name is Jemma, owned by Miss Anne-May Wilson Watson, of Peeler Plantation, formerly of New Orleans, Louisiana."

I stood straighter, pencil ready, as the first girl stepped down, name written in fat block letters pinned to her dress, *Cynthia*. Her new name, given by Anne-May, was Fidelia. Fidelia was nice, you could tell by her quick, shy smile and hair tied up on her head like five puffy little clouds. Her characteristic feature was a perfectly good, working body except for one hand missing, a smooth little stump there instead. I checked which one, the left, and made note of it. She turned and I saw another characteristic feature: a couple months' worth of baby in her belly.

I penciled in another line. *Fidelia's Baby*. I bit back a smile and crossed fingers I could take care of it like I had with little Toby.

Next to come down the wagon steps, after a shove from Overseer Caruthers, was her soon-to-be husband. The name pinned to his shirt was *Benjamin*. Now he'd be Charlemagne, on account of Anne-May's love of all things royal and rich, but right off, we shortened it to Charl. He was skinny as Fidelia and looked as sad as Fidelia looked kind, holding himself like he's cold all the time. Charl had two characteristic features: a scraggy little beard and ears big as oyster shells, and I put down *25* as age for both those two, a big guess, but better than nothing.

My chest thumped hard as number three stepped down, a girl about my size, maybe a little taller, *Sukey* pinned to her dress, who Miss Anne-May renamed Celeste, on account of it sounding like a Louisiana name. She had pretty almond-shaped eyes, good hair pulled back in a pink ribbon, and skin darker than mine, like an Ethiopian princess I saw in Aunt Tandy Rose's book. I set down my list and stepped closer to the window as Ma and Pa and Sally Smith crowded around her, with big smiles. She smiled back at Ma, showing a pretty dimple in each cheek, and just like that, my pining for a friend disappeared and I hated that girl worse than anything.

Then Miss Anne-May floated down the front stairs all dainty, her hair in sausage curls that bounced around her face as she walked, that I'd set with an iron that morning. She wore a dress I finished for her the night before, of amber and brown plaid silk, with a hoop the size of Chesapeake Bay.

"Let's get this over with," she said in her Southern way.

Instead of her usual cowhide whip at her skinny waist, she wore the little black riding crop, always part of her Sunday best. She held up her skirt to admire her own feet, stuffed into another pair of pretty, new boots from the dry-goods store in town, Smalls and Sons, the fanciest place, where she bought so much they delivered it here in a wheelbarrow. Ma said just plain old bonnets there cost more than Sally Smith ever made on her jelly.

Anne-May hurried out the study door to the wagon in the gravel turn-around, barely making it through the doorway, her hoopskirt so big. Once outside, she clapped her smooth, little hands. "All of you inside right away. Don't you dare touch a thing, 'cept your clothing bundles, and after the ceremony get yourselves gone, down below."

"Down below" was one of the things Anne-May had names for that made them sound better than they were. As if calling a ramshackle slave shack at the bottom of the hill next to the hogs "down below" made it any better.

As the rest of the new folks arrived, Anne-May's husband, Fergus, who wouldn't be called Master, but Mister Watson instead, came out of his library like a snail out of his shell, since he didn't like people much. He was a homely man, with a face long as Abraham Lincoln's and a beard with two white stripes down it like a skunk's tail. I once heard Anne-May tell her sister she thought her husband had eyes like the frogs he studied, but he left us alone. He was always happier walking the bay, head down, looking for dead crabs and weeds to put in his leather pouch, so much he smelled like shore water, which is not so bad. Better than pea soup like Overseer Caruthers.

Once all seven of the new ones came down from the wagon, they walked into the study, looking all nervous, and I handed out their clothes to them, while Pa gave out the leather shoes he made so well, with the pegs drove in the wood soles.

I handed Fidelia her bundle, a pretty blue calico head rag on top, and she leaned in and whispered, "You eat good here?"

"Never enough but Sally sneaks us extra, best she can."

"Summer and winter suits?"

"Both. Summer, each girl gets a sleep shirt, what Aunt Tandy Rose called a 'shimmy.' Just thin linsey, took me one minute to sew. And I think I got the size of your dress just right. And that's me put felt inside the cuffs. Made the underthings, drawers and top, outta softest flour sacks we had and sewed a dress pocket just here. Everybody deserves a pocket, don't you think?"

Up close I couldn't help look at her smooth little stump. What happened to her hand? Chopped off in a cotton gin, most likely.

She hid her stump in her pocket and leaned close enough to kiss me. "Just so's you know, I heard the overseer say war's started. Mister Lincoln's fixin' to get us free."

A thrill ran through me top to bottom and I looked to Ma. She looked around, as usual, makin' sure she didn't show one bit of emotion to give Anne-May an excuse to go after her. Chin up high, arms folded across her chest, Ma kept watch on us all, her blueberry-color cloth tied up extra special for the welcome day. Did she know about the war? She opened her eyes a little wider and sent me a look that says all this: *Yes, I know and it's good news, but don't get your hopes up and we'll talk about it all down below,* because in one look Ma could say all that.

Next up came the new girl, Celeste. I shoved her bundle at her, happy the dress was probably too big.

"Age?"

"Sixteen, maybe, or thereabouts," she said.

Anne-May stepped to the parlor doorway and called out, "Hurry now!"

"I'm sixteen, too," I said. "But I know my birthday. May twelfth."

Celeste smiled and stepped closer. "I always wanted a June birthday, but I don't know when I was—"

All of a sudden, like a hawk on a squirrel, Anne-May came down on

Celeste and whacked her shoulder so hard with her crop she fell against me.

"I said *hurry*," Anne-May said as she prodded Celeste with her crop toward the parlor. "Get in there. We can't take all day for this."

Celeste rubbed her shoulder, tears in her eyes, and I felt for her, even though she was stealing my spot in the family, but she had best get used to the ways of Miss Anne-May.

Once we got the new arrivals their clothes, Sally Smith arranged all six of the marrying new folks in twos. Since Anne-May said she would have *no jumping-over-the-broom nonsense in her parlor, which once hosted George Washington himself,* Fidelia and Charl stood with the other two couples, looking itchy, as Pa said a few words he knew from the Bible. The more I got used to them together, the more they seemed to fit, his arm around her waist like he was holding her up, and maybe he was.

Before Pa even finished talking, Anne-May clapped her hands again. "There. That's done."

LeBaron Caruthers walked to the front of the room, red-eyed from a spell of drinking the night before, the iron nails he pounded into the bottom of his boots jangling on the wood floors, mouse-brown hair long to his shoulders, greasy and limp as boiled laundry, and started in on his usual welcome address.

"Y'all get down below, now. You'll hear the horn at the crack tomorrow and you best be up and ready. Here in Maryland we work in all weathers, dawn to dark. You'll get your allowance first Friday of the month. Six pounds fatback, ten pounds cornmeal, and a quart of blackstrap."

Fidelia's eyes widened at that, molasses being the greatest of all human luxuries.

LeBaron kept at his list of rules, counting on his fingers. "And you need a pass from me, mind you, to hunt or fish. And we'll have none of that at night. You can forget any talk of emancipation. You're slaves for life. Remember that. The worst fire of hell will rain down on coloreds who impose grievous harm on their masters."

Out of the blue he looked right at Charl. "What you say, boy?"

Charl looked at the floor. "Nothin', suh."

"I've got my eye on you. Way I reckon, it's worth half a cent to kill a darkie and half a cent to bury one. You cross Miss Anne-May, I won't think twice."

Maybe sensing a fight, Ma stepped toward the door and Anne-May waved everybody off. Ma and Pa took to their heels and the rest followed, out the door and across the grass, down the hill to the cabin, and I mustered my courage and stepped to Miss Anne-May.

"I'm visiting town, Jemma," she said.

"I can stay here and clean—"

Anne-May twisted back at me like a stuck snake. "You think I'm stupid?" She grabbed my arm and pinched it tight till it burned. "You just want to stay here and eat cake. Who's the stupid one?"

I stared at the pattern of the rug, little diamonds.

"Who's the stupid one, Jemma?"

"I am, missis."

"That's one thing you got right. After all, who started that fire in the barn?"

I held my belly like it was about to fall out. "I'll go to town, missis."

"Better believe you'll go. And if I hear another word from your stupid mouth, you'll get it bad—make Clementine's passing look easy. Hear me? Now go get my gloves. You'll come with us to town and do the cleanup when we return tonight."

Holding my head high so no water'd run out of my eyes, I ran and snatched her best lace mitts from the box and helped her fingers find all the right holes and then slunk back to the window.

Rubbing my pinched arm, I watched the crowd of new folks walk off down the hill, Ma with her arm wrapped around the new girl, Pa leading them down with a big smile on his face, and I asked Jesus for any life but mine.

Anne-May

✴

UNLESS IT'S YOUR OWN, A WEDDING IS A TERRIBLE BORE. Especially a colored wedding, where they tie the bonds without even a minister present. Since they're not married in the eyes of God, they sin each time they lie together, putting their souls well on the path to hell. It's no wonder they steal and cheat us blind, already bound for eternal damnation.

I stood at the upstairs window and finished dressing for one such charade, the union of our new servants at Peeler Plantation, the finest tobacco plantation in all of Maryland. How good it was to survey my property, to be, at the age of only twenty-five, the mistress of one hundred acres overlooking the wide Patuxent River, which runs out into Chesapeake Bay.

To the west, acres of dirt tobacco fields stretched out, with their neat rows of mounds, like overgrown anthills, waiting for their tender young shoots to rise. Hard to believe our sad little herd of field hands made three thousand of those a day. I pressed my face to the glass to look east and down below, to the whitewashed cabins and hog pen. Even with the window closed I could smell the foul odor of both.

Farther back stood the new tobacco barn and the stables and the little round whitewashed smokehouse with the black pointy roof, like something out of a fairy tale.

I sipped blackberry brandy and ran the edge of my new diamond down the middle pane of glass, etching in script *Mrs. Fergus Watson 1861*. I smiled, knowing the ring had passed the test, for paste diamonds don't cut glass. Perhaps Jubal Smalls would notice it at the benefit that night. Handsome Mr. Smalls knew quality.

"What're you doing, Anne-May?"

I turned, not a fan of surprise attacks, to find my husband of six months, Fergus. "Just writin' out my new name, as any newlywed in love does."

Fergus came and encircled me with his slender arms, the arms of a woman, really. More like a young girl's, smooth and hairless.

He kissed my neck, his lips tepid and wet. "I suppose you earned that ring, making all those clothes for the darkies."

"S'pose I did."

"How'd I get so lucky to marry the prettiest girl in Louisiana?"

I laughed. "Just good, clean livin', I guess."

He looked out across the property, down the sloping lawn to the river. "All this land, so beautiful from up here. Hope Reggie invests our money wisely so we can buy more. As your stepfather he has an obligation, I suppose."

"*Ex*-stepfather, please. And Reggie can't help making money from every investment he's ever made, so your money and your daddy's should grow fast. Millions, someday."

"I'd like to see that happen sooner than someday," Fergus said. "Like he promised."

I slipped out of his embrace and pulled my glass snuff bottle from my pocket, the one painted with roses, the stopper set with jade, a gift from my brother, Harry, the only truly good person in my family.

"Why is it always about money with you, Fergus Watson? You promised me fun when I said I'd marry you."

Fergus slumped into a chair. "Just want to make sure you have enough to run this place in case I head off to fight."

I dipped the brush in the bottle, rubbed the snuff along my gums, and felt the rush of pleasure run down both arms, followed by a perfect quiet calm.

Voices came from the back of the house and I hurried to the window there, layers of white organdy rustling, to find our overseer LeBaron's wagon arriving in the gravel turnaround below. Fergus followed and stood behind me as we watched the first new servant step down. We'd bought seven this time, to replace one lost to scarlet fever and several lazy runaways. Spring was the worst season for that, seeing as how tobacco work is hardest then.

I leaned in for a closer look to see that first one had a hand missing. I turned away from the window, about to lose my morning tea, and made a note to tell Sally Smith to have that one receive her food allowance anywhere but in the pantry with the others, and just half the rations since she could only do half the work.

Fergus hooked one arm around my waist. "I know you wanted a bigger diamond. Like Harriet Smalls's."

He was right, of course. Being a scientist and all, he saw the truth in things. I do like diamonds as much as any girl does. That was half the reason I agreed to my stepfather Reggie betrothing me to Captain Watson's third son to begin with, all that old Watson family money, diamonds and sapphires wrapped in cotton wool and tucked away in strongboxes and safes. In return, Reggie'd done the Watsons a big favor and helped them invest their money. And of course I'd brought the *most* valuable asset to the marriage, when Aunt Tandy Rose willed the house and contents to me.

"Oh, don't be silly, Fergus. It's just fine, though most gentlemen have the ring when they propose, not six months later. In New Orleans no self-respecting lady—"

"You're in the North now, Anne-May, married to the master of a plantation in a house that—"

I felt a high, hot sound in my head like a knife on wire. "*My* house, Fergus, and every servant out there with it. Lord knows they're worth as much as the house."

"Ever feel the least bit of guilt—"

"Don't you dare bring that up, Fergus Watson. My lunatic aunt didn't really want them free. I don't feel guilt at all."

"Aunt Tandy Rose wasn't so bad."

"She was a mean one, Fergus, and smelled of pickled eggs. And loyal to colored folk over her own *blood,* for pity's sake. Letting those girls read her books."

"Not that you read them."

My temple throbbed. "That's beside the *point,* Fergus. Everyone knows learning makes a Negro unfit for service."

He kissed my palm. "Don't get yourself all riled up. We have a party to go to tonight."

"Come if you want, but it'll be mostly sewing-circle ladies, no one who'll talk crawdads and clams."

"Mollusks. And I can converse about any number of things. Let's get this wedding done."

ONCE WE GOT THE wedding over with, I still had to wait while Fergus chatted in the kitchen with Sally Smith, the cook, laughing and carrying on.

He heaved a net bag of oysters onto her black stove. "I'm working on breeding these smaller ones so they're sweeter. Tell me what you think, Sally."

Sally took up that bag, dripping with filthy water. "Yes, sure will, Mister Watson. Settin' aside some of my best quince jelly for you, too, come time to boil it up."

"I don't deserve you, Sally," Fergus said.

Thank goodness Fergus finally pulled himself away before I lost my lunch listening to that foul woman cotton to him, and we rode ten minutes by carriage to the little town of Hollywood. We were already late for the St. Mary's Soldier Dance at Smalls and Sons store, to benefit our boys going off to war.

To call Hollywood a town was an exaggeration. Named for its only distinctive feature, an overgrown holly tree, it was barely a town, with its two sickly rows of shops and sad little church, one potholed dirt road down the middle. But it was better than nothing for the plantations close by and had one redeeming feature: Smalls and Sons Mercantile, where a person was guaranteed to pass a good time.

Its owner, Jubal Smalls, a Baton Rouge native, had built it, a freestanding building smack in the middle of town, with two wide picture windows in front. Those windows were always filled with the best displays, of unspooled bolts of camel hair, the latest ladies' hats from Paris, and every style and shade of parasol. You could find all the comforts of Louisiana there, pictures of Royal Street on the walls, a little shelf of hot sauces up front near the cash drawer. In a little glass box sat little tins of snuff, dip brushes and pipes, and every kind of pretty snuffbox and bottle.

Fergus helped me out of the carriage and I turned to Jemma. "Walk the carriage down the block and stay with it, you hear?"

She took the reins, head bowed.

I shook one finger. "Don't you sulk at me, or you'll feel it good, Jemma."

Fergus and I stepped onto the Smalls and Sons porch as Jemma led the horses away.

"You need to ease up on the whip, Anne-May," he said. "She's just a girl."

"When I came here I let them keep their names, for goodness' sake, and they never said one word of thanks. And they have shoes, better than most."

"And show some kindness to old Sally. She said you made her eat that whole loaf she burned."

"Tattletale. Mama always said, 'You burn it, you eat it.' Guess traditions mean nothing anymore."

"Think how you'd feel if you—"

"If I'd come along to the auction house I'd have picked a better bunch than those new ones. That Fidelia's missin' a hand, for mercy's sake."

"That's not a place for ladies. I loathed the whole thing."

"In New Orleans they sell 'em on the street, along with the pelicans."

"This isn't New Orleans, Anne-May."

"Don't I know it. Miss it every day."

"Slavery's barbaric. Humans weren't meant to be owned by others."

"You wouldn't understand, Fergus, raised up in Delaware. You have to be strict with them. My mother—"

Fergus held up one long-fingered hand. "Please don't bring her up, Anne-May. I want to enjoy myself tonight."

We entered the front door into a cloud of tobacco smoke scented with men's cologne and lemon soap, to find a gathering of all twenty-five adult persons living close by Hollywood. My sewing-circle friend Charlene Tidwell Weed stood in a new baby-blue dress, *tête-à-tête* with the mistress of the party, mousy Harriet Smalls, who lived with her husband, Jubal, and three children right upstairs.

A long counter filled much of the place, a fresh red, white, and blue bunting pinned along its side. Lit by three hanging lamps, the store was portioned into areas: household goods, men's furnishings—and my favorite, fine ladies' wear, up near the front. It was the latter that attracted ladies from as far off as Baltimore. They came to barter or pay cash money for the most wonderful silks and woolens, ribbons and Belgian lace, or latest little straw hat.

Fergus wandered off to find us two cups of claret, and I found Mr. Jubal Smalls, entertaining the circle of ladies around him.

"Charleston women are known for being handsome, graceful, and ladylike."

"How about Richmond?" old Mrs. White asked.

Jubal squinted one eye. "Richmond ladies are famous for their aversion to labor and love of pleasure."

"And what about New Orleans ladies?" I asked.

Jubal turned and trained his gaze on me. "Mrs. Watson. Well, everyone knows New Orleans ladies are known for their feminine taste for juleps and champagne."

Perhaps Fergus's complete opposite, Jubal was the fine-looking type of man you find in Baton Rouge, always dressed according to the latest fashion, with his gold-headed walking stick in hand. He had a fine, high brow, deep-set dark eyes, and was a hand taller than Fergus, with long legs and an elegant way of standing that showed off his powerful chest. His expression seldom softened, leading every Hollywood lady to feel a surge of accomplishment at having teased out a smile.

The little string band in the corner struck up a lively rendition of "Soldier's Joy," and Jubal took me in hand, demonstrating a popular step. As we danced, he leaned close, releasing a wave of heady, woodsy scent.

"You're the best dancer in Hollywood, Mr. Smalls," I said. The music ended and I took out my snuff bottle.

"Are you happy with your choice?" Jubal asked. "I only get a small amount from Paris."

I brushed a bit of snuff under my tongue. "Oh, the Golden-Banded Oco? It is very much to my liking, sir."

"Famous for its stimulating properties."

"I find it calms me like no other."

"Then I shall set another tin aside for you. My treat."

"*Vous n'allez pas faire une chose pareille,* Mr. Smalls."

"Yes, I'm serious, Mrs. Watson, and I do enjoy hearing French spoken again. Am I back in the French Quarter?"

I capped my snuff bottle and let my hand linger under the light.

Jubal took my hand in his, warm and soft. "What a lovely ring, Mrs. Watson. European center-cut diamond surrounded by eight smaller stones. Almost a carat altogether?"

"I don't believe Fergus would take kindly to us discussin' the value. It's a Watson family piece."

"I hear your home is one of the finest on the river, Mrs. Watson."

I leaned over to brush dust from my décolletage and felt his glance down my dress front. I lingered a perfect second and then straightened and met his eyes.

"It's no plain old Louisiana shotgun house, but architecturally pleasing in every way. Please come anytime, Mr. Smalls."

"I hope Mr. Watson doesn't mind me visiting his place."

"He spends a good deal of time in his shack down by the river." I held my pinkie finger under my nose. "I do believe I've taken too much snuff."

Jubal handed me his handkerchief. How soft it felt in my hand, made from dove-white China silk and linen, edged in a manly border of plain Irish lace. I ran one finger down the handkerchief's fat *S* monogrammed at one edge, and even without lifting it to my nose I caught the scent of his cologne.

"Thank you, Mr. Smalls. I'll return it, of course."

He bent at the waist. "I look forward to that day."

Fergus joined us and handed me a glass of claret. I made introductions and Fergus raised his glass.

"Here's to free enterprise, Mr. Smalls. My wife tells me this is the finest apparel store in St. Mary's County."

"And I hear you have the prettiest house in Maryland, Mr. Watson. Let's hope we can hold on to them through this war."

"How'd you end up in these Northern parts, Mr. Smalls? Isn't cotton fever continuing down South? Seems that's where the money is."

"We moved to Hollywood to help with my wife's dying father in Leonardtown and decided to stay put for a while."

Fergus pulled at his collar. "Northern troops are already in Washington."

"Back in Baton Rouge, they're eager to fight those Yankees, Mr. Watson."

"I suppose I'm one of those Yankees, Mr. Smalls."

"Maryland was a border state last time I heard. Your loyalty could just as easily lie with the South."

"Well, since the Union army is buying our entire tobacco crop this year, my loyalties lie with Mr. Lincoln."

"My customers prefer Virginia tobacco."

Fergus raised his glass in a toast. "Well, Honest Abe himself tried ours and proclaimed it the best for his troops."

I set one hand on Fergus's arm. "At least you've got enough slaves to keep things going when you march off, Fergus."

Fergus drained his glass. "Barely."

"My husband's ashamed of having slaves on the property," I said to Jubal in a mock whisper.

"I only keep a few slaves, myself," Jubal said. "Don't want to risk the thievery." He reached down and rubbed his left shin. "And I'd enlist but I'm laid up with an old injury."

Fergus bent to examine Jubal's calf. "You appear to dance just fine, Mr. Smalls."

"I could never walk a mile in formation, Mr. Watson, but I'll do my part here at home. Keep an eye on the ladies."

Fergus set his empty glass on the counter. "Anne-May needs no looking after."

" 'Course not. She's a strong Louisiana girl. They've got fight in 'em."

"You don't need to lecture me on my wife, sir. I see she has your handkerchief?"

"Jubal was gentlemanly enough—"

"Kindly hand it back, Anne-May."

I felt the color rise in my face. "I will not, Fergus. Mr. Smalls was simply bein' polite."

Jubal fixed his gaze on Fergus.

Fergus stared back. "You are not a gentleman, sir."

Jubal stepped away. "If it makes you feel better, I don't buy Highland Plantation's tobacco either."

Fergus grabbed my hand and yanked me toward the door, causing my sewing-circle ladies to stare. "Come, Anne-May."

The screen door banged behind us, and Fergus called for Jemma to bring the carriage round. As we rode toward home Fergus ranted about his run-in with Jubal.

"I detest such a character. He avoids riding to war and promotes divisiveness and malice."

I simply fixed my attention out across the dark fields and held that handkerchief to my nose, breathed in the scent of pine and clove, and imagined exactly how I would return such a fine gift.

Georgy

✳

I GAINED CONSCIOUSNESS AND FOUND MYSELF SPLAYED UNCER-emoniously on the floor, my associate nurse dipping her fingers into a tumbler and splashing my face with water before offering me a drink from it.

Dr. Prentiss stood over us. "I did suggest a chair, Miss Woolsey, but I'm afraid your weak constitution and pride have marked you as unfit—"

I struggled to sit up. "Please, Doctor, this has never happened before."

Dr. Blackwell arrived, carrying a folder in the crook of her arm. My face burned at the thought of her seeing me on the floor.

"Miss Woolsey fainted during a simple wound probe," Dr. Prentiss said.

Dr. Blackwell dismissed him with a wave and knelt next to me. "So the nurse has become the patient," she said, brow creased.

"I don't know what came over me."

She leaned closer. "The same thing almost happened to me in Paris. You must harden yourself, Miss Woolsey." She stood and took me by the hand. "Up you go now."

I stood. "Please don't declare me unfit, Dr. Blackwell."

She crossed her arms over the folder at her chest and considered me. "Do you think you deserve to join the ranks of the war's first nurses?"

I brushed off my skirt. "I do, actually. I've worked to memorize every—"

"Take a breath, Miss Woolsey. I just wanted to see you stand up for yourself. You'll need to do that a lot with the life you've chosen."

She pulled a certificate from her folder. "You may want to keep smelling salts handy. Because soon you'll be a very busy young woman." She handed it to me, a smile in her eyes. "Welcome to the United States Sanitation Commission, Miss Woolsey."

THAT SPRING, THE WAR began in earnest. New York mobilized, with regiments arriving daily en route for Washington. By June, our town house thrummed with war preparation day and night until all other activities practically ceased and our home became headquarters for all those fighting to end slavery and to preserve the Union. The first skirmish between Northern and Southern troops had just concluded in western Virginia with a Northern victory, and Union supporters floated on optimism.

One morning, in an attempt to stay busy and not think about where I'd be assigned for my first nursing post, I asked Margaret to help me assemble and wrap in newspaper an endless number of ham sandwiches for the departing troops.

In the front parlor, the air was full of fluff from lint making, the only sound the occasional tear of muslin. I sat with Mother and my sisters Hatty and Carry as we performed our various chores while waiting for our sister Eliza, on her way down from her upstate New York estate, Tioronda. Only the prospect of the Great Soldiers' Benefit Ball that night at Hotel Brevoort held us in good spirits.

We arranged ourselves about the room, not a hoop worn among us, only moderate crinolines, due to space constraints. Mother sat in the center of it all, at her bandage roller and lint press attached by vises to the strong little mahogany table her uncle Admiral Newton had ordered made aboard his flagship, *Pensacola,* fifty years earlier.

"We will get ourselves ready for the ball only after we have a carton each of bandages and socks," Mother announced.

Once our most formal space, decorated with overstuffed horsehair settees, the parlor was now piled high with Abby's boxes from the House of Industry, where women of reduced means learned sewing as a paying occupation. The boxes stood bursting with items bound for our troops: shirts, drawers, socks, handkerchiefs, cologne, and books.

Our little white mongrel, Pico, originally Mary's dog until she reluctantly left him with Mother upon her marriage to Robert Howland, sat atop a pile of woolen drawers, licking one paw. A skilled singer, known to accompany Eliza at the piano, Pico had adopted the way of any man who lives among a great many women, a stoic air of acceptance.

"Must every bedsheet be scraped for lint?" I asked.

"Do we really need sheets when a blanket will do?" Mother asked, keeping her gaze on her press.

Mother, who left that table only to eat, sleep, and read the war news, had directed us to haul from the attic trunks filled with every sort of old textile treasure from our Newton and Woolsey ancestors—heavy ochre britches, calico dresses, and muslin petticoats—all to scrape into lint. We surrendered stacks of lovely old table linens from the Newton family, to rip for bandages, each napkin and cloth embroidered with an elaborate *N*.

I sat, practicing my bandaging skills on my youngest sister, Carry, a copy of *Manual of Surgical Bandages, Devices and Dressings* borrowed from the hospital library open on my knee. I had almost completed a grand four-flap dressing, winding Mother's soft bandages about Carry's arm, making my reverses perfectly.

My sister Hatty sat near the hearth knitting a sad-looking sock, dropping stitches here and there. How robust she seemed after traveling through Italy, as Mother insisted we each did by age twenty-four, accompanying Mary and Robert and their children. She set down her sock and smoothed back her dark hair.

"Must I knit? I'm miserable at it and Carry gets to be bandaged by Georgy."

Mother turned. "You've spent three months abroad attending eggnog parties with dashing soldiers, my dear, with Carry left here sewing shirts."

Hatty was often described as Mother's favorite, so it was somehow satisfying to see Mother deny her any little thing.

Hatty unraveled her sock and started anew. "I spent much of that time helping Mary with the babies. And where is our brother? Why should Charley be exempted from the pleasure of this?"

"He is bringing Frank Bacon from the train," Mother said.

Two sisterly glances slid toward me.

I rested the spool of bandages on my lap and turned. "Frank Bacon can walk here himself, Mother."

"He's bringing something down from New Haven, on his way off to war, and Charley offered assistance."

"A diamond ring, perhaps," Carry said, making me regret not bandaging her mouth.

"Certainly must be an extraordinary one if he needs help," Hatty said.

I closed my bandaging book. "The only extraordinary thing about Dr. Bacon is his aptitude for stepping on the hems of women's dresses."

"Such a small complaint by which to reject a man," Mother said. "He certainly is devoted. And about to march off to battle. Please be kind, Georgy."

Hatty tossed down her sock and needles. "Permission to gossip? He's under the impression you are the mirror to his soul. I heard him tell Mary so. Such a tender story."

"You declined him once," Carry said. "Perhaps this time he'll bring a love token. Charlotte Benson has hers affixed to a link bracelet. If you accept, it's a pre-engagement."

"What is this?" Mother asked.

"Everyone gives them, Mother," Hatty said. "An ardent suitor etches his initials into a Liberty dime."

Mother sat back from her press. "Seems ruinous to the poor dime, if a simple declaration of love would do."

I continued bandaging. "I'll not accept any such thing from Frank Bacon. And please don't encourage him or I assure you he'll be disappointed."

All at once the door opened and Stanislaw Moritz stepped in, doubled over, Eliza's Goyard trunk strapped to his back with a fat leather belt.

"It is I, Stanislaw Moritz."

Hatty stood and ran to him. "Moritz!"

We were all happy to see Stanislaw Mortiz Von Schulman, Eliza and Joe's manservant, including little Pico, who jumped up at him like a circus dog, expecting a morsel of the dried tenderloin or desiccated liver Moritz kept in his satin-lined vest pockets. Half German and half French, Moritz was infinitely kind and doted on us all. A small, well-muscled man, he often carried Eliza's oversized trunks on his back, much as an ant carries a crumb three times its weight.

Behind him came Eliza, done up in a traveling dress of apple-green silk moiré. She wore the perfect little lacquered straw hat, ribbons down the back, and held a bouquet of lilacs, their stems wrapped in cotton wool.

I rushed to her. "Heavenly day, I've missed you. So much has happened."

"You're a nurse now! I'm terribly jealous, Georgy. My nursing training has consisted of bandaging and holding hands."

I linked arms with her, breathing in her scent of lily-of-the-valley and sweet country grass. "Are you still keen to try find a nursing post together?"

"Most keen."

"Good. I've scheduled your training with Elizabeth Blackwell herself and I know she'll adore you. I'm to tutor you as well."

Eliza squeezed my arm with hers. "Could this be more exciting? Joe's regiment will be encamped near Washington—west of Alexandria at Cameron Run."

"Perhaps we can request a Washington post."

"And follow Joe? That would be splendid, Georgy."

"Let us all share Eliza," Mother called, from her lint press.

With one hand Eliza removed her bonnet and handed it to Moritz.

"You would begrudge me one minute's conversation with my best friend?" I asked.

"A sister can't be a best friend," Carry said.

"In this case, she can. That is my place in this family, let us be honest. Eliza Woolsey Howland's best friend."

"Will you all come out to see Joe's Sixteenth Regiment march off?"

Eliza asked. "You won't believe the flag I've had made by Tiffany for them. A fine indigo blue with gold lettering. Joe says his men are overjoyed to march with it."

"Where is the famous Joseph Howland now?" Mother asked.

Eliza stepped toward Mother. "I left my dear husband in Washington Square with the regiment, seeing to last details. He has asked for a cookery book, can you imagine? To make gruel and stew."

She offered the lilacs to Mother to breathe in. "They're the last of them from Tioronda."

Moritz spirited the bouquet off to the kitchen and Eliza sat, her lovely skirt puffing out as she descended.

"Glorious war," Carry said as she straightened the bandage on her arm.

"They leave by transport ships for Elizabethport—and from there by rail to Washington."

"If only we could accompany them," I said.

Eliza smoothed Mother's hair back from her forehead. "Joe tells me the young boys back up in Fishkill have organized a company and are drilling under the name of the Howland Guard."

Mother turned from her press. "Perhaps they should be called *Mrs.* Howland's Guard."

All at once the front door opened and our brother, Charley, bounded in carrying a long, white box.

"Hi ho! Look who I've brought."

Fresh from the train station with Dr. Frank Bacon, Charley stood tall in the front entry. At twenty-one years old he stood taller than Father had, more like Mother's Newton family, lanky and broad-shouldered, with two clouds of blond muttonchop whiskers and Father's bright, inquisitive gaze.

Frank came to stand next to Charley. Steady, safe, and a good fellow, Frank looked his usual self, mildly distinguished in his blue U.S. Army greatcoat, with his silly little king's beard, black leather French medical bag in one hand.

We rose to greet them and both men pulled off their hats.

"How is the splendid Woolsey family of New York?" Frank asked.

The son of Leonard Bacon, the colossal, cloud-bearded New Haven pastor who occupied the most conspicuous pulpit in New England, mild-mannered Frank had inherited little of his father's magnetism.

Charley handed me the white box. "From Frank."

I lifted the box lid to find two bunches of long-stemmed red roses.

"Thank you, Dr. Bacon. Very kind of you." I whispered to Eliza, "I shall miss not him, but only the roses."

Mother pulled the box from my arms and handed it to Margaret. "Do get these a drink and a fresh cut, dear."

Carry helped Frank remove his coat and revealed quite a nice government-issued uniform, probably tailored by his lovely mother, a deep blue frock coat with two rows of gold buttons down the front, dress trousers, and black boots.

Frank Bacon stepped to me, twisting his hat in his hands. "Georgy, I thought we might take a turn around the block, before the ball tonight. I'm sure I'll lose you there to every man in New York."

"But—"

"Pico does need a walk," Mother said. "Perhaps you two could take him?"

"Capital idea," Frank said.

I sent Mother a dark look and reached for Pico's leash. "If he can accomplish his business quickly."

Frank assisted me down the steps to the sidewalk and we'd stepped barely ten yards along when he abruptly halted.

"You may be worried about me going off to war, Georgy, but I assure you medical officers do not draw fire."

"I'm not worried, Frank."

"I've often wondered where your affections stand. When you presented me with bay rum soap last Christmas, I dared hope—"

"It was a friendly gift, Frank; the proceeds went to Carry's orphan asylums. I simply enjoy the scent."

"And I never even returned the favor, so caught up with work. I know I haven't been the most devoted suitor, and last time we discussed this I didn't have a tangible evidence of my feelings—"

"We've been over this, Frank."

He reached into his trouser pocket and pulled out a silver coin no bigger than my thumbnail and offered it to me on his palm.

I leaned in to examine it. "A token, Frank?" Engraved with an *F* and *B* entwined, it was a lovely little coin, quite well done.

"Do I need to bore you with the details of my attachment one more time? We are meant for each other, Georgy, I'm convinced of it. Thought you might wear a physical indication of my deep regard."

I closed his hand around the sweet gift. "It is lovely, Frank, but I'd be dishonest if I accepted it. I don't want to misrepresent my affections. And with you joining your regiment and my head full of nursing curriculum, it's not a good time to consider a pre-engagement."

He slipped the coin into his pocket. "At a later date, then?"

"Let us get Pico back, Frank. I'll teach you to knit. And you'll help us get to that benefit ball sooner."

WE HURRIED TO DRESS for the ball, our maid Margaret lacing, buttoning, and tying us into our finest, and we made it to Hotel Brevoort just as the last carriages arrived. One of the most fashionable hotels on lower Fifth Avenue, the Brevoort had stood a stone's throw from our town house, at the northeast corner of the intersection with Eighth Street, for the last seven years.

We came by foot, all seven Woolsey sisters, with our brother Charley, Joe Howland, and Frank Bacon bringing up the rear, each of us carrying a paper carton of items to donate to the U.S. Army troops.

As Abby groused about the necessity of having to buy new gloves for such an event, and Jane bossed us all about, we passed the sidewalk opposite the hotel, which stood teeming with citizens waiting to view guests arriving for the ball. Carriages rolled to the hotel entrance, and ladies sprang from their doors, sparkling with diamonds and awash in lace, and the crowd shouted with happiness.

Dressed in our own best silk dresses, cashmere shawls, and more paste than precious jewels, we entered the frantic promenade into the hotel ball-room. Mary had made us each a Union ribbon, resembling a red, white, and blue bull's-eye, and we wore them with pride, pinned to our chests. We gasped at the canopy formed of star-spangled banners, the walls draped with patriotic silk, all lit by two enormous chandeliers. We admired Eliza's magnificent flag she had commissioned for Joe's regiment, the deep blue field with a golden eagle atop the regiment's crest, as it hung with the other regimental flags on the ballroom wall.

We joined the parade of gowns, slowly melting into that bouquet of rustling beauty, and breathed in the scents of the fragrant roses and lilies lavished upon tables and doorways, plucked from the Empire State's best gardens and hothouses. We passed the mountain of blankets, sheets, socks, and other war supplies deposited by the guests near the dance floor in a heap and added our offerings.

As a patriotic quadrille played, we gathered around our beloved mother, petting and arranging her ribbons and sleeves, each of us wanting our time with her.

Mother took in a glorious spray of tulips and narcissus. "The hospital should have so many flowers."

Hatty tucked a lock of Mother's hair back under her little white cap. "It is a party, Mother. We'll take them to Bellevue tomorrow."

I scanned the crowd and recognized Frederick Law Olmsted, ringed by a throng of admirers pushing their way to meet him, their champagne flutes held high. He was a great celebrity at the time, known for his work on the Central Park, and the previous day had been featured in the news-paper, having been appointed head of the Sanitary Commission.

I pulled Frank Bacon aside. "Frank, you know Mr. Olmsted. Would you be a dear and introduce us?"

"To pester him for a Washington post for you and Eliza?"

I turned my gaze toward the crowd. "We simply want to serve our country, Frank."

Frank looked to Olmsted. "He's the toast of New York right now. But I'll see what I can do," he said, and headed into the crowd.

It took some time, but Frank Bacon finally returned to us, the man of the hour in tow. "May I introduce Mr. Frederick Olmsted from Connecticut, on his way to Washington?"

Upon closer inspection, Mr. Olmsted was a slight, balding man with a bristle-brush mustache and a pleasant yet efficient way.

Frank made a sweeping gesture toward Mother. "Mrs. Woolsey. The heart of this glorious family. Brought up in Cameron Run, Virginia, by her Aunt Ricketts."

"Of Ricketts Flour?" Mr. Olmsted asked.

"The very one. And Mr. Woolsey was a New England merchant. Headed his own prosperous company until his untimely death over twenty years ago."

"Charles Woolsey of Boston? I knew him by his excellent reputation."

Mother curtsied. "Oh, Mr. Olmsted, we *do* continue to enjoy your park. What a triumph."

"I meant it to be a botanical garden, but, without the budget for that, opted for more park than garden."

"For once I am glad of an inadequate budget, Mr. Olmsted, for it is perfect as is. It must have taken a legion of workers to complete such a project."

He smiled. "Four thousand, actually. It was originally mostly swamp."

Frank made a grand gesture toward us. "You've met Joe and Charley, and Mrs. Woolsey, but let me introduce the Woolsey sisters, whom I've known since they first beat me at jacks. Allow me to start with Abigail."

Abby nodded, blinking as if caught in the light, not used to such attention, and pulled her shawl closer. Taking after Mother's side of the family, with her piercing blue eyes and strong brow, Abby gazed at him, her face without a trace of rouge or powder. After extreme pressure from us all, she'd relinquished her black silk and wore her only smart dress, a gay blue silk.

"Abby is the Woolseys' firstborn and the head matron of the Ladies' House of Industry, a place for the less fortunate to learn a trade. So far they've fitted out half the Union army. Not a fan of dancing, Abby would much prefer to be at Cooper Union in the front row of an abolitionist speech. And do not attempt to play a game of checkers with her, for she is a master of it and will swear you off the game forever."

Frank continued down the line. "Jane Woolsey." Jane made a lovely slow curtsy, dressed in a costume of her own making, the peach silk almost liquid in the lamplight, the perfect color to complement her red hair.

"Jane keeps the child welfare books for the Colored Orphan Asylum and acts as nurse in the clinic there, and Mr. Stewart's department store considers her one of their best customers of bonnets and gloves, after Mrs. Lincoln."

Jane's garnet earbobs swayed, catching the light. "Wearing a well-made wardrobe is a patriotic duty, Dr. Bacon. The government needs revenue from the importation of ribbons and lace."

Mr. Olmsted smiled. "Indeed, Miss Woolsey."

"And may I introduce Mrs. Robert Howland. Mary to us."

Mary stepped to Mr. Olmsted in her gentle but intimate way, blush rising in her cheeks, and offered her gentle hand. "An honor to meet you, Mr. Olmsted. I accompany my daughters to your park almost every week."

Mr. Olmsted seemed quite taken by her and no wonder, for Mary was known as the prettiest of the seven Woolsey sisters, and was once described by a friend as "a flower with a soul in it." She looked especially stunning now, in her morning-glory-blue dress, which showed off her white shoulders, and with creamy freesia artfully arranged in her dark hair.

Frank continued. "Mary assists her husband, the rector of the Church of Heavenly Rest on Fifth Avenue, and has raised untold sums through organizing their bazaars, *and* is an accomplished painter and poet."

Mr. Olmsted smiled. "Is there no end to these sisters' accomplishments?"

"Next comes Mrs. Joseph Howland—Eliza, wife of Joseph Howland here, who is cousin to Mary's Reverend Howland. Our Joe is about to march off tomorrow as adjutant to the Sixteenth Regiment New York Volunteers. Eliza sees to the sick up in Fishkill, New York, at their estate, Tioronda."

Eliza stepped to Mr. Olmsted and offered her hand. She wore her new lilac silk, her dark hair center-parted and drawn back into a low chignon. Light glinted off the gold locket containing a curl of Joe's great-grandmother's hair tied at her throat.

Mr. Olmsted accepted her hand and seemed in no hurry to let it go.

"What a gift you've given us, Mr. Olmsted," she said in her quiet yet inviting way, which made any new acquaintance step closer to hear more. "When we were in London last year, all they could talk about was your park. You are the toast of the Continent."

It was Mr. Olmsted's turn to blush.

Frank led Mr. Olmsted along. "And next we have the two youngest, thick as thieves at all times. Hatty, just back from Italy after charming all of Venice."

Hatty in her new black mantilla, dark eyes downcast, performed a graceful curtsy.

"And here next to her, the youngest Woolsey sister at twenty-three and her partner in crime, Carry, who can be found most days at the Colored Orphan Asylum or the Bloomingdale orphanage up on Seventy-third Street reading to a lapful of parentless children. She just graduated from the Agassiz School in Cambridge, Massachusetts, top of her class."

Carry extended her hand to Mr. Olmsted, who shook it in a brisk, paternal way. She stood a hand taller than Hatty and wore Eliza's old ecru silk, which fit her just fine with an extra ruffle around the hem.

"There were only six in my class, but thank you for the compliment, Dr. Bacon," Carry said, a decided coolness in her manner. "And, Mr. Olmsted, Hatty and I have had a rather personal connection to Central Park."

"Really?" Mr. Olmsted asked.

"We spent many days there passing leaflets about the demolition of the free Negro-built town there, which made way for the park."

"Seneca Village?" Mr. Olmsted asked.

"Three churches destroyed. Good, taxpaying people displaced with no compensation for their land."

Mr. Olmsted turned his full attention to Carry. "We've tried our best to relocate those we found it necessary to resettle."

Carry stepped toward Mr. Olmsted. "There are still hundreds not recovered from their rapid displacement."

Frank clapped his hands. "Perhaps we should move on to dinner—"

Mary set her hand on Frank's sleeve. "But, Frank, you seem to have forgotten our Georgy."

Frank turned to me. "How could I make such an omission?"

I reached out my hand to Mr. Olmsted and took his, warm, in mine. "It is a tremendous pleasure."

Frank came to stand by me. "I was twelve when I first met Georgy, at archery camp, where she threatened to wound the poor instructor, after he called her a show-off for making a bull's-eye first try." He looped his arm through mine and gazed upon my face. "Tolerance is not one of her virtues, but extreme kindness is. And don't ask her to play the piano or speak about her behind her back—"

I unhooked my arm from Frank's. "And I just completed a nursing course at New York Hospital."

Carry stepped forward. "She knows how to bandage a fractured clavicle. Trained with Dr. Elizabeth Blackwell, the first woman doctor, herself."

"She only fainted once," Hatty said.

I nudged Hatty aside. "Mr. Olmsted, we hear you are going to head up the Sanitary Commission, which means we will have the extreme pleasure of working for you. Eliza and I would like to offer our services as nurses in Washington."

"I'm on my way there now," he said. "I've been asked to improve daily life for the men of Lincoln's army through discipline in diet and hygiene."

Eliza stepped to Mr. Olmsted's side. "Georgy and I would be most appreciative if we could serve nearby my husband Joe's regiment in an official capacity."

"These nursing positions are risky, Mrs. Howland. The commission is still in its infancy, and we need flexibility in our nurses, to serve where needed as the battlefield conditions change. Right now we're staging from Washington. Next month it could be Virginia or a hospital ship off the shore of Maryland. This is the nature of war."

"We are at your disposal, Mr. Olmsted," I said. "But a hospital ship would be our first choice. We are not your average ladies, but come to you as doers, with clean aprons and kind hearts."

"And so modest," Carry said.

Mr. Olmsted leaned closer. "I will try to put in a word for a Washington posting and then take it from there."

Eliza and I exchanged jubilant glances, only tempered by the grave expression upon Mother's face.

"Don't worry, Mother," Carry said. "They say this war will be over in weeks."

FRANK BACON STAYED AT my side the entire ball, so it was a relief when the festivities wound down and I could release myself from his company and return home to my bed, the weeks of nursing training and war work catching up with me. I asked Frank and Joe to escort Mother and four sisters on the short walk home, while Jane, Charley, and I stayed to help the ball organizers wrangle the donated goods into barrels for shipment.

It was close to midnight when we finally headed for home, with Charley, inspired by the evening's patriotic music and speeches, having decided to enlist.

"I've already inquired about a regiment," he said. "Joe offered his own as a possibility."

"The Sixteenth?" Jane asked. "They leave any day. You've not enough time to prepare."

Charley smiled. "You just want to keep me in cotton wool for the duration."

"Not true at all," I said. "You'll bankrupt us all, the way you eat. Better the U.S. Army pays for your beans."

Jane and I linked arms with our brother, happy to have him to ourselves. To we Woolsey women, he was our sun, moon, and stars. After Father died, all seven sisters doted on the boy, yet somehow he'd escaped the least trace of entitlement or conceit.

The streets had cleared of carriages from the ball and the sidewalks stood mostly empty of foot traffic and, halfway home, we walked three abreast, and sang a popular abolitionist hymn, a favorite of Mother's:

"We only ask, O God, that they,
Who bind a brother, may relent:
But, Great Avenger, we do pray
That the wrong-doer may repent."

Just then, an unaccompanied colored woman, slight in stature, came walking toward us carrying quite a full carpetbag, almost half her size, the bottom of which gave way just as our paths crossed. The contents spilled upon the sidewalk, a mass of linens and clothing cast down, and Charley stopped to help the woman. At the same time, three men who had been walking slightly behind us caught up.

"Move along," the tallest one said to the woman, lowering his cane to block our access to her. "Your kind is not welcome here."

She hurried to gather her clothing, eyes downcast.

All three men were dressed in finely tailored cutaway coats, top hats, and neckties, but reeked of whiskey and upon closer inspection appeared disheveled and most decidedly drunk.

Charley addressed the man with the cane. "Christian Longworth?" Charley later revealed the manner of their acquaintance, for the man was a former boarding school classmate of Charley's, dismissed for behavioral offenses.

"Woolsey. You've become famous since school. Correction, your darkie-loving family has."

Christian stepped closer to Jane. "You attract dangerous elements to good neighborhoods with your Union ribbons and songs."

Jane drew herself up and faced the man. "Yes, this woman looks to be a scoundrel and a terrible threat to you men."

"Sarcasm does not become you, Miss Woolsey. And that moderate mindset is exactly what keeps coloreds coming around here."

Charley stepped to Christian. "Step away from my sister, sir."

The woman tried to lift her broken bag. I bent to help her. "Take all the time you need."

Christian glared at me and leaned in toward Jane. "You abolitionist types are so self-righteous. Probably in the front row at Dr. Cheever's talks. But do you know how that is hurting industry? You people garner headlines, but make no mistake, conservatism is alive and well here in the North in her commercial marts."

"Kept alive by the profits of the Southern trade," I said. "Great Britain is doing without that stain. Very well, in fact. Perhaps your family will have to learn a new trade once slavery is gone."

The man turned toward me. "I believe in this country the U.S. Constitution leaves that up to the states."

"I believe the war will decide that, sir," I said. "Though you three don't appear ready for any battle other than a crude street fight. Not one of you wears a uniform."

"Nor does your brother, the colored-lover."

"At least I've put my name in," Charley said. "I'm no coward."

Charley bent to resume helping the woman retrieve her clothes and Christian, by use of his cane, pushed him by the shoulder down on his knees.

Charley pressed two hands to the sidewalk to boost himself up, as Christian lifted his cane above him.

"Come to think of it, let us make sure you never fight, Woolsey."

"No," I cried out as Jane and I both lunged toward Christian, but it was too late to stop the terrible thing that came next.

Jemma

PEELER PLANTATION, MARYLAND
JULY 1861

B Y JULY IT GOT HOT SLEEPING UPSTAIRS AT PEELER PLANTA-
tion and I stood and fanned Anne-May and Mister Watson most nights
with Aunt Tandy Rose's old gray peafowl-feather fan.

I never got used to sleeping apart from Ma and Pa and Sally Smith, and
hated my place at the end of Miss Anne-May's four-poster bed, lying there
in my shimmy, under my blue-checked scrap of a blanket. I most of all
hated trying to sleep while listening to them make a baby. She and Mister
Watson would forget I was there and Anne-May'd fuss so bad about having to do her wifely duties, same old conversation every time.

"Why must you touch me so, Fergus?" she'd say. "I'm tired."

And he'd say back, "But you're my wife." Then he'd finally roll over
and let her be, and set to snoring. Then she'd rub on herself, breathing fast
and smelling on that pretty man's hankie she got in town, until she was
quiet and snoring, too.

That was my sign to sneak out and go down below, since once those
two were snoring even God's worst thunder couldn't wake them. And tonight, best of all, it was a full moon night when the old man in the moon
could light my way down to the cabin.

I threw on a blanket and crept out with nothing but my shimmy under it, hurrying down the carpeted stairs, out into the cool night, my bare feet cold to the ankles in wet grass. I got to the first cabin, pushed the cloth door aside—Aunt Tandy Rose's old yellow bedspread she gave us when she burned a crispy little black hole in it smoking her pipe in bed. Coming or going, pushing that cloth aside you'd still get a whiff of her too-sweet rose perfume.

I found Ma and Pa asleep near the embers of the fire, Fidelia and Charl sleeping in the corner bed, Charl's hand on the blanket over Fidelia's belly. From the loft came Sally Smith's snoring and I figured Celeste was up-stairs with her.

I stepped to Ma and Pa asleep on their straw mattress, their mud-caked hoes leaned up against the fireplace. They'd been up by moonlight tilling their patch. It smelled good in there, like sweet earth and soap and the fish brine that kept the dirt floor smooth. I wiped my feet on my shimmy, pulled up the cover, and backed in close to Ma, so warm. Her name other than Ma was Sable and fit her just right, for she not only had the smoothest skin, but she carried herself like a fine lady—even out in the field she had the gentle way of royalty.

She snugged me close like always, and I drifted off with them as the pine knots popped in the fireplace, and I was home.

I WOKE BEFORE DAWN, well before the signal, for once that horn blew, everyone in that cabin would be running like scalded ants to get out to the fields. It was hard to leave that warm bed next to Ma, but I was visiting my twin sister, Patience, that day and everything had to go perfect. Since Anne-May was going to Leonardtown, the big city where the train came in, she sent me to Ambrosia Plantation next door to bring over a box of pota-toes and fetch home some fabric for Miss Anne-May's new dress she wanted me to start cutting out.

I left the bed, wrapped my blanket around me, and stood for a long second taking in Ma and Pa dreaming together, his big arm across her hip. Then I went to Fidelia's bed and found only Charl, the covers on her side thrown back. I stepped outside and found her bent over near the hog pen, her good hand on the split rail fence. She stood in nothing but her shimmy, Sally Smith's white shawl wrapped around her shoulders.

It won't be long now, Sally Smith had said.

I stepped closer to her. "Couldn't sleep?"

"This one's a fighter," she said, her voice soft and pretty in the morning air.

"Can I feel?"

She took my hand in hers and held it to her belly and I felt a funny sliding, just the way Toby'd felt inside Ma. Tears came to my eyes and I couldn't talk for a second or two and we just listened to the crickets sing.

"You have enough to eat? I know Anne-May cut your rations."

"Charl's been going out for pickerel and catfish some nights. Gets a powerful lot and cooks it for me too. That gets me through."

"LeBaron know he's fishing?"

"It's good by LeBaron since Charl gives him most of it. Then his friend sells it for cash money."

"Charl get a pass every time?"

"Deed he does. Signed with LeBaron's *x*."

Fidelia closed her eyes and touched her belly again.

"I think it's a boy, Fidelia."

"Call me Delly. Suits me better. And yup, this one feels strong, all right. Had four girls so far, so chances are against it." She stopped and listened to the birds sing their wake-up songs. "They say once I have twelve I get free."

"How old were you when you had the first one?"

"Thirteen. By my reckonin', you're overdue three years."

We both startled as LeBaron came around the side of the shack, a silver wrench in his hand, and nearly scared us both half witless.

"What's happening with that baby?" he asked.

I stood between him and Delly and took her cold hand in mine.

He walked closer. " 'Bout time it come."

"It's a long way off," I said, my hand starting to sweat on hers.

"You shut your mouth. Babies take nine months. By my calculatin', she's close."

I put one arm around Delly, felt her shiver like a bucket of cold water fell on her.

LeBaron came closer and lifted one end of Delly's shawl. "When the time comes, it needs to happen out in the tobacco barn, y'all know."

The barn. Just the mention of it made my stomach sick.

I drew Delly closer and muttered, "May happen in the field."

LeBaron let the end of the shawl drop and shook the wrench in my face. "I'm talkin' to *her*. And it happens where I say it happens."

He took one long look at Delly and walked off.

We both finally breathed and I gathered Delly's shawl closer around her. "You need to rest now. You've got a while to sleep before that horn goes off."

She held her belly. "He wants the baby born in the barn so he can take it."

"LeBaron's gone now."

"He'll be back. He comes every day checkin', just so he can sell it. I seen it all before."

"Charl. Pa. They won't let that happen. Sally Smith'd rather die than see your baby took from you."

"Had four babies so far and can't keep one. It's always the same. 'You can keep the next one, I promise.' Then they sell 'em off and tell Mistress they died. She don't care. Wants me back in the fields. I'd rather see this chile for real dead than let him go."

"Don't you say that."

"It's the truth. Can't give up another one. You don't know what it's like."

"That baby comes, send Pa to find me. Promise on the Bible?"

Delly just looked away and started back inside. I got her settled back in her bed and stood there watching her sleep, her snugged in there, one arm cradling her big belly. I felt sick thinking she'd have to be up so soon and out to the fields hauling tobacco, in her advanced condition.

I left the whole shack sleeping and ran up to the chicken coop, to feel under the warm hens and steal their eggs from them, for Anne-May's breakfast.

LeBaron Caruthers would not touch that baby if I had a thought left in my head.

I GOT ANNE-MAY PRIMPED, curled, and all her chin hairs pulled, then saw her off in the carriage, made up the bed, washed the breakfast dishes, sewed a rip in Mister Watson's coat, helped Sally Smith pluck a chicken, picked up the chicken feathers in the yard, cut a big piece of Sally's cornbread and wrapped it in a cloth napkin, slid it in my apron pocket, loaded a crate of pig potatoes, cut one of the first sunflowers blooming near our kitchen window, laid it atop the potatoes, and set to my last task before I could go, getting the eleven o'clock water down to the field, my one time of day to see my folks.

I stood on the porch overlooking the tobacco fields that ran down to the river, Ma, Pa, Celeste, and Delly bent at the waist over the young tobacco plants. That scene from up there'd take your breath away, the wide river beyond, until LeBaron rode into view, up on his horse with his whip coiled at his thigh, and you remembered it was all just a place to keep us chained for their own use.

Even from so high up I could see the flash of LeBaron's metal bottle he drank his whiskey from flash in the sun as he raised it to his lips. I didn't even notice Charl wasn't there.

I took my gourd, filled it with cool water at the pump, with a touch of blackstrap snuck in for Delly and the baby, and started to head down. Halfway there, Charl came walking along the road from the woods, toward the field.

I turned and looked back up at the porch and saw Mister Watson'd come out and stood looking over the scene. Mister Watson did the same thing every morning, walked the property along the river, with his shotgun and game sack in case he bagged a rabbit.

LeBaron musta seen him too, since he rode to Charl in a sudden way.

"Where you been, boy? Sent Clem after you. Looks like you thought twice about runnin' away."

Charl stood in the road looking up at LeBaron, hands at his sides. "No, suh."

"Then where you been?"

"Just fishing, suh."

"You gotta pass?"

"From you, suh." Charl offered up a paper slip. "With your mark just there."

LeBaron slid down off his horse, whip in hand, looking up at Mister Watson. "I didn't give you no pass to fish in work time."

Charl looked down at the pass and just like that, LeBaron unfurled his whip and struck Charl, sending him down on the ground, one hand to his neck.

At the sound of the crack Delly started off to Charl but Ma held her back.

I dropped my gourd and ran back up onto the porch. "Mister Watson, come quick."

"What'd Charl do, Sally?" he asked, squinting down at the little scene.

"Nothing I can tell. Maybe that's a little show for you, suh."

Mister Watson stepped off the porch and called down. "LeBaron, you leave Charl be and get him back to work."

LeBaron paid him no heed, just wound his whip back up, eyes on Charl, fixin' to hit him again.

"Stop that now," Mister Watson called down. "We can't lose him this time a year!"

Charl struggled to stand, as LeBaron drew back his arm, aimin' to crack his whip again at him.

That's when Mister Watson raised his shotgun to his shoulder and blasted a shot into the air. That startled us all and caused LeBaron to jump a little.

"You all get working now," he shouted down.

LeBaron got back on his horse and wound his whip back up but even from that far off the hate in his pig eyes was plain as day.

———

MISTER WATSON TOLD SALLY we could fix Charl up so we brought him to the cabin and she put a plaster on his neck where LeBaron got him good with the bullwhip and let him rest, while LeBaron sulked and worked the others extra hard.

So it was late afternoon by the time I finally set off for Ambrosia Plantation, still shook up by the sight of Charl falling to that bullwhip. It was a half hour's walk through the woods to drop the potatoes, and I looked for devil's dung along the path to make tea of for him when I got back.

Ambrosia was half the size of Miss Anne-May's place, and more stuck in the woods, so they didn't grow tobacco, just indigo, made dye and sold it to places in the North, which made denim cloth for working clothes.

The path was sheltered from the wind off the river by trees, and that walk was a pretty one, with glimpses of the river along the way, so I took my time. That day you could barely smell what Aunt Tandy Rose called the Big Stink, officially named Douglasville Swamp, where that boggy smell'd rise up, from water sitting too long. It was just south of us at Peeler, and the kind of place snakes go to raise a family. Jagged stumps and cypress trees rotting. The butcher from town killed hogs and cows and old horses at Butcher's Dock, just south of there, and left the parts nobody'd eat, hog maw, feet, and hocks, for Sally Smith to come get, so some hot days when the wind was right, blood and swamp together made the Big Stink. Pa knew that swamp inside out, and found his wood there to make furniture with. He'd catch muskrat, mink, and raccoons and bring home lady slipper orchids for Ma, never once bit by a copperhead snake.

Not more than ten minutes down the path, I saw something that caused me to stop in my tracks, the birds calling to one another in the trees the only sound. There, tied with twine to the gray gate that once led to old Farmer Burns's farm, was a pretty sunflower finished with a neat bow. Mr. Burns'd been dead for years. Was it sign of a party? Barn dance?

"Anybody here?" I called out, but only the cicadas answered back.

I set down the crate, wiped my face with my hem, and stepped up on it, one foot on either end, and saw only part of a saggy old barn.

I picked up my crate and kept going, hands rubbed raw in spots by the rough wood, but I didn't care once I saw Ambrosia in the distance. I was going to see my sister, Patience—the nicest girl in the whole world, and maker of the best indigo mud in Maryland, for which Miss Charlene prized her highly, since every indigo plantation tried for the brightest and cleanest tinge on their blue cloth.

I'd give Patience the cornbread and laugh with her for a bit. Maybe see her new place.

"Hurry up, you!" A white lady on the back porch was waving me toward her like she was fanning flies off herself. "Not around the front, you dimwit. The back door."

Even from far off I could tell it was the mistress of Ambrosia, Miss Charlene Tidwell Weed. She was one of Anne-May's sewing-circle friends, even skinnier than Anne-May if that's possible and with yellow hair instead of dyed brown. Today she was wearing a dress the color of a fresh-stuck pig's blood.

As I stepped across the dirt yard at the back of the house, not half as pretty a place as Anne-May's, Miss Charlene's dogs started barking out in the wood-slat pen by the barn. At the sound of those hounds my legs got all wobbly and I slowed up at the sight of them jumping against the slats, slobbery teeth bared. LeBaron loved those mongrel dogs, with their big heads and starved down to the ribs, and said they came from Mexico, trained to run slaves.

"I feed them Indian cornbread and meat only when they catch a runaway darkie," he said.

He'd given them the scent of each of us, through a shoe or shirt. After that they knew us by smell half a county away.

"Hurry up!" Miss Charlene called out. "For the love of Jesus, do you know the word *hurry*? What is the matter with you?"

I crossed the yard and stepped up to the kitchen door.

"Don't you dare come in," she said from behind the screen, like she might catch the typhus. "Set that crate right here next to the door and be off with you."

I set down my crate, happy to be done with it, and pressed my blistered hands against my apron. Then, still behind the screen door, Miss Charlene stuck one arm out and handed me a tin bucket with some yellow cloth inside.

"There are seven yards of silk here and a box of buttons. Make sure it gets back to your mistress."

Then she sent out a hunk of what looked like bacon wrapped in newspaper, the grease bleeding through with a yellowish stain. "And this here's a rasher of bacon. Do not put it in the bucket and stain the cloth, you hear me?"

I took the bacon in my other hand. "Yes, missis."

"Go right home and deliver it and do not bother your sister while she's working."

"Yes, missis."

I walked back past the hounds as they howled worse than ever, probably smelling the bacon. I traveled back the way I came and, once out of sight of the house, doubled back toward the hut down on the way to the river where Patience worked the indigo. Every time I made a delivery, it was the same, Miss Charlene would warn me not to go see my sister and I'd go anyway.

I found Patience in the field closest to the water, with six others, all wearing the same blue kerchiefs tied around their heads, bent over, planting tender green indigo plants.

Patience saw me coming and walked toward me; with that limp of hers, she looked like a boat out at rough seas. Every time I saw her walk like that, I went back to that night in the barn. The fire rose up in front of me like it was yesterday and I waved it away.

My elder by one minute, Patience was a good bit smaller, with skin a shade lighter, but in most other ways we were the same. Liked to laugh. Read books. And sew.

Patience hugged me around the middle, and I could feel her ribs plain as day, skinny from working so hard, soaking plants in the big iron vats and straining out the dye.

I returned the hug, my tears soaked up in the homespun of her shift, so happy to be with her.

"Let me look at you," I said, holding her away from me. I took her soft hands in mine. They were dyed deep blue to the wrist from the indigo she worked, a stain that would never wash away. "Miss Charlene feed you anything?"

She just smiled and leaned on my arm like always and we walked past the shed with the fat iron vats where they cooked the indigo, toward the shacks.

"Gotta hurry. Miss Charlene lets the dogs out at five. She gave you bacon? Miss Anne-May must be a good friend. That woman's stingy with her bacon."

We made it to the cool of the cabin, almost the same as ours at Peeler Plantation since Pa made both, two floors each, only this one had a wood floor 'stead of dirt downstairs. The same wood plank walls, a rickety table and chairs near the fireplace, a bucket of water aside it, six corn-husk-filled sacks on the floor for beds, smaller ones for pillows, all dyed indigo blue, and more beds upstairs. My sister had a way, even with nothing, to make it homey and nice, with wildflowers set in jelly jars all about the place, since she came home every day smelling like indigo, like peas in a bad way, and flowers covered the smell.

I set my tin pail and bacon on the table and handed Patience two letters. "One's from me. Made up a new code."

Ever since we first learned our letters from Aunt Tandy Rose, Patience and I had written to each other in all sorts of codes so Ma and Pa, or anybody really, couldn't know our secrets. We wrote letters backward and upside down, and wrote whole letters in pictures. It came in handy when Miss Anne-May lent Patience out to Ambrosia, and we mostly talked by way of those letters.

"This other letter's from Ma, wrote down by me. She misses you and wants to visit but Anne-May won't give her a pass to anywhere these days. Scared she'll run and she'll lose her best worker, next to Pa."

Patience rubbed Ma's letter in her fingers and teared up. "Miss her, too."

I handed her the sunflower. "This'll cheer you. Very first bloom this year. Don't let the boys eat those seeds. They're for you."

Patience stood and stuck the yellow flower in a jelly jar. "Big for the first one."

I leaned against the table. "Doesn't smell like much but sure makes a person happy, don't you think?"

"I've been thinking they mean something else of late," Patience said. "There was one tied on the fence to old man Burns's farm."

"Just saw that. On the gate."

"Seen them other places, too. Seems like some warning. It's scary."

A chill ran through me, turning the sweat running down my back cold, and I shivered. "You want to know about scary? Pa's making knives. Has ten now under the boards upstairs."

Patience sat. "That's bad, Jemma. LeBaron's going to—"

I leaned in and kept my voice low. "Heard Pa tell Ma we're leaving once Delly's baby is born. Said he can't see one more child raised here. So we'll come for you soon. He said it'll be some night when it's raining. Make it harder for the hounds to follow."

"All of us together? He'd have a better chance alone."

"He'd never leave us. Besides, he knows how to get us through the swamp and down to the dock. Not sure after that."

"I don't know if I can do it, Jemma."

"We'll help you walk it."

"You can't carry me the whole way. And the *swamp*. I wake up nights sweatin' about it. The snakes—"

"Just have to be strong, that's all."

"I'm not like you, all courage. Sometimes I think Miss Charlene's not so bad. Why not just stay here?"

"Do you hear yourself? That's just your bad leg talking. We're the queens of strong. Look what we got through. The fire. Aunt Tandy Rose passing. You sent here. But we have to fight."

Patience dipped her hands in the water bucket, trying to wash the indigo stink off. "Miss Charlene did say if the North wins the war and we're set free, she'll have to turn us out like cattle."

"All the more reason to go. Get situated now."

"Don't think I could live with myself if I slowed you down so much we got caught."

"Well, we're not leaving you. And we can't stay here forever. I want to see things. New York City—"

"Would you stop about that? Who knows if it's even real."

"It's real all right. They have a library where you can read any book you want for free. Why should we die without living life like other folks? I want to have things to look forward to like Aunt Tandy Rose said."

"Suppose so."

"And I want my own full name. Don't want to be just Jemma."

"Who cares about a last name?"

"Every free person has one. Means you matter. You give it to those who come after so they matter, too."

"If you go to New York you could see Carter again."

My breath caught in my throat. "He's there? Says who?"

Patience shrugged. "Just grapevine news. But old Daniel heard LeBaron tell Miss Charlene that he ran off from them who bought him. They think to New York."

I swallowed hard. "That's true?"

"Reckon so. Any more letters?"

"Just the one. It's worn thin as cobwebs I read it so much. He most likely has a new girl by now."

"Ma and Pa were young when they met." Patience dried her hands, lifted her pillow, and pulled out two cloth dolls. "Speaking of Ma, can you give these to her on her birthday?"

"It's Pa and Ma," I said, for she'd captured their likenesses perfect. She got Pa's face spot on, in brown homespun, his coat indigo blue, two jet button eyes and his mouth done in red thread, some curly wool for his little beard. He even wore his Sunday-best waistcoat, white with red stripes and shell buttons.

She handed me the Ma doll, same brown homespun face, rooster-comb-red lips, and a necklace of oyster shells like the one Pa made her, only doll-size. She had a soft piece of mink fur for hair, wore a calico dress and little flowerpot bonnet just like the one I made Ma.

Patience watched my face. "Sybil got me the mink fur from the inside of Miss Charlene's cape for Ma's hair. What do you think?"

I clutched them to my chest. "She'll cry for sure. Just wish you could give 'em to her yourself." I stopped short of telling her the new girl'd taken her place. Didn't want to make her sad.

I slid the dolls in my bucket under the silk so Anne-May wouldn't see them and tucked the bacon under one arm.

"You better get home before those dogs come out," Patience said. "Got your pass?"

"Wrote my own. Miss Anne-May doesn't care. I make her signature better than her. Might just walk down a ways past the gate to old Mister Burns's farm."

"Go straight home, Jemma. I don't like the way that LeBaron looked at you when I was over there last. And he's building a place for himself at that old farm. Wouldn't put it past him to get you there and do what he liked."

"I'd throw myself in the Patuxent with rocks in my pockets."

"You need to bring somebody on your walks here."

"He won't do it again—after he tried to get Ma into the tobacco barn and Mister Watson slapped him down. Never seen a man so hangdog. Plus, Anne-May holds my paper. He won't trespass on her property. There's a fine."

"Come on now, Jemma. She won't care if LeBaron tarnishes you. Sheriff won't make him pay no fine either."

"I can outrun him any day."

"LeBaron has his ways. Heard Clementine—"

"I know all that." I started to walk off and turned. "Don't worry about me. I can fend for myself. But you just be ready to go any time Pa gives the word. You and me, we're getting away from all this, going to New York City. We're gonna be free."

THE WIND PICKED UP as I said goodbye to my sister, turning back three times until I promised to stay gone for good. I missed her right away as I took the long way around Miss Charlene's hounds and found the path home.

It went quicker this time without the potato crate, and I found myself back at the sunflower gate right quick, but now it was open and faraway voices came from somewhere down the path. I stepped through the gate and wandered down the path a piece, and saw a clearing up ahead with some pine-knot torches lit up at what looked like a campsite. My heart skipped a beat when I saw another sunflower, this one tied around a sapling next to the path, the wind blowing its leaves as I passed.

I kept on down the little road, my tin bucket creaking, doing my best to see through the trees, holding the bacon so tight to my chest it grew warm and slippery through the newsprint.

The voices came louder as I crept to the edge of a clearing. In the distance stood dead Mr. Burns's barn, the roof sagging in the middle like an old horse's back, and next to it a clearing with one gigantic tree, a sycamore with fat, gnarled branches spreading out, swaying in the wind like a creeping spider.

Patience was right about LeBaron's shack he was building—almost done, it looked like. In the clearing LeBaron's pattyrollers stood on horseback around a fire, talking and joking, each holding a flaming pine knot. One lifted a flask to his mouth then tossed something in the fire. They were LeBaron's friends from around the county who went to the different plantations, usually on Sundays, ransacking our cabins and closely examining our conduct. Anyone found without a pass'd get thirty-nine lashes then and there.

On the biggest horse was a man named Chester, skinny and bowlegged. He was the one who found Sweet Clementine and brought her body back to the house.

They say LeBaron had his way with her, Sally Smith had said.

A shiver ran through me and all at once it was darkening quick. I turned and made my way back toward the road, hoping those men in the clearing didn't see me.

Anne-May

❋

IT WAS HOT AS TOPHET THE MORNING FERGUS AND I MET MY SISTER, Euphemia, and my brother, Harry, at the train station in Leonardtown. And that didn't help the dull ache in my head, which caused everything to be seen through a thick fog, the direct result of runnin' out of snuff.

When had I last seen my siblings? At my wedding, of course, which Aunt Tandy Rose put on eight months ago right here at Peeler Plantation. Thanks to Mama it was as lavish as any could be, with a French-made trousseau, a Belgian lace wedding dress, second-day and third-day dresses, too. Lasted a whole week, night and day, ending with a dance in the new tobacco barn.

The train disgorged a surprising number of passengers for such an un-popular little town, several blue-uniformed men among the crowd. Soon my younger brother, Harry, descended, running one hand through his au-burn hair, and a load of pure joy ran through me. Now twenty-one, he'd grown a bit taller, but still looked to be the same good-hearted boy, dressed in casual traveling trousers and jacket, a knapsack slung over one shoulder. Harry turned and helped Euphemia down the train steps. Tall and plain as paint in her serviceable calico dress, like a lost dog she scanned the crowd for a face to recognize and take her home.

Euphemia, with her manly walk, came to us first and reached out to Fergus, causing him to bend at the waist and kiss her lace-mitted hand.

"Hope your trip went well," he said.

"Have you found the *Callinectes sapidus* yet, Fergus?" she asked with a little smile and flutter of her cow eyes. Even the most unattractive women in Louisiana knew how to flirt.

Fergus smiled back at her. "Have indeed. Good to see you, Euphemia."

Harry ran to me, threw his arms about me, picking me clear off the train platform. "My dear Anne-May! How is married life?"

My fog lifted as he kissed my hand.

"I have *missed* you, Harry Wilson."

He sent his mile-wide smile my way. "And I you, Anne-May Wilson Watson."

"You're growing more handsome every time I set eyes on you. It's just not fair the only boy in the family got the prettiest eyelashes. Now, I have so many things planned. First, a trip into Hollywood to Smalls and Sons, they have all sorts of new—"

"Woah, now," Harry said, fake-angry. "Can't a man get settled? You know how I am about social calls. And when I was here at your wedding, I promised Sally Smith I'd build her a window."

"Sally Smith can go to blazes. Must you do carpentry? I want to feed you. Show you the town."

Harry ran his fingers down my sleeve. "Just take a breath, Anne-May. We'll have a good time, all of us together." His touch soothed me like nothing else.

"Well, you have to eat *sometime,* so—"

"Hold it right there, Anne-May. I have a surprise for you."

He hurried to his trunk and came back with a fabric-covered box the size of a loaf of bread, the front covered in a screen, ribbons tied on each side.

"What in heaven's name, Harry?"

He unbuttoned the top and lifted out upon his palm a perfect ball of taupe-colored fuzz, ears singed black. "She's from Siam and she's for you.

Hope you don't mind I named her. Saint Joan. Like Joan of Arc. Doesn't that fit her? They say Saint Joan had blue eyes, too."

"How precious, Harry." I reached out to pet her, but she hissed at me like a snake and I snatched my hand back. "Well, Saint Joan hates me, that's for sure."

"Give it time, Anne-May." He set the kitten back in her carrier. "These carriers are all the rage in Paris. French women tie them to their back and take their cats with them around town." He tied the ribbons at my waist, the box to my rear.

"The French are so clever," I said, happy to own something from France, even if it did hold a spitting cobra of a cat.

Harry turned to greet Fergus, and Euphemia held out two hands to me, with that same sad look she always had. "How are you, sister?"

I took her hands in mine. "Just fine, Euphemia."

She reached to my rear, unbuttoned the carrier, and lifted out Saint Joan, who relaxed in her arms.

"How's Mama?" I asked.

"She sends a message: that when she gets Harry's uniform made up from Shreveport and mailed, if it isn't too much trouble for you to fit in—with your fancy balls and dresses—that you make sure he receives it."

I stroked the kitten's head and she swiped at me with her paw. "Mama wrote me she's pushin' Harry into it. I just hate to think of him going off to war for her glorification."

Harry took my elbow. "I couldn't live with myself if I didn't serve."

"Thank the Lord Mama's not here," I said. "Don't think I'd survive it."

Euphemia placed Saint Joan back in her carrier. "She means well."

The ache in my head came back and I felt about to explode if I heard one more syrupy platitude from my sister, so I turned to Harry and took his arm.

"Let us go, my handsome man, off to Peeler Plantation."

ONCE WE ALL ARRIVED HOME and my siblings finished arguing about who should stay where—Harry wanted Euphemia to have the best guest room, overlooking the river, and she insisted he should have it—Harry waved off my most extravagant refreshments made up in his honor, downed a cup of tea, and then took his tools to the shack down below to work on the window Sally Smith had conned out of him, probably in exchange for some of the opium she grew. A sharp operator, old Sally had hoodwinked my husband Fergus, too, and cooked up his favorite oyster gumbo and corn fritters, but underneath it all she was a fat rat, making up her jams and jellies, pushing them on townsfolk, and hoarding the proceeds. Harry and Fergus had sure fallen for her act.

Having no Harry to show about, I had LeBaron bring the buggy round and took Euphemia to town, since she was in need of entertaining, the albatross around my neck for the foreseeable future. We brought Saint Joan along to show Jubal Smalls, and set her on the buckboard between us.

"How kind of Fergus to give you his mother's ring," Euphemia said.

"Not that she wanted to. Took almost a year to pry it out of her jewelry chest. She has six rings, for pity's sake, and one's a sapphire the size of Baton Rouge."

"I tried to deter Harry from fighting for the South, but his mind's made up. Papa wouldn't let Mama push him if he were alive."

"I refuse to think about that on such a nice day, Euphemia. They say this war will be over quick, so let's hope Harry never marches off, and right now we have shopping to take our minds off it, after all."

Smalls and Sons was full of patrons that day, drawn out by the warm summer weather. I tied on my carrier and stepped in with Euphemia to browse the snuff, as Jubal Smalls strode from the back of the shop.

"And who is this pretty lady, Mrs. Watson?" Mr. Smalls asked, proof Louisiana men are adept liars.

"My sister, Euphemia Anne Wilson. Euphemia, meet Mr. Jubal Smalls, owner of this whole establishment. He lives right upstairs with his wife and three precious children."

"It's a lovely place, Mr. Smalls."

I turned to show Jubal my back. "And look what my brother brought me all the way from Louisiana. This type of carrier is all the rage in Paris."

Euphemia lifted the kitten out and showed it to Jubal like a butcher shows off a pork roast, and Saint Joan growled at him, from deep in her throat.

He bent at the waist, one hand to his heart, and turned to me. "Mrs. Watson, that is the sweetest little Siamese cat. Sadly, I can't get too close on account of the fact they make me sneeze. By the way, I have that snuff I set aside for you."

"Thank you, Mr. Smalls. I will take two tins if you have them, and put it on my account."

"Only have one today, but I'll have more soon." He took a tin from a low shelf behind his counter and placed it on the glass countertop. "How is Mr. Watson?"

"Just fine, thank you. I must apologize for his unbecoming behavior at the dance."

"The war has everyone on edge. Is he serious about enlisting for the North?"

"I believe so. Looking at the First Maryland Volunteer something."

"Regiment? Mustering out of where?"

"I don't know really. It's hard to keep it all straight."

Mr. Smalls slid a red Moroccan leather book off the shelf. "Well, this is my gift to you, Mrs. Watson. You just write it all down in here; keep it nice and organized."

"I'm not the best writer."

"Doesn't have to be perfect. All the best women keep a record of their husbands' exploits in travel and war. The wives in Paris do it. We can work on it together while he's gone." He leaned in closer. "I hear some of your darkies can write. Have one of them transcribe for you."

Mr. Smalls walked us out front and handed us up into the buggy, with Euphemia driving as she always did, since her sturdy constitution was suited to reining in horses.

"I'll have your handkerchief back to you soon, Mr. Smalls, clean and pressed," I said.

"You just come back soon, both of you."

I smiled as Euphemia drove the buggy on, and turned back to find Mr. Smalls watching us leave.

"Be careful there, Anne-May," Euphemia said, her gaze on the road. "Mr. Smalls. He's not to be trusted."

"Don't be ridiculous."

"Parceling out that snuff you like. I saw several more tins of that on his shelf. Why would he tell you an untruth? He wants something from you."

I felt a hot bee buzzing in my head. I took the snuff from my bag, wet my finger and dipped it in the fragrant powder and ran it around the inside of my mouth.

"He flirts with you in such an outrageous way."

"You know how Louisiana men are."

"And he does not strike me as the type of man who'd give someone a Morocco book for nothing in return. And all those questions about Fergus. It's not right."

Soon the snuff worked its magic and I found myself in such a better temper even Euphemia's prattle was not a bother.

As my sister drove on, I opened the little leather book, the virgin paper smooth and white, to find an ivory-colored silk bookmark, a pretty little magnolia embroidered at the top. I ran one finger down the silk, so much like the lacy underthings he sold at the shop.

"You're right, sister. I'll take note."

No matter what she said, I would record whatever I pleased in that book.

ONE MORNING A FEW days later, we set off for the church fair, my Harry driving the carriage, me next to him, ready to show off my handsome brother to all of St. Mary's County. Fergus had taken Euphemia earlier that morning, to set up her single-lady's lunch basket for the church auction, the most popular event at the fair. My poor sister had labored over her lunch for two, hoping to attract a male bidder, and had cooked it all herself: Mama's favorite, Chicken Purlough, Sally Smith's yeast biscuits, chocolate bread pudding, cherry iced water, and Robert E. Lee's favorite gingersnaps, the hypocrite, since her political sympathies clearly lay north of his Stratford Hall. She denounced good General Lee for leading the

Confederate army but still ate sheets of his cookies. The meal took a heavy toll on our already low sugar supply, but if it helped Euphemia secure a husband and take her off my hands, it was well worth it.

Harry turned to me and grinned, his hair, deep red as an Irish setter's coat, shining in the sun. "You're in a fine mood today, sister."

"Who wouldn't be? Riding up here, wind in our face on this hot day, wearin' my best blue silk, with my handsome brother. I'll have to beat the eligible ladies away from you with a switch."

"I get too shy around ladies. Rather pound nails."

"The shyness looks good on you, Harry. You have all the things ladies love. A comely expression. Youthful frame. And there isn't a kinder person in all Christendom. Daddy said you and Euphemia were God's two angels."

"Guess that makes you . . ."

"The devil, I suppose. Least Sally Smith'd say so."

"Wish you'd let up on them all."

"Ever since the wedding you've been their biggest friend. But I can't be good to them. They'll knife me in my bed just like Daddy if I don't keep the upper hand."

He reached over and covered my hand with his, and even through the crocheted mitt I felt the warmth. "I know you're good as any of us, Anne-May."

I raised an eyebrow. "What do you know?"

"Remember when you carried me home from school on your back when I stubbed my toe?"

I smiled. "You going barefoot like a little colored child. And you bled all over my yellow dress."

We entered the yard behind the church, and as I predicted, the ladies gathered as Harry bounded down and I took my sweet time as he helped me from the carriage. The atmosphere was that of high carnival spirit as we strolled the fairgrounds, arms linked, drawing admiring glances, and took in the wooden booths arranged in a square, an open lawn in the center.

They had every sort of amusement, fate ladies giving risqué fortune readings, and a pretend post office where male customers could always find an eager young lady ready to write them personal mail for a small fee. Booths that sold needlework and pen wipers, a tree covered with gilded apples.

At once I spotted Fergus in deep conversation with the county fishmonger and steered Harry clear of them. I looked over the crowd of Maryland ladies in their best summer calicoes and a few gentlemen, several in Yankee uniform, but did not see Jubal Smalls. Harry and I stood and admired the tethered hot-air balloon, hoses pumping it full of hot air; soon it would take fair patrons up above the grounds to see the whole county and then float back down to earth.

We found Euphemia in the church hall on the low stage with the other single ladies, their quilts made for the occasion spread out in front of them, a picnic hamper atop each, flaps open to advertise their wares. A little chestnut box sat on a table in front of the stage into which fairgoers slid their bids for the right to spend picnic time with the various ladies. Each lady adorned herself in fresh ringlets and lace, hoping one of the handful of single men that weren't decrepit or off serving or suffering from some sort of disease would drop a bid ticket in the box for them. They'd brought out the good earbobs and dressed as if their lives depended on attracting a man that day, which of course they did.

Euphemia stood with them, perspiring profusely and fanning herself. She snapped her fan shut as we approached. "Thank you for coming. Don't think I've had one bid yet. No one's even glanced at my lunch."

Harry peeked into the hamper. "Looks fit for a king. And it's early still for bids."

"If someone does bid, I hope they don't get to keep my hamper," I said.

"No, just the quilt. And any lunch not bid upon goes to the troops." Euphemia folded her arms across her chest. "This is all just one big opportunity to show off new clothes and talk to gentlemen without introduction."

"You should be on your knees thanking Jesus to talk to a man without introduction, sister."

Euphemia looked to the ceiling. "I'll never get a bid."

"Julia Hammond had men all over her basket," I said. "Looks like she took great care in her appearance."

Tears came to Euphemia's eyes. "I was up most the night finishin' my quilt."

"You could have thrown on a spot of rouge. And for pity's sake flirt a bit. You'll never get a man looking at the floor."

"I don't want a man I have to reel in like a fish. I'd prefer to be alone."

"With me taking care of you in your old age? Think of others for once."

Harry stepped between us. "Much as the parish'd like to see you two in a regular fist and skull fight, maybe you need a break. Pheme, how about you go freshen up and we'll hold down the fort here?"

Euphemia smoothed her skirt. "Could use some air."

Harry smiled and held up one hand to help her down from the stage. "Walk around and show the men of St. Mary's County how charming a lunch partner can be."

Euphemia smiled and hurried off.

I pulled a bid form from the table and filled it out in pencil.

Harry looked over my shoulder. "You filling it out for Euphemia?"

I dropped it in the box. "Don't you dare tell."

Soon fairgoers started gathering in front of the stage and Euphemia returned and took her place behind her quilt, dark rings staining the silk under her arms.

Fergus joined us. "So what happens here now?"

"They read the bids from the gentlemen and the ladies go off for a picnic with the highest bidders."

"Seems sinful, the church selling off women," he said.

"Hush, Fergus, they're starting."

With a great flourish the parson gathered the bid cards from the box, read through them, and made a dramatic pause. "And Julia Hammond with a high bid of fifty dollars goes to William Parker of California, Maryland."

Mr. Parker helped Julia off the stage as Euphemia and the other single ladies, wearing tight smiles, applauded.

The parson read the bid cards of the two other single ladies, causing them to pack up their quilts and hampers and walk off with their winning bidders, which left Euphemia onstage alone. She sent me a nervous look.

The parson smiled, felt around the bottom of the box, and at long last pulled out a card, causing Euphemia to breathe a relieved sigh.

"Miss Euphemia Wilson, this lovely quilt, and the most delicious-smelling Chicken Purlough in St. Mary's County goes to Mr. Fergus Watson of Hollywood, Maryland, for twenty-five dollars." The crowd clapped as Fergus turned to me with a quizzical look.

I urged him forward. "Git now, she's waiting."

Euphemia burst out into a smile the size of Louisiana and handed the hamper down to Fergus.

Harry leaned closer to me. "Like I said, there's good in you, Anne-May."

Fergus led Euphemia out of the hall, the two smiling at each other, him guiding her with one hand at the small of her back.

"Just don't tell anybody," I said, as I watched the two of them hurry out the church hall door.

Georgy

✦

CHARLEY CRIED OUT AS MR. CHRISTIAN LONGWORTH BROUGHT his cane down at a ferocious speed and plunged the silver tip of it into our brother's right hand, which proved a perfect target, splayed as it was so innocently there on the sidewalk. Charley groaned upon feeling the stab of the cane and Jane and I recoiled at the sound of breaking bones.

While Christian hurried off, Jane and I, and the woman with the carpetbag, helped Charley back to Brevoort Place to withstand the indignities of so many sisters clucking over him, and Frank Bacon, after tending his wound, telling him he'd not be eligible to enlist anytime soon.

In the end the night turned out fortuitous in three ways; the first being that the woman with the carpetbag, named Lucy Locker, went on to become a most valued sewing instructor at Abby's House of Industry and a dear friend and ally. The second, the vile Mr. Longworth was taken into custody of the police, paid a pretty fine, and spent two nights locked up. And third, Charley's hand wound, though not dangerous, was serious enough to preclude him from battle at the start of the hostilities, saving Mother a great deal of anxiety, at least for a short while.

———

A DISHEARTENED CHARLEY ACCOMPANIED us as we all gathered to see Joe Howland march off down Broadway with his splendid troops. Frank Bacon had also marched off that morning, and it was hard for our brother to stay behind and nurse his hand, but he knew not to sulk, at least around Mother, for it was her greatest peeve.

We stood amidst the crowd, three miles of flags and people, and soon began to see in the distance the glimmer of bayonets approaching. Before long the immense throng parted and pressed back upon the sidewalks and the regiment came—first the Artillery Corps and then company after company in solid march with fixed faces. The cheers were like cannonade, people shouting and waving handkerchiefs, crying and praying.

Then the Sixteenth came by, led by a serious young blond color-bearer holding Eliza's magnificent flag aloft. We caught a glimpse of handsome Joe, looking younger than his twenty-seven years, despite his formal gray trousers and brass-buttoned blue coat. The men glanced neither right nor left, but marched as if at that moment they were marching into the thick of battle.

They were not long in passing, and the crowd closed in upon them like a parted sea. I linked my arm in Charley's and a shiver ran through me as we watched the shining bayonets as far and long as we could, a late beam of sunshine touching the colors as they disappeared.

THAT SUMMER, AS MOTHER, Eliza, and I cut out cloth for uniform shirts in the front parlor, windows open to lure in a breeze, a telegram arrived at Brevoort Place. Carry, who spent most of her time lurking near the door for such an opportunity, intercepted it.

"Georgy, Eliza! A telegram addressed to both of you."

"Bring it here, Carry."

She opened it and read.

To Miss Georgeanna Woolsey and Mrs. Eliza Howland,
   Please report to Sanitary Commission headquarters address Washington as soon as possible. Further orders furnished upon arrival.
                                        Frederick Law Olmsted.

Eliza turned her wondering gaze upon me. "It's *happening,* Georgy."
I took Eliza's hand. "At last."
Mother looked out the window. "I will not survive it."

WHEN ELIZA AND I arrived in Washington to begin our nursing careers, we set up at Ebbitt House, a serviceable boardinghouse and restaurant, a favorite of Washington journalists.

Eliza alighted from the carriage. "At long last, that famous city, Washington," she said, looking up at the wide façade.

"Famous for dust," I said, following her down out of the carriage to supervise the unloading of our first trunks, with Mother sending more soon.

We settled quickly and outside our window, a hot wind blew down F Street and flies plagued us all, blackening the tablecloths at hotel tables and flying into one's mouth while dining. The war everyone had predicted would be a quick defeat for the South forged on, three months in at that point. Once the U.S. Army suffered humiliating losses at Big Bethel and Bull Run, where Joe Howland and Frank Bacon both fought, Union morale sank to an all-time low. Our cousin Theodore Winthrop, Abby's beloved friend, had been the first casualty of rank for the North to fall in battle, at Big Bethel, and we dressed in mourning black.

Soon after our arrival, Eliza received a letter from Joe, sent from his camp near Centreville, Virginia:

ON THE BATTLE FIELD NEAR BULL RUN,
JULY 21, 1861

Dear Eliza,

Our brigade is making a demonstration in the face of the enemy and a fight is going on the right of the line five or six miles off. We see im-

mense masses of troops and the supposition is that the enemy is try-
ing to outflank us on the left. Everything points to a great battle.

Most lovingly, Joe

We stood in great suspense as to the outcome of the battle until the next day, when the following little note, written in pencil on a scrap of soiled and crumpled paper, made its way to us at Washington and told the story:

Dear Eliza,

A complete rout at Bull's Run. The Sixteenth safe.
We are making a final stand.

J.H.

After what Joe described as "never a more complete defeat of our Union forces" by the Southern forces, rumors flew all about Washington that the capital would fall to the Confederates, and we woke each morning to the going and coming of squads on foot and horseback, the incessant drumbeat in the streets.

We soon rejoiced to receive our first Sanitary Commission orders. While not assigned to a hospital ship as we had hoped, we were to arrange a make-shift hospital on the top floor of the local Patent Office, the war having inter-rupted its construction. We embraced the project and soon, once Eliza caught up on Dr. Blackwell's nursing curriculum, had the place fully operat-ing, along with a rotating roster of doctors who left much of the work to us.

I was relieved the Sanitary Commission assigned us fewer critically in-jured troops, and mostly typhoid fever, measles, or malaria patients, which I had learned to treat during my time with Dr. Blackwell. But we still had our share of heartrending deaths unattended by a chaplain, since they were in short supply, none having been officially hired by the President.

AT EBBITT HOUSE, ELIZA and I had just unpacked the last of our trunks Mother sent down when we received our first guest. Our rooms stood on the bottom level of the hotel and people would often stop by on their way along the street and share something with us, a gross violation of our privacy, which we at first abhorred and then quickly grew accustomed to, becoming a walk-up window of sorts for visitors.

It was terribly hot for July and we kept the window open to catch a breeze, the draperies swaying gently. We took turns fanning each other as we unpacked our hulking black trunk we called the Ark, which we'd shared all through Egypt, and which stood in our room covered all over with chalked names of the hotels we'd visited, when Uncle Edward presented himself at the window.

"Hi ho, ladies. They told me at the front desk I could find you both here."

We turned to find his head and shoulders framed by the window, his black armband tied about his upper sleeve for Theodore, black top hat shining in the sun.

I stepped to the window. "Uncle. How good to see you, but how freely they divulge our room location."

He removed his hat. "You shall soon find Washington to be one big unhappy family."

Eliza joined me at the window. "This is so unexpected, Uncle."

Behind him a regiment marched by in their woolen uniforms, swatting the flies away, one soldier with a loaf of bread impaled on his bayonet.

"Poor things," Eliza said. "They must be so hot."

Uncle Edward turned and watched them march on. "They're the lucky ones. Not dead at Bull Run. Headed to their camps along the Potomac. Can't bathe there, though. Swarming with snakes."

"Do come around for a proper visit, Uncle," I said. "As much as we do like chatting through the window."

"Little time to visit, I'm afraid. I have received an invitation just this morning." He handed Eliza three ecru cards.

Eliza fanned herself as she read. "The President and Mrs. Lincoln request the honor of Miss Georgeanna Woolsey's company at a reception Tuesday at seven o'clock."

"That's tonight!" I said.

"There is one here for me as well. How extraordinary, Uncle."

"The food is uninspired, mostly claret and crackers, since it would be bad form to be too extravagant with the troops in need, but could be worth a look."

I waved a fly off Eliza's sleeve. "It's too hot for dressing up."

She turned to face me. "You would pass up a chance to meet Mr. Lincoln? I will certainly attend. There will be glorious and terribly important people there to whom we must represent the Sanitary Commission. And perhaps we can hear some war news not in the papers."

"I suppose."

Uncle Edward replaced his hat. "No need for finery. Just come as you are."

Eliza closed her fan with a snap. "Uncle, it is the White House."

He started off. "I will return at half past six with the carriage."

THOUGH IT WAS A quick walk from our hotel to Pennsylvania Avenue, Uncle had insisted on arriving by carriage and drove us past the nearby Capitol building, decapitated and awaiting the addition of a new iron dome, construction having been halted due to the war. Union soldiers stood and drilled on the grounds there, brass buttons gleaming in the sun.

"Those lucky soldiers live there," Uncle Edward said. "There are twenty ovens in the basement to bake bread for all the troops in the city."

As we came back toward our destination, I became curious to see the President's house, that famous place built by slaves, which now lodged a man who seemed determined to end their suffering.

Eliza and I wore our best black silk dresses, pagoda sleeved, with mourning veils, and the carriage windows provided welcome breezes. We must have lurched forward and stopped abruptly one hundred times as our line of fine carriages wound its way through the black iron gates and around the driveway, toward the vast pillared portico.

Eliza leaned toward me, her palms pressed together. "At the reception, darling, please keep conversation to general topics."

I looked out the carriage window at the troops lined up on the lawn, guarding a young boy, whom I assumed was the President's son, while he played.

"Must you muzzle me?"

"Is it so taxing for you just to remark upon the furnishings or the shape of the room?"

"Yes, actually."

"Then just say 'How do you do?' and leave it at that, Georgy. Uncle Edward has friends here."

"Perhaps I could ask Mr. Lincoln to approve official chaplains for the troops?"

"I wish you wouldn't, dear. To badger our chief executive with a request for pastors may be considered a terrible lack of manners."

"To provide our men with God's agent to hear their last words?"

"Perhaps a letter would do, Georgy?"

We drove under the vast portico and uniformed footmen handed us out to follow the crowd into a wide hall, handsomely carpeted, around which several grand doorways stood.

Uncle Edward leaned toward me. "In some ways it resembles a run-down hotel, don't you think? Not one picture on a wall."

"I rather like it," I said. "A severe simplicity."

Eliza looked toward a long metal and glass screen walling off an area to our right.

Uncle handed his hat to an usher. "That screen is an attempt to get the Lincolns some privacy. Separates their quarters from the public spaces. Poor man has every opportunist in town here all day asking for handouts. Sees every one. How does he find time to run the country?"

The Marine Band played a Grand March Medley as Uncle Edward guided us into the Blue Room, already full of guests, many men in uniform, ladies in sherbet-colored dresses and ornate hairstyles—their maids had evidently been busy all afternoon braiding flowers into their tresses. There were a good many black dresses in the crowd, since war casualties had already been high in number.

One could not escape noticing the furnishings, upholstered in blue and silver damask, the woodwork of the chairs in gilt, a blue and white carpet, and blue and gold tapestries on the walls.

"They took the Blue Room name to heart," I said.

Uncle Edward pressed the seat of one chair with his fingers. "Congress allocated twenty thousand dollars for decorating. Can you imagine such spending in wartime, Mrs. Lincoln here hanging drapes with Rebels ready to march in at any minute?"

"Mrs. Lincoln is criticized for breathing," I said.

Uncle pressed on. "It's been only four months since the family has taken residence and Mrs. Lincoln is already over budget. She wouldn't even tell the President. Just sent the bills to the Commissioner of Public Buildings."

"Would a man be criticized so?" I asked. "No paper would print it."

Eliza took my hand. "Come see the view."

Having brought no hoops due to our service as nurses, we wore only stick-out petticoats, making it easier to navigate the wide hoopskirts and caged crinolines in the room. We pressed into the crowd, brushing by smooth silks, organzas, and cashmere shawls, through a heady cloud of rose and lily toilet water and cigar smoke. Hardly a satin lapel or décolletage stood without some Union patriotic badge or rosette.

We broke out of the crowd and stood at one of the soaring windows, taking in the view, by far the finest aspect of the room. Shadows grew long across the rear grounds as twilight fell, the wide Potomac River glittering in the distance.

"What a splendid scene," Eliza said.

A shortened drape next to the window caught my eye. "Look at the fabric here. Souvenir hunters have already taken their spoils."

Eliza bent to examine the carpet. "They've lopped off a whole edge here as well."

Soon Uncle found us and set to flagging down officials of note as one hails a hansom cab on Broadway. "Edwin!"

He drew the attention of Mr. Stanton, Secretary of War, a bespectacled man with a nose like a small turnip, who wore his gray beard natural and untrimmed. He nodded hello as he hurried by.

"Mr. Secretary, may I introduce Eliza and Georgeanna Woolsey, the great-nieces of Admiral Newton?"

This earned the secretary's attention for a moment.

"Fine man, the admiral," Stanton said as he passed.

Uncle Edward called after him. "They're here working for the Sanitation Commission."

Secretary Stanton waved as he hurried by. "I am on my way to send a telegram, but at your service at all times, ladies."

The secretary vanished into the crowd as a vaguely familiar woman hurried toward me.

"Miss Georgeanna Woolsey?"

Uncle Edward drew himself up taller. "Mrs. Gibbons?"

I recognized her from newspaper illustrations as Abigail Hopper Gibbons of the famous Philadelphia family of abolitionist Hoppers. Mother and my older sisters knew Mrs. Gibbons from the Cooper Institute and told remarkable stories about her and her father, who often directly confronted those who kidnapped fugitive slaves.

The illustrations showed Mrs. Gibbons as any other well-groomed, melancholy woman in her sixties, dark hair simply styled. However, after meeting her in the flesh, with her Quaker lilt to her voice, strident way, and gift for conversation, Eliza and I found her a most engaging companion.

"I've searched the whole party for you, Miss Woolsey," she said, as if it were the most charming compliment.

"Oh, Mrs. Gibbons. How delightful to finally meet you. May I introduce my sister Eliza and our Uncle Edward? We all admire the work you and your family have done for the cause."

Eliza stepped closer to Abigail and spoke in low tones. "Your father's work with the Underground Railroad has been inspiring. Can you speak of it?"

"I cannot take credit, but let me just say I am thankful for the cover of night."

"I hear it's to be disbanded soon," I said.

"I'm afraid I cannot say much about it. We are one of the few organizations that don't crow about our accomplishments. But I'm proud of our work."

"What brings you to Washington?" Eliza asked.

"To see you both, in truth. Your sister Jane wrote that you might help me secure a nursing post with the Sanitary Commission. I can no longer sit with my hands folded."

"We have just arrived, Mrs. Gibbons," I said. "But I am happy to make—"

She slipped a card from her little drawstring bag of Chinese satin and handed it to me. "If you would be so kind to make introductions by way of correspondence, I would be indebted."

Mrs. Gibbons swept off, saying as she hurried away, "Be sure and make the President's acquaintance. So he can someday say he once met the Woolsey women!" and was gone as quickly as she'd arrived, no doubt in pursuit of another charitable errand.

Before we could protest, Uncle took us each by the arm and led us to the group surrounding the President. It was easy to spot him amidst the crowd, standing a head higher than the tallest among us.

Uncle plowed us through the cluster of admirers, who crowded about Lincoln like a pack of hounds.

"Mr. President, may I introduce my nieces, Mrs. Joseph Howland and Miss Georgeanna Woolsey? Here at Mr. Olmsted's request to represent the Sanitation Commission. They've made a fine hospital out of the Patent Office."

The President turned to Eliza. "Would your husband be Joseph Howland of the Sixteenth New York?"

A scarlet blush rose in Eliza's cheek. "Indeed, Mr. President."

"They served well at Bull Run. Wish we had one hundred Sixteenth Regiments."

"I will tell him you said so, sir."

Mr. Lincoln turned his sharp gaze to me and I became tongue-tied as his great hand grasped mine for a moment. "And how are you today, Miss Woolsey? How is life as a nurse?"

My mind went blank. "Quite good, sir."

He leaned down ever so slightly and smiled. "Pardon me, but I must move on to the remaining invitees. It is like the line at the barbershop. Each one must be seen."

I tried to summon my ask about the chaplains but instead only laughed, a hyena-like bark, unable to formulate even a common sentence.

He addressed us both with mock seriousness. "You will notice that our visitors have taken a great many tokens of our furnishings as souvenirs. Please be kind and cut samples only from places that cannot be seen."

Eliza and I smiled at that and stood, stunned we had met the President and watched as he quickly became overrun, a woman leaning on his arm begging a job for her nephew.

"Mr. President," I said. "Just one more thing."

Eliza sighed.

He turned to face me.

"We've had patients pass away on our watch, good soldiers who ask for a chaplain before they go, which we cannot supply, having no direct order from you, sir."

"Who hears their dying words?"

"We do, sir. These men die for their country. Don't they deserve the simple last comfort of a chaplain's hand? A proper funeral?"

He looked down at his hands for a moment and then returned his gaze to me. "How many do you need, Miss Woolsey?"

I glanced at Eliza. "Well, sir, one hundred would be a good start. For the hospitals here and field hospitals, as well."

"Can you do me a favor, Miss Woolsey? Write to General Van Rensselaer's office to ask for names of chaplains who might be willing and able to assist?"

"Yes, Mr. President."

"Then you shall have them, Miss Woolsey. Anything else?"

"No, sir."

He started off but turned back. "If we don't win this war with the Woolsey sisters on our side, then I am no judge of wars."

Jemma

✵

AFTER COMING UPON THOSE MEN IN THE CLEARING, I BEAT it quick as I could back to the path toward home, the frogs starting their nighttime songs, the trees tall and dark above me.

I was almost home, when out of nowhere someone grabbed me from behind, by the arm. My heart went right solid standing there on the path and I thought I'd fall.

Slowly I turned around. "Mister *Harry,*" I gasped. Every inch of me went limp with relief. It was Anne-May's brother, who'd been so kind to us at her wedding. "When'd you get here?"

"Just today and I'm glad I did. This is not a good place for a young lady, Jemma."

"I was just curious about—"

"Walk back to the house with me. And how about we get Sally Smith to fry us up some of that bacon?"

IT WAS A FINE TREAT having Mr. Harry with us all summer. He talked Anne-May into letting Patience come visit us for Ma and Pa's wedding anniversary, and I helped her bring over a whole armful of sunflowers from

Miss Charlene's patch. You've never seen a happier ma than ours when we handed her those big-faced flowers, and she gathered us to her and held us like she'd never let go.

By the time the leaves started turning, Harry and Pa had built us a set of stairs in the shack; a whole new, bigger hog pen; and a window with glass for Sally Smith up in her loft. Only trouble was, having him around made Miss Anne-May care so much about her looks, I spent an extra hour each day on her toilette, even on Sunday, our one day of rest.

One Sunday, on Ma's birthday, it took me all morning to get Anne-May ready for church. First I sugar-scrubbed her face and neck and feet, then got out her box with the secret compartments where she kept her lotions and creams. She thought they made her look younger and I smeared them all over her face and arms. Then I mixed India ink, burnt clove paste, and charcoal to just the right black-brown and slopped it on her head so her regular yellow hair wouldn't show through.

"Why was I born with blond hair, Jemma?" she'd cry. "It's a deformity."

Then she had me tap beetroot on her face, fill a cotton bag with Venetian talc and dab it all over, on her arms and on her face to cover up her freckles, and smooth castor oil on her eyelids. Only then did she let me go see my family.

Finally, I got to run down below and give Ma the present I'd been working on—a flowerpot bonnet, the bonnet part wove around one of Miss Anne-May's clay flowerpots and tinted a nice light brown with my walnut shell dye. Ma called those bonnets I made "trash bonnets," meant in a nice way, because I decorated them with what I called my "trash roses," flowers fashioned out of scraps from my ragbag. Yellow silk roses with green organza leaves. Pink flannel carnations so real a bee tried to land on one.

Under her chin, Ma tied the blue ribbons I'd scavenged from Anne-May's sewing basket. "Thank you, Jemma. You sure know my colors."

I gave Ma the dolls from Patience, which made Ma cry a little. Sally Smith gave Ma a new head rag, red and yellow check she hugged to her chest. Then Pa gave her a fine wood cross on a chain, all made from one piece of wood that he'd been working on all summer. Then Celeste just said some old poem that made Ma smile and she gave her a big hug. That's when the green-eyed monster slithered out and just about drowned me in envy and I stood, arms folded across my chest, watching those two.

"Patience should be here with us, not some new girl," I said. "She spent months making those dolls for you."

Ma took me by the arm, walked me outside and down the road. "You and Patience will always be my girls."

I kept walking, hands in my apron pockets.

"Celeste needs a good word and you don't seem to have one. I'm gonna put you two together and I want you to be kind."

I shrugged. "I didn't do anything."

Ma smoothed back my hair. "That's the problem. You know it's on you to reach out, Jemma. When you mess up, fess up."

I kicked a stone down the road.

Ma linked arms with me and bent so close I could smell that morning's ashcakes she'd had with Celeste on her.

"We're going to church, Jemma. You two stay here and work it out."

MA LEFT THE TWO of us alone in the cabin and we sat on opposite sides of the room, her on Delly's cot, me on the stairs, and stared at the floor for a while.

Celeste played with a quilt square that'd flapped loose. "Nice folks you got."

"Suppose so."

"Ain't got kin of my own."

"Don't say *ain't*. 'Ain't ain't great.'"

"Sally says you can read. Know your letters, too."

"Aunt Tandy Rose let us read before Anne-May came. Taught myself to write some."

"Almost went to school down in Carolina but then I got sold off."

"How was that?"

"You're lucky you never done it. Worst day I can remember. In Charleston." She bowed her head, two fists under her chin. "They get us all clean and fattened up, then after the sale off you go in chains, walking barefoot, no food for days."

"They put you up for sale?"

"Yes they did. Being up there on a table, all the men liftin' my skirt. Sold off to the worst farmer in the South for picking rice. Shoulda seen the look on my ma's face when she saw me go. They took my brothers off, too." She wiped a tear. "Don't know what they're doing without me."

I leaned in closer. "Sally Smith says just saying the words makes you feel a heap better."

She slid a little white card out of her pocket. "My ma gave me this right before they took me off. Well, not my blood ma, but close enough. Name was Alice." She handed me the card. "Thought you might read it for me."

"Well, I suppose." I took the card. "It says *Mrs. Charles Woolsey, 8 Brevoort Place, New York City.*"

I had to read those last words twice. "New York *City*? Where'd you get this?"

Celeste shrugged. "Ma told me the lady who gave it to her said if she ever came to New York, to come find her. Said she seemed nice."

We both sat listening to hogs rooting around in their mud.

"Wonder what Brevoort Place is," Celeste said.

"Aunt Tandy Rose said in New York City they have a big park where everyone walks in fancy clothes and you can buy rides in a little cart pulled by a goat and there's Barnum's museum with whales in tanks and a seal that talks. Patience and I want to see it something awful, but I suppose you can come, too."

"I'll come, sure. Maybe I can learn to read and write a bit."

I took Pa's paper and pencil. "How about I teach you to write your name?"

"You can? Teach me to write Sukey Celeste, my two names together? And add Wilson Watson."

"Why d'you want Anne-May's last name?"

Celeste shrugged. "Better than none."

Once I showed Celeste how to hold the pencil proper, she was sure good at writing and wrote her name ten times over, down the page. "You help me write to my ma?"

"You bet."

Then Celeste started to cry for real, fat tears, her shoulders shuddering.

She wiped her face with two hands. "Just happy tears. Can't believe I can *write*."

"That's just the start." I scratched down the alphabet on the paper. "And to read, you just learn these letters and then you can read whole books one day."

"Never saw a book up close before," she said, wiping the last of her wet face with her sleeve.

I stood. "Let's go get us one. Anne-May's at church."

"What if she comes back early?" Celeste said softly.

"We'll be fine. I do this plenty."

I took her hand, her palm rough and tore up from tobacco work, and led her in a run up to the house. Double-quick we stepped down the hall and stood in front of the closed library door catching our breath.

Celeste hugged her belly. "I'm sure scared."

I pulled the key from my apron pocket and held it up and paused to show off a little and opened the door. "Nothing to worry about. This is what best friends do, pull mischief."

Celeste stepped to the middle of the room and looked around at all four walls covered with glass-doored cases filled with books. "So many books. Why they behind glass?"

I opened one door. "Keeps the dust off. I'm in charge of keeping the glass clean."

"Every day?"

I ran one finger along the shelf. "Most days. Wipe it with a special vinegar."

"Can I hold one?"

"If you're careful." I slid a book from the shelf, *Villette by Charlotte Brontë* written down the spine, drawing of a white couple on the front.

"This one's about this girl Lucy who likes this doctor, John Bretton, who marries somebody else."

"Is it true?" Celeste asked.

"No, these are all made up, but meant to seem true."

"Sounds sad."

"S'posed to be, I reckon."

Celeste tipped her head to one side. "Think I'd like a happy ending."

I set *Villette* back on the shelf and pulled down another, *Uncle Tom's Cabin* written down the spine. *H. B. Stowe. VOL I.* "I read this one once. Want to read it again. It's pretty good."

Celeste took it and smoothed one hand down the front. "So pretty."

I smiled, nose in the air. "All Aunt Tandy Rose's books have leather covers. Anne-May only cares about how pretty they are. Doesn't read any, especially this one, since it's about slaves. Patience says almost as many folks've read it as the Bible." I ran my hand down the gold decoration on the cover. "This's called embossing. I'm taking it."

"Oh no, Jemma."

"Quit your worrying. Not a soul would come in here to find it gone, except Miss Euphemia sometimes and she doesn't notice much." I moved the other books to fill the empty space.

"Where'll you keep it?"

I shrugged. "Wherever I like. Sometimes I read while I'm sewing when Anne-May's napping, and I keep it in the linen closet."

"Is it scary? I'd give anything to read it."

"Since we're best friends now, I'll teach you." I took Celeste's hand. "Let's go down below and start."

"We'll get in all sorts of trouble."

"Don't worry one bit. You're with me. You'll be just fine."

WE SAT SIDE BY SIDE at the table back at the cabin, with the book set before us. "I'll write some letters in the back of the book and you copy them," I told Celeste.

Pretty soon she was writing almost good as Patience.

"Hey, I got an idea." I took out the letter from Carter I kept in my pocket always. "Let's read this together. It's from the only beau I ever had, that Aunt Tandy Rose sold off on account of him looking like her brother, who was his daddy."

"That's mean."

Guess it was my time to cry, not blubbery, just a few quiet tears. "She had a heart of iron when it came to him. Since he so looked like her brother, Wilfred, he was a constant reminder her brother forced hisself on one of her slaves, over on the beet farm."

Celeste set her hand on mine. "Where's he at now?"

"Carter? Last I heard, Alabama. But let's read this and you can hear his voice in a fashion."

I spread out the letter between us and followed the words with my finger:

PORTLAND, ALABAMA

Dear Jemma,

Here in Portland I miss you every day but found someone who promises to bring this letter to you by hand. If you are reading this, picture me at my candle, eyes shut tight, remembering you and Patience. Hope you think of me, too. I know you can't reply, but you are in my heart every day but Tuesday, when I drive the hogs to town and can't think of much else. This is all I can write at present. Direct your letters to Bailey Plantation, West Portland, Alabama. In care of R. W. Samuels.

Yours very truly,
Carter

Celeste smiled her sweetest. "He esteems you, Jemma. And he's sure good with a pen."

"Isn't he? I taught him." I folded the letter with care and set it back in my pocket. "Bet you find a boy someday, good as him."

"Thanks, Jemma. You know, I was sure jealous of you when I first come here. Thought you were pretty fulla yourself, up in that fine house with such nice clothes and talking like a white lady. You even know your birth-day."

"Nice clothes?" I smoothed one hand down the once-yellow calico skirt of my dress, worn smooth and practically white, the flowers faded out. "This is Anne-May's old calico I made over." Didn't tell her about the only other one I had, a threadbare green cotton, patched with every green type of cloth in Anne-May's rag bag, and worn white in spots, but I saved it for best. "When you came I was pea green with envy over your dimples."

She smiled and tilted her head to the side. "But for all your fancy ways, I think you're nice."

I slid the book toward her on the table. "You're nice, too. Why don't you take this one for yourself?"

"For keeps?"

"Learn to read with it, then we'll get you more. Careful though. You change once you read some books. Get more thoughts about things."

"Can I write my name in it?"

I shrugged. "I suppose."

Celeste took the pencil and wrote inside the cover: *Sukey Celeste Wilson Watson.* She then slowly copied the address from her card: *8 Brevoort Place, New York.*

I watched her, proud of my first student. "But just hide it well. Anne-May finds it, there's no telling what she'll do."

ONCE THEY ALL GOT BACK from church, Charl went into town, and Ma and Celeste went off to hunt blackberries. They asked me to go, but I said no, wanting to stay with Delly and help Harry and Pa set up out by the squash patch. They were making two doors to stand up in place of the old blankets we tacked up.

Pa sanded while Harry shaved the wood with a metal piece, taking it down nice and smooth, sending that good pine smell into the air. Pa squeezed old leather bellows on a fire they used to make nails.

He never looked so happy as when he was making something with wood. When he wasn't in the fields, he did carpentry, like building Mister Watson's science shack down by the river and making outbuildings for Anne-May. A man from Leonardtown paid him twenty dollars to make him a maul to split logs with, and said it was the finest wooden hammer he'd ever seen, the long locust-wood handle polished to a soft shine.

Pa was sure proud of his smokehouse that he built for Anne-May out back near the new barn. Turns out white people killed more food than they ate so they hung it up in the smoke house and cooked it with smoke to stop it goin' rancid. It was a round building of whitewashed brick with a black pointed roof, a little bigger and taller than our cabin. Only went in there once, when LeBaron left it unlocked by mistake. Got the creeps as I stepped in the little door, saw the fire pit in the middle stacked high with apple wood, and hams hung in burlap swaying from the ceiling. Pa said you couldn't even see your hand in there, the smoke'd get so thick.

Anne-May gave Pa paper and he sketched with a pencil to make her tables and chairs or whatever she dreamed up. Taller by a bit than Mr. Harry, he smiled ear to ear when he had a hammer in his hand. Pa's name other than Pa was Joseph, which fit him, seeing as in the Bible Joseph worked with wood. But Pa had a third name, Kofi, his own Pa's name, a name given in Africa to boys born on Friday. That was his secret name, just with us.

Pa had another secret, too. He'd been making something else, by the fire at night. I saw when he thought I was asleep, him shaving down the wood handles, the silver blades shining orange in the firelight. Heard him put them up under a board of Sally's loft.

Delly and I leaned against the new hog pen fence watching Sally toss a whole bucket of peanuts to the hogs to top them off before killing time. They rooted around after the peanuts, mud splashed on their black-splotched fur, ears flapping. Then Sally strolled by me and Delly and slid us each a handful of peanuts into our pockets, and kept walking.

Peanuts never tasted so good, there taking in the sun with Delly, watching Pa and Harry work, the little curlicue shavings flying off the wood, the stink of manure mixing with the pine smell in a good way. But then, along came LeBaron, his fat friend Clem, and three other pattyrollers ridin' down to the shack, kicking up a cloud of dust, Miss Charlene's dogs at their heels. They wore their crazy clothes, coats inside out, handkerchiefs tied over their mouths, tall, pointy hats they'd made. Clem kept a whistle in his mouth, tweeting it, all just to scare us.

They stopped next to the hog pen and sat in their saddles, holding half-empty liquor bottles on the Lord's day. LeBaron's skinny-neck friend Chester was there, too, and wore the same phony silver star as LeBaron did.

Harry glanced up from his shaving. "No need to act the fool on the Lord's day."

"Africans scare easy, that's a fact. Gotta keep that fear of God in 'em." LeBaron slid down off his horse. "We're celebratin', too. Got word of another bluebelly surrender."

As LeBaron stood near me I got a good look at his tin star pinned to his vest, RUNAWAY SLAVE PATROL etched in the middle. Someone had crafted it with loving care, decorated it with little swirls and flowers here and there.

The hounds came sniffing and growling at Delly and me as Chester led the others into our shack, where they set about pawing through our things, all serious.

Pa's knives. Every part of me froze up as I listened to them upstairs in Sally's loft. I looked to Pa, but he kept sanding, couple beads of sweat come out on his forehead.

Harry continued his shaving. "That so?"

LeBaron lifted the flask to his lips, lost his footing a touch, and drank. "Indeed it is. Lexington, Missouri. Union colonel James Mulligan surrendered. We got 'em on the run, I tell you, sir." He pointed one finger toward Pa. "And once we Rebs win, all you coloreds is here for good."

"You and your pattyrollers signing up?" Harry asked.

"For the fight? No time soon. Got to keep these darkie best friends of yours here under control. You?"

"Joining the First Maryland Infantry CSA if they'll have me."

Pa stopped sanding and looked at Harry, sadness in his eyes.

"You don't say," LeBaron said. "Harry Wilson fightin' for the Rebs. Thought for sure you were a Negro Crusader at heart."

Harry took off his hat and rubbed his forehead. "I'm more of a gradual emancipationist."

LeBaron kicked the dirt. "And that's what?"

"I'd like to see the slaves freed slow. Make sure it's done right."

"So why fight for the South?" LeBaron asked.

"Seems we're right back at the revolution with this invasion of Northern power. I'm not for slavery, but you can't just take that much property from people overnight. It'll ruin Louisiana."

LeBaron drew on his flask, and then waved it toward Pa. "Long as it's them pickin' tobacco, not me."

"Besides, God will protect me." Harry set back to work. "I choose to fight for what I believe in. What do you believe in, Mr. Caruthers? Getting drunk and riding with your boys?"

"This ain't about me or the boys, Harry," LeBaron said. "I'd enlist. But can't go off leaving Miss Anne-May with all these darkies."

Over at the shack Chester and the others laughed and joked as they pulled the place apart, dumping the corn husks out of our mattresses.

"Why tear their place apart?" Harry asked.

LeBaron shrugged. "Got word somebody's making knives."

Harry smiled. "Who'd have the time to do that?"

LeBaron stared right at Pa. "You tell me."

Pa kept his eyes on his door shaving.

LeBaron turned and stepped to Delly. "When's that baby coming? Must be close to time now."

She smoothed her good hand down over her belly and I shimmied closer till the sides of our hips touched.

"What's it to you?" Harry asked. "Bringing babies is women's work. That's not your bailiwick."

LeBaron stepped closer to Harry and made a little circle in the air with his finger. "This whole place's my bailiwick."

Harry stopped his shaving and stood straighter and puffed his chest out. "From what I've seen, babies don't follow schedules."

LeBaron stepped closer to him and stuck his chest out, too, so they were like two ornery roosters.

"I'd be careful if I was you, Harry. Where Anne-May's property's concerned, she sides with me always."

"Well, well, well," Chester called down from the loft. "Lookee what I found."

We heard him tumbling down the steps and he shuffled out the cabin with something hid behind his back.

He came to LeBaron and showed what was in his hand. "It's a book."

Every part of me relaxed when I saw it wasn't the knives he found. Until I saw what book it was.

LeBaron snatched it from Chester. "Looks like one of Mrs. Watson's fancy ones." He held it away from him, reading it slow. *"Un . . ."*

Chester read his shoulder. "Says *Uncle Tom's Cabin.*"

"It's just a fiction book," I said. "Pretend."

"Let's see here." LeBaron opened the book and turned it to us to display the picture. "It's got pictures. Happy, free darkies."

Chester chucked a stone into the woods. "That's pretend, all right."

LeBaron ran one finger along the inside cover. "What's this writ here?"

Chester took a close look. "Says *Sukey Celeste Wilson Watson.*"

LeBaron shut the cover with a terrible snap.

"Guess we now know who it belongs to. That new girl, Celeste. She'd be in a whole heap a trouble, having stole a book like this and taking Miss Anne-May's name in it, too."

"It was me who gave it to her," I said. "Not her fault."

LeBaron looked at me, eyes half-squinted. "Don't know what Anne-May'd do if she found out, now do we, Jemma?"

ONCE HARRY WALKED LEBARON back up to the house, Pa turned to me.

"You put Celeste in danger, Jemma. No more books for now and don't leave her side for the next week or so. You come find me if LeBaron gives her trouble. Same goes for you, Delly. We all know why Mister Caruthers is so interested in the welfare of that baby of yours. When you feel it coming, you need a signal to call for help. There's strength in numbers."

Pa hustled into the shack and came back with an old bean can, the lid flapped up. He went to the road, scooped up stones into the tin, then came back to the fire and held the hot poker around the lid. He blew on the top, stepped to Delly, and handed it to her.

"Careful—it's still plenty hot."

"What's this?" she asked, with her pretty smile.

"Shake it."

Delly shook the can and the rocks rolled around inside.

Pa folded his arms across his chest. "*Really* shake it."

Delly shook that can harder and it made a noise so loud the old sow in the pen woke up with a snort.

Pa threw his head back and laughed. "Thatta girl. And don't be shy about usin' it. We'll all come running."

Delly's eyes got all watery and she looked away, off toward the river. "That's mighty kind."

Pa went back to his sanding. "One thing's for sure, LeBaron Caruthers is not gonna touch that baby. Long as I have breath in my body."

ONE DAY ANNE-MAY CAME to me while I was helping Sally shell peas, and slid a pretty red leather book across the table to me, and a pink-ribbon-tied packet of letters.

"Take this book and copy down these letters into it for me."

She had me write a whole pack of Union war tales from Mister Watson's brother's letters, all about some battle in Virginia he was fighting in. He told of how it wasn't so good for the North, and all the particulars of the forts they were building around Washington so the Rebels wouldn't get to the capital. When I finished, Anne-May made me take the book over to that terrible Mr. Smalls, and I felt bad with good Mister Watson not knowing his wife was telling all his brother's secrets to that snakiest snake.

I thought about heaving that evil book into the woods and fibbing it was lost, but Anne-May'd give it to me bad or have LeBaron tumble me down the hill in his tobacco barrel with the nails inside, or worse. Thought about smashing my own hand with a hammer to get out of writing, like Harry told us some soldiers did to get out of serving. But I was too chicken to take a hammer to a perfectly good hand.

LEBARON KEPT HIS SECRET about having that *Uncle Tom's Cabin* book so long I almost forgot what he had over Celeste and me.

One sweltering day I walked off to Ambrosia, a paperboard carton of chicks for Miss Charlene held against my belly, my bare heels hitting the hard dirt path. The chicks peeped, poking their orange beaks out the air holes, and I breathed deep the parched grass and honeysuckle smell of late summer. How lucky I was to have a sister, and now a new friend, Celeste, and planned to have the three of us take a good long visit after church if Miss Charlene said yes to that.

Even all that ways away from Peeler, I could hear Ma singing in the tobacco field, leading Delly, Pa, Celeste, and Charl in "Old Virginia Never Tires," with her own made-up words:

> *A jaybird sat on a hickory limb,*
> *He winked at me and I winked at him,*
> *I picked up a stone and hit him in the shin*
> *Says you better not do that again.*

The sound of her singing hurt my stomach, since she sang mostly when she was sad. That jaybird was Anne-May, of course, though she was never smart enough to figure that out. Made Ma feel a little better, making up those songs, her way of fighting back.

I felt the horse's hooves on dirt before I heard him, coming from the hardpacked path behind me, and turned to find LeBaron atop his horse.

I squinted up at him against the sun.

"Like you to do me a favor, Jemma."

I turned and kept walking, eyes fixed on the path in front of me.

"I'm gonna ask you nice, now," he called after me. "And I want you to think about your answer long and hard before you give it. Not that I need your say-so."

I kept on, my palms wet on the cardboard.

"I want you and me to take a little stroll together. Maybe have a talk."

I tripped on a root and almost dropped the chicks, but righted myself.

LeBaron urged his horse closer till she was practically breathing down my neck and I could hear the horseflies buzzing around her head.

"I expect a little something back from you, Jemma. You're just as bad as your ma, disrespectin' me." He leaned down his horse's neck. "Ain't right me offering an invitation with no reply."

I kept on, making him no answer, just saying *I'd rather step on a snake than touch you* to myself.

"Mister Watson won't be here forever to protect you all, if that's what you're thinking."

LeBaron reined in his horse and stopped. "I'll give you one last chance to reconsider."

I picked up my pace, and got a ways ahead, finally a little cool wind in my face. I glanced back, saw him up on his horse, face red as a swamp crayfish, but turned and kept going.

"You know that word *regret,* Jemma?" he called after me. "Hope so. 'Cause you sure are gonna regret this."

Anne-May

ONE HOT FALL DAY FERGUS AND HARRY BOTH MARCHED OFF
to war, Fergus in his sky-blue uniform, north with the Yankees, U.S. Army,
First Maryland Volunteer Infantry. Harry went south to join the Confederacy, First Maryland Infantry CSA, with his butternut-yellow jacket from
Mama under his arm. We weren't the only ones in a border state with family members fighting on opposite sides, but that didn't make it any easier.
I ached for Fergus to stay by Harry's side to protect him, but instead they
parted ways at the fork in the road.

In the kitchen before they left, Harry embraced Fergus like a brother,
bringing a tear, possibly genuine, to the eye of Sally Smith. Harry and Fergus had never been particularly close, but a person couldn't help but be
touched to see the two of them part ways, knowing they'd be fighting on
different sides.

"I hope to see you again soon," Fergus said.

"Not too soon," Harry said with a smile. "You're too good a shot."

Harry had spent the morning saying goodbyes to his colored folk down
the hill, rather than get a proper send-off from his own kin.

Fergus spent the morning drilling me with instructions as we sat at the
dining room table, Saint Joan asleep there, the shiny surface her favorite

spot. I considered it a victory that after almost two months of living with me, on rare occasions she finally allowed me to pet her without biting my hand.

Fergus slapped his pad of paper on the table and my head hurt at the thought of a math lesson.

"Since the investments Reggie's made with our money have not yielded the intended results, I'm afraid I leave you with less than adequate funds, Anne-May. I will send my pay, and that will have to sustain you all. You'll have last year's leaf and the new dried by spring and ready for auction. But you must tend to the new shoots come April."

"Surely you and Harry'll be back before then."

"Make sure Joseph and Sable plant the tobacco seeds in the barn a few weeks after Christmas as always. Transplant into the mounds. And when it comes to the leaves, the seconds come first—"

I waved him away. "Hell's bells, Fergus, that makes no sense."

"I learned this in one day, Anne-May."

"But you went to school to learn plants. All I learned was my stitches."

"Just pay attention, that's all. Remember to weed carefully and top off each plant so it doesn't spread and make sure they get all those tobacco worms."

"I can't go near those worms, Fergus."

A dull ache gripped my skull and I felt for my snuff bottle. Had Jemma misplaced it?

"Attach the leaves to the stakes and dry them in the barn. Then sort, bundle, and pack them in the crates. LeBaron will ship them up to New York."

He rolled out a map on the table. "Now, these fields will need to be planted for corn, and the hogs, they're like money in the bank. Sell five at a time if you need emergency money or have Joseph slaughter one, only when you . . ."

Why hadn't I listened to Mama when she told me plantation life is so hard? I looked out over the river in the distance. *How nice to just float down that river out to the bay, far from—*

"Are you even listening, Anne-May? And I left my father's silver brushes in my top drawer if you need to pawn something as a last resort. And don't let that cat get at my turtles. And water my terrariums—"

"You know I don't like goin' in your office, Fergus. That lizard . . ."

"It's a chameleon and Euphemia's promised to feed it crickets. Don't you worry. Just a cup of water once a week in each terrarium. You can do that, now, right?"

AT FIRST, AFTER FERGUS and Harry left, the farm practically ran itself. I busied myself taking stock of my wardrobe, choosing what to wear to the Harvest Ball in Leonardtown, leaving me with the impression I sorely needed a new dress.

The windows at Smalls and Sons were no longer full of the finest fashions, and just months into the war the best imported cloth and notions were already hard for Mr. Smalls to find. They were down to their last seven yards, twenty-five dollars' worth of gray China silk that, with my meager budget, would most likely end up on the back of Miss Charlene Tidwell Weed.

A week after the boys marched off, a letter from Fergus came, penned in his looping hand.

My dearest Anne-May,

I've thought of you often on our journey to Phillipsburg. They have put me in charge of a company at the rank of captain and my men seem to be happy to follow my lead. One is a former classmate of mine at Harvard, in my same chemistry class if you can believe it. The first task I have been assigned is to guard an old store near the railroad depot, which holds some very important equipment (if you can believe your botanist husband has been given oversight over an actual powder keg). I cannot tell more, since my orders come sporadically, but trust that I love you and . . .

I stepped to Jemma and handed her the red book. "Copy from the letter and write it in here. Just the part about the train."

"Yes, missis."

"Make it your best writin', now."

As Jemma wrote, slow as cold molasses, I went to the kitchen, separated off from the rest of the house in case of fire. That room induced great satisfaction, with wide windows offering a view across the long slope of grass to the river. For all old Aunt Tandy Rose's faults, she knew how to furnish a kitchen, with sturdy wooden counters and a wide porcelain sink.

The only blights on the scene were the ugly cast-iron pots placed around the room, one on the counter next to the stove, from which at least a hundred wooden spoons stood, like decapitated flowers, old Sally Smith's collection, to which Fergus had contributed, when, in his travels, he came upon a spoon with an unusual carved handle or rare wood. How often had he stepped into that room, brought his hand round from behind his back, and presented her with a new wooden spoon for her collection.

"Aw, Mister Watson. You made it your own self? You are one talented man."

That's how she wound him around her pinkie.

Sally Smith stood with one of those spoons, stirring something steamy in a pot, skin dark as the iron stove. For all I knew, she was cooking up one of her old African remedies she drug out every time Fergus sneezed, instead of working on a decent dinner.

"You have any money, Sally?" I asked.

She just peppered the pot.

"I'd like you to lend me some. Need things at the grocer. Flour, soap—"

"Write it down and I'll send Charl to town."

I massaged my left wrist. "You know I can't write since my injury."

Sally glanced over. "Was your right hand last week."

"You know I'm not good at writin', Sally. Don't give me that look. I can read, for goodness' sake, I just choose not to write. The important thing is we need things. Rice—"

"Got a whole barrel of perfectly good rice in the pantry untouched."

"Well, if you hadn't rudely interrupted me, I was about to say I also need to buy some new cloth to make winter coats for you all."

Sally banged a pot into the sink. "You know what I'm saving up for."

"Already *told* you I won't sell that girl for any amount. Besides, Jemma isn't worth spending money on, Sally. She wouldn't last five minutes as a free girl. She's too stupid."

"*She* knows her letters."

A hot wind blew into my head. "That jelly business is illegal, Sally. Mister Watson may turn a blind eye, but one word from me to the sheriff—"

Sally Smith waddled to the pantry.

I looked out the window to the river as I waited. "Any more sass from you and I have a mind to put you in my pocket."

"Mister Watson'd be mad you sell me off, Miss Anne-May," came Sally's muffled reply from the pantry.

"He'd survive just fine. You may backtalk Mister Watson, but I hold the paper on you, Sally, and don't you forget it. High time you remember your place around here."

Sally returned from the pantry, eyes properly downcast, with a rolled-up wad of bills in hand. "Only have twenty-five."

I plucked it from her fingers. "That'll do for now. Tell a soul and you'll be gone by morning."

EUPHEMIA AND I DROVE into town, bought the seven yards of dove-gray silk and a few other things, Jubal Smalls nowhere to be seen, just his house woman Doreen and her four boys, crowded around her like always. We went on to old Dr. Gardener's house, or rather, that of his widow, Beulah Bickford Gardener, the frequent hostess of our gatherings.

With its wide porch and fall roses, sunflowers, and foxglove growing in her front garden, it was the prettiest house in Hollywood, though that was not sayin' much. Euphemia and I stepped into the house and went straight to our places at the sewing circle, around a blue and gray Flying Geese quilt to auction at the soldier benefit, more than halfway done.

"My nephew Phillip's finally sent a letter," Widow Gardener said.

"Isn't he in my Fergus's regiment?" I asked.

"The same. Says they march for the Shenandoah Valley."

My mind wandered at the mention of a battle. Unless my Harry was in it, they were all just confusing names. To make it worse, the North and South called them different names.

I yearned for the cool breeze of a fan but Widow Gardener only had one servant left, crippled-up old Bitty May. She'd freed the rest and sent them north, after her husband contracted typhus and died after doctoring one of the slaves over at Ambrosia.

Old Bitty set a cup of tea down next to me, a piece of paper poking out from under the cup. I checked her face and found no trace of understanding about that note, just the usual dumb look all coloreds have. I picked up the cup and saucer, lifted the cup, and read.

My love, Meet me in the butler's pantry. J.

I excused myself and, under the watchful eye of my sister, stepped out of the room. In the pantry I found Jubal leaning against a flour barrel, smoking a cigar.

"You're eavesdroppin', evil man."

"Just delivering some flour to an old widow woman."

"Who might just have some Union war secrets from her nephew?"

"Thought you might like a little present." He slipped a tin of Golden-Banded Oco snuff into my pocket.

"I take that back about you bein' evil, Jubal."

He ran one finger down my bodice and gently tugged on the jet button at my chest. "Certainly fine jet buttons."

"Found them in a little shop in New Orleans."

"All the way from England most likely."

He continued to play with my button, rolling it between thumb and forefinger.

"Do you know everything there is to know in this world, Jubal Smalls?"

All at once the button came loose with a little pop and he handed it to me. "Many pardons, Mrs. Watson. Seems I don't know my own strength."

I slipped the button in my pocket. "I better get back in there."

"Got that book?"

"Could be."

He smiled. "C'mon now."

"What are you doing with all this? Sellin' it? They hang spies, you know. I rather like my neck."

"I do as well." He ran one finger down my throat. "But this is just between us."

I pulled the book from my pocket and handed it to Jubal. "Had that girl of mine write it."

He slid the book into his coat pocket. "You don't say."

"Jemma's stupid, but she's a fair writer and will hide the book well. The coloreds are masters of stealing and secreting things."

"I'll send it back when I'm done."

"There isn't a whole lot of war information in there. Fergus packs his letters with more poetry and science talk than military factuation. If you're not sharing it with anyone, why do you want it?"

All at once Jubal pulled me close, softly pressed his lips to mine, and kissed me, long and slow. I pushed him away, my hand against his chest, but then slipped one hand inside his shirt. I ran my fingers along his warm skin and he kissed me deeper.

He gently drew his lips from mine, but still held me tight. "I can taste the Golden Oco. It's good on you."

I pulled away and straightened my skirt, my whole body trembling. "You should give a girl a warning, Mr. Smalls."

"That would spoil the fun, don't you think? There's more where that came from, Anne-May. Now you get back out there and find out more."

"Maybe I will, maybe I won't," I said with a smile.

I hurried out of the pantry, a bit dizzy in the head, and took my place next to Charlene in the sewing circle.

She looked up from her quilting. "Where'd you go all this time?"

"To the necessary room. Feelin' a bit queasy."

"Must be all that snuff you dip." Charlene leaned in close. "You reek of tobacco and your hands are shaking."

Euphemia scowled at me across the table. "And you lost one of your jet buttons."

I smiled at Euphemia. "Sorry to interrupt the conversation. Where were we about the Shenandoah Valley? Please tell me every little thing about it. There's no place more fascinatin'."

Jemma

✹

PEELER PLANTATION, MARYLAND
OCTOBER 1861

A FEW MONTHS PASSED AFTER LEBARON THREATENED ME
with bad things if I didn't play nice with him. As summer moved into fall
and nothing ever happened, I figured he'd forgotten about it and life
went on.

I couldn't wait to get to Pa's secret nighttime meeting, but the afternoon dragged, since once Anne-May started dipping snuff all day and visiting Mr. Smalls she got more particular than ever. She pitched fits at me as
I stood behind her chair, shooing the flies off her with the peafowl-feather
fan, and complained all day.

"My back is itchy, Jemma," Anne-May'd said. "Why did you draw such
hot bathwater this morning?"

But bad as it was, it almost made me forget how scared I was about
LeBaron threatening me.

ONCE I FINALLY GOT Anne-May to sleep that night, I snuck down to the
shack for Pa's secret meeting. It was plumb dark in there, Sally, Ma, Pa,
Celeste, and me around Pa's little pine table, only one little lard candle lit

so no pattyrollers would see us up past nine o'clock lights-out. But night was our day, only time we could have a little freedom.

Smelled good and bad in there, like Sally's gumbo and smelly Devil's Dung drying by the fire. Pa let me sit on his lap like always even though I was too old for that kind of thing, and I settled in against his chest and felt the thump of his big heart against my arm.

Ma had her hair wrapped in her favorite pink head rag, tied up high. When Anne-May came to Peeler, she made all us ladies start wearing head rags, like they did by law in Louisiana to mark folks as slaves, when before we only wore them to work if we wanted. Only time we got to wear bonnets was on Sunday. Ma knew Anne-May's rule was just trying to keep us down, and took that as a test to make her head rags the prettiest, tied up in a fancy new way every day, just to spite Anne-May.

Sally Smith never wore head rags, just cream-colored sugar sacks she rescued from the kitchen and washed up soft and tied up her hair in. Even washed, those sacks gave Sally a sweet smell all her own.

A little pang of missing Mr. Harry went through me when I looked at the sturdy whitewashed steps he'd made, winding their way down from the loft, a smooth rope hung on the wall to hold on to.

Charl stepped down those stairs, wearing the coat Delly made over for him, a fine brown wool castoff of Mister Watson's, which proved her skill, having only one hand to sew with, though Ma threaded her needles for her.

Charl set himself down next to Ma. "Delly's finally dropped off."

"Good," Ma said. "Poor girl, working the fields with that much baby in her belly."

"My great-great-grandma Fari came with a baby too, right here to the front lawn of Peeler, in the year 1720, on the *Generous Jenny* straight from Africa," Sally said.

Ma sent Pa a look that said, *Here she goes.*

"Old Captain Smith, who the Peelers bought this house from, traded twenty-nine bedsheets for her. Highest price of any of the eighty-nine slaves on that ship, since she was a royal woman."

Ma looked bored, but I could hear that story a hundred times and still want more.

"She look like you?" I asked.

"Way taller and hair out to here, men stopped in the street when she walked by, stunned by all that beauty."

Pa sat up a little straighter. "Before we start, I wanna give Jemma something I've been workin' on as a reward. Carved out of deer bone."

I sat up straighter, all puffed up with pride.

"For her reading to Pastor Kearn's blind ma for all these weeks in the vestry while the rest of us are enjoying the service." He handed me a bone cross the size of my thumb, perfectly carved. "She's a lucky woman to have you read scriptures to her so pretty, Jemma."

Ma smiled as I turned and hugged Pa, a pinch of feeling bad nipping at me, since I liked sitting with Mrs. Kearn. It got me out of regular services, and she had her girl make me a strawberry fizz every time I said Peter was my favorite apostle, while it was really Thomas, the only one who had the good sense to not accept a person rising from the dead without at least a little investigation.

I smoothed the cross in my fingers. "Thanks, Pa."

Pa held up another bone cross, just the same. "And I'll keep this one so we're connected. Wherever we go, you and me, we'll always have this."

Celeste smiled, looked happy for me.

"So, now," Pa said. "Anybody have news to share?"

Pa asked this in his lawyer way, since he'd been lent out by Aunt Tandy Rose to work for one in Leonardtown when he was younger.

Charl leaned in. "LeBaron finally took the block off once Mister Watson gave him a talking-to."

After LeBaron had got embarrassed in front of Mister Watson, he'd made Charl wear a wood block chained to his ankle for days. Even worse, out in the fields, made him wear Delly's shimmy, too, but Charl wouldn't talk about that.

"Also heard Anne-May's sister sayin' that the Rebels were thinking about using slaves to fight for the South, but decided not to. And heard LeBaron boasting about another defeat for Lincoln. Place called Ball's Bluff. A whole lot of men drowned in a river there."

"Anything else?" Pa asked.

Sally Smith leaned in. "Well, Anne-May took twenty-five of my hard-earned dollars. Said it was a loan. To make us coats. Really? And buy *rice*. Can you even believe that woman?"

"None of them eat rice up there," Ma said.

"What kinda people don't eat rice? It's just not right."

"Don't give her a penny next time," Pa said.

"She threatened to put me in her pocket."

Ma laughed. "Sell *you*? Just hide your money better next time."

"Already have some stashed in every tin and box in that pantry. Heard some good house talk, too."

I leaned in, happy to hear it since Sally got the best news when the other cooks came to buy up her jellies.

"Widow Gardener's old Bitty May said Anne-May spent my money at Smalls and Sons on silk for herself. Can you imagine? In wartime no less. *And,* at sewing circle Jubal Smalls wrote Anne-May a note asking her to meet him in the pantry. Called her his *love*."

I leaned over the table. "Did they kiss?"

"Bitty said they were in there for a good long time."

Celeste smiled and covered her mouth with her fingers.

Ma sent me a worried look. Every day, she and Pa did the work of six slaves, to keep Peeler on track and makin' money, so none of us would get sold off. With Mister Watson away, Anne-May havin' an expensive tumble with Jubal was a threat to our little family Ma couldn't control.

"Next matter?" Pa asked.

I folded my hands on the table. "Anybody else seen that sunflower tied to the gate on the way to Ambrosia? Seen more, too, all down the path to that spidery tree. What's that mean?"

"No idea," Ma said.

Charl pulled his coat tighter around him. "Go down North Carolina where I come up and you see that a lot—one tied to a tree or a post, any-place that's dangerous to us."

"It's a warning?" Ma asked. "From who?"

He shrugged. "Mostly colored folks who know who to stay clear of. Some white folks do it, too."

"I'm off to Leonardtown all tomorrow to fetch Anne-May's walnut," Pa said. "I'll ask around."

Ma turned to me and Celeste. "Meantime, if you see one, don't go near it."

Pa leaned in and shifted me to his knee. "Next thing to talk about: I suggest we move to Fort Monroe and offer ourselves to the U.S. Army as contraband soon, maybe early as the new year."

"What's contraband?" I asked.

"Any of us who surrender ourselves to Union soldiers," Pa said. "They call us contraband of war and keep us safe."

"The *new year*?" Charl asked. "Two whole months?"

"LeBaron won't look for us when we're off for Christmas. My hope is we move on from there to New York."

Everything in me fluttered at the words. *New York.* Celeste and I met eyes, hers wide.

"We should fight," Charl said. "Mutiny. That's what they did in the islands."

Pa leaned in and spoke low. "I got a plan to assemble some knives."

Charl slammed one palm on the table, making the candle jump. "Knives? Powder and ball's the only thing they understand."

"We can't appear sneaky," Pa said. "Gotta be patient."

"Patient? Delly's about to have that baby any day. Can't be patient. I'm so tired of being judged by white folks. If we're quiet, we're sneaky. If we stay in the fields, we love being slaves. If we run away, we hate work. If we sing, we're childish. If we frown, we're sassy. Can't win. Only choice is to go to Canada."

"Quiet, Charl," Ma said. "You'll wake Delly."

Sally leaned in. "Can you tell us what happened to her . . ."

"Hand?" Charl asked. "Not sure she'd want me—"

Ma looked to the stairs and then we all did, as Delly came down in her shimmy, holding her belly, the baby quilt Sally made around her shoulders.

Delly sat on the second stair and pulled the quilt closer. "I don't mind sayin', but it's not an easy story for the younger ones."

"We're plenty old," I said.

"Okay, then." Delly looked down at her bare feet. "All started down in Georgia, on my third baby in as many years."

"Girl or boy?" Ma asked.

"A girl." Delly smiled. "She was good from the start, came out easy, and just one day old had a sweet little nature, you could tell, with them bright eyes. I try to hide her, since I knew like always Mister Fisher the speculator'd come. Take her away and sell her for a hundred dollars. So he come all right. I told him she was dead, but he turned the place upside down and found her where I left her in the drawer. He took her and got on his horse, holding her under his arm like a bread loaf, and I run after him.

"'Please,' I called after him. 'I'd give my left hand to keep that child.'

"He laughed and said, 'I'd like to see that. Might just be worth leaving this pretty baby behind.'

"I ran to the chopping block, where I must've helped two hundred chickens meet their Maker, took that ax and chopped off my own hand, clean at the bone, and left it there on the block. I'm soft in the head, you might say, but no, I was thinkin' clear. I would have done anything to keep that girl. I got dizzy, but I run back to him, already rode away a piece.

"'Mister Fisher,' I called, my one arm up, blood running down my arm thick. He stopped his horse and turned up there in his saddle and looked right at me. He tipped his head to one side for a long second, and then turned back around and rode off."

We sat quiet, listening to the crickets sing.

"Got sewed up by the animal doctor in town and nobody gave it another mention. Only I think about her every day, her not knowing I wanted her so bad."

Delly stood. "Don't think I can give another one away." She started back up the stairs. "So you'll forgive me for doing what I have to do when Mister LeBaron comes and I have to give this one back to Jesus."

I MANAGED TO GET the hens to lay extra so Anne-May'd send me over to Ambrosia and I'd get to see Patience and it worked like magic. The next day I got sent to deliver a dozen fresh eggs to Miss Charlene. As I walked I thought about LeBaron and how he'd come after me like he had after Ma so many times, though I wasn't anywhere near as pretty as her. It was just a matter of time before he managed to do whatever dirty thing he would to me and I did my best to not look pretty at all.

BY THE TIME I got to Ambrosia I was excited to see Patience, but got the bad news from my least favorite person when Miss Charlene's house girl, skinny little Sybil, came out the back door, just as black as me but somehow thinking she was Miss Charlene's best friend.

"Hope you don't think you're gonna see Patience. She's in the west field today."

"Fine," I said, setting my eggs on the back porch.

"I told Miss Charlene, you know. How you sneak back there for a visit when you stop by. She tole me I can let the dogs out anytime you're here, on account of that."

"How'd you get so sweet, Sybil?"

"You better get off now," she said with a bitter smile. "It's feedin' time and I'd hate to leave the pen door open."

AS I WALKED BACK, and after I drummed up ten ways to get back at Sybil, I thought about Delly and her saying she'd kill her own child. How could she even say that out loud? Probably made Ma think of little Toby and how he died.

I came to the end of the path, where it opened to Peeler and the outbuildings, and saw a mess of gray smoke chugging out of the smokehouse chimney. Ma and Sally stood nearby the little whitewashed house, walking in circles, doubling over at the waist now and then, and wringing their hands.

Ma hurried to me, tears in her eyes. "Jemma—it's bad."

"What?" I walked on to the smokehouse.

Sally joined us. "You better not look, girl."

I picked up speed. "*Tell* me."

Ma followed. "After Pa left for Leonardtown, that's when LeBaron went to Anne-May with a book he said Celeste took from her and wrote her name in."

"I heard it all from the kitchen," Sally said. "LeBaron told her, 'Look at the address she wrote in that book. That's up in New York City. Probably where they all go when they run.' Then Anne-May took one look at that and had a fit like you've never seen. Came down here, yellin' and cussin', all foamy at the mouth. Cornered Celeste and got her with her switch."

Ma walked back and forth, hands clutched at her chest. "Anne-May whipped her so bad, and then told LeBaron, 'Do your damnedest to that colored thief,' and he did and she watched the whole thing, too."

Sally leaned in. "Then he got a fire going in the smokehouse. Celeste knew what was coming, so she tried to run, but LeBaron's locked her in there and done Lord knows what to her, she was screaming so bad. LeBaron's pattyrollers sat on their horses waiting around, too."

I started off toward the smokehouse. "So let's get her out."

"LeBaron said he'd kill us all if we set foot in there. He's out cold in his shed, key on a ring on the wall."

Ma tried to hold me back, but I ran off to LeBaron's shed, which looked more like a jumble of boards holding one another up against the tobacco barn. I opened the door a crack to find LeBaron asleep on the dirty blue-ticked mattress, lyin' up drunk, empty whiskey bottle under his cot, and dirty dishes in the washtub. The key on the ring hung there next to him on the wall, a little glint of light catching the silver of it.

I opened the door wider till it creaked. A jolt went through me and I looked at LeBaron, still sound asleep, mouth open. I stepped slowly to the key, through the smell of dead mouse, the flies having a party on a peach pit left on the floor.

I lifted the ring off the hook, gentle as I could, and stepped out quick, not stopping to close the door, and ran back to the smokehouse as Sally and Ma followed.

I set the key in the lock, my fingers shaking so bad I could barely turn it. When I got the door open, a powerful wave of smoke rushed out and sent us all coughing. I stepped in, waving the smoke away, and searched the room for Celeste, the fire logs still glowing red. Two ladders stood leaned up against the wall for fetching the hams down, the dirt floor empty.

I turned to Ma, relief going through me. "She's not in here."

Those two stepped in behind me and looked around.

Then Sally looked up through the smoke. "Lord in heaven, what has he done?"

MA AND I STOOD frozen for a second, looking up at Celeste, hung up there with the hams, down to her sugar sack underthings, the rope tied around her middle, arms hanging down limp. Coughing out the thick smoke, we got the ladder and set it up under her and I scrambled up. Took me forever to untie the rope. She hung there eyes closed, mouth sagged open. I ran one hand down her back.

"It's me, Celeste," I said, but she didn't come to.

I finally handed her down below to Ma and Sally and we hustled her back to the cabin and set her in bed. She wheezed something awful and even with every quilt on her she shook bad with chills.

Sally shook her head. "The lungs are the hardest. But I'll try pokeweed for the skin."

I stepped to the bed and sat gentle on the side, Celeste there shivering. I helped Sally cover her up with pieces of wet, torn-up sheet, green poke-weed under each.

Ma kept the fire going long as she could and then dozed off and I sat up with Celeste, replacing her cloths and squeezing the blood into the basin, her going in and out of sleep.

As the night went on she finally spoke, her voice faint.

"Jemma."

"Quiet now. Rest yourself."

"May need to retch."

"I got the basin." I smoothed back her hair, the smoke still in it. "I should've known LeBaron would find that book. I was so stupid to let you write in it."

"You're not stupid. It's just my time. Anne-May sure was mad, though. Kept asking if I was going escape here and go to New York. But I didn't tell her one thing. That's what friends do, right?" She was quiet for a minute.

"And, Jemma, I want you to steer clear of LeBaron from now on."

"Already do. Who'd want to smell that?"

She got an extra pained look in her eyes. "I mean never be alone."

My blood went cold. "What'd he do to you, Celeste?"

"Think you know." She looked away. "Can't say, it's so bad."

I took her cold hand in mine. "You squeeze my hand if he took you in a manly way out there in the smokehouse."

"It's too awful to think on."

"I know. Just this once you tell me, Celeste. Then we don't have to talk on it again."

She looked down at her hand and squeezed mine best she could and turned her gaze to me.

Her eyes filled with tears and mine, too. "I'm so sorry, Celeste."

"Fought him best I could. I just don't want him to get you, too."

I rubbed her cold hand warm. "Quiet now and just get better. You can't leave me with no friend to fight him off with."

She lay quiet for a minute. "Want you to have my card."

"I can't take that."

"It's under the mattress here. If I go, you keep it. No use in LeBaron havin' it."

We listened to the fire spark and pop.

"Your pa gonna make me a box?" she asked.

"He'll be dead in the ground before you, Celeste."

She was quiet for so long I thought she fell back asleep.

"Wish I knew a birthday for my grave marker."

"Well, I got a mind to go on up to that house and look in that big book she keeps up there and see what your birthday is."

Celeste tried to smile. "You would?"

"Why not? Got the key. Anne-May's asleep."

Celeste thought for a second or two. "I'd be much obliged."

"You wait right here. May take me a little time."

I stepped outside the shack and walked down the road a piece and stood and looked at the stars thrown across the sky and asked Jesus to keep my one friend who'd done nothing wrong, except write her name.

Once I spent a fair amount of time outside, I walked back into the shack, and sat down next to her on the bed. "Good news, Celeste. You're not gonna believe this, but I saw your birthday written up there in that book."

"Sure it's mine?"

"Right next to your name, plain as day, next line down from Delly. And it's June, of all things."

She smiled a bit. "Just like I thought."

"June 26, 1845, plain as day."

Celeste rolled slowly toward me. "Happy day."

"You're sixteen just like me."

"I'm powerful cold, Jemma."

I pulled back the quilt and lay in next to her as Ma and me always did, pressed myself gentle and warm against her and fell asleep the two of us, my best friend and me.

WE BURIED CELESTE NEXT to Sweet Clementine, with Ma, Sally, and me crying so hard we used up all our tears. I'd tried to keep her warm enough in the night, but by morning she was cold and Sally and Ma lifted her out the bed and wrapped her in a blanket. Once Pa got home, he started building her box, fat tears wetting his face. He made her a fine wood cross, too, and burned into it her June birthday and set it at her head, then said some Bible words and we stood there and sang every song we knew from church.

Sally Smith stood wiping her eyes and looking down at the grave. "What'll we leave on her cross to take to heaven with her? What'd she do best?"

I pulled Pa's pencil from my pocket and set it atop the stone. "She was a fine writer, even brand new to it."

Ma set a little straw basket there. "She picked a good basket of berries, too."

I lingered a long time there, hard to leave my friend in the ground, wondering if it did any good to pray for her soul. While it was my own stupid ways that got Celeste killed, teaching her to write her name and all, it seemed to me God was hell-bent on taking everything good from us. Little Toby. Clementine and Celeste. Only had Delly and Charl and family left, Ma, Pa, Sally, and Patience.

When I told Ma and Sally what LeBaron did to Celeste before she died, Ma broke down worse than ever.

Sally linked her arm in mine. "LeBaron is the devil himself, no better than a rutting hog. And I pray to Jesus he doesn't catch you alone before we can leave this forsaken place."

IT WAS HARD SHAKING Celeste's sad end, especially when I had to live in the same house as Anne-May and she'd been the one that killed her. Day after, she nearly killed me too, same switch.

"Get to the pantry. Giving you thirty for teachin' that girl to write."

"Yes, missis. But—"

"That'll be thirty-five for talking back. Get in there and take down your dress, now."

I went to the pantry, unbuttoned my dress to the waist, and waited, my hands braced against the shelf, fingers around the pretty red cloth Sally Smith lined those shelves with, with the paper lace edges. Anne-May took her sweet time, too, knowing the worrying about the pain to come was almost as bad as the whipping.

She finally came with her switch, and her cat ran for the hills when she started hitting me with all her might cross the back. It stung worse than ever, on top of the pain of losing Celeste, and I held my breath and prayed for it to stop.

Anne-May leaned in to her work. "You may as well have killed that girl yourself when you put that pencil in her hand. It'll cost me one hundred dollars to replace her."

By lash number seven the blood ran warm down into my waistband, and I rested my head against the edge of the shelf, breathed in the nutmeg and flour, and bit my lip, knowing better than to cry out. That just added strokes. I tried setting my mind on good things about Celeste. Her dimples and stories she told about her little brothers, but the whip kept bringing me back.

Sally banged pots around in the kitchen, her way of showing she was mad about it, then came by the pantry and peeked in. My eyes filled with water from the pain and the shame, but mostly the shame of Sally seeing me like that.

"I'm stoppin' at twenty," Anne-May finally said. She took a kitchen rag, wiped her switch clean, took down a bottle of vinegar from the shelf, and opened it, the terrible smell of it filling the pantry.

Sally knew what was coming.

"Miss Anne-May, ain't the girl suffered enough?"

"You'll be next, you sass me again."

I braced for the splash but when the vinegar hit my back it took my breath clean away, making each lash come alive again but double.

Anne-May handed me the vinegar bottle and the rag, my blood fresh on it.

"Now button yourself up. I'm plumb wore out. While I rest, start on the front parlor windows."

I pulled my dress on over the sting of the cuts, whole back on fire, and holding my head high so no more water'd run out of my eyes I took the rag and bottle.

I stepped to the front parlor window and shook the vinegar on the rag, blood and all, and set to wiping one pane. I was wrung out, my back so hot, I rested my forehead against one pane of glass, my palm against the other.

I sent myself away from that place, above the trees and off north to New York City, to the Central Park, the grass so green and fresh I could smell it, and then over the museum with the seal in it, to the crowded streets where I could just get lost. Felt good to go away from there, even for a minute.

Then all at once I felt my hand grow warm on the pane and I lifted my head to find my ma there on the other side of the window, standing on the porch, up from the fields, her hand pressed up against mine, only glass between us. Her eyes were full as mine and she just nodded her head, with that look of hers that said, "I miss Celeste, too, and what Miss Anne-May did to you was a sin and I have you in my heart and we'll get you out of here if it takes my every last breath to do it," because she could say all that in one look.

Ma stepped away from the window but I kept my hand there on the glass. I watched her go all the way back down to the fields and then got to my own work, and stood a little straighter. Because after that I knew we'd be getting away from there.

The very next chance we got.

THE NEXT DAY, ANNE-MAY came to me as I washed the front entry floor, my back on fire worse than ever. She leaned in, pulled that red book from her pocket, and whispered, "Got a letter I need you to copy in here."

I took the book.

Could barely look at Anne-May, hating her so bad, and the last thing I wanted to do was write in that book of hers, but figured she'd have LeBaron smoke me, too, if I refused, and what good would that do? LeBaron. How could God make such an evil bag of parts? How could he let him do that to Celeste, the kindest girl to walk this earth, who never said a cross word to anyone? Sad truth was, couldn't count on God to keep any of us safe.

Tears pooled in my eyes as I sat on the pantry floor, careful not to set my back against the wall, and copied another long tale into that book, took word for word from Mister Watson's letter, the daylight in there so dim.

My dearest Anne-May,

Still on railroad guard duty here in Annapolis, there is talk among the men that we are about to march to Winchester, Virginia, soon. As much as I pride myself on making living things grow, by all accounts, my commander is confident in my ability to understand how to blow things up and has given me sole jurisdiction over a bridge that must be defended at all costs and force the Rebs to take the long way round. . . .

The fire in my back made it hard to keep my mind on the letters and I wrote slow as I could, to form them all right, and pricked myself with thoughts of Celeste, and how I'd been the one to teach her to write and the one who killed her, my one true friend.

THAT AFTERNOON, ANNE-MAY SENT me to Hollywood to deliver that book to Jubal Smalls. It sure was hot for October and as I walked the sweat ran down my back, stinging the lash marks even through the poultice Sally Smith made me. With Mister Watson and Harry gone I worried full-time. About Pa hiding knives. About the baby coming. I had dreams about that spidery sycamore tree, me strung up on it on account of my spying with that book.

I was parched by the time I made it to the porch of Smalls and Sons, a fancy men's coat and a few shotguns in the window. The three Smalls children, all the opposite of the name and fat and pink as piglets, sat on the porch steps throwing jacks. The one almost tall as me spit in my path as I passed.

"Damn darkies. Don't know enough to courtesy to their betters when they pass 'em on the street."

"Curtsy," I said.

"What you say?"

"The word is *curtsy*."

Mr. Smalls's house lady, Doreen, came to the screen door, two of her four little ones around her. Mr. Smalls worked his slaves hard, and even the little ones had jobs to do.

"Time to come in for lessons," she called out to the Smalls children.

They stood and each kicked dust in my face and piled in through the door.

Doreen came out onto the porch and smiled at me. "You here to see Master Smalls?"

She was Ma's friend so I knew I could talk to her.

I nodded. "Miss Anne-May sent me."

She stepped closer and spoke in low tones. "You be careful of him, now, you hear? And I know how you like lemonade. I'll send Terrence out with some."

Once she went inside, my favorite of Doreen's boys came out with a glass, cold by the look of it, little drops like sweat on the glass. Terrence was a couple years younger than me and a sweet boy, smarter than any other his age.

He handed me the cup. "For you, Jemma. Just the way you like it."

You've never seen such perfect, yellow lemonade. My mouth watered just looking at it.

"Made it myself. Taught Ma how to take the seeds out with a new lemon press I made."

"You're my favorite, Terrence."

He sent me a shy smile and whispered behind one hand. "That's because I give you licorice whips from the candy case."

I was about to drink the lemonade when Mr. Smalls came out the door and shooed Terrence off.

"You Jemma?" he asked.

He stepped to me and took the lemonade from my hand.

"Why, thank you," he said.

I gritted my teeth as he drank my perfect lemonade in one long swallow.

He set the empty glass on the porch step. "Like to come on inside?"

"No, suh."

"You take snuff?"

I shook my head.

Most folks would say Mr. Smalls was a handsome man, his way of talking smooth and Southern. But he gave me the creeps just looking at him. Something about his way reminded me of a snake I saw one time, that caught a baby rabbit and squeezed it up tight in its coils and licked its head nice and slow before he unhinged his jaw and swallowed the poor thing whole.

He leaned down. "You got that book for me?"

I handed it to him, careful not to look him in the eye.

He held it up with one hand. "What you think about all this in here?"

I made him no answer.

"Anne-May good to you, Jemma?"

What slave would be so dumb as to advance honest opinions?

I kicked the dirt with my foot and then nodded. "Yes, suh."

"You know the word *loyal*, Jemma?"

I nodded.

"Bad things happen when a person has no loyalty. Understand? Like what happened to that friend of yours. Heard she put up quite a fight."

I stepped back. How'd he know so much about it?

He came closer. "I have a secret for you."

I stood my ground.

"You know LeBaron Caruthers?"

I nodded.

"He sure thinks you're nice."

I looked around me to check if anybody was listening.

He crouched himself down in a frog squat. "I leased him some property. Couple acres of old Mister Burns's farm I just bought, on the way to Ambrosia. Sold him the lumber he's using to make that new little house for hisself with. So nice and private."

I started walking away, back toward the road home.

"So you keep your mouth shut, you hear?" he called to me. "Or else I'll make it extra easy for him to take some nice young girl back there."

I took a quick peep back as I walked and he stood there watching me, big snaky smile on his face.

"Because that's where girls with no loyalty go, Jemma."

CHAPTER
1 2

Georgy

WASHINGTON, D.C.

DECEMBER 1861

EARLY ONE MORNING I ANSWERED OUR EBBITT HOUSE DOOR to find Mr. Olmsted standing there, accompanied by his aide, Mr. Knapp, an unassuming man who we later found acted as his fleet provisionary.

"Good afternoon, ladies. Forgive my haste, for I have little time, but I'd like to offer you each a position in our company to serve aboard the hospital ship *Wilson Small.*"

Eliza and I only dared glance at each other.

"Yes, Mr. Olmsted," I said. "We would be most honored to serve."

"So we will travel on the ships up to New York?" Eliza asked.

"No, you will transfer your wounded to transport ships going north and stay here with your base ship *Daniel Webster No. 1.*"

I slid my little paper book and pencil from my pocket. "Our duties on board?"

"For now you will simply ready *Wilson Small* for use until a Christmas furlough. You will stock pantries and prepare linens, make patients' beds. When you return after Christmas, you will assist in surgeries, devise locked storage for wines, spirits, and other expensive items and guard it well, dedicate yourselves to patient comfort, and generally make yourselves available to Dr. Robert Ware and the other doctors. The conditions are not elegant or spacious."

I copied down the list. "Understood, sir."

"And these positions are not without grave risk. It is one thing to read about war in the papers, another to put oneself in the eye of the storm."

I took Eliza's cold hand. "And when should we report, Mr. Olmsted?"

He looked to Mr. Knapp.

"Immediately?"

"Of course," I said.

Once Mr. Olmsted and Mr. Knapp took their leave, we seized our carpetbags and pitched our belongings in every which way, our underthings mixed with dresses and wrappers. There was no time for elegant storage. We were sailing into the eye of the storm.

TO MEET OUR SHIP, Eliza and I boarded the tugboat *Wissahickon,* whose captain agreed to deliver us. We stood on the deck, cold wind in our faces, and chugged down the Potomac, past the vast fields of the tobacco plantations along the banks of the river, legions of slaves, even in the December chill, bent over in their fields, a vivid reminder of what we were fighting to end.

It all seemed peaceful enough below deck, neatly made beds, the sounds of a well-tended ward, sepulchral whispers and a few moans. But I could feel it coming.

That peace would not last long.

THAT CHRISTMAS EVE THERE was a lull in the war action and Eliza and I returned temporarily to our little front parlor rooms on the first floor at Ebbitt House. We stacked in the corners abundant hospital supplies we'd scrounged from various places, and set up a kitchen to rival Paris's Hôtel de Vendôme, complete with a camp stove I lifted from the Sanitary Commission stores, an old toaster found sitting next to the hotel trash bin, and tea and coffeepots, all set on a scavenged plank atop two sawhorses.

With Moritz off visiting friends in Baltimore, and Joe tied up with military efforts and unable to visit us from nearby Camp Franklin in Virginia, we stayed in our morning dresses and wrappers, making our own Christmas dinner. It was hard having Joe so close and not be able to visit. But we had each other and knelt next to our makeshift dining table, two wooden crates united, a linen cloth over both. Eliza and I took great care unwrapping the treats Mother had sent down packed in wood shavings: date bread wrapped in waxed paper, a little pot of marmalade topped with a pinking-sheared calico scrap, and a burlap package of coffee.

We toasted each other with a jelly jar of port. "Here's to having made the hospital ships."

Eliza pulled out a tin of sardines. "This is a feast. Too much for us, Georgy."

"Don't we deserve a bit of Christmas cheer?"

A knock came on the door and Eliza hurried to it. "If it's the desk clerk with another package—"

She opened it to find her husband, Joe, standing there. She rushed to him with a fervent embrace and then took his hands in hers.

"Oh, Joe. You came after all."

No person could approach Joseph Howland without feeling they were in the presence of a noble man, and every Woolsey swelled with pride that he and Eliza made such a good match.

In physique, he was not strong or broad, and therefore unsuited to the work of soldiering. But his early education under the best masters had strengthened his constitution and developed a mind of great cleverness. His honey-blond hair, clear blue eyes, and warmly handsome visage helped make him a man all welcomed and the Sixteenth of New York idolized.

"I've known for days but wanted to make the surprise." He presented Eliza with a bundle wrapped in linen, the scent of ginger perfuming the room. "Terribly sorry, but I bring no presents, just horse-cakes. An Alexandria institution."

Eliza opened the linen to find gingerbread cut in the flat, rude shape of two prancing horses with very prominent ears. "Oh, Joe. Mother has wonderful childhood memories of them."

Joe stepped into the room. "And I also bring the good wishes and ardor of the men of the Sixteenth and Old Scott of course."

"You rode him all this way?" Eliza asked. "You love that horse more than us, I believe."

I hurried to Joe and took his hat. "You bring yourself, the best gift, and you're just in time for the feast. Coffee or port?"

"Coffee, please." Joe knelt with us by our little table. "So sorry I couldn't provide a more elegant dinner."

Eliza set one of her china teacups she'd had sent down from Tioronda in front of Joe and poured coffee into it.

"This is actually just the way we wanted it, isn't it, Georgy? Mother sent us a Christmas banquet."

"I'm just happy to have a respite from bad coffee and beans," he said.

"Though this is quite different from our Christmas in Italy," Eliza said. "Wasn't that a lovely trip?"

We all grew quiet and conjured images of one late-night holiday dinner with Mother's friends at the Malabaila di Canale estate, the Alps as our backdrop, tables groaning with stuffed capon and cod, yeasty panettone, and endless Barolo from the ancient cellars. And then, as snow fell as if on cue, Joe had proposed to Eliza while I, sworn to secrecy, watched from the garden.

I offered Joe a plate of date bread. "Can you tell us what is in store with regard to the war?"

"I have sealed orders, Georgy, and wouldn't tell you if I could. You'll find out soon enough out there on the hospital ships."

"The Winthrop brothers wrote of all their military passages."

"A letter home is different, Eliza, safe in the hands of a loved one."

"General McClellan has some reason to keep you camped in Virginia, right there on the river," I said.

Joe held out one hand. "Would you pass the butter, please?"

"Camp Franklin is the perfect place to wait, poised for an attack on

Richmond. What better blow than to take the Confederate capital? Capture that and the war's is over."

Joe smiled. "You'd be a better general than McClellan, Georgy."

Eliza stood and retrieved more port. "Mr. Olmsted said essentially the same thing. I quote, 'Georgy would, upon orders, take control of the naval fleet, arm and provision them, and lead her sailors against the enemy better than any landsman I know.'"

"I must learn more about the geography," I said. "If I'm about to become a general."

"Well, here it is in a nutshell." Joe inverted his hand. "If you think of the peninsula as one large green mitten, the top facing down, surrounded by water, Richmond their capital sitting adjacent to it, to the west . . . *If* our General McClellan decided to run his troops up the rivers on either side to attack Richmond, and that campaign produced casualties, Sanitary Commission ships would ferry those wounded out to sea, up to Northern hospitals, and then return. You can see how dangerous that is and why Olmsted was reluctant to have you on the ships."

Eliza handed Joe a napkin. "We feel like the Sixteenth is our regiment, Joe. We want to be close and help with your wounded."

"You two don't know what it will be like on those ships. You've dealt with measles and malaria. Important work, but nothing like a transport hospital. I would prefer you were safely back in New York, but I must have faith the good Mr. Olmsted will protect you. In the meantime I will tell you what little I can."

"Don't string us along, Joe," I said.

"As you do to poor Frank Bacon? He showers you with compliments and gifts and you rarely even smile at his jests."

"Not sure we're compatible."

Joe sat back. "Well, he's been serving our country in mortal combat and is coming to Washington tomorrow and plans on calling on you. You could be kind to such a faithful servant of the U.S. Army on Christmas."

"Of course I will treat him kindly, Joe. He's a dear friend."

Eliza poured me tea, the steam curling the hair at her forehead. "He may find himself on bended knee this time, Georgy."

"I certainly hope not. Marriage is so constricting. Plus, Frank hardly sees me as an equal. Talks right over me sometimes."

"Well then, cut him loose, Georgy," Joe said. "He thinks the world of you and he's a faithful friend. It pains me to see him trifled with."

ONCE FRANK BACON ARRIVED, he told us he wanted to visit the so-called contraband on Christmas Day, at the troop barracks on F Street, where the fugitive slaves had come for protection. He'd visited the area in a medical capacity and described the need for care and comforts.

Eliza and I had delighted in the paper box Abby and Mother had sent down for us, filled with soft coverlets, fresh handkerchiefs, waxed-paper-wrapped peppermint sweets, and little blue-striped ticking pillows Carry had made. It seemed in keeping with the spirit of the holiday to share our good fortune with those living there.

Frank and I arrived at the low gray barracks not far from Ebbitt House on Christmas morning after church. We stepped inside to find mostly women and children, and a few older men, sitting on their cots or gathered at the fire, and Frank and I went about, offering medical care. It was hard not to survey the group, who'd come so far, so patient and full of hope, and not wonder if President Lincoln wasn't doing them a great disservice, sending them unprotected into a perilous battle of their own.

I approached Frank, who knelt bandaging a child's foot.

"Georgy, do you have a pin?"

I pulled a safety pin from my pocket and handed it to him. "I've been thinking, Frank. We can heal their complaints, but what about their lives going forward? The mothers here with their children—how will they make do day-to-day?"

"Fetch me the iodine, Georgy."

I handed him the bottle. "Did you hear my question, Frank? What if we helped them learn the fundamentals of nursing?"

"The government is looking after them."

"That's not my idea of freedom."

"Most of these women cannot read."

"That can be fixed. What do you think?"

He handed me a basin without looking up. "Hold this?"

A dark-complexioned young man approached us, dressed, as any true gentleman would be, in a gray worsted wool frock coat and paisley cravat. "They call me Nathan. Thought I'd offer my help."

Frank turned his full attention to the man and extended his hand. "How do you do, Nathan. We could use the help."

I had trouble not staring at Nathan's lovely, dark-lashed eyes, a vivid green-blue, the color of an angry sea.

"I lived with a physician down in St. Mary's County. Once he died, I got my freedom, and I came here to doctor to this group since they need it so bad."

Frank smiled. "What an admirable thing to do, Nathan."

Nathan knelt before the boy, and Frank turned to him and said, "This child has a festering foot."

"Iodine?"

"Yes. But the bandages they sent are—"

"Too wide, sir, that's right. I will cut them if you apply the iodine."

The two of them worked in silence.

"Excuse me, Doctor," Nathan said. "Your medical bag label says 'Nanterre, France.' Have you been there? The doctor I worked for in Maryland told me they've made great medical advances."

"Yes, I've been and intend to return as soon as this war is over. The French are years ahead of us."

Frank and Nathan walked the room, stopping here and there to inquire about complaints, and I followed, fetching bandages and basins at their request. We came to a man presenting with a bad tooth, the pain exhibited on his face.

Frank pressed a tongue depressor into the man's open mouth. "You must have that pulled."

"Perhaps he can try powdered alum?" I asked.

Nathan hunched down and squinted into the man's mouth. "The decay is quite deep."

I stepped closer to the patient. "According to Dr. Blackwell's instruction, alum will not only relieve the pain, but prevent further decay. May be a good short-term action to consider."

Frank moved on without answering me, and bent to study the next patient, conferring with Nathan.

After two hours of bandaging, lancing, and prescribing beef tea, which I boiled up, we stood and surveyed the group as they settled in to sleep.

"What would you say to a paid position, Nathan?" Frank asked. "Assisting me in my work?"

"I would very much enjoy that, sir."

"It can be perilous at times. I often find myself in the line of fire."

"Understood, sir."

"You will sleep in my tent with equal privileges and may leave anytime you feel the need."

"Right, sir."

"I ride for Fort Monroe soon. In the interim we will find you a doctor to cover your work here. Satisfactory?"

"Very, sir."

Frank offered Nathan his hand. "Welcome to the U.S. Army, Nathan."

The children slept, heads in their mothers' laps, as we stood and raised our voices with all those there, our hushed and gentle "Go Tell It on the Mountain" filling the room.

NEW YEAR'S DAY, BEFORE Frank Bacon was due to ride back to report to Fort Monroe, he walked me back to Ebbitt House. He grew quiet and developed an attitude of even greater stiffness than usual, so I filled the empty air.

"How good that Nathan has agreed to join you."

"It will be a godsend. I'm shorthanded every day out there. Would you ever consider joining me and Nathan? A U.S. Army tent is not Ebbitt House, but we have our little comforts."

"That *is* a fine offer, Frank Bacon, but first of all, I have a new position aboard a hospital ship. Second, I think Washington would be aghast at the impropriety of it. By strict social law we should not even be out here walking unaccompanied."

"There is a way to solve that impropriety."

"Frank—"

"I think you may have some notion of what I wish to speak with you about."

"Again, Frank?"

"This time I've taken the liberty of speaking to your mother and Uncle Edward. They gave their heartiest good wishes to the idea. My mother, when told, practically leapt to her strongbox and pressed her mother's ring on me." He patted his coat pocket.

"Not the ruby."

"They feel as I do, Georgy. As I told you before, I've loved you since we were small. Mother hinted she would support a marriage in New Haven and a reception at our house. I'm hoping your feelings have changed toward me. If not, I promise never to broach the subject again."

"I've always pictured being married at Brevoort Place."

"Father would prefer the ceremony be performed at his church."

Almost at the hotel, I stopped and turned. "Frank, you know I care for you very much, but I crave an equal partnership."

"I consider you my equal in many ways."

"But you don't show it. I say Brevoort Place and you override me with New Haven. Just last week you ignored my thought on offering nursing training to the women."

He waved the idea away. "Such small things."

"You also ignored my idea about the bad tooth. You and Nathan chose a course of action between you with no consideration of my experience or opinion."

"But we know medicine, Georgy."

"And I do not? I was taught by Elizabeth Blackwell to be a true partner in medicine. Should I not be consulted as Nathan is? I want a relationship like that of my parents. They counseled each other on all things."

"In most things, men must lead."

"I would rather never marry than be diminished daily."

"So, I diminish you?"

"You don't understand. I'm trapped in a peculiar bind. My mother made sure I was handsomely educated, but having nothing formally devised to employ that education other than charity and child-raising, I must go out and find something I do well. I believe I've found it in nursing."

"Surely you have a womanly desire for children?"

"I don't know, Frank. I wish I could be more like Mary, living a life of fealty to her husband, giving birth each year, but I've grown fond of my vagabond life. Perhaps I'm not right for marriage."

"So you'd choose to remain unmarried?"

"I want to live a different kind of life—to travel freely once the war is over. I want to see far-flung places. Peru and Africa—to start a school for women nurses where they can learn the proper way to tend patients—to have the excitement of my own career, doing things as *I* see fit."

"Perhaps you crave excitement to assuage the wound of your father's death."

"What a ridiculous notion."

"Don't you see? It is simple avoidance. I've seen it treating soldiers. If a person doesn't confront their problems their psyche grows stunted. You don't cry, Georgy."

Frank reached for my hand and I pulled it away.

"I might say the same about you, Frank."

"Do you ever get close to the wounded in your ward? Eliza says you prefer meal prep and organizing the storeroom to the simplest contact with the men."

I clasped my hands at my waist. "So I am mentally unhinged because my sister and I prefer to split the labor?"

"Your mother couldn't get you off that beach after you got the news of your father's death. Seven was a tender age to undergo such a terrible ordeal. You must see—"

"I declare myself unworthy of you, with these distressing issues in my life. You're not capable of an equal partnership, anyway."

Frank tried to take my hand. "Georgy, please."

I pulled away. "This conversation has fixed in my mind the idea that, forgive my directness, I never could feel for you in an amorous way."

Frank searched my face. "I must admit that is not the answer I had hoped for."

"I'm truly sorry, Frank. But I will always keep you near my heart as a dear friend."

He took a step back. "At least now I know, Georgy. I won't ask again."

Frank took one last look at my face, tipped his hat, and walked off toward Fort Monroe.

Jemma

✳

T HE CLOCK ON ANNE-MAY'S DINING ROOM MANTEL STRUCK NOON Christmas Day. It was all I could do, standing behind her chair, not to tap my toe for her and her sister to eat faster so I could run down the hill to see Ma and Pa and, if the good Lord smiled on us, a new baby soon. That child had gotten so used to being in Delly's belly he got so big she looked about to bust.

As it was, Anne-May'd spent half the morning giving me a terrible Christmas present, having me brush her hair and her cat's and taking me through every little thing in her sad old memory book.

Christmas was our day for family to be together. Even Anne-May knew it was tradition to let us rest on Christmas Day, past lunch. A few snow-flakes drifted down outside the windows.

Anne-May and her sister sat at the long table I'd polished that morning with wax, the fruits of some poor bees' labor they had to give up for Anne-May to see her sour face in that shine. What she called the dining room was a big room and was cold all the time in winter, even with me throwing a log on every five minutes, but Saint Joan the cat seemed just fine stretched out right on the table, never giving Anne-May the time of day. When Sally

Smith came to the doorway and saw that cat eat from Anne-May's plate and then stretch out on the table, she just shook her head.

I stood behind Anne-May's chair just as she liked it, straight as a soldier, wearing my starched white apron over my green dress. Now and then she'd hand me a bread plate with the part of the chicken she didn't like and make for me to take it outside in the cold and eat, acting like it was some big treat, while I just tossed it out in the yard for the crows.

She sat and pushed the roast chicken around on her plate, fought with her poor sister about money, and cussed her out for not keeping better track of how much sugar they bought. Made me nervous Anne-May was having money troubles, spending so much on her precious snuff, and fish for that cat. I could tell since, for a woman who ate less than a parakeet, she suddenly kept a hawk eye on the food stores, counting out the sugar and flour by the pound and ounce. She learned exactly how much flour made eighteen biscuits, each just the size of a lady's palm.

Little did she know Sally saved her best cooking for our family on Christmas Day. She baked up as many ashcakes with jelly as we could eat, and every kind of sweet thing she could make from the sugar she'd been pilfering from Anne-May all year. Only thing we'd miss was my sister, Patience, since Miss Charlene kept all her slaves on Ambrosia Plantation on the Lord's birthday, right back to regular work the next day, while Mister Watson set in stone that we got most of Christmas week off from tobacco work and housework, except for Sally, who still made dinners, not that we didn't work other ways, like weaving in the loom house and knitting Anne-May's gloves and tending the livestock.

Soon as the clock struck one, I walked calm as could be to the kitchen, untied my apron, and hung it in the pantry, and just about tore the hinges off the kitchen door before I ran down that hill like the devil himself was after me, and I didn't once feel the cold for the joy.

But once I opened the door and stepped into that shack, I knew something was plain wrong, with no fire in the hearth, Delly on her bed, a bundle in her arms, Sally Smith next to her, Ma and Pa with long faces.

"What is it?"

Ma looked away.

"Come sit, Jemma," Pa said. "Child's born dead. Charl went to get LeBaron to dig the hole."

Every part of me sank like a rock. "No."

Sally wiped her eyes with the back of her hand. "A boy."

I stepped closer to Delly, sitting there on the bed looking down at her bundle.

Tears blurred my eyes. "Born dead or did she kill it?"

Ma stepped to me. "Don't you say that, Jemma. Delly's out of her mind sad."

"Are you?" I asked Delly. "I don't see one tear. Shame on you, killing your own child Christmas Day."

She held the boy closer and avoided my gaze. "He came in the night. I must've rolled over and smothered him."

She handed me up her bundle and I took it in my arms, the quilt wrapped around a good-sized infant child, hands crossed up under his chin like he's sleeping, skin tinged with blue like Sweet Clementine's had been.

I touched his little hand, cold. "I'm so sorry, Delly."

LeBaron came in the door, blowing air on his hands to warm them and stamping his feet like he's cold. "Where's that baby?"

Charl followed him in and went to sit next to Delly on the bed.

I turned to LeBaron, baby in my arms. "He's dead." A tear slid all the way down to my neck.

"Let me see for myself."

I stepped to LeBaron and pulled the quilt back so he could see the poor dead baby's face, even more blue in the light coming in the door. "Died in the night."

LeBaron leaned down, took a good close look, and then stood straighter. "I'm not buryin' it. Ground's froze up. You see to it yourselves."

He shoved his hands in his pockets, turned, and left, and Charl went to the door and watched him go, the only sound my crying, worse than ever.

Soon as LeBaron was down the road a piece, Charl shut the door, careful not to slam it, and turned to Sally Smith.

"He's gone," Charl said.

All at once everyone jumped up. Never have you seen a dead group of people spring to life so quick.

Sally Smith pulled the child from my arms and laid him on the table. "Hurry now."

Delly and Charl jumped up from the bed and gathered round and Ma and Pa, too. Sally opened that poor dead baby's mouth and poured in some red water.

"Get a log on that fire," Sally said.

Delly stood, looking down at the baby, terrible fear on her face. "It's not working, Sally."

"It's in God's hands now." Sally wrapped the boy up in the quilt and handed him to Delly.

We held our breath as a whole minute went by, then she felt the baby's hand. "I think it's warmin'. Feel it, Charl."

Charl felt the boy's hand. "I feel it, too."

We all gathered round that baby and saw one of God's great miracles happen, as he finally breathed a little breath in and made a little sound like a kitten, his skin already losing its blue.

Ma held my hand and we looked at each other with shock and happiness all mixed up together.

"Jesus did this," I said.

The child moved his arms, and one little foot escaped the quilt.

Ma choked back a sob as she watched Delly and Charl look down at the boy. "Sally Smith did it. Used belladonna to put him to deep sleep just temporary and then brought him back with a tonic."

Sally came and smoothed one finger down the baby's cheek. "Seen it done down in rice country. Can be dangerous, too much, but you gotta know how to do it."

"Why didn't you tell me?" I asked.

Sally rubbed my back. "Needed you to cry real tears to fool LeBaron."

I knelt at Delly's feet, cooing over that child. Every little move he made I smiled at, and Ma looked down, so happy. Was she thinking about her little Toby?

"What's his name?" Sally asked.

Delly looked at Charl. "We thought Kofi'd be a nice name."

We all liked the sound of that and Pa swallowed hard and looked about ready to cry himself.

Sally Smith started the song we sang for the birth of a child, "Let Us Break Bread Together," Ma keeping time for us all, tapping on the table.

We sang it, quiet, Pa's two fine doors keeping the wind out, a good fire in the hearth, and soaked in the joy of that happy, happy time.

ALL CHRISTMAS WEEK I helped Charl and Delly care for the baby. With no horn blaring in the morning, we all got to sleep past dawn, me in the loft bed upstairs with Sally Smith.

Kofi was a good baby, quiet most times, and I gave him Ma's dolls to snug in with and a bird folded from paper, which he liked to stare at like it was some wondrous thing, and Charl sometimes set it dangling over the basket with a bent twig and piece of string. I thought a lot about Carter and where he was and how if I ever saw him again he'd love Kofi, too, since he always took to children. Even from when we were little we'd played at us being Ma and Pa to doll babies, him tucking them in their beds and kissing them so tender on the head. But I was too busy helping Delly fuss over the baby to think too much about old almost-sweethearts.

Good thing that Kofi was on the quiet side, since we all lived in fear LeBaron would come back and see that little boy right as rain and put him in his pocket.

One morning we woke to find a box put inside our shack, next to the hearth. We all stood looking down at it until Ma squatted next to it, opened it up, and pulled out a good wool blanket and the tiniest knit cap.

She looked up at Sally Smith. "Who knows about this baby 'cept us?"

Sally shrugged.

"It was Patience that left it," I said.

Ma looked at the fire. " 'Course it was."

———

PA SKETCHED A TINY COFFIN and set to making it, for our pretend funeral for baby Kofi. Then he and Charl used the poker and shovel and dug a hole out near Sweet Clementine's and Celeste's graves, which took a long time since the ground really was froze up hard.

While the grown-ups made a big show of their phony service and buried an empty box, I got to mind the baby. I laid him in his basket Pa had made for him, which I set by the fire, next to his dolls and looking up at his paper bird, and got to thinking how much Celeste would've liked him and how my sister, Patience, might never see him.

LATER THAT WEEK, all the women gathered in the loom house to work on our sewing and weaving and to love on our precious baby Kofi. My job was to keep him quiet and happy, so LeBaron didn't hear him, no small task with any baby, no matter how good.

Of all the outbuildings Pa made at Peeler, the loom house was my favorite, where all the cloth for the whole of Peeler and Mister Watson's beet farm got made by us. Anne-May's tablecloths, bedspreads, napkins, chair pads. Cloth for field clothes. We sewed quilts there and Ma wove homespun and linsey-woolsey. We crocheted Anne-May's gloves and knit Mister Watson's socks.

It was a snug little room, with a low ceiling and a stone fireplace big enough to stand in. The oak table Pa made stood in the middle, a big old blanket chest in the corner. To one side, far from the fire since it made her too hot, Ma sat at the big old wooden loom, pulling the shuttle back and forth with her hands and dancing on the pedals with her feet, working up a sweat.

She was making a cloth for Anne-May's kitchen table, a nubby, speckled weave we all called "nits and lice," but not in front of Anne-May. Ma was the best weaver in those parts, good at all kinds of cloth: muslin, homespun, wool, you name it, and all dyed natural with persimmon juice or walnut bark. She gave me the thrums, the leftover ends of the threads from the loom, and using them together with cloth scraps, I made my trash flowers.

At the table, Delly and Sally sat working projects, Delly, with one hand, embroidering daisies down the edge of a pillow slip she made and Sally knitting socks to send to Mister Watson, pointer finger forever crooked from the needle hitting it funny all those years.

It smelled good in there, like honey, cedarwood smoke, and home.

I sat cross-legged on the edge of the stone hearth, my bottom warm, folding tablecloths and napkins and shawls to bring up to the house, little Kofi beside me in the swamp-grass basket Pa made. I blocked the fire so it wasn't too hot on him, and if he got fussy, I dipped my pinkie in a glass of honey warming by the fire and let him suck on it, so Delly could work. It felt good, his hard little gums on my finger.

I'd just changed his homespun diaper cloth, no bigger than a ladies' handkerchief, and set it by the fire to clean later. A happy child, he only cried when hungry.

"He's getting bigger, don't you think?" Delly asked.

The day after he'd been born, Sally'd snuck the kitchen scales down to the cabin and we'd weighed Kofi at almost five pounds.

"Never seen a happier one," Sally said, trading a look with me.

I knew she was thinking what we all were. What would happen to the baby when Delly went back to the fields?

"He smiled at me this morning, after I nursed him," Delly said.

"He's too little," Ma said. "That's just wind."

Delly tied off a thread with one hand. "Swear on ten Bibles, he smiled."

"Makes sense," I said. "All we do is grin at him like crazy people."

Sally looked to Delly. "What'll gonna happen when you go back to work?"

Delly waved like she was shooing a fly. "Deal with that when the time comes."

Sally glanced over at Ma. "Can't keep him secret forever."

We all stayed quiet for a bit, only sound the whoosh of Ma's loom.

"S'pose the good Lord will come through," Sally said.

I felt the gust of cold air, and in came LeBaron through the doorway, sending my whole insides to ice, and I set a homespun shawl over the baby in the basket. Outside, two of his dogs jumped up at the window, whining.

LeBaron closed the door and studied the room with his pig eyes. "I come to fix the loom."

Just seeing him made my insides boil. I had to look away and grit my teeth hard to tamp down the thought of him ruining Celeste like he did.

Ma barely turned to him, kept at her weaving. "Fixed it myself."

LeBaron smiled and stepped to the loom. "Look at you, so good with tools, Sable." He ran one finger along the back of her neck, but Ma kept working.

"She is," Sally said from the table.

Under the shawl Kofi wriggled a bit in his basket. I dipped my finger in the honey, offered him my finger to suck, and he took it.

"You need somethin', LeBaron?" Ma asked.

The dogs scratched at the door.

LeBaron rubbed his stubbly chin. "Think we got another runaway. From the beet farm." LeBaron wandered to the blanket chest and lifted the lid. "Seen anybody?"

I peeked under the shawl to make sure Kofi was breathing.

"Not a soul," Ma said.

LeBaron sniffed the air, like one of his dogs. "Smells funny in here."

I slid the balled-up diaper behind me.

Ma waved toward Sally. "That's just old Sally. You know, getting the wind now she's older."

LeBaron squinted one eye. "Dirty old woman."

"You know dirty," Sally muttered.

"Watch that mouth, Sally. With Mister Watson gone, you might trip and fall in your old age."

Kofi released my finger, cooed, and I coughed to cover the sound.

LeBaron stepped to me. "You sick?"

Kofi turned in his basket, sent one little foot up and kicked the shawl, and a jolt of fear went through me. I couldn't meet LeBaron's eyes to see if he'd seen it, too.

"Think Jemma's just got the grippe," Ma said.

"Or maybe it's the fever," Sally said. "We all got it."

LeBaron took a step back. "Don't come near me, then. I sicken easy."

The dogs scratched harder at the door, banged it open, and ran in, slobbery and fast, dog number one to the loom and number two right to the honey on the hearth next to me, flicking his long, pink tongue into the glass.

I broke into a cold sweat as dog number one pounced to the basket, and I barely breathed as he nudged the swamp-grass weave with his nose. Once he finished the honey, number two joined him at the basket, sniffing under the shawl.

I kicked number two away and he snapped at me.

"You hurt my dog?" LeBaron asked.

I pulled the basket closer and kept my gaze on the hearth. "He ate the honey."

Dog number one bit the shawl and started to drag it off, and I held it fast, in a quiet tug-of-war.

LeBaron stepped right to me and looked down at the basket. "What you got in there, anyway? Stole some food from Miss Anne-May's house?"

Just then a man's voice came from outside. "We got a scent, LeBaron!"

"Comin', Clem," LeBaron called over his shoulder.

LeBaron moseyed toward the door. "Just remember, harboring a runaway's just as punishable as being the runaway yourself."

He didn't have to say *what* punishment. His own special branding with a hot iron, an *R* for runaway, to the chest. Only seen one of us get it, old John-William over at Ambrosia, but LeBaron seemed itching to do another.

"Yes, sir," Ma said, her eyes on the basket.

LeBaron put two fingers in his mouth and whistled, and then cried, "Come!" but his dogs just burrowed their noses deeper into my basket.

My heart beat out of my chest.

"Hey—" LeBaron called out. He trudged back to the basket, pulled one dog by the scruff and dragged him back to the door. The second dog followed and relief washed over me as they all tumbled out.

Sally stood and rushed to look out the window. "He's on his horse. Dogs close behind."

Ma, Delly, and Sally hurried to the basket, and I pulled up the shawl to find Kofi chewing on his fist in his cute baby way, right as rain.

Delly heaved a big sigh and slapped her good hand to her chest. "He's fine."

Sally folded her arms across her chest. "Well, I'll be," she said.

Just as that baby broke out with a big old, honest-to-God smile on his little face.

THE NEXT MORNING, I woke in the cabin early and crept downstairs to see the baby. I stepped past Ma and Pa sleeping, fire long since out, but Charl and Delly's bed was empty, baby Kofi's basket by the fire, too. I stepped closer and saw the bed made up as Delly always did it and saw something that caused my blood to run cold for a long second, a shiver shimmying down my back.

Just a dried-up old sunflower set there on the bed.

Anne-May

CHRISTMAS MORNING JEMMA WAS IN MY BEDROOM CHANGING
the slop jar when I handed her the gift I'd wrapped for her in a kitchen
cloth and twine. It was warm by the fire and I thought she might like to rest
a moment, it being Christmas and all. That bedroom was pretty at Yule
time, after Jemma decked the fireplace mantel with evergreens and polished Father's trophy so bright the whole room reflected in it. Saint Joan
sat on my bed exercising her claws on my satin pillow.

Jemma set the slop jar down and stood there looking down on the gift.
"Thank you, Miss Anne-May."

"Well, don't just stare at it like an imbecile."

Jemma untied the twine to reveal a hairbrush.

I pulled the brush from her hand and ran a thumb through the bristles.
"It is a boar bristle brush. See? These black bristles come from a pig. The
best for keeping hair glossy."

"Not my kind of hair."

"It's not *for* your hair, it's for mine. Thought it'd make your job of
brushing me out a whole lot easier." I handed her back the brush. "And
you can start right now. I'm lunching with Euphemia and want to look best
I can with not one decent thing to wear in my armoire."

I sat in the chair and Jemma made long strokes with the brush, those black bristles hitting my scalp in the best way.

"What's that teapot up there for, Miss Anne-May?"

"That's a very important trophy. I won it with my daddy. Dove-shooting contest."

"Why's Harry's name on it?"

"My name's not on it since I shot in Harry's place in the father-son tournament when he took ill. Daddy often had me and Harry pick up the doves he shot down, though Harry stopped doing it, said he felt unwell any time Daddy got his shotgun."

"But you did it."

"I hated it, too, hearing the shot and seeing those sweet birds fall like they did. One still had a beating heart and it cried like a baby, dying in my hands."

"Doves are gentle birds."

"I'd have done anything to be close to Daddy. Just pretended they were crows. Soon as I could hold a gun, he got me shooting. By ten years old I was better than Harry by far. Better than Daddy, too, if I must say." I waved toward the bed. "Go get me my memory book under the bed."

Jemma hustled over and brought back the fat green book, *Scrapbook* printed on the cover in gold script. I turned to the page with a newspaper article pasted there. "Daddy was so proud we were in the newspaper together, though Mama hated it, of course, thinking good ladies are never in the paper except for charity work, but Daddy loved it."

I turned the page to a cutout from *Godey's Lady's Book,* of a model in a silk dress embellished with roses along the middle of the skirt. "Wore to my first cotillion. Mama had it made in Paris, France. My first beau, named Chase William, danced with me all night." I ran one finger down the dance card, a pink tassel hanging from it, Chase William's name penciled in every blank. "Didn't let one other boy come near. Scandalous, really."

"Why didn't you marry him?"

"Wasn't allowed, that's why. Daddy would've blessed that match, a good Louisiana boy, but Daddy was dead by then and my stepfather, Reggie, thought Fergus's family had more money and Mama did anything for Reggie. Chase William was heartsick for exactly five minutes and then went and married his cousin. They have twin boys, both the spittin' image of him, can you imagine?"

Jemma pulled the brush a little too fast and tears came to my eyes. "Stop that now."

"Yes, missis."

I slapped at her with my fan. "*Git.* Leave me alone and go help Sally Smith with Christmas lunch. I don't know why you always get me talking about the past. It's not good for a person."

ONE GOOD THING THAT CHRISTMAS, I had a letter arrive just before the post office shut for the holiday week, from my brother, Harry. I ripped it open before I got back to the carriage, and read:

Ever Dear Sister,

With a thankful heart I take up my pen to address a few lines to you to let you know that I am still in the land of the living, quartered in Centreville, Virginia. We drill relentlessly under the skilled command of Colonel George Steuart, whose love of strict sanitary rules keeps us all hale and hearty, and we often play football before evening parade. We have seen no action, though many here are still filled with tremendous pride for their victory at Manassus, what they call Bull Run up north, and hope this buoyant morale will propel us to continued success. My only concern is that I might come up against Fergus on an opposing Union side, but trust in God we will not meet. I have purchased an insurance policy on my life, to cover the costs of internment and relieve you of the burden of arrangements in the event of my demise. But with the strength of my fellow soldiers and Colonel Steuart on our side, I may have little use for that enclosed piece of paper. Write as soon as you get this and let me

know how you are getting along. Give my love to Euphemia and tell
Joseph to recaulk Sally Smith's window nails with winter coming
on.

> *This from your*
> *affectionate brother—*
> *Harry Wilson*

P.S. I came across this poem in camp and thought you might like
a copy.

> *A Rainy Day at Camp*
> *by Anonymous*
> *It's a cheerless, lonesome evening,*
> *When the soaking, sodden ground*
> *Will not echo to the footfall*
> *Of the sentinel's dull round.*
>
> *God's blue star-spangled banner*
> *To-night is not unfurled;*
> *Surely He has not deserted*
> *This weary, warring world.*
>
> *I peer into the darkness,*
> *And the crowding fancies come:*
> *The night wind, blowing northward,*
> *Carries all my heart toward home.*

Except for the part about Sally Smith's window, it was a splendid letter, and I read it at least hourly, the sound of dear Harry's voice in my head.

CHRISTMAS DINNER WAS A dreary one with the boys gone and only Euphemia and the cat for company, Joan stretched out on the dining room table as usual. Though that cat was a beauty, she'd turned out to be runty, not much bigger than a large kitten. But what she lacked in size she made up for in hostility toward me, no matter how many of her favorite tinned kippers I put in her bowl.

As the war kept on, the cost of everything necessary to running a household went through the roof and the money Fergus sent didn't last long. At least old Aunt Tandy Rose had six bottles of good sherry in the wine cellar. I cast my eye about the dining room, considering items for sale. Perhaps Jubal would buy the gold mirror. No way in Hades I'd part with the blue Sèvres vases on the mantel.

I motioned for Jemma to pour more sherry into our glasses. "We could sell off some hogs."

"Fergus said only as a last resort. We need those to eat."

"That gold stickpin of Fergus's, then? Or Tandy Rose's candlesticks."

Euphemia waved the sherry bottle away. "But they've been in our family for—"

I set down my fork. "Well then, you tell me how to feed and clothe ourselves and all those darkies. The tobacco won't be ready for market until when?"

"February."

"You could at least speed it up."

"It has to dry, Anne-May. And I'm worried the barn roof might leak if there's a bad rain. But I don't need anything much in the way of clothes and food."

"You need to eat. And we go through entirely too much sugar in this house."

"Every time you scrub your face, you use a cup, for pity's sake."

"You check the receipts like I asked? When did we last buy sugar? Flour?"

"Not sure," Euphemia said, head bowed.

"For the love of Jesus, I don't ask you to do that much here, Euphemia. Is it that hard to keep track of the receipts?"

Color came to Euphemia's cheeks. "I do your share and mine of the tobacco work, helping Sable with all those seedlings, and keep Fergus's office in order, since you won't go in there. I spend half my day keeping the cat out of the cricket box. And I think she ate one of Fergus's salamanders."

Saint Joan averted her gaze.

Euphemia went on. "And if you'd learn to read and write, maybe you could take on recording half the receipts."

I shifted in my chair. "I can read. Just the writing I'm not good at. Mama didn't have the time to teach me."

Euphemia buttered her second biscuit. "You spend so much time on your looks, but you could be good at many things. Have you thought about you and Fergus starting a family?"

"We would if he was capable. Don't think he's shooting with live ammunition, if you catch my meaning."

"Maybe if you ate more and loosened up your corset. Mama says—"

"Would you just keep quiet about Mama? Or I'll send you back home to her, since no one else'll have you."

Euphemia examined her knife. "Fine, then."

I slid some dark meat and a gizzard onto a plate, a special Christmas treat, and handed it to Jemma, behind me.

Euphemia dabbed her lips with her napkin, dainty for such a tall girl. "You shoot good as I do, Anne-May. You should come out with me. Got a rabbit this morning. Gave it to Sally for their dinner."

"They eat better than we do, for pity's sake. I'm sure the Jubal Smalls family is sitting down to more than one skinny chicken. Maybe I should ask him for a loan."

"You've become talked about, you and Jubal, you know. It's no wonder. He rarely attends church."

I took a long sip of my sherry. "He doesn't like all the darkies there."

"They sit in the back, not bothering anybody."

"Can I not be friendly with a man, Euphemia? This town is entirely too small."

"A married woman associating with a man who has a wife and children won't end well."

"I don't see many men flocking here callin' on you. Let's be honest, you have no fortune and even less natural beauty."

Euphemia looked toward the fire.

"Sorry to be so cruel, Pheme. It's the money troubles weighing on me. You have, well . . . pretty eyes. And you know I covet that dark hair of yours. But you could at least try a little rouge."

Euphemia smoothed back her hair. "Bachelors are a shy game. When convinced of deception, they may imagine many more. If a man rejects me for lack of cosmetics, so be it. And besides, beauty won't pay the bills."

"It's the only currency I have left."

"Beware of Jubal, sister."

"You use the tools in your toolbox and I'll use mine."

WHILE THE DARKIES LAZED about and had their dull little Christmas, I took Euphemia into town for the ladies' sewing circle Christmas party at Smalls and Sons. I wore my gray silk, my little white fur muff, and at my chest, Fergus's gold stickpin with the seagull with the ruby eye. Then I tied on the smart flowerpot bonnet Jemma made me, with the pretty little flowers she made up from scraps, closest thing to French couture this side of New York.

Old Widow Gardener rested her blue-veined hand on my arm. "Lovely bonnet, Anne-May. Did Jemma make that for you?" As usual she was more interested in my servants than in me. "You'd swear every one of those little flowers was real, with their fabric stamens and petals."

"Jemma did make it, yes."

"Sally Smith have any of her jelly left? May come by and get some more after the holiday. Dr. Gardener always loved it so."

Fearing another lecture on the personal beauty of Abraham Lincoln, I excused myself and left Euphemia and Widow Gardener talking *tête-à-tête,* the two of them fast friends since my sister joined the sewing circle back in July.

After looking all over for Jubal, I found him toward the rear of the place, near the storeroom.

"How are you, Mr. Smalls? I'd like to buy more snuff, but I need it on account."

"All out, so sorry, Mrs. Watson."

I unpinned the seagull pin and stabbed it through his lapel. "Merry Christmas, Mr. Smalls."

He looked down at the little golden bird and smiled. "Well, isn't that that sweetest gift I've ever had." He took my hand and pulled me toward the storeroom. "I need to show you something."

He pulled me into the little room, closed and locked the door, and lit a candle, which illuminated a wooden table in the middle of the room and a stack of boxes against the wall.

"I can't be here with you, Jubal. You know that. Open the door."

He tossed the match on the dirt floor. "Knowin' you were there at that party was too much for me, Anne-May. I can't stop thinking about you."

"Your wife—"

"All she talks about is her service work and won't let me near her 'cause it's her time. I may go mad here in this house."

He pulled me by the waist and kissed me in that slow Southern way of his, long and lingering, but urgent, too, as I reveled in the scent of earth, match sulfur, and his orange spice cologne.

He put one arm up my skirt and rubbed me all the right ways under my silky underthings. Before long I was backed up against the table as he kissed me harder, the sounds of the party coming through the door.

"Jubal, if you'd please keep your tongue out of my mouth."

Jubal pressed his soft lips to my ear. "Come up to my bedroom."

A knock came at the door.

Jubal straightened, and smoothed his hair. "Who is it?" he called.

"It's me, Jubal," came the voice of Harriet Smalls. "I need to get in there."

I hid behind boxes while Jubal opened the door and talked to his wife and then finally closed it.

"I can't do this anymore, Jubal. She'll find out and tell everyone."

"Since when did Louisiana women care about conventions?" he asked, blew out the candle, and pulled me to him.

Georgy

✳

ONE MAY DAY, MR. OLMSTED CAME TO US ONBOARD THE *Wilson Small.*

"The military situation is developing rapidly, ladies, now that we're on the march to Richmond. General Lee will put up a fierce fight and we can expect heavy casualties. Can you be packed and move to the *Daniel Webster No. 1?*"

"Of course, sir," I said.

"Mrs. Howland, you may be interested to note Colonel Howland and his men can be found on *Daniel Webster No. 2,* which you will pass today on your way to Ship Point. Let's all say a prayer we don't end up seeing much of his Sixteenth Regiment in the wards with us."

ELIZA AND I TRANSFERRED to our new ship by tug. Just past the mouth of the York River, we passed the *Daniel Webster No. 2* and we held hands, knowing we were finally close to our Joe. We pulled up alongside our new home, the *Daniel Webster No. 1,* a fine old side-wheel steamer with two tall black smokestacks, U.S. HOSPITAL written in white on its paddlewheel housing, and were handed up onto the deck by a male nurse. He, along with his nineteen colleagues, bid us no greeting.

"Ward floor is downstairs," one particularly unhelpful young nurse said, pointing a finger toward the hatch without even a glance at my face.

We descended the ladder and arrived below deck to find a surprisingly wide, high-ceilinged ward, with army cots lined up down each wall, a few beds occupied by sick and wounded troops. The boat rocked gently, water lapping its sides, while our male counterparts joked and arm-wrestled on deck, locked fists banging the barrel tops above to choruses of jeers.

As we arrived, our two fellow female nurses rushed to greet us: Christine Griffin, a slight woman with expressive blue eyes and a bright way, and dark-haired Katharine Prescott Wormeley, a dear friend of the family, for our mothers knew and liked each other. They were the kind of women who dedicated themselves to selfless causes, not sewing circles, which met amid extreme social exclusiveness to embroider tablemats for the rectory.

"It's good to see you both," Katharine said. "I knew this would be a worthwhile endeavor when I heard you two would be joining us. They say this ship is the one that will bear the brunt."

From a good Newport family, Katharine had been born in England as I was, and had lost her father at a young age as well, so we had much in common and deep mutual affection. Though she might be described by others as homely, I saw nothing but a lovely face, full of wit and good cheer.

"We've been hearing such good things about you both," Christine said. "You studied with Dr. Blackwell, Georgy? And asked Mr. Lincoln himself to secure chaplains? Everyone is talking about it."

They were sensibly dressed, as we were, in black silk dresses without hoops, just simple petticoats, our own little army of four.

Katharine waved us to follow her. "We will catch up later, but for now, we are glad to have your help. We found the ship disgustingly dirty and it still hasn't been cleaned to our satisfaction, since the male nurses do nothing but complicate our good works."

Christine leaned in toward Eliza. "Stay clear of them if you can, though that's close to impossible, there being fifty of them. Most are former patients serving here to avoid returning to the fight."

Katharine forged along. "These wounded have been here for one day, their injuries the result of recent skirmishes onshore. Three or four amputations, one lieutenant shot through the knee and in agony, poor man, and a young boy of seventeen shot through the lungs."

Christine spoke quietly. "Every breath draws a hissing sound through the wound. Just terrible."

Eliza and I followed Christine and Katharine down the rows of sick men, most of them asleep beneath clean linen.

"We also have several typhus and malaria cases," Christine said.

Katharine stopped and adjusted one soldier's bandage. "We begin the day at five o'clock by conveying the breakfast trays, and then the surgeons make their rounds and we assist in the wetting of wounds and the changing of bandages. This morning we had to hold our ears, the cries of pain so torturous."

Katharine stopped at another young soldier's bed, a drummer boy no older than fifteen, his arm in a sling.

"Will I die tonight, ma'am?"

"Oh, pooh," Katharine said. "You'll walk off the ship at New York. Take your tea when it comes."

The tour continued.

"We then give clean handkerchiefs dampened with cologne to the men," Christine said. "Sponge the wounds over the bandages, write letters home for them, and give medicine or brandy. They say all ninety beds will be full soon, so we must prepare the remaining cots, fill the linen closets, and, when we go onshore, look for a second hospital stove to pilfer."

I looped one arm through Eliza's. "We shall become devoted kleptomaniacs."

"Expecting action in Richmond any day now," Christine said.

Katharine leaned in. "Dr. Ware is our head doctor. Only twenty-six years old, but full of good humor."

Christine leaned in toward me. "Dr. *Rogers* is an entirely different sort of animal—a real show-off, but a fairly competent surgeon when he's sober, though he holds his knife clenched in his teeth while he operates."

Katharine turned to Eliza. "We hear your Joe is fighting with the New

York Sixteenth. Of course you know we're moving nearly abreast with them as we advance upriver."

"Yes, we know," Eliza said. "Though I've not had a letter from him in days. It's the lack of information that's unbearable."

"We've heard rumors the Rebels may be advancing toward us," Christine said.

"Please don't draw it mild for our benefit," I said.

"Yes," Eliza said. "Any news is appreciated."

Katharine pulled us close. "Well then, I just heard from the steward. Now that Grant is winning in the West, Lincoln's pressing McClellan to go on the attack and take Richmond. So the next few days will tell the tale, if we can seize it from Lee. He said some of our troops have gotten so close they can hear the church bells there. Let's just hope McClellan will finally get aggressive."

"And the war will be over?" Eliza asked.

"If we take their capital? It would be a crippling blow to the Confederacy. I've heard your Sixteenth is being considered to move into place for the attack."

Eliza sent me a dark look.

Katharine tugged my carpetbag from my hand. "Let us get you settled quickly, there is much to be done. We'll know a battle is happening when we get the order to steam farther up the Pamunkey River to White House Landing and await the wounded."

WE TOOK OFF OUR BONNETS and got to work, and as night fell we surveyed the fruits of our collective labor, weary and hungry, but with pride. From hold to hurricane deck, the floors were clean and waxed, each unoccupied cot perfectly made with hospital corners, a regulation underquilt added, along with army blanket and one plump pillow in its starched pillowcase. I arranged the linen closet with neat stacks of linen, hospital clothing, socks, bandages, lint, and rags and checked the medicine closet and found it well supplied, but lacking in sufficient brandy. That would have to be resolved, for this often served as our only anesthesia.

Then all at once, a stream of male nurses descended the ladder and ambled down the rows of empty beds until each chose one to lie upon—some dismantling the linens, pulling out the underquilts, others climbing beneath the sheets with their boots still on, many with brandy on their breath.

I stood over one. "I hope you've not helped yourself to alcohol from our pantry, sir."

He grinned up at me. "Dr. Rogers gave it to us. Had some himself."

Katharine came to my side and swatted him out of the bed. "You get out with your dirty boots."

Eliza and Christine pulled another from a bed. "These are for sick men who've been in battle. Go to your bunks."

One leaned close to me, brandy on his breath.

"I'm afraid I must report you, sir," I said.

"We don't need you here. Maybe go tell that to Mr. Lincoln," he said with a smile as he threw his head back and drank the last of our medicinal brandy.

WHEN WE WOKE ON May 31, not one of us was prepared for the frenzy of suffering and death that would descend upon us so quickly.

Orders came at dawn to sail up the Pamunkey River, and we did so at close to full speed, our smokestacks sweeping the hanging branches along the banks. Eliza and I stood on deck, and as we drew closer to White House Landing, Virginia, we saw Martha Washington's former home, an unpretentious white cottage, standing atop a green lawn sloping down to the river, and a stream of wounded being carried to the grassy shore.

Dr. Ware came to stand near us on deck and I admired his wide-spaced, kind eyes and quick smile. "The Confederates attacked outside of Richmond," he said. "Lee got McClellan's left flank near Fair Oaks Station. Massive casualties on both sides. Wounded've been arriving at the train depot. We'll go ashore and see what we've got."

We anchored in the bay and took rowboats bound for land, the air hot and heavy. As we neared the grassy shore, scores of wounded lay piled up there, left by medics, crying out from the pain of every sort of grievous wound. Once our rowboat landed, we hurried to the wounded, but as more army trainloads arrived, entirely unattended, we were quickly overcome. Streams of men arrived, alive and dead together in closed boxcars, and others came on horse-mounted stretchers and by ambulance, until the entire shore stood full. Staff soldiers dumped the wounded on the riverbanks, leaving them to cry out in agony for help.

It was my first encounter with the fresh wounds of battle, some inflicted with bayonets and sabers, but the vast majority by means of soft lead bullets known as minié balls. These bullets flattened as they met flesh and splintered bones, creating festering wounds that almost always required amputation.

We all carried the wounded to our shore hospital tent, many with bones protruding in such a manner as to make such cases nearly hopeless. Each stretcher that passed seemed to bear men with wounds more horrible than the last. A man with both legs gone, hastily bandaged. One man's lower face blown away, exposing neck bones and teeth.

Dr. Ware came to us. "We've almost got our ninety, those with good prospects to survive. We'll leave quickly."

"We can fit more patients, Doctor," I said.

"There isn't time. We can't be caught here with no means of defense. Then none of us will survive it."

I trailed Drs. Ware and Rogers as they circulated among the sea of crying wounded, choosing which surgical cases to admit, and wrote their names in my little book, which I now wore tied to my belt. They chose probable amputations, and left the worst cases dying in the grass, those poor fellows with chests blown open by gunfire or with bowels and soft tissue exposed and inflamed, sepsis already setting in.

Back on board, the wards filled with the grossly injured. We breathed through our handkerchiefs, for the stench of suppurating wounds produced vomiting in the strongest of us, even those habituated to attending the sick and wounded.

Eliza and I eased the patients into beds, the air filled with the sound of men calling out for their loved ones and moaning with thirst, hunger, and pain.

Dr. Ware rushed to us as Eliza and I applied a new bandage to the stump of a private's lower leg.

"Have you assisted at an amputation, Georgy?"

"I watched one in training in New York, Doctor. But from afar."

"And you, Eliza?"

"No, Doctor."

"Dr. Rogers needs assistance with one. I told him you might need some instruction. He can talk you through the process."

We barely nodded and Dr. Ware stepped away and called back over his shoulder, "He's operating in the foredeck!"

We found Dr. Rogers, unshaven, his apron soaked with blood, operating in the low-ceilinged open space at the front of the ship. He stood at the side of a young man lying on the table usually reserved for staff meals, fully awake and restrained by male nurses as one shaved the upper part of the man's arm. The doctor's wooden surgical kit lay open on a table next to him, the silver instruments glowing in the sun streaming through the hatch.

As I stepped closer I saw little sign the man was in need of amputation.

"It is about time you got here," Dr. Rogers said. "He's had his brandy. Helps the chloroform take effect."

As I drew closer it became clear that the smell of brandy was coming not only from the patient, but from Dr. Rogers and the male nurses as well.

"Ware says you've never seen such a surgery, and today you'll learn from the best. I've done hundreds of these."

"Where would you like us, Doctor?" I asked.

"Both of you administer the chloroform. One come to the head of the table and form a cone with that towel. The other drip in a tablespoon of the chloroform."

"Please, no," the man on the table said. "I farm my land in Quincy. Can't plow if you take the arm."

Eliza and I sidestepped a pile of severed limbs, some legs still wearing shoes or boots, as I took my place at the head of the table and lay my hand on the man's good shoulder.

The private looked up at me. "Please don't let them, ma'am."

"You need to live to see your family," I said and took the towel and folded it into a cone as Eliza dripped the chloroform into the cone's top. All at once the man became more exercised and thrashed about.

"The towel won't stay a cone, Doctor," I said.

"Do the best you can. It's just the chloroform causing the agitation."

The patient calmed and Dr. Rogers wasted no time. Chloroform's length of sedation varied, so surgeons were praised for their quickness. He tied off the upper arm with a tourniquet.

"Once I tie off, I shall address this wound, what we call primary amputation with uncontrolled hemorrhage."

"It does not seem to be hemorrhaging, Doctor," I said.

"There is a bullet wound to the joint there, Miss Woolsey."

"A surface wound."

"Tut, tut, Miss Woolsey. You're about to learn from the best. If you feel faint, step away from the table."

"Perhaps we should consult Dr. Ware."

One of the male nurses leaned toward me. "He's in the middle of a surgery himself."

"Now that I have compressed the main artery against the bone, Nurse, retract that skin."

The doctor brandished his knife. "Behold Liston's small amputation knife, the hardest worker in the kit. I make an incised circle around the arm and through the musculature to the bone." Eliza and I exchanged dark glances. How sickening to see an honest man's perfectly good arm sacrificed to another's hubris.

"Now the skin must be further retracted, thank you, Nurse, to permit the bone to be sawn thus, with a common bow saw. You will see many of these in your time at the table. Makes quick work of the bone thus."

As he cut I blotted the blood with a clean towel and Eliza and I held the table edge, forcing ourselves to tamp down our anger and study his method.

And with a few rasps of the bone saw the young man's arm fell away and Dr. Rogers tossed it on the pile. There was clearly not ample skin or tissue of any kind left to cover the bone.

I held the towel firmly to the wound. "Dr. Rogers, in nursing school they taught us that there must be more than ample skin left to cover—"

"I've given myself more than ample skin." He turned to me, linen thread in his needle. "I get the distinct impression that you believe yourself a doctor, Miss Woolsey. First, questioning this soldier's need for an amputation."

"I believe his arm could have been saved. You robbed him of his livelihood all in the service of your own vanity."

His face grew a deep red-purple. "*Second,* questioning my technique. I suppose you're covering that in the nursing handbook you're writing."

"How did you know—"

"The male nurses know everything, Miss Woolsey."

"They've rummaged through my private effects?"

"I believe they find your treatise amusing."

"If you must know, it's a serious concern. I'm writing a handbook for a school I'd like to open one day, for female nurses. And, yes, proper surgical technique will be covered."

"A handbook for lady nurses?" He choked back a laugh. "I'd like to see that." He turned suddenly serious. "But a few days of nursing school does not give you permission to question a surgeon of ten years. When I am done here, you will escort this patient back to the main ward. And I will not see you at my operating table again."

AS THE PATIENTS SETTLED in, Eliza and I slept sitting up, with our heads on our arms and only for brief spells, to make sure we could minister to our "criticals." The majority of them required constant attention, such brave boys, so young and uncomplaining. We watched over them during the most urgent phase of their recovery, fetching them brandy milk punch or a little piece of meat to suck as men died all around us.

That night we felt our ship move, clawed by the little tugs on either side of us, sending us on our hasty retreat down the river, to transfer our wounded for their trip back north.

I came up on deck for air as we got under way, and saw at least a hundred of the poor hopeless cases onshore, still alive, watching us go. I was heartsick to leave them behind, but relieved we had not yet recognized one face from the New York Sixteenth among them.

Jemma

✴

PEELER PLANTATION, MARYLAND
APRIL 1862

THREE MONTHS AFTER DELLY AND CHARL AND THE BABY DIS-appeared, I still missed them bad. Once I found that sunflower on their bed, we took it as a sign we should keep their sudden vanishing a secret, and LeBaron didn't find they were gone till we all came back to regular work and those two didn't report.

I was down below with Sally when LeBaron, having found out, stomped into our shack with Chester and Miss Charlene's dogs. He let the dogs run up and down our place while I just closed my eyes tight and hoped they wouldn't lift the floorboards to find Pa's knives.

LeBaron, red in the face and wild-eyed, shook the handle of his whip in Sally Smith's face. "If I find out you're hidin' them, you black witch, I'll see you swung up the limb of the sycamore myself."

ONCE DELLY AND CHARL disappeared with the baby, things got worse at Peeler. It was harder for Ma and Pa to do the tobacco work alone so I pitched in where I could. Then some of the harvest got wet in the barn, the worst thing for a crop of leaf, and Ma worried day and night that Anne-

May was running Peeler into the ground. Aunt Tandy Rose had been a frugal one, though she had a sense of humor about it, renaming the main road from town to Peeler *Moneysunk Road* since that big place was expensive to keep up. But everybody knew Anne-May spent money like nobody's business. One day that spring she up and sold ten hogs for no good reason and went to Smalls and Sons for shopping soon after. Even the hogs thought selling them was dumb, since when the pig drovers came from Leonardtown to get them shouting "Soo-ee!" they kept running back to their pen. Drovers finally had to sew their eyelids shut before the poor things would go quiet to the big slaughterhouse.

So it was no wonder I couldn't wait for Pa's next secret meeting that night. Anne-May was fit to be tied, losing Charl and Delly, two good workers, and as punishment ordered Sally to feed our cornbread mush to what hogs was left, but by that afternoon she'd already moved on and wanted a new dress made up, so that kept my mind off my rumbling belly.

Due to the war, it was hard to find as many fancy doodads and frills for decorating clothes. It was a miracle Anne-May found silk cloth. She told me to take back the cast-off gown she'd given Ma, to use the black cloth for embellishments, but Ma used that as her church dress and there was no way I would take that back.

Instead, I found an old mint-green bombazine dress of Anne-May's, took Mister Watson's old umbrella that went inside out on him in a hurricane, cut up the black cloth from it for pretty tracks to run down the skirt, and had Pa smooth down the bone handle for buttons and sewed them down the front placket.

After an hour or so of sewing, my mind wandered to Anne-May's jewelry case and Ma's earbobs in there. I stood and stepped to the case, a deep-maroon leather box with black velvet inside. I opened the case, the jewels arranged just so. Anne-May had lectured me on each piece when she first came, along with warnings of the bad things to happen to me if any went missing.

I pulled out one of the amethyst earbobs Aunt Tandy Rose gave Ma, and I held one up to the window, the purple stones alive with light. She gave them to Ma back when the bad thing out in the tobacco barn happened, when we kids were playing out there. Tandy Rose made her that present to help Ma feel a little better, and she did for a while.

But once Anne-May came, Aunt Tandy Rose wasn't in the ground one hour when LeBaron told Anne-May that Ma had those earbobs and she sent him tearing up our whole place to find them. Until Ma handed them to him and said he couldn't take Aunt Tandy Rose's esteem for her away, too, and he smacked her hard across the face with his whip handle, and the metal of it left a little half-moon on her chin. Every time we saw those purple stones hanging from Anne-May's ears, glittering so pretty, I felt Ma's blood boil.

Anne-May's voice came from the direction of the stairs and I dropped the earbobs back onto the velvet and shut the lid.

She stepped into the room, one eye half-shut. "What's going on in here?" She peered around the room.

"Just finished your new dress, that's all."

She stepped to the jewelry chest and opened the lid. "You were in here, weren't you?"

"No, missis."

"Things are not as they were. Get down to the pantry."

"I swear on the Bible I wasn't—"

"Don't you defile the Lord's name. You get to the pantry or I'll whip you right here twice as long."

THAT NIGHT AFTER ANNE-MAY fell asleep, tired from whipping me, we all met down below. Pa set me at the table while Sally put every remedy she had on my back and fretted over me, dabbing chamomile tea on my wounds with cotton wool.

"I have a new plan," Pa said.

Ma paced, the candlelight catching the tears in her eyes. "I'm tired of *plans,* Kofi. How much more can we take? I won't stay here one day more. I'll swim the river, I don't care, my girl will not suffer like this again. Plus, it's just time before LeBaron gets her like he did Celeste and does his worst. I'll take her to Fort Monroe myself if I have to."

Pa handed Sally more cotton wool. "I have a new plan, better than Fort Monroe. We're going to Point Lookout, a Union army camp set up just down the peninsula from here. There's a contraband camp there, they'll take us in."

"Says who?" Sally Smith asked.

"Freed shop boy in Leonardtown where I get my paints. Says we only have to get there. They'll put us all to work for pay. Some get on boats due north."

Ma sat next to me. "Fine with me. But it better be soon."

"How do we get there?" I asked.

"We'll go through the swamp. Jemma, you get word to Patience."

"The swamp?" Sally said, then set her lips together hard.

Just the idea of it got my hands shaking. "Is there another way, Pa? Patience is scared of the snakes and the dogs know me too well."

"Can't just walk the main road. You don't know what you can do until you have to, Jemma."

Ma held my hand.

"We'll be just fine," Pa said, no smile in his eyes. "We're close to free, I can feel it."

Anne-May

EUPHEMIA AND I SAT IN THE DINING ROOM ONE MORNING, the cat swatting at the little chenille balls on the window curtains, the buzz in my head growing louder since I ran out of snuff, my mind on going to town to see if Jubal had gotten any more in, when we heard the sound of wheels on gravel. We hurried out to the courtyard to see a wagon driven by two top-hatted men, remarkably fresh-faced and cheerful for people in their business, a gray metal coffin in the back of the wagon.

Euphemia leaned her full weight on me. "Fergus."

I pushed her upright and smoothed back my hair as the men alighted and came to us.

"Sorry, ma'am, to bring bad news, but this is a delivery for Miss Anne-May Wilson Watson."

"That is I."

"Where can we deliver the deceased? We'll need two sawhorses and a place to lay out the remains."

"Fergus Watson? Oh my." I took a step back. How awful, Fergus dead. It was all so unexpected. And just like him to leave me with no money and a plantation to run.

"Take him in the front parlor, I suppose, like we did for Aunt Tandy Rose. It overlooks the river. One of the finest views in Maryland, boys."

Euphemia pulled a hankie from her sleeve. "Fergus loved that river."

I turned to the coffin boys. "How much do we owe you gentlemen? We haven't much, I'm afraid."

"Not a cent, ma'am. He prepaid. Probably had a feeling his time was up."

"Oh, Fergus," Euphemia said. "He was so thoughtful that way."

Once we repaired to the front parlor, Euphemia started that blubbery cry of hers.

I shook her by the arm. "Stop this now. It's like *you* were married to Fergus, for pity's sake. It was just his time. Have Joseph take down the door and set up two sawhorses for the coffin and get Sable and Jemma to prepare the body."

The coffin boys followed me. "He's had preserving liquid pumped through him at the battlefront, so he can be viewed for a week—maybe more—without rotting."

"How comforting, when you put it like that," I said.

Once Joseph took the door off its hinges, set it on two sawhorses, and Sable and Jemma appeared, the men brought the coffin in and set it on the makeshift table.

I hated glancing at that blue-gray zinc box, so morbidly shaped like a man. It was broad in the shoulders, and had a refrigerated chest of the same material fixed atop it.

"Just sign these papers here and we'll take the coffin away once the remains are in place."

One of them removed the refrigerated box to reveal the coffin below and the writing chalked across the top, *Harold Wilson. Deliver to Miss Anne-May Wilson Watson, Peeler Plantation, near Hollywood, Maryland.*

I stepped back. "I don't understand."

"I told you he prepaid. Bought the full insurance package."

"I mean I don't under*stand.* This is not my husband, Fergus Watson?"

"No. This here's Harold Wilson. Wrote this address. Look, we have another drop-off, ma'am. We need to take the box."

"Of course." I could say no more, as a dizzying emptiness came over me, like staring into a chasm.

Euphemia grasped my arm. "Oh no, not our *Harry,*" and started to wail.

They crowbarred the metal top off the coffin and set it aside.

"Care to view the body? Been fixed up according to the contract. A gentleman at the battle site made sure it shipped."

On shaking legs I stepped forward to see my brother, my handsome boy, eyes closed, a lifelike color in his cheek. I locked my fingers under my chin as they lifted him from the box, dressed in his uniform.

"Had to change the shirt. Shot in the chest. No one makes it home alive from that. Charge went clean through. Didn't suffer, that's for sure."

How could it be Harry, so cold and white, like he was sleeping, ugly blue around his lips, mouth half-open like nobody sleeps, arms at his sides?

The cat jumped up onto the sofa and peered over at Harry. Tears filled my eyes. Did Joan remember him?

Euphemia hurried upstairs and took to her bed as Sable, Sally, and Jemma crept toward the body, heads bowed, each holding a basin half-filled with water and clean rags, and set to work. I stood numb as they removed my brother's uniform jacket and trousers, folded a towel over his privates, then sent that rag up his side and down one last time as Sally set out his grave clothes on the sofa like he'd be up and putting them on any minute.

"Make sure you wash him good, now," I said, from somewhere far off.

Sable just nodded as she ran the rag down my poor brother. "Yes, missis."

We all jumped as the back door slammed and a voice echoed through the house.

"Is it true? Where's my son?"

A hot pain stabbed my eye.

Mama.

"Good to see you, Mama. You got here so fast."

Zoretha Wilson Stickman brushed into the room, bringing to mind a skinny little hornet in a black teaspoon bonnet, her black bombazine dress, one of three she'd had made up, anticipating this occasion.

"I'd only just got to cousin Sissy's in Baltimore when I received word. I still can't believe it. Not my Harry."

"Yes, it's true, Mama," I said.

I stood back to let her pass, the scent of gardenia thick in her wake.

Mama pulled off her gloves, tugging one finger at a time. "I must remove my own gloves? I forgot how backward you are up here."

"Jemma's busy now."

She stepped to Harry and looked down on him. "My boy." She reached out to touch his shoulder and then snatched her hand back.

"Where's the bullet hole?" she asked, to no one special.

I stepped to Harry's side and pointed to the horrible, red-ringed hole just off the center of his chest. "Right here, Mama."

"Lift him up."

Jemma and Sable just looked at each other.

"Lift him *up*, I say. Christ Almighty, what is wrong with you people?"

I could scarcely look as they tried lifting my Harry up like he was sitting, but his poor, gray-white body was still mighty stiff and Mama had to bend low to look at his back.

She stood up, a queer little smile on her face. "There. I knew it. The exit wound is much bigger than this here in the front. He died with valor, shot face on, not runnin' away."

I took her by the arm. "Come, Mama. Sable has to finish up so folks can come to the viewing."

Zoretha looked at Sable as if for the first time. "Get them out of here."

I tried to lead her out. "But they have to finish."

"I don't want them touching my boy. Get your sister."

"But, Mama, Euphemia's resting, all broke up about Harry."

Zoretha took a deep breath and said in an even voice, "You get these black bitches out of this house this second or I will take a gun from that closet and shoot them each dead, do you hear me?"

Sable and Jemma hustled out, leaving my brother naked on the makeshift table.

"Will you not say a prayer for Harry? You've barely looked at him."

"In time, Anne-May. I must get settled first. I'll be taking your room. I need the view to calm me."

"You don't care about Harry at all. You sent him that uniform for your own glorification. He died because of you and you don't care one bit."

Mama stepped to me quick, her eyes bright with tears, and jabbed one shaking finger into my chest. "Don't you dare question a mother's love for her son. He was my moon and my stars from the moment he came into this world, more than either of you girls could ever be, and there will never be another person I loved more. He was good and kind and a balm to me, delighted to be at my knee, more like your father than you girls. You will have him cleaned up and I will view him properly this evening with the rest of our guests. Have my trunks sent up and have Sally send tea to my room."

HALFWAY THROUGH HARRY'S VIEWING DAYS, Fergus came home by ambulance, one leg shot clean off.

Euphemia ran to the courtyard as two attendants pulled him out on a stretcher. "Fergus," she cried out as she went to him. "We've missed you so."

I followed. "Hope this ambulance is paid for, since we don't have a dime, Fergus."

Right there in the gravel turnabout, the attendant pulled down the blanket and exposed Fergus's stump of a leg, the sewed-up end still bleeding through the bandage.

He handed a paper bag to Euphemia. "Major Watson's wound requires a bandage change and iodine twice daily."

I turned away, about to lose my breakfast, as Euphemia heeded the medical instructions like a bird dog on point.

The attendants helped Fergus up to standing and arranged a crutch under each arm.

"That will be all, Private," Fergus said, and Euphemia helped him turn toward the house and make his way to the door.

I followed them. "Don't know if you heard, Fergus, but Harry's dead. Here inside." Tears filled my eyes.

"We fought in the same battle, Anne-May. I'm the one who finalized his arrangements."

"How did it happen?"

"Not sure. I knew we were fighting his regiment—"

"And you went anyway? You could've refused to fight your own brother-in-law, run away."

"They shoot deserters, Anne-May. I tried to look for him."

"Why didn't you save him, Fergus?" I folded my arms across my waist. "You know how precious he was to me."

"Did my best, Anne-May. I was lucky I could make sure the body got shipped home. Often those insurance writers just leave the bodies."

Euphemia helped Fergus along.

I followed. "You promised me you'd protect him."

He turned to me, eyes dull. "There was no protecting anyone, Anne-May."

Euphemia helped him struggle along; the wood ends of his crutches stuck in the gravel now and then.

"He had no business in that ridiculous war," I said. "He was a gentle sort."

"And I'm not? I've never seen such a poor reception for a fallen soldier. I was close to death myself, Anne-May."

"Well, it's been hard on us here. Just want you to know, Fergus, Sally Smith has been stealing this house blind. Took your gold stickpin and sold it. Has the money hid all over the pantry. You should think hard on selling her soon as you can. Jemma's been trouble, too."

"How did the tobacco auction go?"

"LeBaron had nothing to take. Last year's leaf got wet from a hole in the roof."

Fergus stopped in his tracks. "So we have no money for the year? Why didn't you have LeBaron get up there and repair it?"

"Joseph got on a ladder and went at it with hammer and nail but there was still no way that leaf'd be dry by auction."

"Should've known I couldn't depend on you, Anne-May." Fergus forged on toward the house. "And now, if you'll allow a man to enter his own house in peace?"

I let that comment about this being his own house slide. A movement above caught my eye. I looked up to my bedroom window to find Mama, her black veil down over her face, pull back the curtain with one hand, look at Fergus with stone-cold disgust, and then retreat into the darkness.

EVEN THE LITTLE BIT of snuff Jubal dropped off for me couldn't help me through Harry's funeral. Mama could barely stay still at the service, like she was sitting on a hot biscuit. When it was done, she wandered up to the casket and stood there, stroking it with one hand. "My boy. He's with God now," she said, swaying to some song in her head. It had been hard on her, the wake and viewing for Harry, a lot of people she barely knew coming by the house, from the other plantations, all over St. Mary's County.

Back at the house after the funeral, always the consummate hostess, Mama sat next to Widow Gardener at the dining table and told her that her husband was a fool to doctor coloreds and deserved to die, as she offered her the decanter of blackberry cordial.

"And you will burn in hell for supporting the Yankee cause," Mama said.

She then stood and told anyone who'd listen that in Maryland, Lincoln only got one thousand votes out of thirty thousand.

After that, Mama cozied up to Jubal, despite the dowdy Mrs. Smalls, paler than January, hanging on his arm.

"If they took all the attractive men in Louisiana and rolled 'em into one, it'd be you, Jubal Smalls, with your handsome looks and even handsomer manners. No wonder every woman in this town is downright mad for you."

Jubal leaned down. "I never set eyes on such a comely woman as yourself, Zoretha."

His affection for her may have had something to do with her buying a black cashmere shawl and jet earbobs at Smalls and Sons the day before.

Jubal was in a fine mood, walking about my house, inquiring about every little thing, while Fergus eyed him from his seat near the hearth.

"What year was this place built?" Jubal asked.

"Perhaps you'd like to move in?" Fergus asked.

Always with a sense for quality, Jubal eyed the blue Sèvres vases. "Perhaps I would."

Mama trailed Jubal like a hound on scent. "If only Anne-May'd met you before Fergus," she said, no attempt to lower her voice.

Harriet Smalls turned to Mother. "I understand you're mourning your son, but that is my husband you reference."

"If you want to keep him, you'd better start taking care of yourself."

Was that a hint of a smile on Jubal's face?

As Mama leaned in toward him, her cordial overflowed its rim and sloshed onto her skirt. "I see the way you look at my daughter. And me as well. Louisiana boys do love their mothers."

Before Mama could offend every person in Hollywood, I sent her off to bed and watched Jubal usher his wife out the front door. He turned and smiled at me and I knew right there I could have him if I wanted.

ONE DAY BEFORE MAMA left to go stay with her cousin Sissy in Baltimore, the two of us went on a mission to town. Dressed head to toe in black, with net veils over our faces and loaded with a cargo of men's socks, we drove the carriage to the Hollywood post office.

"You and Fergus going to have a baby?" Mama asked, her gaze on the road.

"Not sure that's in the cards, Mama."

She thought for a moment. "Maybe it's for the best, there bein' half a chance the child would favor Fergus."

"Think I'd be a good mother?"

She checked her lumpy little yellow beaded purse she always carried, which held her pills and comb and perfume pots. "I believe I left my rouge at home."

"You're not so good at changing subjects, Mama."

"You barely show that cat of yours affection, Anne-May, never mind a child."

"Come now, wouldn't you love a little grandbaby?"

"I suppose you'd be a passable mother."

We pulled up to the dingy little post office and stepped inside. That place brought to mind a tomb, tight and airless, a small desk and chair the only furnishing, a bespectacled, balding man seated behind it. My mind flashed to Harry's lifeless body stretched out in our front parlor on that first night and I took a deep breath.

We'd come to send to the troops the sewing circle's three paper cartons of socks we'd worked our fingers to the bone knitting. I'd argued to Widow Gardener that some should be mailed to Confederate troops, but she sent Euphemia a pencil list of only U.S. Army troop addresses, written in her looping hand. Places I'd never heard of, like Kernstown and Newtown, all in Virginia. She'd asked Euphemia to send the packages, seeing as those two were practically married, but my sister had taken to bed with her head-ache powders, perhaps brought on by Mama's expert pestering and prov-ocation, so the job fell to me.

I handed the list to the postmaster.

"Most folks bring packages in here ready to go," he said, and he copied the addresses onto the packages so slowly a line began to form behind us.

"Most postmasters don't sass their payin' customers," Mama said. After a whole five minutes had passed, he finally finished, writing *Stras-burg, Virginia,* and set down his pen.

Mother lifted back her veil. Mourning had brought a gray pallor to her cheek, as if in sympathy trying to match dear Harry's color. How flawless her skin was, even well past forty years old, from years of sleeping at night with thin-cut slices of rare beef on her face.

"The framers of the Constitution took less time writing it," she told the postmaster.

The postmaster removed his spectacles. "You can take that Southern attitude of yours and go right back where you came from."

Mama leaned in over the desk. "Don't see you in a hideous Yankee uniform."

He glanced at the clock. "This is a U.S. government establishment and I will tolerate no treasonous language, madam."

Mother rolled her eyes at me and mouthed the word *asswipe*. "My son was killed by the very men who will wear those socks."

The postmaster answered without looking up. "Perhaps he was on the wrong side."

Mama's mouth tightened. "Perhaps the wrong country."

"The law's clear. I can have you locked up for disloyal thoughts, words, or actions without any just cause."

"What about free speech?" I asked.

"This country is at war, madam. You live in a border state. There is no freedom of speech here."

"No honest elections, either," Mama said. "Y'all stuffing ballot boxes."

The man shrugged. "I fear much worse if the Union falls apart. And I'd be careful if I were you. U.S. Army's locked up others down at Point Lookout for saying less."

Mama looked out the window. "Where's that?"

The postmaster finished a return address with a flourish. "Just south of here, down the end of Point Lookout peninsula, bunch of rich people's houses they turned into a camp. Got a Rebel prison for smugglers, traitors, spies. They hang them by the thumbs down there."

Something in my belly turned over and I smoothed back my hair. "Certainly not ladies."

The postmaster applied the last stamp. "Hear they got four there right now. Traitors to the Union. Spies giving aid and comfort to the enemy."

He handed me back the pencil list and Mama and I stepped out onto the porch.

I crumpled the list into a ball. "Good riddance. Hope Widow Gardener's happy."

Mama took the ball from my hand, pulled it out flat, leaned in, and said with a low voice, "There must be someone you can share this with, Anne-May, who can put these addresses to good use. It shows where the Yankee troops are. Do it in the service of justice for your brother."

I plucked it from her fingers. "Certainly will, Mama."

That afternoon I slid that list into my red morocco book and sent Jemma back into town with it. Jubal would surely be pleased.

And my Harry, cold under the ground, embalming fluid still fresh in his veins, deserved to be avenged.

Georgy

Dear Mother,

Our whole fleet of hospital ships made our way to Fort Monroe, cut off from all communication with the army and our special part of it, Joe. There are rumors that Joe and the 16th are on their way to a place called Gaines Mill and are expecting a great engagement with General Lee. Eliza and I are on edge. A mounted messenger just announced that Stoneman's cavalry were worrying them till we were safely off, so we steamed away. The most interesting thing was the movement of the slaves, who, when it was known that the Yankees were running away, came flocking from all the country about, bringing their little movables, frying pans, old hats, and bundles to the river side. There was no appearance of anxiety or excitement among them. There was plenty of deck room for them on the forage boats, one of which, as we passed, seemed filled with women only, in their gayest dresses and bright turbans. Now and again the roar of the battle came to us, but the slave women were quietly nursing their children, and singing hymns. The day of their deliverance had come and they accepted the change with absolute placidity.

Your loving Georgy

As we headed for Fort Monroe, casualties continued to stream in. We battled on, doing our best to tend the terrible injuries, until Christine fell ill with malarial fever and left on a transport, in bed next to the wounded soldiers sent north. I contacted Mr. Olmsted, who sent relief in the form of a lovely young novitiate from the Sisters of Charity.

"Miss Woolsey?"

I turned to find a novitiate standing in the doorway, no more than a girl, her brown eyes shining.

"I am Sister Marguerite. I came with two others from my order but they left since there is no chapel on board. But I shall stay if you would like me to."

I stepped to her and took her hand. "Very much, Sister. I'm sorry we have no place of worship for you."

She leaned in with a smile. "This whole ward will be my chapel."

THAT AFTERNOON WE ASSISTED with the worst cases, dealt with six deaths, and attended at three amputations with Dr. Rogers, his manner cool to us after I had questioned him.

Sister Marguerite was initiated by fire, took charge of the washing machine, and proved to be a charming and steely addition.

We were on constant watch for men we knew from Joe's regiment, afraid we'd see members of the Sixteenth, but still wanting news from the front, until we finally found one, the flag bearer of Joe's regiment. He lay in his bed, so young—and so thin one could count every rib in the poor thing's rib cage—with a bullet wound to the right eye, which left a gaping hole in his face, requiring a bandage change hourly. It was a miracle he lived, and we made him our pet patient, sneaking him extra jellies and milks.

Eliza held his hand.

"You had our flag made, Mrs. Howland. It got pretty beat up, last few days."

Eliza smoothed back the hair from his forehead. "You carried it valiantly, I'm sure."

"How is Colonel Howland?" I asked.

"The colonel acted so bravely, riding up front with the men. He stayed in his saddle, until . . ." The boy glanced at me and then back at Eliza.

"Until what, Private?" Eliza asked.

"I can't tell you, ma'am. It's not right to hear it from me."

"Please, Private."

"Well, I saw his Old Scott tied to a tree watching Colonel Howland. They took him away in one of those new ambulances, face as gray as your cloak. I hate to tell you this, but not sure he made it, ma'am."

TO KEEP OUR MINDS off Joe's possible mortal wound, Eliza wrote letters home and I began, once my shift was done, to finish my female-nursing handbook, complete with chapters on managing wounds, proper hygiene, and diet, including some of the patients' favorite recipes: raspberry milk punch, cherry cobbler, and Mother's beef tea. I imagined it as a blueprint for a nursing school curriculum I would adopt and teach one day and finished two copies quickly, having spent one entire night writing my hand numb.

I delivered a copy the next morning to Dr. Rogers's assistant, a bitter young man named St. Pierre who rarely made eye contact with the female nurses.

"Please make sure the doctor receives this, Nurse, for he expressed a desire to read such a book. And if you would be so kind as to circulate it among your brethren."

"*The Nursing Handbook*?" he read from the top sheet.

"It contains everything necessary to know about the profession."

He smiled. "I'll let the doctor know. Sure he'll get a kick out of this."

THE NEXT NIGHT ELIZA and I slept sitting up, dozing between calls from men in need of a cold compress or a shot of brandy for the pain. Sister Marguerite made midnight rounds, stopping here and there to fetch a cup of milk or hear a story from a sleepless soldier.

We'd just drifted off when Sister Marguerite gently touched our shoulders and we woke and found the sight we feared most had appeared in our ward, Captain Holland of the Sixteenth New York, standing at attention.

"Mrs. Howland, ma'am, a message from the field."

We rose slowly from our chairs and Eliza reached for my hand. "I cannot bear this alone."

Captain Holland stood straight, his gaze straight ahead. "Colonel Howland has been wounded, ma'am, and is on his way here by ambulance."

Her grasp on my hand tightened. "And the nature of his wound, sir?"

"He requests I tell you it is a slight wound, ma'am."

"Thank you, Captain," she said.

The four of us stood silent, the question hanging in the air.

"Is it, Captain?" Eliza asked. "Slight I mean?"

The candlelight caught a tear in the captain's eye. "After Colonel Howland fell from the saddle, his old horse Scott kept watch over him." He wiped his eye with his cuff. "I have no further news to report, Mrs. Howland."

He stepped toward the stairs and then stopped and turned. "Thank you for all you and your sister've done for us, ma'am."

Eliza stepped to him and touched his sleeve. "You are most welcome, Captain."

"We've been the luckiest regiment to serve under Colonel Howland. No man was ever braver in the face of the enemy."

TWO ARMY MEDICS ARRIVED before dawn, bearing Joe on a stretcher. One of the medics stepped to Eliza, removed his kepi cap, and saluted. "Reporting from Gaines's Mill, Mrs. Howland. Colonel Howland requires immediate medical attention."

We transferred Joe to a bed, where he lay unresponsive, his chin slack. I tried to keep the shock from my face for my sister's sake. We'd seen that peculiar shade of gray-green on the faces of soldiers, and each time pulled the sheets up over them.

Eliza knelt at Joe's side and took his hand. "Joe, it's me."

She looked to me, her eyes dark. "He's not responding."

"Marguerite, fetch Dr. Ware," I said.

She hurried off.

The medic stepped closer. "Our surgeon in charge regrets he could not accompany Colonel Howland. He is besieged with casualties and felt it best to leave the removal of the bullet and any further surgery to Dr. Ware."

I held one hand to Joe's cold cheek. "The nature of the injury?"

"Colonel Howland rode along the front line with his men and took enemy fire, shot through the thigh. He continued on and led the charge with them, even with the air thick with iron. There's been a tremendous loss of blood."

"Thank you, Medic," Eliza said.

The medic saluted. "If you'll excuse us, Mrs. Howland, we have other patients to attend to."

The medics hurried off toward the stairs as Sister Marguerite returned, leading Dr. Rogers and three male nurses in his wake.

Even from where I stood, I could smell the brandy on him. "Marguerite, would you please call Dr. *Ware* for Colonel Howland?"

"Ware's been ordered to shore," Dr. Rogers said, barely addressing me. "Report details from the field."

The medic took a step back toward us. "My orders are to report to Dr. Ware."

"I am the doctor in charge here and you will report to me."

"Thigh wound, sir. Bullet not found. Severe inflammation. Wound was suffered a few days ago, but Colonel Howland stayed in the saddle to complete the battle."

Dr. Rogers looked down on Joe. "So, a glorious death."

"Case complicated by malaria. The chloroform administered wore off but we're all out."

"As are we, Medic."

Dr. Rogers threw back the blanket to reveal Joe's leg: the trousers had been cut away from it, and a plaster bandage covered his thigh. Rogers pulled away the bandage in one piece, exposing a black entry wound wiped with iodine, ringed with pus, swollen and inflamed.

Eliza cried out and pressed two fingers against her lips. We had seen countless serious wounds like it, few with good results.

Dr. Rogers tossed the blanket back over Joe's leg. "He's septic. Get him to the table."

Eliza looked to me. "Georgy, no."

I clasped my hands at my waist to stop the shake. "We shall wait for Dr. Ware."

Dr. Rogers turned to me, unsteady on his feet. "Dr. Ware is an hour from here, needed at the battle site, and I'm in charge. This man has a putrefied, suppurating wound. Every minute you wait increases his chances of a fatal event."

I stepped closer to him. "You are inebriated, Doctor, and Mrs. Howland and I will not allow you to operate on Colonel Howland."

"Well then, you are damned fools. Even taking the leg might not save his life. But if you don't try, he'll die for certain."

"He is not leaving this bed," I said.

"Very well." Dr. Rogers turned to the male nurses. "There is no reason why we should not perform our duty right here. Prepare this patient and escort the ladies out."

The orderlies pulled Eliza from Joe.

"No, please, Dr. Rogers," she said. "I must stay with him."

Sister Marguerite tried to hold on to the bed frame and Eliza and I struggled against their firm grasps, but the orderlies soon triumphed and hauled us to the stairs.

"Wood's circular amputation knife," Dr. Rogers said to his audience of orderlies as he presented his blade.

Jemma

✳

PEELER PLANTATION, MARYLAND
JUNE 1862

IT WAS A DRY SPRING AND BY THE TIME JUNE CAME, I WONDERED every night if it would be the one when we'd leave, until one Sunday Pa said we'd go that next night, down to Point Lookout, and turn ourselves in as contraband. Made sense, because I could see the undersides of the leaves and rain was coming.

"We going through the swamp?" I asked.

"Only way," Pa said. "Pray for a good rain. Dogs won't track us so easy."

The next day, I had much to do before I could leave to warn Patience we were going that night: feed the chickens, finish Miss Anne-May's new bonnet, and wash and hang out the bed linens. Only then did Anne-May say I could deliver her eggs to Miss Charlene.

I wore my green cotton dress, my best flowerpot bonnet with the lilac ribbons Anne-May said weren't good for her coloring, got Delly's old can of rocks, and then set off toward Ambrosia to tell Patience the good news.

Ma was working in the field nearest the house, while Pa worked in the house.

Ma waved to me as I passed. Her mouth said, "Hurry back now." But her eyes said, *Tonight we're gonna be free.*

———

I PASSED THAT OLD gray gate again, one of the season's first sunflowers tied there now, and tried not to look at the spidery sycamore tree in the clearing. The tin can grew slippery in my grasp as I hurried on to Ambrosia Plantation. I went straight to my sister's shack and left a note under her pillow, that we would see her that night to go north, and hurried back to pack.

On the way home, fierce-looking black clouds came overhead, it grew darker, and I nearly ran the whole road back. I was almost to Farmer Burns's gate when LeBaron busted out of the woods on his horse and the breath caught in my throat.

"Got your pass?"

I tried to sidestep him and his horse but he blocked my way.

"You don't understand what your place is here, Jemma. When I say where's your pass, I expect an answer."

He slid down off his horse and walked to me. "This won't be so bad. Once you relax."

I stepped back, every part of me filled with dread. Just like Celeste. "No—"

He reached out one hand. "This is gonna happen, Jemma. You might as well come quiet like."

I shook my can of rocks hard as I could and it echoed through the trees.

"You want to do it the hard way?" LeBaron grabbed me by the arm and dragged me down the path toward his shack, me shaking that can of rocks so loud, until he finally chucked it in the woods.

I fought so hard my bonnet fell off, but after a time he managed to drag me inside his little house, which still smelled like new pine, the only furniture in there one iron bed and a chair he stole from Anne-May. He pushed me onto the bed and yanked his belt through the loops in one pull. I kicked and punched, but he still got a hand up my dress and pulled my underdrawers down to my knees.

That's when the door opened and Ma rushed in out of breath and started hitting LeBaron's back. "Leave her be."

He stood and stepped to Ma. "You know I can do what I want."

I pulled up my drawers.

"Take me instead," Ma said. "You want someone that knows how to do things. Not a child."

LeBaron smiled. "Well, 'bout time, Sable. If you'd offered long ago, my needs would be met, and this one wouldn't be tempting me."

Ma's eyes flashed to me. "Well, you and me, we never get a chance to talk, LeBaron."

LeBaron smiled and walked closer to her. "Well, now. There's an idea. C'mon and sit and we'll talk."

With a little tilt of her head, Ma motioned for me to get up.

LeBaron came to her and pulled her shawl off with one slow tug.

"So you finally come around to me, Miss Sable."

"Let the girl go," Ma said. "I feel more relaxed just the two of us."

"I'm not stupid. She'll go right to her pa and tell all and then where'll we be?"

"Her pa's gone to town."

Our eyes met. That was a bald-faced lie. Pa was fixing Anne-May's sticky dresser drawer.

I thought I'd upchuck my soup when LeBaron started kissing Ma's neck and touching her all over. I squeezed my hands into two tight balls standing there, not knowing what to do.

Then LeBaron took his nasty old belt and looped one end through his iron bedpost and the other around Ma's neck. "Not taking any chances with you runnin' away."

Ma's eyes met mine, scared, and that's when I ran, out of there and over to Peeler.

I found Pa kneeling at Anne-May's dresser.

"LeBaron's got Ma in his shack," I said, and he was up and out the door and running fast down the hill, past the smokehouse and off toward that shack.

I followed fast as I could and got there just as Pa ran in the door. By the time I stepped in, he had LeBaron up against the wall, knife at his throat, and Ma pulled me close.

Pa tossed him hard against the floor. "Don't you ever touch her again."

LeBaron just lay there rubbing on his neck, his special brand of hate in his pig eyes.

IT DIDN'T TAKE LONG for them to come get Pa. They showed up at our cabin just before dark, LeBaron and four of his pattyrollers, all on horses. LeBaron had his big black club and the rest had every kind of nasty-looking stick you could dream up. Chester dragged a long chain, the fat kind they pull logs with, and just looking at that made me turn to ice all over. Though Ma had tried to get Pa to go tell Mister Watson or Anne-May his side, they were nowhere to be found, and Pa didn't even try and run as one of LeBaron's men tied his hands behind his back.

Then the men scuttled all over our little shack and one came down from the loft with a knife in his hand. "Look what I found up here. Must be twenty knives. Looks like they're packing up to go somewhere."

That made the men whoop and holler and they held one of those knives to Pa's throat and told him, "Git."

They looped the chain around his neck and pulled him down the path toward Ambrosia Plantation, and Pa looked back at us, such terrible sadness and fear in his eyes. Ma followed them, begging LeBaron to take her instead, and Sally Smith and I ran up to the house, her screaming.

"Mister Watson! Come quick! LeBaron's got Joseph and he's gonna kill him."

We hollered all over the house for him, and down by the shore, but nobody came, and I led Sally back to the shack by the sycamore, thinking that's where they'd take Pa. She fell in the road and I ran back to get her.

"Just leave me," Sally said, but I had her lean on me and stopped every now and then for her to catch her wind.

By the time we got there, they'd put Pa up on a little stage made of four low barrels, a fat plank set on top, and LeBaron stood close by, a broom in his hand. They'd pulled that chain tighter around Pa's neck and thrown it up and over a limb of that tree, his hands still tied behind his back.

Ma was crying and falling on the ground, flailing around in such a frightful way I could barely stand it. I looked back to the road for Mister Watson.

He'd always thought highly of Pa. For sure he'd come help.

LeBaron took the broom handle and shoved Pa toward the edge of the stage with it.

"No!" I said, and ran toward them, but Sally held me back. She tried to cover my eyes, but I watched as LeBaron pushed Pa off the plank.

Georgy

JUST AS WE REACHED THE LADDER OF THE *DANIEL WEBSTER*, hustled off by Dr. Rogers's orderlies, Frank Bacon hurried down, medical case slung over his shoulder.

"There will be no surgery, Dr. Rogers. The medics have briefed me and you will yield this case and those nurses to me."

Dr. Rogers stood taller. "I'm doctor-in-charge and you're subject to my authority."

"I am Dr. Francis Bacon, Chief Medical Officer of Provisional Brigades, and you will step aside, Doctor, along with your orderlies."

Every part of me rejoiced to see Frank, the front of his blue frock coat dark upon the breast with blood, as if stained with blueberry tea. His black hair had grown past his collar and down over his forehead.

"Under whose directive?"

The whites of Frank's eyes flashed in the near darkness. "My own and Dr. Ware's. He's close behind."

Dr. Rogers hurried off, spouting foul language and wagging his finger back in our direction. "I'll go directly to Olmsted with this."

Frank stepped to Joe's bed. "Has the bullet been removed?"

I joined him. How good it was to have Frank take charge. "The field doctor at Gaines's Mill felt it best to wait and remove it here."

Eliza knelt next to Joe and took his hand.

"Probably saved Joe's life," Frank said. "But the malarial fever presents a complication."

"Shall we bring him to the operating room?" I asked. "Sister Marguerite can assist us."

"No, he mustn't be moved. But I can't see a thing in this darkness. Bring every lamp you have. Bandages and three basins of clean water and a small table."

"We have no chloroform, Frank. Brandy either. Only scant quinine."

Sister Marguerite brought the table and Frank unpacked his medical bag onto it. "I brought everything we need," he said.

Frank stepped to the head of the bed and found Joe barely responsive. He brushed Joe's hair back from his forehead, so quick and tender in his sympathies.

"You've been through a great deal, Joe. The bullet is still in your thigh. We're going to remove it. You must rest."

I fetched a spirit lamp from the galley, set it next to the bed, and turned the flame up, casting Frank's shadow black upon the wall. The flame lit his grave gaze, his eyes the color of strong tea, the black stubble of his beard. Eyes trained on Joe, Frank unbuttoned his coat with haste and I helped him out of it, releasing the scent of horse and gunpowder and night air. He rolled up his sleeves, cheeks hollowed out in the shadows, and handed Eliza a bottle of chloroform and a metal rectangle the size of a bar of soap, with two prongs at one end.

"Sister Marguerite, remove his boots. Eliza, you stay near his head and administer chloroform through this inhaler. Slow and steady. It will keep him lightly sedated. Georgy, find a basin and assist me. And, Sister Marguerite, if you would send our most fervent prayers to the Almighty. We'll need all the help we can get."

———

WHILE SISTER MARGUERITE TOOK Joe's clothes to the laundry, I spread a clean sheet beneath Joe's leg and Frank began to probe the wound. "It's of the utmost importance we find the bullet, for left inside, this wound will not heal."

"Perhaps it went right through his leg?" I asked.

"Bring the lamp closer, Georgy."

With his silver retractor, Frank gently probed the depths of the wound. "It may have nicked the bone here, but where is the damned bullet?"

Sister Marguerite appeared behind us, bearing one of Joe's boots. "Dr. Bacon, I was cleaning Colonel Howland's boots and found this inside one. I thought it might be important."

She held out in her palm a misshapen gray metal pellet the size of the top of a man's thumb.

Frank lifted the bullet from her hand, held it to the lamp and examined it, and his gaze met mine, eyes wet with relief.

"How that bullet caused this wound and ended up in his boot, I'll never know," he said with a smile. "But thank you, Sister Marguerite. And I suspect thanks are also due to our Maker. I believe we can close now."

I STOOD TRANSFIXED AS Frank worked with balletic skill. He swabbed Joe's wound with iodine, closed with metal sutures, and finished with alternating layers of our best lint and collodion, a syrupy solution that formed an adhesive film as it dried.

Frank's expression remained somber as he watched Joe sleep and checked his pulse at intervals, two fingers on Joe's wrist, glancing at his father's gold watch. Soon he made the rounds of the other patients, pausing here and there to raise his lantern to a soldier's face, to feel a forehead for fever or leave a kind word. I had always wished Frank to be more like his father, unreserved and charismatic, but that night I saw Frank with new eyes, and found his quiet power more appealing than his father's bombastic way could ever be.

Joe woke before dawn, and as Frank helped him drink a mixture of quinine and whiskey the color slowly came back to our patient's face. We placed a pillow behind Joe's head and plied him with every comfort.

Frank packed up his bag. "I cannot inoculate Joe for smallpox until he regains his strength. You and Eliza are eligible, though, and I recommend it."

"You brought the kit with you?"

"Always. I have pure U.S. Army cowpox vaccine."

"Is it dangerous?"

"It's more dangerous to be here nursing soldiers, unvaccinated. The public has become lax with vaccines and smallpox is back on the rise."

"But all soldiers are required to be vaccinated."

"With the rush to get troops on the battlefield, we're finding a great many are not."

"I am not prepared to—"

"As a Sanitation Commission nurse, you should always be prepared, Georgeanna. *Semper paratus.*"

"Fine, then. How is it done?"

"We must go somewhere private. The galley will do."

We stepped into the ship's kitchen; Frank closed the door and set his medical bag on the counter. "I will need your upper arm exposed."

I met his gaze for a long moment and then reached behind my neck to unfasten my buttons. "Remember when you tried to vaccinate Mother and she ran from you?"

Frank smiled and turned to wash his hands and scalpel in the sink. "Your dear mother thinks coffee cures asthma."

I pulled my dress down, exposing my arm to the chill of the room, and gathered my dress to my chest.

Frank turned and took in my exposed skin—a queer look on his face— and then shook a bit of iodine on a patch of lint.

"You are going to feel a bit of a chill here."

My breath caught in my throat as Frank swabbed cold iodine on my upper arm.

"You know, Dr. Rogers says your ideas about the little bugs that cause infection are insane ramblings—that surgical fever is God's way of purifying the wound."

"The little bugs, as Dr. Rogers calls them, are indeed deadly. In France, they've used carbolic acid to kill them and it's been found to prevent inflammation and disease progression. Wish I could get my hands on some here. It would give Joe a much better chance."

Frank took his scalpel in hand. "Avert your eyes, Georgy. I am to make three cuts in your upper arm and introduce a small amount of serum in each."

"I'll watch, Frank. In order to know the procedure."

Frank hesitated a moment and then made his three incisions with precision and lightly touched the serum bottle to each. As he placed a square of lint on the incisions and wound a bandage around my upper arm, I felt light-headed and lost balance, but Frank caught my arm.

He raised one hand as if to smooth back my hair but then seemed to think better of it and held back. "Are you unwell?"

I stared at him, so close, and breathed in the scent of him, of bay rum soap and iodine. I looked down at my bodice and pulled it up over my shoulder.

Frank turned me around and buttoned up the back of my dress. "All you need is a bit of brandy and you'll be fine. The arm may feel sore for a couple of days, but nothing compared to the pox."

"You have a good touch, Frank Bacon. Perhaps you should think about a career in medicine."

Frank kept his gaze on his bag. "I need to go. I'm leaving a vaccination kit, in case Eliza chooses to inoculate herself later. Joe must stay in bed for a full three days, more if he'll tolerate it. There's a good chance the bullet nicked the bone, so no weight on that leg and let no one disturb the dressing—leave that for Dr. Ware. The metal sutures and the syrup make it airtight, and he'll judge the day to remove it. Administer the quinine I left every two hours. If you see marked improvement by week's end, I suggest you and Eliza accompany Joe back to New York. The fresh air at Tioronda will help the fever, better than these swamps." Frank stepped closer. "And it is becoming more dangerous by the day out here. Lee is proving himself to be a tremendous asset to the Confederates and will not hesitate to fire upon our hospital ships if they get in his way."

"Can you not stay, Frank?" I longed to take his hand. "Once I do morning rounds, we can have tea."

Frank left the galley and headed for the stairs. "I am expected onshore, but Dr. Ware is due back this morning. Have him contact me if Joe's condition worsens."

I started after Frank. "I'll stay even if Eliza and Joe go. Will you not visit again?"

"Needed elsewhere, I'm afraid."

"Frank, about what we spoke about at Christmas, I—"

"Goodbye, Georgy." He tipped his hat. "May God bless you."

JOE RECOVERED SLOWLY, BETTER one day, relapsing the next, and I sat with Eliza at his bedside and tried to keep his spirits up with letters from home. Abby's, reliably full of opinions about Union general George McClellan, were always a favorite of Joe's:

Dear Georgy,

General McClellan's "caution" in battle has ruined the country. It is too expensive a policy. We are bankrupt already. Stewart's and Lord & Taylor began yesterday to give change to their customers in postage stamps, handed Carry a tiny envelope stamped U.S. 50 cts., in change for something, which she in turn handed out as payment for a piece of ribbon at Aitkin & Miller's, all right, no words exchanged. So we go! Uncle Edward is blue as indigo. I would give every dollar of mine if it would end this accursed war and slavery to boot.

Your loving Abby

Soon Eliza and Joe left the *Daniel Webster,* transferring ships with all their possessions, for their long journey home to Tioronda. It was a bittersweet goodbye: I knew Joe was finally on his way to safety, but I would miss them both terribly.

There was little time to dwell on it all, for the wounded kept coming at a steady pace and the male nurses did everything in their power to make the female nurses look bad, disregarding their laundry shifts, and forcing the lock on the liquor cabinet and pilfering the restocked medicinal brandy, despite my many complaints to Dr. Ware, who tried his best to admonish them.

To keep my sanity, I began a series of nursing classes to share the knowledge I'd learned from Dr. Blackwell, with Katharine Wormeley and Marguerite as my inaugural students. I set up three chairs in the liquor closet, a snug room for my first class, with one counter and square bottles lined up in wooden slats to keep them from spilling at sea.

I'd made it midway through my lecture on bandaging techniques when the door abruptly opened to reveal the orderly named St. Pierre, who stood there looking uncharacteristically chipper.

"So sorry to interrupt, ladies, but I bring a message from headquarters." He paused for dramatic effect. "Effective immediately all female nurses are to leave the premises, to board a steamer due north. Your services are no longer required and will be taken up by a team of additional *male* nurses just authorized by Congress."

"This cannot be," I said. "Does Mr. Olmsted know?"

"He's the one who told me, and is preparing to leave himself." Mr. St. Pierre tossed three yellow booklets onto the counter. "And I thought you'd like to know the surgeon general has prepared a manual of procedures for the new nursing team."

I picked up one booklet. "*The Hospital Steward's Manual?*" I asked. "By Dr. Winslow Rogers."

"Dr. Rogers's new book. Going to be the Bible for all us men."

I flipped through the pages while Katharine looked on. "This is the exact text I lent to Dr. Rogers."

Katharine Wormeley stood. "It contains Georgy's most celebrated recipes. Her bandage diagrams. Her entire curriculum."

Private St. Pierre shrugged. "All I know is all you women're leaving tonight. And just make sure you leave the key to this closet. We need to have a big old celebration when you're gone."

Jemma

✳

LEBARON LEFT PA FOR US TO PULL DOWN, AND MA AND SALLY held him up down below as I climbed in the dark up the sycamore's bark, slippery and wet. *Please let Pa be alive, at least a little,* I said to myself over and over. I talked to him, too. "If you can hear me, Pa, just hold on." It took me forever to undo that chain, but I finally felt it loosen up and let his body fall to them below.

I scurried down as Ma cried over him and I laid my cheek on his chest and waited for the thump of his heart. I slid one hand under his shirt and felt the skin on his chest grown cold. I dry-heaved there, hands in the mud, and felt like I was falling down a hole, with no one to catch me.

"Please, Pa," I said, ten times over, like that would bring him back.

It took all three of us to pull Pa back to the house in the dark through the mud, all three of us crying, not sure what was rain and what was tears, like God crying with us.

We stayed up that night, Pa laid out on his bed, skin shining in the glow of the fire, us wiping the dirt from him. Once I cried myself out, the hate started up inside me and grew quick, black and cold.

The next day, before supper, Sally Smith and I sat in the speculator's two-horse wagon, waiting to be sent off. I'd managed to hide Pa's cross in my palm before the man had tied our hands and feet up tight with rough twine that cut our skin.

We waited there in the drive, up at the house, the horses pawing the gravel, ready to get along. Sally thought Mister Watson might come and help us. I watched the windows up above and saw the curtain upstairs in the bedroom move and figured it was him. Why sell us off? Empty inside, I looked down to the cabin, Pa still inside, stretched out stiff. Who would bury and say words over him? Make him a pine box?

The speculator came along and heaved my flowered carpetbag up alongside me and then climbed up on his buckboard. Ma was working in the far field and I just stared out there hoping she'd come say a goodbye.

The rain started as Miss Anne-May stepped out from the house and sidled up to the wagon.

"Why do we have to go?" I asked.

"It was all because of you we lost Joseph. He was one of our best hands. Fergus thinks you're just more trouble waiting to happen, and Sally . . . she knows what she did."

Sally turned her face away. "I did nothin'."

Even all cried out, I felt new tears come. "Why didn't you help my pa? He did everything for you."

Anne-May leaned in close to me. "Where you put that book, Jemma?"

I just stared at Anne-May's curls starting to go limp out in the rain. She must've done them herself that morning, didn't get the iron hot enough.

"The red book you done the writing in. Took to Mr. Smalls."

"Your spying book?" I asked.

Anne-May looked toward the speculator. "You keep your voice *down*. Do you have it with you?"

I turned away. "Bet the newspapers'll be interested in it."

She thrust out her hand, palm up. "Tell me where it is this instant."

I nodded toward the house. "It's where I always keep it. Practically in plain sight."

The rain started down harder, splattering the wooden floor of the cart. "Move on!" the speculator shouted to the horses, and we started off with a jerk.

Anne-May took a step after us. "Where's it at exactly, Jemma?"

Out of nowhere, Ma came running, barefooted and fast as I ever seen her run, splashing through the puddles, hair tied up in her bright blue kerchief.

The horses picked up a trot and Ma followed, but soon we got too fast for her and she stopped, just ahead of Anne-May.

"Don't you dare lose hope, you hear me, Jemma?" she called to me, hands cupped around her mouth. "You *fight*."

I couldn't say anything as Sally Smith and me bumped off to somewhere in the growing dark. I heard her, but was just too numb to care.

PART
TWO

..

Georgy

AFTER BEING UNCEREMONIOUSLY EXCUSED FROM THE *DANiel Webster* the summer before and replaced by male nurses, I found myself back home at Brevoort Place. I was happy to see that little had changed except the addition of a handsome Lloyd's map of Virginia in the front parlor. So we could follow troop movements, Mother had hung it above the sofa, under the picture of the Virgin, where we all sat and read the papers. I was more resolved than ever to start my own teaching hospital for female nurses. Not that my sisters assisted me with that goal or even treated me with the respect I deserved, since coming home always revived the old pecking order of childhood.

"That was a brief yet distinguished nursing career," Jane said as I came in the front door.

I directed the porter to bring my trunk up the front stairs and then set my net bag of apothecary jars on the front parlor carpet.

Abby helped me off with my coat and bonnet. "You'd better not leave your leech jar in the dining room."

"In the kitchen, then?" I asked.

Much had happened in regard to the war since I'd gone home, including a Union victory of sorts at Antietam in the fall, near the Maryland-Pennsylvania border, which in one day's fighting left more than twenty-two thousand soldiers killed or wounded. Lincoln had replaced his overly cautious General McClellan, and Union supporters hoped his replacement, General Ambrose Burnside, would bring a quick end to the war. We prayed our own men would stay out of harm's way, with my brother, Charley, his hand almost fully healed, working with the New York City Home Guard collecting books for soldiers. He groused to anyone who'd listen about his desire to sign up, which Mother countered by distracting him with new charitable projects, just delaying the inevitable.

Up at their lovely estate in Fishkill, New York, Tioronda, Joe was recovering nicely with Eliza's help, though tireless in his efforts to rejoin the fight. And Frank Bacon continued to serve on the battlefield with his regiment, though he could no longer be counted as one of our men, since I'd rejected his proposal, something that pinched me with regret now and then. But most of all I wished to get back into the fray and lose myself in the practice of nursing.

As the battles continued, with neither North nor South soundly winning, the wounded troops kept coming and our old friend Katharine Wormeley wrote that Mr. Olmsted had asked her to head up a new U.S. Army hospital up in Portsmouth Grove, Rhode Island. He had suggested my sister Jane and me as head matrons, and though Jane fretted about one hundred little things, I accepted at once for both of us, eager for the chance to spend the winter there, finally useful again.

We arrived at Portsmouth Grove unexpectedly early and found our high-ceilinged wards cold, the washing machine broken, and the sixty iron beds stripped to the blue ticking. But we soon had a fire burning in each hearth, and patients brought into freshly sheeted beds, and the scent of roasting chicken wafting through the wards.

Later that week, Katharine came to us while we changed our morning linen. "I've received a rather curious invitation to a ball in Newport."

She handed me the invitation, printed in gold ink on ecru card stock.

THE SEACREST WHITE BALL.
NUMBER ONE BELLEVUE AVENUE.
NEWPORT. RHODE ISLAND.
SEVEN O'CLOCK.

We had seen some grand homes in Newport from afar, but never stepped foot inside.

"Why have we been invited?" I asked.

Katharine slipped the letter into her pocket. "I haven't the slightest. I assume it's to benefit the troops."

Jane shook out a crisp white folded bedsheet. "We do our share for the troops, I would say. It's like the dark ages here, hand washing bed linens."

"Perhaps we could raise funds for things we need," I said.

Jane flew the sheet into the air and it billowed down to the bed, puffing up her red hair around her face like a halo. "I have a great many copies of Mary's poems we can sell."

"And who can refuse Katharine once she presents her canister?" I asked. "It will afford us the means for a new washing machine before the dancing is done."

KATHARINE, JANE, AND I arranged for other nurses to cover our wards and arrived at Seacrest Cottage at the appointed hour, having borrowed the hospital's failing buckboard.

Visible from a mile away, Seacrest stood tall, a vast timber-framed summerhouse on fashionable Bellevue Avenue, featuring numerous gables and dormers, an expansive veranda that wrapped around the house, and an ornate porte cochere, through which a stream of fine carriages was now flowing.

We took our place in line, and as we inched closer Katharine gasped upon seeing the other guests' manner of elaborate dress, the ladies emerging from carriages, out from under fur rugs, in the very latest white organzas and silks, with diamonds at their throats, the men in formal cutaway coats and military uniforms. As the guests entered, the colored footmen, dressed only in their shirtsleeves and britches, took charge of the horses.

Jane, who had, as usual, assigned herself as driver, urged the horse along. "The guests are all dressed in white. Why do I suddenly feel like the poor cousin?"

"We're here to get their money for the cause," Katharine said. "Can't look too prosperous."

We entered the front parlor, larger than the entire footprint of our Brevoort Place town house, with a wide staircase curving up to our right. We stared at the atrium ceiling, open to the elements in the center, and the nubile gilt statues, strewn with white floral garlands and stationed about the room.

"They do like their gold," Katharine said.

Jane looked about. "Ill breeding never appears so ill as when it is heavily gilded."

We declined a trip to the ladies' dressing room, since we had thankfully little toilette to adjust and were perfectly capable of drawing on our own gloves.

Liveried footmen handed each of us a dance card, a booklet of paste-white paper with ecru fringe, *Seacrest Ball* printed in elaborate gold script, a pretty little pencil attached with silk twine. We opened our books and found each page inside headed with *Order of dances,* the program listed below. *Grand March. Polka. Waltz.*

"Twenty-five dances?" Jane asked. "This is going to be a long night."

Katharine pointed to the bottom of the page. "Look, it says *Men requested to pay five dollars per dance.*"

I shut my booklet. "Jane, you set out with the poem sheets, and Katharine, take your canister. I will find our host."

After the call of the trumpet indicating the festivities would begin, a tall gentleman immediately inquired if Jane would care to dance, but she waved him off, intent on selling Mary's poems. Katharine went off into the crowd shaking her coin canister, soliciting funds.

I had just set out to find our hostess when Frank Bacon stepped into my path and stood before me, adjusting his cuffs. He looked particularly well, clean-shaven and dressed in his uniform, the deep indigo color of it bringing out the blue of his eyes.

"Hello, Georgy."

I felt my face flush. "Oh. Frank Bacon. What on earth are you doing here? Abby told me you've been reassigned to a hospital in Louisiana."

"Twenty-day furlough to visit my mother, who's suddenly taken a turn for the better since I arrived. How did you come to be here?"

"Nurses at Portsmouth Grove with Jane and Katharine."

"Your mother must've been sorry to see you go. How is she?"

"A bit on edge. In her latest letter she says she feared a pastor that came to tea had made off with some Woolsey silver in his pocket but was soon relieved to find Margaret polishing the missing spoons."

Frank smiled wide. The old Frank.

"Well, your mother will always have a special place in my heart."

"But what brings you all the way here from Connecticut?"

Frank turned toward the center of the room. "Hold on, they are about to release the surprise."

The orchestra played a drumroll and all attention turned to a white-satin-covered box in the center of the room.

"What is it, Frank?"

A man opened the box lid and released a great flock of white birds into the air. All around us guests gasped as the birds soared as one about the room, and then flew out through the open roof.

"How lovely," I said. "But perhaps that's taking the white theme too far?"

Frank leaned in. "They have been kept from seed and water since Tuesday to keep them from defiling the crowd."

"How do you know all this, Frank?"

The music rose with a voluptuous swell, a waltz, "Our Honorary Members."

Frank offered me his hand. "Perhaps a dance and we can talk about that?"

We danced a waltz, his arm around my waist both snug and familiar. "You've been practicing, Frank."

With my face at his shoulder I could hardly escape his familiar scent, of bay rum soap mixed with the lovely aroma of coffee.

He smiled. "Indeed I have."

"I'm afraid I did not dress in white."

"Can't imagine you in white silk, Georgy. Besides, you are dressed in the most comely costume there is, that of the U.S. Army nurse."

"So what is your business here, Frank? You must come out to the hospital. We could use your help. Not that we can offer you ice cream and fresh ladyfingers at tea. It is fairly Spartan."

"I'm only here overnight—"

"You mustn't keep me in suspense, Frank, as to why you're here. My mind is conjuring any number of reasons. A rich aunt died and left you a fortune. The cure to some dread disease lies in Narragansett Bay."

"Actually, a bit of both."

"That's a shame. At first I thought you might have come all this way to see me."

The music stopped and we all clapped.

"There's no danger of that, Georgy. A lot has happened recently."

"Frank, about Washington. I don't know what got into me to say—"

A dark-haired woman wearing a salmon-colored confection of a dress, draped low off her shoulders and profusely trimmed with flowers and bows, came to stand at Frank's side. She wore her hair center-parted, with a thin braid looped under each ear, and held her fan, of pink silk with ivory sticks, in her right hand, telegraphing she was unmarried. She slipped her hand through the crook of Frank's arm.

He nodded toward her. "Georgeanna, may I introduce my nurse assistant, Miss Bethada Barnett."

I stepped back. "Assistant?"

She and Frank exchanged glances. "I put out an advertisement and Miss Barnett responded. I couldn't believe my luck, with all the experience she has."

Despite my initial impulse to escape altogether, I remained, and nodded to Miss Barnett. Upon closer inspection, she possessed slightly equine features, I was happy to see.

"A pleasure," I said.

Bethada nodded in return. "Frank has told me about all of you Woolsey sisters." She leaned in and widened her eyes. "Hard to keep you straight, though, all seven of you."

I leaned in myself. "Perhaps take notes, Miss Barnett."

"I've been nursing wounded down in Louisiana and have seen every injury imaginable. I find tending to the sick so rewarding."

"And how are you connected to this party?" I asked.

A frock-coated waiter offered glasses of champagne on a silver tray and Frank seized one.

"My aunt, Mrs. Cherie Barnett, is our hostess. My uncle recently died, typhus they suspect, and she is most interested in investing a portion of Uncle's considerable assets in medical advances. She has invited Dr. Bacon to describe his research in disease prevention."

I turned to Frank. "How fortunate for you. *And* you get to gaze upon a whole museum's worth of gold statuettes."

He sipped his champagne.

Bethada played with the locket at her throat. "Miss Woolsey, how curious you chose not to wear white as the invitation requested."

"My sister and I and our friend Katharine Wormeley, who accompanied us, are nurses at Portsmouth Grove. Came directly from the wards. And you chose not to wear white as well, Miss Barnett."

"That was deliberate on our part. Auntie and I chose to stand out in this sea of white, as the only ones wearing color. And here comes Auntie now in her blue."

A woman swept toward us through the crowd, much as a steamship parts the briny seas, leaving guests jostled and turning to look for the cause of their disturbance. One had the impression Mrs. Barnett was an inflated version of her niece, awash in a mountain of baby-blue polished cotton and chiffon, diamonds big as signal lights at her throat.

Bethada offered her aunt a glass of champagne, which she waved away. "Auntie, we were just speaking of you and how interested you are in Dr. Bacon's research."

"I'm a force to be reckoned with when I want something," Mrs. Barnett said. "And I've asked Dr. Bacon here to serve as my personal physician."

"You would leave the army, Frank?" I asked.

"None of this is confirmed," he said.

Bethada plucked a champagne flute from the tray. "He'll leave it once the war is over, of course. In the meantime, Auntie shall carry on and hold balls such as this to support the troops."

"Northern or Southern troops?" I asked.

"Wherever I see fit," Mrs. Barnett replied.

I turned to her. "Your husband made his fortune in cotton?"

Mrs. Barnett surveyed the crowd. "Among other things. I don't meddle in my dead husband's business."

"Surely you know Barnett Industries is the second-largest manufacturer of cotton fabric," I said. "A product of slavery."

"And what concern is that of yours?"

"It should be everyone's concern. I'm also concerned about your colored footmen out in the cold in their shirtsleeves—"

"Ah. An abolitionist, I see. So noble and selfless. *We* hope to raise five thousand dollars tonight. The best way to support a cause. Money." Suddenly she fixed her gaze upon me. "Which is why I prefer no solicitations at the party."

"Are you referring to me, Mrs. Barnett?"

"I would prefer that your sister—Jane, is it?—not ply the guests with requests to buy her poetry."

I folded my arms across my waist. "It is my sister Mary's poetry, actually. Jane is only asking a penny a sheet."

"A woman profiting from writing?" She glanced at Frank. "Is this how ladies are raised nowadays?"

Frank smiled. "The Woolsey women are a fixture in New York. Highly esteemed by all."

"New York," Bethada said. "Who would raise a family there?"

"Mary's poems are very popular with the troops," I said. "One inspired a Winslow Homer painting."

Mrs. Barnett fanned herself, sending her curls dancing at her forehead. "I want this ball to be a place where my guests can *relax* and enjoy themselves. If your Miss Wormeley fills her dance card, *that* will raise funds to support the troops, not shaking her canister at every guest. Not that she will be deluged with offers."

I stepped back. "Mrs. Barnett. I will not hear a close friend disparaged in such a way. We are simply trying to raise funds for a new washing machine for the hospital—"

"And I am simply trying to entertain my guests. Perhaps they can take their efforts into town on the village green tomorrow. If you will excuse me?"

Mrs. Barnett stepped away and Bethada followed, with a meaningful glance back at Frank.

I straightened my gloves. "I will go tell Jane and Katharine we should take our leave."

"Look, Georgy—"

"I understand, Frank. Not every man can stand up to that kind of a woman."

"Her intentions are good."

"There was a time when you yourself shook the coin canister on Union Square. You do realize Barnett Industries has made millions off the backs of slaves by selling cotton? How can a captain in the U.S. Army associate with such an enterprise? Your father rails against it from the pulpit."

"I'm simply here as a guest. Is it wrong to take that money and fight disease?"

"You have Bethada at your side, Frank. Every jewel on her, courtesy of the enslaved. I thought I knew you better."

I turned to leave.

Frank held my arm. "Perhaps this is all because you regret your choice to decline my proposal."

"Quite to the contrary, Frank." I wrested my arm away. "I've never been happier with a decision."

Jemma

✳

HAGERSTOWN, MARYLAND

JUNE 1863

SALLY SMITH AND I ENDED UP IN HAGERSTOWN, MARYLAND, WITH a new owner, skinny Mr. D. W. Swift, *photographer of fine art,* as his cards I passed out in the street said, which most people tossed into the trash bin. *Fine art.* More like pictures of dead babies I had to make look like they were sleeping and a portrait of every soldier who passed through, Confederate or Union, same price.

We'd been there a year and come to the conclusion that Hagerstown was no New York City. Lots of people rushed around the potholed streets, and some tall buildings lined Main Street, but the biggest attraction was a weathervane of a German soldier everyone gawked at on the top of the Market House. But I didn't see much of it, working under Mrs. Swift's eye most the day, except when hauling ice from the icehouse or a rare trip to the mercantile.

That spring day, cold for June, Mr. Swift had me standing out front of the studio, passing out his card to any person who'd take one. I stood in the middle of the street, where carriages came by fast, the wind trying to blow one of Mrs. Swift's too-big cast-off cotton dresses up around my knees. I was in a bad mood that day to start, having had a dream about Pa being alive again and woke up to find it not true, and standing in that road made it worse.

I shoved a card at a man in a top hat and he hocked a wad of spit on one of my too-tight tie-up shoes Mr. Swift's nephew Jim had grew out of, the soles worn through.

I offered a card to a woman and she hurried her children away like I had the typhus. The scent of Sally Smith's cornbread floated out of the kitchen on the breeze and my stomach growled. There was nothing to look forward to in that place. Even Sally's cornbread was off limits.

Mrs. Swift called out to me from the door.

"Jemma, get in here. Just got another big job. A whole regiment."

"Yes, Mrs. Swift."

Mrs. Swift was built upside down, arms like fat pillows tied around the middle with twine, with a solid figure no hoopskirt could hide. Where her husband could blow over in too strong a wind, she had the physique of a circus strongman, and I curled her hair up just as she wanted it, lying on her head like fat little Spanish sausages.

I walked back to the room I shared with Sally, to change for picture work. Just off the kitchen, it was two beds squashed into a former pantry, with shelves wrapping round the room, the scent of flour and vanilla baked into those walls. My flowered carpetbag sat on my bed. I stepped into an old pair of threadbare trousers Nephew Jim had abandoned, patched in the rump, what Mr. Swift liked me to wear when I assisted in his picture work. That way I could climb all over his front parlor in service to his photos, standing on tables with his lamps held high and hanging from the ceiling with a metal sheet to get him more light.

Least it made the time pass quicker.

I came into their kitchen, where Mrs. Swift stood runnin' a straight razor up and down a razor strop, and without a word she shoved me down in a chair. At first I thought maybe she was planning on cutting my throat, which I welcomed in a way. Put an end to my missing Ma and Pa and Patience.

Soon Mrs. Swift started stroking that razor across my scalp, and not gentle, either, tearing it up good.

"Sit still. You coloreds fidget so."

She decided Sunday morning was a good time to shear me like a sheep, the one day Sally and me was supposed to do as we pleased.

Mrs. Swift shaved down the side of my head and nicked my ear. "I found a hair in the developing bath and it was yours, I'm sure."

Sally Smith stepped into the kitchen, drying a dish with her apron. "I'm happy to do this, ma'am. So you can sit and have your breakfast."

"So you can access this razor and do us grievous harm? No, thank you, I will decline that offer. Got a mind to sell you back, Jemma, since you're not the worker they promised, your mind always somewhere else. Haven't even followed through on that black lace teaspoon bonnet you promised me. When we bought you from Mister Watson, he never said you'd be trouble."

I turned in my seat to face her. "Mister Watson you bought me from? But it's Miss Anne-May who owns me."

Mrs. Swift pushed me back around. "No difference. We'd keep Sally, mind you. Mr. Swift can't do without his cornbread kush and quince jelly. Not that I eat kush, on account of all that lard." She smoothed one hand down her fat belly. "I keep my figure trim with consistent movement and prayer."

Sally already had her new jelly business up and running, bringing all of Hagerstown to her back kitchen doorstep, looking for the quince kind especially.

Once Mrs. Swift had made a big production of folding up her straight razor and making us close our eyes so we wouldn't see what pocket she put it in, she left to join Mr. Swift in the dining room for breakfast.

"You gotta eat something, Jemma," Sally said.

"Let's get you ready for church," I said, not wanting to talk about the ache in my belly that kept me from eating much. It was from missing Pa and Ma and everyone else God took from me. Talking only made it worse.

We stepped to our quarters. I got Sally into her best stick-out petticoat and then stood on the bed, the corn husks in the ticking crunching under my feet, and slipped Sally's best dress, a black silk I made over from one of Mrs. Swift's castoffs, over her head.

Sally smoothed her skirt. "Come to church with me."

"I'm done with church." I placed her bonnet on her head, the black teaspoon I'd made for Mrs. Swift but ended up giving to Sally, since it flattered her face so nice. "Once God took Pa, that's it for me. Didn't even get a box to be buried in."

"Rail at them who did it, not God."

"I'd rather sleep, truth be told."

"Your pa's gone. Now what? Don't do nobody good to shrivel up and die."

I tied the ribbons at her chin. "Church won't help. Besides, that preacher only talks about how slaves need to obey the law or God will punish us. Tired of it. Anyway, this morning we got two dead ones coming in, and after that, some troops having a picture made."

"On the Lord's day?"

"The Lord turned his back on me a long time ago."

"Don't blaspheme, Jemma."

"Next thing you know, he'll punish me for writing those things in Anne-May's book for her."

"Still stewing about that book?"

"You heard her ask me for it before we left. Said she'd hunt me down to get it."

"That woman couldn't find a donkey in a barrel. You're miles away now."

"Anne-May gets what she wants. And she still owns me by law, if Mister Watson did the selling."

"Well, even if she did find you, Mr. Swift won't give you up to her, and with me here she can't hurt you. And she's just gonna have to do without that devil book." Sally took my hand and held it tight, hers so soft from years of kneading bread dough and carding wool.

I held out her good purse, navy blue, with the handle sewn back on, and she slipped it over her arm.

She leaned in, so close I could smell the sugar in her hair, and whispered, "I like where you hid it. No way nobody'll find it there. Pretty funny, too."

She shook all over with laughter as she walked out and let the back kitchen door slam behind her.

I had to smile, too, thinking of my hiding place. No way Anne-May'd find that book there.

Anne-May

✳

A YEAR AFTER WE BURIED HARRY, I WAS STILL HAUNTED BY dark thoughts, replaying the terrible day he came home in that box. I barely slept, with Fergus making a racket, up and down to his science shack till all hours, and the grief like a bull sitting on my chest. Then one morning two men arrived in our front courtyard, and with Jemma no longer there to shoo them off, I woke to the pounding of fists on the front door.

Euphemia made it downstairs just before I did, gathering her wrapper around herself like a modest maiden, as if anyone would be even vaguely interested in looking at her. She did have a different look to her, though. Her room was right next to the guest bedroom where Fergus slept. Were those two visiting at night? Euphemia didn't have it in her, though she did hang on my husband's every word.

The men stood just outside the doorway, outlined by the morning's harsh light, and removed their bowler hats in unison. One was older, a thin, severe man with a devil's beard. The other resembled an overgrown baby, dressed up in his father's coat and trousers, his thin blond hair in wispy curls any mother would cut and save, tied with blue satin ribbon.

"Mrs. Fergus Watson?" asked the devil man.

"Yes. And my sister, Euphemia."

"E. J. Allan, ma'am, and my investigation assistant, Detective Toden-hofer." He offered me a card and I plucked it from his fingers.

Pinkerton National Detective Agency. Just reading that card made my head hurt. I handed it to Euphemia.

"What could you possibly want here with us, Mr. Allan? My crippled husband is sleeping upstairs."

"Yes, we know. I hope Captain Watson's doing well. But we are here to see you, Mrs. Watson. You are the sole owner of this house?"

"Why, you certainly do know a lot, don't you, Mr. Allan?"

"We're paid to know, Mrs. Watson. In the service of the U.S. government."

I tilted my head and smiled. "How important you both are."

"We have just been to see a Mrs. Beulah Gardener, on Myrtle Street in Hollywood."

The acid taste of nausea rose in my throat. "Such a lovely woman."

"We inquired about a series of packages, each containing . . ." He referred to his paper notes. ". . . twelve pairs of socks made at her home."

"Can't imagine what this has to do with me."

"She told us you mailed those packages."

I turned to Euphemia. "Wasn't that you?"

"Mrs. Gardener told us she gave your sister a list of the addresses, but she provided the packages to you to post. A conversation with the postmaster, one Donald Wetstone, confirmed you and your mother completed the postal transaction. He especially remembered your mother." He read from his paper. "Called her a *disruptive force,* in fact."

"That description does fit my mother. But what's the problem, Mr. Allan? Do you trouble every woman in Maryland who serves her country sendin' socks?"

"You may have heard of the Battle of Sitlington's Hill?"

I waved a fly off Euphemia's sleeve. "There are so many battles these days."

"Took place just last year. Something troubling about it, though."

I opened my eyes wide. "What is *that,* Detective?"

"The commanding officer tells us no one knew those soldiers were stationed there, in the woods of McDowell, Virginia. They went to great lengths to keep this operation secret: the troops were not allowed to send letters home and they arrived under cover of darkness. *Yet,* they were somehow ambushed by Stonewall Jackson and his men. Thirty-four men were killed."

"That *is* a terrible shame, Mr. Allan."

"In the course of our detective work, we've determined that your package of socks was the only piece of mail in or out of that area. Therefore, the only persons who knew that troop location, outside of the U.S. Army staff, are you, your mama, Mrs. Gardener, and the postmaster. Now, correct me if I'm wrong, but old Mr. Wetstone doesn't seem the type to pass on U.S. Army secrets. In fact, he assured us he'd take a bullet for Mr. Lincoln. And we talked to Mrs. Gardener, who denies any wrongdoing and tells us you've made comments that lead her to believe you're a Confederate sympathizer."

"I don't know what you're talking about, Mr. Allan."

He slid a pair of handcuffs from his pocket. "If you wouldn't mind turning around, Mrs. Watson?"

Euphemia gasped, one hand to her mouth. "I'll get Fergus."

I stepped to Mr. Allan and touched his arm. "On second thought, sir, I do have something to tell you. As hard as it is to admit—"

"We don't have all day, madam."

"I regret saying this, for it is a terrible blight on the family, but—"

"Mrs. Watson—"

"My mother, Zoretha Wilson Stickman, she's advancing in years and may not even remember this, but she may have somehow given that pencil list to the Rebels. After her son was killed fighting the U.S. Army, well, she has been suffering from severe nostalgia."

"Where might we find her?"

"I'm afraid she's gone to visit her cousin Sissy in Baltimore. If she's left there for home, you can find her at number six Chartres Street in New Orleans, Louisiana."

Georgy

NEW YORK CITY
JUNE 1863

T HE JUNE AFTER PORTSMOUTH GROVE HOSPITAL CLOSED, I moved back to Brevoort Place, no longer caught up in the stimulating practice of nursing soldiers, and waited every day for the newspapers. With Joe up at Tioronda with Eliza, recovering from his injury, and my ties with Frank Bacon severed, we'd lost our most reliable correspondents of war news, so the newspapers and letters from my sisters became our everything. Jane wrote from Litchfield, Connecticut, where she and Carry were spending time:

THE AMERICAN HOTEL,
LITCHFIELD, CONNECTICUT

Dear Georgy,

As we welcome warmer days in lovely Litchfield we follow with great interest the growth of the 19th regiment, recruited in that county, all the little white crumbs of towns dropped in the wrinkles of the hills sending in their twenty, thirty, fifty fighting men, clubbed by the very little villages, marching under our windows every day to

the camp ground. Almost all the young men in Litchfield village
have gone; the farmers, the clerks in the shops, the singers in the
choir. Who is to reap next year's crops? Who is to sow them? They
understood very well to what they were going; disease, death, a com-
mon soldier's nameless grave. . . .

> *Your loving sister,*
> *Jane*

Once I was no longer needed in Rhode Island, it had been nice to return and see Mother's brick town house standing strong. But after weeks
of sharing a room with my sister Carry, and dispensing doughnuts and
comics at Bellevue Hospital, I longed to return to the thick of things. Our
brother, Charley, tired of working with the New York Home Guard, was
set to sign up with a regiment and march off any day, and I hoped to be
assigned near him. I petitioned Mr. Olmsted, and wrote to Dr. Blackwell,
but received no reply. I tried filling my days going door to door with Carry,
begging quinine from households, for a severe shortage was leaving troops
dying near the swamps of Maryland, but it proved a daunting task, since
we found not one bottle.

ONE WARM JUNE MORNING, a courier delivered to our door a hastily
written message from Carry, from her place of work, at the New York Orphan Asylum, where she spent days at a time performing charitable work,
often with six children fixed in her arms and on her lap.

Georgy,

Please come immediately. One whole ward is down with fever. The
situation is most dire.

> *Carry*

I hurried up by carriage, five miles north of New York City to the asylum, a venerable institution once helmed by Alexander Hamilton's wife,

Eliza, and located on West Fourth Street, now moved up to a mansion in the lovely, rural Bloomingdale area north of the city, named for the old Dutch village of Bloemendael, which meant "Valley of Flowers."

Mother's driver sped the carriage up the long drive to the massive stone English Gothic building, the minaret-like spires shining in the distance. The house, donated by a wealthy businessman, stood with several other colossal weekend and summer houses of wealthy New Yorkers. It was delightfully situated on the brow of a gentle slope on the banks of the Hudson River, where magnificent weeping willow trees swayed in the breeze, all just out of the reach of the miasma of cholera and typhus that hung over New York City.

As my carriage arrived at the front steps, a few children, toddlers to those of sixteen years or so, gathered there, well dressed in clean second-hand clothes, their hair cut in the signature Bloomingdale orphanage bob.

I hurried through them up the stone steps, my nurse's bag in hand.

One young girl stood. "You gonna leave, too?"

I bent to her. "What do you mean?"

"Doctor was here and left. Said he couldn't do anything for them."

"There's always something to be done," I said, and continued up the stairs.

Carry met me at the oak front door, holding a pair of towheaded, slap-cheeked twin toddlers, one at each hip. "Hurry, Georgy. The whole ward is down with something. A doctor came by but left just as quickly."

"What are their symptoms?"

"It's the youngest girls' ward. Fever mostly."

We rushed into the ward, which had once served as the dining room in the former house, the vaulted ceiling and walnut-paneled walls a sharp contrast to the rows of white iron beds, each filled with a small blanketed form, the great fireplace dark. Carry handed the twins to an older girl near the door.

"There are thirty of them," Carry said. "Too sick to leave their beds this morning."

"Heavenly day, Carry, how did this happen?"

"No idea. It came on suddenly."

"Have they traveled anywhere?"

She smoothed her hair back with one hand. "Not recently. Just the excursion last week when it was so warm."

"Excursion to where?"

"Up to see the new aqueduct."

"Near the swamp?"

"Yes."

Carry stepped to the closest bed and held her palm to the forehead of one dark-haired patient, her body so small under the blanket. "This is Constance. Her father went to heaven at Bull Run and her mother left us just last month from the grippe. Constance is the apple of Mrs. Peabody's eye and very brave. Just eight years old."

Eight years old. Just one year older than I was when I lost Father.

Constance looked up at Carry. "I'm terribly cold, Miss Woolsey."

Carry held her hand. "They woke this morning, all the same, with chills and fever."

A slender, handsome woman dressed top to toe in black silk entered, skirt rustling.

"What is going on here?" she asked, unsmiling.

Carry stepped to her. "Mrs. Peabody. The little girls woke this morning with fever and chills."

"And I was not told? I'm practically right next door, for heaven's sake."

"My first thought was to call upon my sister Georgeanna, a nurse with the Sanitary Commission."

"And where is the doctor?" Mrs. Peabody asked.

I stepped forward and extended my hand. "I am Georgeanna Woolsey. I served aboard the hospital ships."

Mrs. Peabody ignored my hand, stepped to the bed, and looked down upon Constance. "Yes, I am quite familiar with the commission. But you have no business treating disease. We'll wait for a doctor."

"Dr. Simpkins was here," Carry said. "Told me he could do nothing for them."

I removed my bonnet. "Mrs. Peabody, it will be difficult to find another doctor in New York who will neglect their military patients to come this far north of the city right now. I'm confident I can treat the girls here."

"You think quite highly of yourself, Miss Woolsey."

"She was taught by Dr. Elizabeth Blackwell herself," Carry said.

Mrs. Peabody turned to me. "Mostly learning to brew beef tea and write letters, I hear."

"No, Mrs. Peabody. Dr. Blackwell taught me a great deal more. True, we are committed to offering soldiers daily comforts, but I can now treat everything from fractures to disease—intermittent, eruptive, and continued fevers." I unbuttoned my cuffs and rolled up my dress sleeves. "In fact, I'm considering opening a school for nurses."

Mrs. Peabody swatted the air. "I've never heard of such a thing."

"Only for women. Perhaps your girls, once they reach a certain age, would be candidates to earn their certificate there."

"And catch the smallpox? Not to mention death to their reputations. These girls will be seamstresses, not nurses."

I pulled a blanket from the foot of the bed up over Constance. "I suggest we proceed with the treatment. First, we must light a fire to fight the chills. And then an extra blanket for each."

"How do we even know what they suffer from?" Mrs. Peabody asked.

"At first I suspected typhus," I said.

Mrs. Peabody drew herself up. "This is not some fifth-rate, bedbuggy concern, Miss Woolsey."

"Typhus can strike anywhere, Mrs. Peabody. But I've determined it's not typhus, but malarial fever."

"How can you be so sure?"

"I've seen both typhus and malarial fever in great numbers in Washington hospitals and on the hospital ships. In typhus, the fever is accompanied by a rash, headache, and cough, but these patients display only intermittent fever and chills, which indicates malaria. They contracted it on their excursion last week, no doubt. However, we have no quinine. There is a severe shortage throughout the hospital system. Soldiers are dying every day for lack of it."

Mrs. Peabody held Constance's hand. "I will not just let them suffer. I have dedicated my life to these children."

"We must employ our resourcefulness," I said. "Do you have turpentine in your cupboard, Mrs. Peabody?"

"Most likely."

"Carry, fetch it and we will rub it on the girls' chests. A fair substitute for quinine. And those willow trees near the riverside? Have their branches cut and brought up straightaway and we'll brew willow tea. Mixed with whiskey, it's not quite as effective as quinine, but will fend off fever in these little bodies."

Mrs. Peabody sent two footmen to fetch willow branches, we made our tea, and the three of us went from bed to bed through the night. We sang lullabies, rubbed turpentine on the young girls' chests, and offered sips of willow water until our sweet charges slept soundly.

It wasn't until the sun peeked over the horizon that we took a moment to rest near Constance's bed.

Mrs. Peabody came and stood in front of us, a wool blanket folded over one arm. "I must admit you are fairly good at this, Miss Woolsey."

I gazed at her directly. "I do have a talent for nursing."

"Some might call that vanity."

"Is it wrong to recognize a talent that is employed in the service of others?" I asked. "Is a man accused of vanity if he admits to a gift for law or banking?"

"I've not seen a gifted doctor display false modesty," Carry said.

I turned to pack up my nurse's bag. "I must be going. I'm sorry I don't fit your idea of the ideal woman, Mrs. Peabody, but I hope the children recover well."

She held out one hand. "Please wait." She looked to young Constance, asleep in the bed. "Perhaps my thinking is a bit backward. My affection runs so deep for these poor children, sometimes I get overprotective."

Carry and I exchanged glances.

"I owe you both an apology and will spend some time thinking just how to reward you." Mrs. Peabody smoothed the blanket at the foot of the bed. "Expect my thank-you to arrive in New York City very soon."

———

THE DAY AFTER MY visit to the orphanage, our brother, Charley, prepared to leave Brevoort Place to enlist and join the war. Mary and her daughters sat in the dining room sorting books for the troops, and the rest of us followed suit and did anything we could to stay occupied and not think of our precious brother marching off. I skated in and out on my parlor skates, retrieving cartons of books from the front vestibule and delivering them to Mary. Our little dog, Pico, sat at her feet, rarely moving from her, as usual when she visited.

How good it was to spend time with "My Mary," the name I had called her since I first could speak. Now she held her plump one-year-old daughter Georgeanna as she helped Una, three, Bertha, four, and nine-year-old May sort books, the children thumping tomes into the various boxes, labeled *Great Literature, Comics, Periodicals.*

I heaved a carton of books onto the dining room floor.

"Must you skate today, Georgy?" Mary asked. "It won't help Mother's mood."

I lifted my skirt to display one metal skate, attached to my boot by means of leather straps.

"You really should try them, Mary. I can get from the front parlor here to the dining room in eight seconds."

That dining room had hosted our most contented times, warmed by a happy fire, its table laid with a white tablecloth over a heavy felt silencer and set with the Woolsey family silver, it had always been a magnet for guests. Add Mother's famous Norwich baked beans and the prospect of a rousing game of chess with her, often lasting well past midnight, and the guests reliably returned. But now with boxes of war supplies and books piled high on the table, that room seemed small and claustrophobic, with reminders of Father's death on every wall.

Mary held one hand to her midsection as color drained from her cheek.

I pulled a chair near her and sat. "You're not feeling well."

"Just a light head."

"Baby number five?"

"Perhaps. Can you imagine?"

Father had delighted in all seven of his daughters as children, endlessly shuffling on hands and knees across the front parlor carpet, riding us about on his back, and Mary's children would have been no exception. How he would have loved sweet May and little Bertha, so poised, her laugh so ready and clear. And Una, who favored Mary so, with her startlingly blue eyes and sweet, light touch. And the baby Georgy, who had a lovely way of resting her sweet head on my shoulder as I held her, so round and pink with wisps of golden curls. She was—I liked to think—the most gifted of the four, and bound to be spoiled by me for life, if just for her name.

Mary helped May choose a box for her book. "What a blessing a fifth would be."

"Mary, perhaps four is enough. You run yourself ragged with Robert's congregation and the girls and helping Mother here. And we should tell Mother that Charley should pack his own luggage. He's twenty-three."

That morning Charley had received word his hand wound had healed to the satisfaction of the draft surgeon and he was assigned to the Army of the Potomac, to report immediately, creating a panic in Mother to prepare him for battle and seek out and pack up half of the house. He was reporting right to the middle of what was predicted to be one of the worst conflicts of the war. Confederate General Lee had soundly defeated the U.S. Army at Chancellorsville, Virginia, south of Washington, and we'd heard he'd marched his forces north, reaching and occupying southern Pennsylvania, his sights no doubt set on soon invading our capital.

Mother hurried through the dining room, her white cap askew. "Where is Charley's blanket?"

I slid another book into the box. "Have Charley find it himself, Mother."

Mary held one hand out to Mother. "Rest a moment. He's no longer a child, and can do it himself."

"I heard that, dear sisters," Charley said with a smile as he charged into the room, dressed in his new uniform Mother had sewn him, complete with a fine navy-blue jacket, two rows of brass buttons double-sewn down the breast. "You would deny a soldier a blanket?"

Mary and I caught our breath to see our little brother in full lieutenant's uniform, looking so tall and soldierly we scarcely knew him.

He stopped short. "Oh, Georgy, did you make the sandwiches?"

"As promised, but they will only be delivered once a 'thank you' is heard."

"Without too much meat? The boys don't like them too thick."

"You really should stay here with the Home Guard, Charley," I said. "This will be terribly difficult for Mother."

"It's worse to have a coward for a son."

I skated to him. "At least put a piece of paper in your pocket with your name and address here, in case—"

"What a ghoul you are, Georgy. I'm to be a simple secretary for General Meade and will probably see very little real engagement, unless you count corresponding with the bank manager."

Mary brought his blanket and all three of us helped him strap it on under his backpack.

Mother handed him a gold watch. "This was one of your father's. To have a piece of him with you."

"Don't cry, Mother." Charley slid the watch into his coat pocket and kissed Mother's cheek. "I'll be home by Christmas, you'll see."

He grabbed the sandwiches I'd wrapped in newspaper, and the little girls climbed onto dining chairs and offered their cheeks for his kisses. We then gathered on the front steps and watched him go. Mary and I stood on the steps, Mother between us, the baby in her arms, Mary's older girls at our feet.

"He has wanted this for so long," I said.

Mother watched him go, her face drawn. "I have given my all to this campaign, but must I give my son, too? Your father wouldn't have wanted it. If only he could have been here to stop it somehow. He would have worked his influence and arranged a safer post for him. No one could say no to your father."

Mary tucked back a lock of hair that had escaped Mother's cap. "Charley is also stubborn like Father, and you've raised him to be a valiant man.

We should be proud he would not let someone pay three hundred dollars to keep him out."

"I don't know how I will manage the worry."

As Charley walked off to join the Army of the Potomac, so full of optimism, I tried not to think of all the countless wounded men I'd sat with, and how easily those poor dears had slipped away, their hands falling from my grasp.

MOTHER, MARY, AND I spent the following two weeks immersed in emptying every home in New York City of gently used clothing for the troops, and carting it over to Abby at the Ladies' House of Industry. Once a serene place where needy women of all shades sat quietly sewing to earn a wage, it had become, with our sister at the helm, a Swiss watch of a distribution center for donated war supplies.

Charley had sent us a brief letter in which he mentioned heading for Gettysburg, Pennsylvania. Once June ended, Jane stalked the poor paperboy for the newspapers each day, and we swiftly scanned the columns, hungry for news of Pennsylvania, but found little. When Carry finally brought in a telegram from Uncle Edward from Washington saying the battle had started, the first day of fighting had been immense, and the reports he'd heard predicted no early end to the battle, Mother stood and called Margaret for her coat.

"My Charley," she said. "I must go down there now."

Harriet pulled Mother back to her chair. "He's been gone less than a month, Mother. You must calm yourself. Besides, they won't allow you on the battlefield, dear, though you'd fight a good deal better than some of those generals."

ONE MORNING MOTHER AND MARGARET minded the children while Mary and I walked cartons of donated books to Abby's House of Industry. We stepped into the little wooden house on Sixteenth Street and looked about for our sister. What a satisfying, snug place it was. In 1854, Abby had helped raise funds to purchase the former residence for sixteen thousand dollars and turned it into a hive of charitable activity.

Mary and I peeked into a sewing class in one room, where young women, colored and white, six to sixteen years old sat at desks and received embroidery instruction from Lucy Locker, preparing them to support themselves with steady income. We walked down the hall, bumped and jostled by men and women coming and going, finding each room filled to the ceiling with boxes marked *Shirts, Havelocks,* and *Tinned Meats.* I especially liked the look of the house's gift shop, a tidy store no bigger than our pantry, where the pupils sold their carefully sewn little iron holders and pen wipes, women's dresses, and men's wrappers, all benefiting their cause.

It smelled like progress there, the fresh cedar from the crates, paper cartons of spiced cologne, and leather field bags, all going where I longed to be.

Abby rushed to us. "Isn't it all so energizing? We have two pallets of havelocks coming. So good to keep the sun off a soldier's neck."

She rushed off to the gift shop as Mary and I set our books down.

Mary pulled a small green book from her box, *Merry's Book of Birds,* embossed in gold on the brown cover. "This reminds me of Frank Bacon. He does love birds."

"Did Eliza tell you Frank has a new ladylove?" I asked.

"Yes, she may have mentioned it, but she didn't say much. We know you don't like us talking about you. Do you regret turning him down in Washington?"

"Perhaps a bit."

"Frank has been such a good friend to the family. Perhaps you only saw him in that light. Almost like a brother."

"But I saw him in a different way in Rhode Island. He now seems more open to female equality." I struck an air of nonchalance. "That's where I met his new companion."

Mary searched my face. "Sometimes competition sparks new interest. And I hear the beard is gone. That may be the greatest factor."

"It may have improved his chances."

"I know it's hard for you to be on intimate terms with people some-times, Georgy, after being so close to Father."

"Perhaps in the past, but now I find myself missing Frank."

Mary set one soft hand on mine. "It isn't too late to tell him."

All at once there came a great commotion at the front door of the house and a familiar woman strode in, followed by a phalanx of liveried footmen bearing paper cartons, which they set upon the hallway floor.

"Where might I find Georgeanna Woolsey?"

Abby stepped into the hallway. "And who may I say inquires?"

"Mrs. *Peabody*," I said.

She waved the stream of footmen in. "Why the surprised expression? I told you I would bring a gift."

"Frankly, I'd forgotten. Mrs. Peabody, please meet my sisters Mary and Abigail. Abby runs this—"

Mrs. Peabody barely glanced at my sisters, who stood, stunned by the great ziggurat of cartons in the hall. "You won't forget *this,* twenty-four cases of some of the best quinine money can buy."

Abby stepped to the cases. "Johnston's Quinine. They keep this brand at the White House."

"Where on earth did you find it?" I asked. "The surgeon general him-self is at a loss where to find adequate stores."

Mrs. Peabody folded her arms across her chest. "I pressed a certain neighbor for the cartons he was stockpiling, hoping to sell at higher profit once the need became dire, terrible man. When you said there was a short-age, I knew that was the way to show my appreciation for your charity to my girls."

"And how are they progressing?" I asked.

"Every child has not only survived, but thrived as a result of your care, Miss Woolsey, and that of your sister. I am not usually in the habit of pass-ing out checks with abandon, but I am giving you this one today, Georgeanna. It's to be used toward the establishment of the nurses' school you so convincingly advocate. My bank will honor it."

She held out an envelope.

"I don't know what to say."

Abby took the envelope and handed it to me. "Well, this has made my day. Seeing Georgy speechless."

"Just say you will build the best nursing school for women anyone has ever seen. And make sure the New York Orphan Asylum girls are among your first ranks."

MRS. PEABODY SWEPT OUT, barely allowing us time to take in the incandescent joy of it all, and Mary, Abby, and I embraced as one.

Mary laced her fingers together at her waist. "What a fine day. The quinine we wished for and a start for your school, Georgy."

"How much is the check written for?" Abby asked.

I opened the envelope, hands shaking. "Five hundred," I said, a bit faint.

Mary gasped. "I've never seen such a fine gift, Georgy."

I stared at the letter, numb with happiness. "This is all Father's doing."

Abby plucked the check from my fingers and examined it. "Father was our savior, but this is all Mrs. Peabody, Georgy."

I tucked the envelope in my pocket and the three of us began lifting cartons of bottles and ferrying them toward the storage room.

"Won't Mr. Olmsted just fall over to see all this quinine?" Abby said.

All at once Mother hurried into the front hallway, wearing no bonnet or shawl and looking about frantically.

We set down our cartons and rushed to her. "What is it?"

"You must come quickly, girls." She caught her breath, one hand to her chest, blue eyes bright with tears.

"Calm yourself, Mother," I said.

She held a yellow envelope we all recognized as that known to hold a telegram. "This just arrived."

"What does it say?" Abby asked.

She held the envelope out to me. "I don't know. But surely it is about your brother. I cannot bring myself to open it."

Mary circled one arm around Mother's shoulders. "It could be nothing at all, dear."

I tore open the envelope and read, trying to keep my voice steady. *"Charles wounded. If you are coming to Gettysburg, let me know."* I looked up at Mother. *"Frederick Olmsted."*

Mary pulled the telegram from my hands. "It says no more?"

Mother reached out to me and gripped my arm. "Georgy, you and I must go at once."

CHAPTER 26

Jemma

✷

HAGERSTOWN, MARYLAND

JULY 1863

THE SWIFTS WERE IN A FINE MOOD THAT MORNING SINCE THEY had two moneymaking opportunities booked in one day. Like many photographers, they made a big part of their living making pictures of dead people, so with all the war and sickness going on, business was good. A picture cost a lot and most times only when a loved one died did a family spend the money to remember them. My job was to make them look as alive as I could.

"Bring it in front-first," Mr. Swift called, to the men carrying in a small wicker coffin. Two children, easy to tell from the small size.

The Swift house stood on the main road of the big city of Hagerstown, rubbing shoulders with other businesses in town. Downstairs was a front parlor where pictures were done, a dining room, and in the back a kitchen and my and Sally's room. Upstairs was one bedroom where the two Swifts slept in one bed, her taking up way more than her share of the real estate.

The ma and pa followed the little coffin, and the men sat it on the front parlor table and lifted the lid off, sending the terrible smell of embalming—mercury and arsenic—into the air. The front door stood open to the dusty street, the hot breeze carrying some of the bad smell away, and the scent of Sally Smith's butterscotch crisps baking in the oven helped a little, too.

I set up the room with the usual things. Fancy cloth backdrop, the velvet couch for the ma to sit on, and the iron stand for the older child. When it came time to charge money for his work, Mr. Swift called those pictures *memento mori,* meaning "remember thy death," but to me they were just plain pictures of dead people, taken so they could be remembered by their kinfolk.

"It's uncanny how at ease you are with those unfortunates who've passed, Jemma," Mrs. Swift once said, scared to say the word *dead.* "You have no qualms about touching the deceased."

She was right. I'd seen plenty of killing. Sweet Clementine. Harry. Celeste. Pa.

After that, touching two deceased children didn't bother me much. At least the last person to touch them was a kind one.

Mr. Swift made the pictures and then, when they put those children back in the wicker box, their ma set to weeping something terrible, throwing herself on the coffin. That's when Mrs. Swift started her best work, selling them another coffin to *guarantee each child sailed to heaven for sure* and two extra-special frames for the pictures, carved with angels, *like Jesus himself looking over them,* that costing extra, too.

Soon as the Swifts got their money and the coffin back out the door, a company of soldiers arrived to have their picture made. They tumbled into the front parlor, most with their hair carefully arranged, like a litter of puppies, at least thirty of them, while their colored cooks and camp followers sat out front.

The Swifts bargained with the troop leader about cost, and a skinny boy who wore his red hair stuck up in the back like a rooster tail and had a big brown drum slung by a strap over his shoulder came to me and poked me in the chest.

"Do us a favor and dress up like our drummer for the picture? We lost Eddie at Fredericksburg and you look about his size."

He took me for a boy, with my shaved head and trousers, so I lowered my voice a bit. "I don't know how to—"

"I'm known as Raymond Gleason, by the way, and that there talking to the owner is Major Ellis. He's the boss. And this is the Fourteenth Connecticut. Nutmeg Regiment. We just need us a boy to wear the shirt and trousers with the stripe and pose with this drum and drumsticks like so. It's not so hard."

I went to the closet and tugged on the clothes and then Raymond slid the drum strap over my head so the big drum rested at my waist. I caught a look at myself in the long mirror and saw why they thought I was a boy, bone thin and bald as a baby bird.

I came out of the closet, tucking in my shirt. "How'd Eddie die?"

"Took one in the head. Never felt a thing. We shared a sack, so I got his stuff. The Rebs aim for the drummers since they direct the company with their beats. Specially when they're dark as you."

"Is it hard? Drummin', I mean?"

"You got to walk beside us in the march, beating your drum to keep us together. Then, out on the field, each of Major Ellis's commands has a beat what represents it."

He rapped out a series of little beats. "This one means 'meet here.' Here's 'forward' for when we march. And best of all, 'the long roll,' which means 'attack.'"

"My ma played the drums. Seems easy."

"Ain't easy at all. When the drummer boys're not needed for sounding calls, they got another job. Stretcher bearers for the wounded to get them to medical care."

"Two rows for the picture, gentlemen!" Mr. Swift called out.

Raymond pulled a cap from his bag. "Here, you wear this. Mine's my pop's, he was wearing it when he got killed at Fredericksburg. Died right next to me." He put the cap on my head and arranged it.

Mr. Swift fussed the soldiers into two rows and pulled his big wooden box camera, set on three legs, closer to the group. Mrs. Swift came hurrying with the wet-plate glass she'd got ready and wouldn't let anybody else touch.

Mr. Swift got under the black cloth at his camera. "Hold still, now. Don't even breathe for ten seconds."

Once it was done, Sally Smith came out of the kitchen and stood near me, holding a platter of her butterscotch crisps, warm from the oven. The soldiers crowded around us and each took a cookie from the plate and thanked her kindly.

She smiled, looking at her near-empty plate. "I've never seen my baking disappear so fast. Except my cornbread kush. You barely see that, it goes so quick. Sure sticks with you. Men known to go all day on one plate."

The major parted the circle and stepped in. "What about pigeon pie? Can you make that?"

Sally smiled, and acted like she had to think about that for a minute. "With or without gizzards?"

"It's her specialty," I said. "Made it for Mister Watson every Sunday down at Peeler Plantation. He liked it brushed with extra butter on top, made the crust nice and crispy."

"What is your name, ma'am?" the major asked.

"Sally Smith, sir."

"And the drummer boy?"

Sally glanced at me and then at the floor.

"Um," I said, searching my brain for a boy name.

The major squinted one eye at me. "Don't know your own name?"

"Jem, sir," I said.

The major stood tall and called to his men. "We're taking these two with us. Heading out, all of you."

The men crowded through the front door and Sally grabbed my flowered carpetbag she'd already packed for us and left at the foot of the stairs.

"Got Pa's cross, too?" I asked.

"First thing I got."

"You planned all this," I said as we walked out onto the street, the drum hitting my thigh in a good way.

"Just the power of cookies, that's all."

I tried the forward beat Raymond showed me, the second-easiest one, and the drum made a bigger sound than I expected, and soon the men just fell in.

Mrs. Swift ran after us, the fat on her pillow arms flapping.

"That is *my* property!" she hollered, as she snatched me by the arm and held on harder than a hawk on a hare.

Raymond came, took the drum, slung it over his chest, picked me up, and threw me over his shoulder, breaking Mrs. Swift's grip. The soldiers just laughed at Raymond carrying me like a sack of turnips and yelled back to Mrs. Swift, "Them's contraband now!"

One tossed her a coin as we marched along and she bent to pick it up.

"Five cents?" she said. "I paid almost a hundred dollars for her."

We just kept walking and after a piece Raymond set me down.

"You are officially conscripted into the United States Army, Jem, my boy. Take good care of that uniform, property of Abraham Lincoln."

"I will," I said, happier than I'd been in a long time. "Where we headed now?"

He looked at me with a smile in his eyes. "Hope you like action. Town called Gettysburg."

Anne-May

ONE MORNING FERGUS CALLED ME INTO HIS OFFICE, A DARK dungeon of a place, paneled in oak, every kind of tobacco box and tin heaped upon the shelves, so he could study the competition. I avoided that place like the pox, because of the glass tanks positioned about the room, each holding some sort of slimy lizard or crab that might scurry out from behind a rock any minute. It smelled like dead snails in there, but Euphemia, lacking all womanly sensitivity, loved that room and enjoyed dangling crickets for all of my husband's crawlies.

I stood in the doorway, the cat at my feet. "Yes, Fergus?"

He sat in his desk chair, what was left of his leg resting on a high stool, as Euphemia massaged the end of his bare stump.

"Come in, Anne-May." He was in a good mood. Nothing like having your stump massaged to make a man jolly.

I stayed in the doorway. "You know I can't abide seeing all that medical stuff Euphemia does to you. Makes me queasy."

He stroked a glass paperweight with a hairy spider frozen inside. "I want to tell you about what's happening in the world—the Emancipation Proclamation for starters."

"That happened last January, for pity's sake. I do read a newspaper now and then, you know."

"Then you must know that black troops can now fight officially, and all slaves are free in areas of rebellion."

"Such as what states?"

"Anywhere south that is fighting. Not Maryland, though."

"Why's that?" I watched Saint Joan creep into the room under the line of Fergus's sight.

"The law does not apply to border states like Maryland. I thought you said you read about it."

Tears came to my eyes and the room swam in a sea of terrarium green. "No need to be harsh, Fergus."

"All the servants have run off, except for Sable. Know anything about that?"

"They don't knock on my door and tell me, Fergus."

"Well, it's for the best they've left. They'll all be free soon anyway, I hope. Once we bring in the tobacco, I'm freeing Sable."

"She's mine, Fergus. You can't do that."

"And we'll buy no more slaves. I'm done with that cruelty. And since you've deprived us of income from this year's tobacco proceeds, we'll have to work this place best we can, with Sable's help if she chooses to stay for wages, along with a few borrowed hands from Ambrosia. Long as you and Euphemia help with field work."

I felt a high-pitched sound in my head, like glass on wire. "Me in the fields? I will *not* be choring around, Fergus. I am the mistress here."

"You've shown recklessness to expense, and if you expect to eat, things need to change."

"I'm worn slap out, Fergus, and I need some sort of lady's maid. I can't find one clean dress."

"Your sister manages her toilette without a maid."

"She's got no toilette to attend to."

Fergus slammed his palm on his blotter. "You will not criticize Euphemia. She keeps this place together with no help from you."

She kept her gaze on Fergus's stump, kneading it like bread dough.

"And where are my silver brushes?" he demanded.

"No need to raise your voice, Fergus. Once you left, the servants all took what they pleased. Isn't that right, Euphemia?"

She shook liniment on a cloth. "Not that I know of."

"Where'd the money from the hog sale go? Freddie Fairchild told me he saw you at Smalls and Sons buying snuff and silk."

"A girl needs dresses, for pity's sake, Fergus. I'm the mistress here."

"Rumor says it was *you* who took Sally Smith's jelly money. I sold her because you told me *she* stole."

"You believe Freddie Fairchild over me?"

"And Jemma. *She was trouble,* you said. *She's seducing LeBaron,* you said. You never told me LeBaron accosted her and Sable in his cabin and that's why he and his men killed Joseph. Had to hear that from Euphemia."

I sent my sister dagger eyes and she just kept to her work.

"And my gold stickpin. Freddie said there's one just like it on sale at Smalls and Sons."

"You told me to pawn that pin if we needed it. And I never took Sally's money, but she stole our sugar to make fancy food for the coloreds, while Euphemia and me went hungry. It's not right."

"All lies, Anne-May. Do you even know fact from fiction? You better start telling me the truth *and* pitching in around here. If we can't pay our taxes, we'll lose this house."

"If I wanted to ruin my skin in a tobacco field, I could've done it with someone who treated me right."

"Like the noble Jubal Smalls? Everyone is talking about you two. You are my wife and it's high time you started acting like it or go live with your ex-stepfather. Get money from him, since he took all of ours."

"Reggie invested it, lucky for you, Fergus."

"We'll never see a penny of that money. I wrote five letters to him, with no answer. It's clear now he pushed us to marry for that reason only—to get my inheritance."

I walked out of that smelly old room and went up to rest, while Fergus called after me.

"You'll be out in the fields tomorrow or I'll call Sheriff Whitman to drag you there. A husband's wishes still count for something in St. Mary's County."

"You just try, Fergus," I called back.

I hurried up the stairs, the cat running beside me. As we reached the landing I noted with satisfaction the cat had one of Fergus's precious baby crabs in her mouth, the creature's legs and pincers flailing.

I bent and patted her soft head. "Good girl," I said, and made a silent prayer of thanks to my brother, Harry, for bringing Saint Joan to me.

TRUE TO HIS WORD, at nine the next morning, Fergus had the sheriff escort me out to the tobacco fields. Fat Sheriff Whitman apologized the whole way and I just went along with it all, and figured if I stayed out there on that great sloping hill of tobacco plants long enough, I could escape to a cool bath and sneak off to see Jubal in town later.

I stood out in the field with Euphemia and Sable and tied on the biggest straw hat I owned, heat already steaming off the plants at that early hour. Sable threw hate looks my way as I bent over a row of green plumes.

"I'm not averse to hard work, it's the worms I can't abide. You know how I hate 'em, Pheme."

"We all have to pitch in now, Anne-May. I don't like killing them either."

As the sun climbed the sky, my back ached from bending over, tying brown paper bags to the plants all morning, to gather the best seeds. I could barely look under the leaves for fear of seeing one of God's most horrid creatures, a horned tobacco worm.

I straightened and rubbed my back. "Fergus loves seeing me out here, humiliated."

Euphemia turned to me. "If we don't get the seeds, there'll be no crop next year."

Somehow blessed with the unique ability to spot the wretched fat green worms that others could not see hiding among the leaves, I spotted a particularly large one, big as a giant's thumb, slinking along a lower leaf. "Lord have mercy, it's a big one. Euphemia, come get it."

She handed me the shears. "You need to do some yourself, Anne-May."

"I just can't. Cutting them in half that way is too much for my sensitive disposition."

Sable marched to me, snatched the shears from my hands, cut the worm in half, tossed the shears on the ground, and went back to her bagging.

"No need to get uppity about it," I called after her. I picked up the shears. Last thing I wanted was to get stabbed in the back by Sable.

Euphemia smiled and looked past me. "Fergus. Look at you walking so well on this uneven slope."

There came Fergus with his peg leg strapped on, limping down a row of tobacco plants, a cane in one hand, wad of papers in the other.

I wiped my brow with the back of my free hand. "High time you came out to help."

"I'm inside, working the books," he said. "Where I've found you spent over one hundred dollars at Smalls and Sons this year, Anne-May."

"I buy homespun for Sable's clothes."

Sable sent me another look.

"Euphemia's cloth, too."

Euphemia kept to her bagging. "I've had no new dresses."

Fergus shook the receipts in my direction. "You purchased mostly snuff and bonnets, from what I can tell. That was fine before Reggie swindled my family. But we now have to watch every cent, thanks to you."

I threw down the shears. "I'm going into town."

Fergus grabbed my arm. "You'll stay here and work."

I shook off his grasp and walked toward the house. "Last time I checked, my name's on the deed of this place. So I'll do as I please. Not that you can chase me."

Fergus hobbled after me. "Going to see Jubal? Word is you two are spying together. They hang spies, you know, Anne-May."

I turned. "Wouldn't you like that? You'd have my house and you and Pheme here can run off together."

Euphemia kept her gaze on her plants.

Fergus stepped toward me. "I don't even know you anymore, Anne-May. When did you become so full of hate?"

"The day you didn't risk your own life to help my brother."

"Sometimes I think I'd have been better off dying that day."

I turned. "Well, finally something we can agree on, Fergus Watson."

THUNDER BOOMED AND IT poured buckets the night I suffered the biggest fright of my life.

I sat alone in front of the dark fireplace, settled deep into a down cushion on the parlor sofa, watching the lightning flash in the sky above the river, while Euphemia and Fergus took their dinner down in his science shack, cataloging and doing God knows what else to lizards and crabs. I surveyed my finest things: the gold chinoiserie mirror above the fireplace, reflecting the black river, lit up now and then by the flashes, and the tall turquoise *bleu céleste* Sèvres vases on the mantel.

All at once I heard the courtyard door bang open and Sable appeared at the door, her calico dress soaked to the skin, a bundle of firewood cradled in one arm.

"Sable. You're just in time to brush my hair."

She dropped the wood into the basket. "Mister Watson had me split the rest of the cord to keep it dry. Wants this firebox cleaned out."

"Haven't had a fire in two months in here and there's still ashes in that hearth. You need to put some elbow grease into the housework, Sable."

"In the fields all day till sundown. Then there's the mending and dinner to cook." Sable gripped the little iron ash shovel, knelt by the hearth, and scooped ashes into the metal bucket.

I sat up straighter. "Tomorrow I want you in here cleanin' those blue vases. There's an inch a dust on them. It's a disgrace."

Sable kept to her work. "Aunt Tandy Rose used to say those vases belonged in a house of ill repute, those half-naked ladies painted on there."

"Well, look at you giving your opinion so freely. Those are Peeler family heirlooms, and only the most cultured of us can appreciate their beauty. Don't expect a woman of your wretched birth to appreciate such *objets d'art.*"

Sable stood, wiping the iron shovel with her apron, just looking at me.

"Well then, git now," I said, waving her off.

Sable took a slow step toward me, shovel at her side, and just stood there, looking.

"I *said* git."

At long last she spoke, so quiet I had to listen hard. "You ever feel sorry for all you've done?"

"You been into the brandy?"

Sable stepped closer, her grip tighter on the shovel handle. "Destroying that letter Tandy wrote freeing us. Getting my Joseph killed. I think you liked it."

I shifted on my sofa cushion. "You put that shovel down, now."

"Smoking that poor girl in the tobacco shed, selling off Jemma and Sally. You liked that we lost our baby son."

"Your Jemma started that fire."

She stepped closer. "It was an accident. Someone knocked over a lantern in the barn."

"It was stupid of Jemma."

Sable stepped toward me.

"You come no farther, Sable."

She stopped. "At least *she* can write. Don't think I don't know about that damn book you made her copy down all your spyin' in. All this evil will come back on you."

"You've never appreciated all I've done for you. I kept that crippled-up daughter of yours working over at Ambrosia when I should've sold her."

"Aren't you kind."

I ran one hand down the silk of the sofa cushion. "I got one piece of news you might want to hear."

She waited a long second. "Well?"

"LeBaron came by the other day."

Sable waited, lips clamped together.

"Out o' the blue, he asked me the strangest question. 'Miss Anne-May,' he says to me, 'what do you think about me buyin' your Patience?'"

Sable gripped the shovel handle tighter and stepped closer to me.

"Hold it right there. You hurt me and you think Joseph got it bad . . ."

"What God-fearing Christian woman would do a thing like that to a good girl who never said a cross word to you? I'll go to Mister Watson."

I examined my cuticles. "Y'all belong to *me,* no matter what delusional world Fergus lives in. And I have a mind to say yes to LeBaron. Could use the money, frankly."

Like a woman possessed by the devil, Sable lunged toward the mantel and sent that shovelhead right through my turquoise porcelain vase. It burst like a hollowed-out egg into a million pieces and I held my hands above me to escape the needles of shattered glass raining onto my bare shoulders.

I screamed. "Those are eighteenth *century,*" I said, heart beating out of my chest. "I'll call Sheriff Whitman."

Sable stepped to the other vase.

"No, no, stop," I begged.

Sable smashed the second vase to smithereens, and then came back and stood over me, ash shovel at her side.

I stood. "You'll pay, Sable."

"Someday I will leave here, and when I do, the earth will open up and swallow this place whole—and you will live to see that, left with nothing."

I brushed glass shards from my hair. "I suppose that's a colored hex you're puttin' on me."

She tossed the shovel onto the hearth with a clatter and clapped the soot off her hands. "Yes, ma'am, that is a colored hex and it won't be long before it comes true."

She walked toward the door and turned back, her dark gaze trained on me. "You just wait and see."

IT TOOK ME DAYS to recover from the fright of Sable destroying my front parlor, for which I received no solace from my sister, and no support from feeble Fergus to punish her, since she was our last servant. Fergus said, "You're lucky she didn't use that shovel on you," and banned me from telling LeBaron. Fergus knew those pattyrollers would not tolerate insubordination, even if he was right as rain with it.

Later that week, I drove into town with Euphemia for sewing circle and was practically dripping by the time we arrived at Widow Gardener's house, the whole of St. Mary's County like one big steam bath, that terrible swamp stinking something awful.

It was the last thing I wanted to do in that heat, sit with a gaggle of old geese and sew, but I hoped Jubal might stop by there as he did do often, to try to pick up information he could pass on. I wasn't looking my finest, though. With Jemma gone and my toilette interrupted, my nails went un-buffed, my hair unwashed for days, not to mention soiled cuffs.

My temple was throbbing after a steady diet of conversation between my sister and Fergus about his crawdads, and I longed to see Jubal and tell him all that had gone on. Maybe he'd bring some snuff or something pretty to cheer me up, after so much sadness and terrible heat. He knew I'd be there. He'd do his best to reach out.

We entered Widow Gardener's front parlor, close and low-ceilinged, with no sign of even the smallest breeze, and took our places at the table and took out the handkerchiefs we'd been working on, to be sent off to the troops, U.S. Army troops only, Widow Gardener had made clear. As I hemmed the linen I dropped stitches on purpose, thinking about the wretched Yankee soldiers blowing their noses on my handiwork.

"What's everyone wearing to the benefit ball?" I asked, hoping to keep the conversation somewhat interesting.

"My old brown tartan," Charlene said.

"I'm wearing my gray silk," I said.

"With the black add-ons?" she asked.

"The one. Don't you think black, well placed, gives value and tone to a dress? So French. The French have an innate sense of color, which one sees in all the trifles that adorn their shops. Any little French box is always painted with two colors, which are so harmonious that it is a delight to look at them."

Charlene nodded. "When the English choose two disparate colors, it only brings trouble to the eye."

Widow Gardener looked up from her work. "My apologies for it being a bit close in here. I've shut the windows to keep the flies down."

Since Widow Gardener had freed her servants, there was no one to fan us and keep the flies off.

"It's just fine," Euphemia said, dark rings under her arms as she worked her needle. "I feel for the troops at battle in this heat. Any news from your nephew, Beulah?"

"Received a letter, which said he's on his way to Gettysburg."

"Where's that?" I asked.

"Pennsylvania," Beulah Gardener said, like I was a child. "Just up from Hagerstown. North of the Maryland border maybe six hours."

"I hear the Yankees are using Confederate skulls from which to drink their sangria," I said.

Euphemia barely looked up from her work. "You heard that from LeBaron? Consider the source. I heard the Confederates made drumsticks out of Yankee shinbones."

Charlene leaned in. "No need to take sides here, ladies. There are well-meaning people on both sides, really."

Widow Gardener dropped her handkerchief and sat back. "Well, one side is engaged in armed insurrection and treason in the name of preserving the right to hold other human beings as property for their own profit. What is well meaning about that?"

Charlene licked her floss and threaded a needle. "Like it or not, it sounds like the South is well on their way to victory." She smiled at me. "According to the *Richmond Enquirer*."

Euphemia poured herself more tea. "Actually, the opposite is true, Charlene. At Vicksburg, Grant has the city surrounded and it appears Pemberton will surrender soon. Grant is poised to control the whole Mississippi, which will turn the war for the North in a major way."

"You won't read about that in the *Enquirer*," Widow Gardener said. "They trumpet Southern victories and downplay Southern defeats."

Euphemia tied off her thread, strangely dainty for a big girl. "The *Enquirer* rarely gives the Northern side of things."

"It covered the hanging of that Confederate lady spy they discovered," Charlene said.

My throat tightened, but I kept my needle in motion.

"Says she collected Northern war information from her captain husband and sold it to the South. Poisoned pies and gave them to Northern troops, too. Killed a young private from Maine."

"Who knows what's propaganda anymore?" Widow Gardener asked. "All these boys dying. It's a crying shame."

Just the mention of dying boys sent a hot wind screeching through my head, and a picture of Harry rose large as life in front of me and made me happy about Yankees eating poison pies. I ached to see my brother's smile again.

I stood. "I'm a bit faint. Mind if I open the window?"

I tugged the window up and caught a glimpse of the back of a man's head—Jubal, his black hair shining in the sun.

I excused myself to the necessary and hurried out the back door to the garden, where Jubal stood, smoking his pipe.

"You are most ingenious in your eavesdropping skills, Jubal Smalls. Why did you not send a note in for me?"

Jubal shrugged, the skin on his face bronzed. He'd been working outside.

"Got any more snuff for me, Jubal? I can pay you once Fergus calms down about money things."

"I don't have any snuff, Anne-May. Do you know what it's like running a store in wartime?"

"You just made a big delivery here, didn't you?" I stepped closer. "Hear what Beulah Gardener just said about her nephew? I may go mad in there from their war talk."

He stepped back. "Put it all down in the book. You're supposed to be getting Widow Gardener to talk about her nephew. Instead y'all are going on about Paris."

"Has to sound natural, Jubal. Did you hear what they said about spies? Widow Gardener looked right at me when Charlene said it. Not to mention the fact Pinkerton detectives showed up at my doorstep the other day asking about the socks I sent to troops and accused me of reporting their locations to the enemy. Had to throw Mama to those wolves."

"Better than them suspecting us. I'm feeling pressure from high places, too. Sheriff says it's been too long since I gave them anything and if I don't come up with new information, he won't do business with me anymore."

"I told you about all those railroad things. And where I sent the socks. It's all wrote in that book."

"They appreciated all that, but they want fresh news. And where *is* that book? Jemma's been gone a good while. You haven't found it by now?"

"Well, that's the thing, Jubal. Jemma told me she left the book behind in plain sight, so I looked high and low. But she lied, evil girl, and I can't find it anywhere. Even searched the tobacco barn and the smokehouse. Could look in Fergus's science shack."

"You always have some excuse about not finding it."

"Lord knows, she might've took it with her."

Jubal clenched his fists. "That book has our entire history in it. I drew maps, Anne-May."

"*Quiet,* Jubal. I'll give it one more look."

"They catch me and I'm dead. My family ruined."

"And me?"

"It won't be pretty."

"Come on over to the house one day soon. Fergus is going to the doctor next Tuesday. Stop by then. We can have ourselves some fun. And find that book."

CHAPTER 28

Georgy

✳

GETTYSBURG, PENNSYLVANIA
JULY 1863

T HE MOON CHASED US THROUGH THE NIGHT AS MOTHER AND
I raced to Gettysburg in a carriage Uncle Edward had secured for us from
Baltimore, and long before we reached the battle town proper, the odors
of the battlefield greeted us. We were twenty-four hours in getting there,
on roads choked with traffic, when in ordinary times it would have taken
four.

We bumped along, the driver seated just in front of us in the dark.

"Taking you ladies to the Sanitary Commission lodge set up by the
train depot, a mile outside Gettysburg."

"Couldn't they set up closer to town?" Mother asked.

"No, ma'am. Wanted to, but the Rebs burned the bridge." We passed
the charred remains of a railroad bridge, a dark hole in the night. "See?
That *was* the railroad bridge. Taking a while to rebuild it."

I looked out into the night. The moon had been just as full the night
Mother and I had retrieved Father from the train station, when I was
barely six. I sat between them on the soft carriage seat, chosen from all the
sisters to make the trip alone with my parents after learning a new piano
solo.

"He's chasing us," I'd said, pointing to the moon. I hid my face in the great folds of Father's soft wool coat.

Father had wrapped his big arm around me, huffed his warm breath on my hands and held them tight. "No man in the moon can get you now."

He'd held my hands the whole way to our home in Boston's East End, as I sat between Mother and Father, cocooned in the hum of supreme happiness, safe from the moon.

What would it have been like to have Father there with us that night, a balm to the soul, always so eager to right wrongs and to see everything in a most humorous, positive way?

Mother cracked her window open, the warm air bringing me back to Gettysburg.

"Regardless, sir," Mother said, "I'm sure the United States government is doing all it can for the wounded."

"Sanitary Commission's the only one doing anything for them. After two days of the most infernal fighting, there's a line of ambulances and stretchers a mile and a half in length moving the wounded from dressing stations to the train, day and night. It's a mess."

"Well, certainly they are expeditiously taking the wounded by train out of here."

"Only two trains a day, single-track line with no turntables, so trains make the return trip back to Baltimore in reverse."

"They back up all the way?" I asked. "It must take ages."

"At least we have modern trains," Mother said.

"Just cattle cars with the cow droppings still in them. They toss straw on the floor and set the wounded upon it. And there's no water on board—along the way, water brigades from nearby streams bring the wounded water."

"These poor boys," Mother said.

I extended my head and shoulders out the window and scanned the fields we passed—and saw humps of dead soldiers and horses and overturned wagons, bathed in blue moonlight. A long ridge loomed in the distant darkness.

"Could you please hurry?" I asked. "My brother's life is in peril." Up ahead the white of tents stood out against the dark night. "There's a lodge in the distance, Mother."

She pulled my arm. "Do shut the window, Georgeanna."

The driver turned in his seat. "This is an active battle area, ma'am. Could be sharpshooters about."

I held Mother's hand, cold against the black leather seat. With her other hand she pressed a hankie to her nose.

"Such a ghastly odor."

"Scent of war, ma'am. They've used chloride of lime much as they can, but there's been two days of fighting here and terrible casualties. You're lucky there's a lull right now. You should've seen it today, iron raining down like hell itself. More tomorrow."

"Surely they will remove the dead from the battlefield," I said.

"No, ma'am. Hasn't been time or resources to remove all the casualties. Many poor souls still alive out there. Listen close and you'll hear them moaning in the fields south of town. They tried to bury one today and he woke up just as the sod rained down upon him." The driver waved one arm toward the ridge. "Our Union soldiers are up on that hill. Good chance General Lee'll go after them tomorrow with all he's got."

Mother clasped her hands in her lap. "I can't bear it another minute, Georgy. Why did I let your brother—"

"Almost there, Mother."

I checked my pocket again for the telegram we'd received from Mr. Olmsted. Anything not to think about Charley. When he was a baby, how we seven sisters had fought to be his nursemaid, so much so that his feet barely touched the ground until he was two. After Father died, he became our everything.

We slowed as we approached the lodge, a series of tents near the train depot, and heard the terrible moans and cries of wounded and dying men. Mother rushed into the first tent and I followed. Though well past midnight, it was lit to brilliance by oil lamps and teeming with uniformed soldiers and doctors going from bed to bed, tending the wounded.

We hurried toward a table stacked with papers, to a private with long muttonchop sideburns.

"I'm sorry, ladies, but inquiries must wait until morning. We have casualties to process and can't be stopping every five minutes. You're the fifth such group this evening, not including sightseers and—"

Mother leaned in. "My son, Charles Woolsey, has been wounded."

The private glanced at a sheath of papers. "No Woolsey on the wounded list."

"Could you check again?" Mother asked. "It is Woolsey with an *e*."

"We have processed one hundred and sixty-three wounded today at this station alone, madam. Forgive me if your son's name is not at my fingertips."

"We received a telegram," I said. "My brother is aide-de-camp for General Meade."

"Meade? We have his adjutant here."

Mother set her bag on the desk. "Thank goodness. May we speak with him, please?"

"I would most certainly arrange it, madam, but you see, he took a charge to the chest and is no longer of this world. He's with the rest of Meade's fallen soldiers out back here for burial. Sixty poor souls."

"And you have no record of a Charles Woolsey among them?"

"Haven't had a chance to catch up on my clerical duties, ma'am, but we only just got them before dark, and bagged their possessions—a few had their names written on scraps of paper or ID disks in their pockets. Most didn't. Come back tomorrow."

Mother stood straighter. "We will see every one of them *tonight*, to ensure my son is not among them. You have a mother, I presume, and understand she would be racked with grief in such a situation? We have been called here by Frederick Olmsted of the Sanitary Commission and have every right to be here, so please proceed, sir."

"Well, why didn't you say so about Mr. Olmsted? I'm Private Trembley. Suppose I could take some time. But it has to be quick."

I turned to Mother. "I will look."

We held hands, both cold through our gloves. "I must come, too," she said.

"You need to stay here in case anyone comes with news of Charley."

She nodded, lips tight.

I followed the private out of the tent, and held back a gasp at the number of bodies lying there, stretching into the moonlit yard.

"How many here, Private?"

"Hundreds. Another six thousand still on the battlefield and at the dressing station tents. Meade's fallen boys are over here. If you're lucky, he'll be recognizable. Some have heads shot clean off. Unless they can be identified, they go in a mass grave."

He thrust his lamp toward one soldier, stretched out upon the ground. "This him?"

I bent at the waist and peered at the terribly young soldier's face, eyes open, mouth agape, blond hair matted to his forehead with blood.

I felt a wave of nausea and pressed my fist to my mouth. "No. That boy is no more than fifteen."

The private shrugged. "Got thirteen-year-olds out here. Lie about their age. Come along, hundred and fifty-nine to go."

"My brother, Charles, was twenty-three. Tall. He carried one of my father's pocket watches."

"Gold? A fancy one?"

I locked my fingers at my waist to keep them from shaking. "Yes."

"A mighty nice uniform, too. Fine buttons?"

Tears came to my eyes. "You've seen him here?"

The private lurched off, his lamp swinging. "Follow me." He stopped, set down his lamp, and retrieved a paper bag nestled near a body.

Was it Charley? It was hard to tell in the semidarkness. The same height, perhaps.

He handed me the bag. "Here's the possessions."

I felt the paper bag, the pocket watch there, heavy and cold.

"Well, best to rip off the bandage, so to speak, get this done quickly. Come closer so you can see better. No fainting, I beg you."

"I was a nurse on the hospital ships at the Peninsula Campaign, sir."

He shrugged. "Had grown men faint dead away out here. Sure you don't want the bucket before you see?"

My knees shook. "Delay no longer, sir."

The private lifted his lamp toward the face and I fell against him, holding his arm.

"Please, Private Trembley, may I see the pocket watch?"

Jemma

✳

GETTYSBURG, PENNSYLVANIA
JULY 1863

WE MARCHED INTO GETTYSBURG AROUND MIDNIGHT, AFTER the day's fighting had died down, our soldiers trooping in lines, towing a fat black cannon and cartloads of ammunition, followed by groups of colored families and attendants and helpers, some free, some not. The moon was out, so we could see the heaps of dead lying in the fields and we could sure smell them, too. Nothing stays fresh in that heat.

As we stepped along to my beat I considered how much easier it was being a boy, like a cow in a herd, just part of the group. Nobody looked at you twice if you wanted to spit or chuck a stone or sit with your legs spread. I had to use the necessary in private, though, or go in the woods, but none of those soldiers paid me no nevermind, just the way I liked it.

I kept the drumbeat low as we approached the camp, a little city of white tents, a few fires lit.

Raymond came to march next to me. "You learned the beats right quick."

Sally Smith caught up with us. "I smell bacon. Hope they got eggs."

We came to a tent and the colonel gave the order to halt and I quit my drumming. I sat on the grass next to Sally and Raymond, my feet aching and blistered, the white tents bright in the moonlight, the smell of tobacco and coffee in the air. Just as I set my drum down next to me, woman about my color, tallest woman I ever saw, hair tied up in a sugar sack, swooped out of a tent, one big arm throwing back the tent flap.

She came to us. "Don't you set down here." She waved off toward a rise in the distance. "You're off for that hill up there. Cemetery Ridge."

Raymond stood. "Well, that don't sound promising. Got any food?"

"You gotta eat quick," she said, wiping her hands on her homespun apron.

"And who are you, bossin' U.S. Army soldiers around?"

"Mag Palm. Live over back of the old fairgrounds. At first I thought you were here to blackbird me and take me south."

Raymond rubbed his sore leg. "Ain't you free?"

"Got the papers to prove it. But you gotta be careful still. People worse than ever want to take colored folk down to Dixie for a profit. They almost did it to me, too."

"How'd they get you?" Raymond asked.

"Tied my hands in front of me, but even tied up I fought hard. Kicked one with my boot in the privates and then bit one of them's thumb almost clear off. Then crippled old John Karseen helped me, beat 'em off with his crutch and untied me." Mag held up her shotgun. "That's when I went home for my best friend."

"I'm here to help with cooking," Sally said.

"You any good at it?"

Raymond stood and brushed the dust off his pants. "After Major Ellis ate her spoon bread, he said he'd marry her if he didn't already have a wife."

Mag waved toward the tent. "You stay near me, good lady."

Sally turned to me. "If we get separated, Jem, we meet back here, same time tomorrow?"

Mag Palm leaned down and peered at my face good. "That's the prettiest boy I ever seen."

Sally Smith paid her no mind and led me off away from the others.

"You just stay back near the major, you hear? Somebody's got to get back and help your ma and Patience."

"What if you're not here when I come back?" I asked, my voice all quavery.

"If we lose each other, you remember, life goes on without me."

"No, Sally."

"Don't you cry now. You're smart and strong. You'll be fine."

She hugged me, neither one of us letting go for a good long while, and then looked me in the eye. "Remember, you may not be of my body, but you are of my heart."

Sally set off for the cook's tent with her new friend.

As they went off into the dark, I stepped back to Raymond.

He looked up toward the dark ridge. "Let's climb us a hill. But first, better kiss this ground, make sure we come back."

TOOK US A GOOD while to walk almost to the top of Cemetery Ridge, and once the sun rose up there it was hot. We camped behind a stone wall, a good strong one some farmers had built. Below us, the hill sloped down, steep and rocky, with our black cannons down there, soldiers gathered around them, just a whiff of death in the steamy air.

Far off, the sound of thunder echoed back.

Raymond turned his head toward it. "That's the sound of battle, Jem, my boy. Won't be long now. Soon Rebs'll be all over this hill like tomtits on a round a beef."

We waited behind the wall, sun blazing hotter still, and he stabbed the sharp end of his gun in the ground and draped his blanket over it and the wall to keep the sun off. The smell of coffee from somewhere rode over on a hot little breeze and made my stomach ache.

The thunder from afar returned, this time louder, and a chill ran through me.

Raymond squinted in my direction. "If you're too chicken for this, better tell the major."

"Not chicken, I'm just not the best luck for folks. Most everybody's died that I've been acquainted with for long."

Raymond shrugged. "I don't go in much for magical thinking, luck and such. Way I see it, you do your best and then die when it's your time. Eat your hardtack."

"It's wormy."

"You sad about something? That can dull an appetite."

"My pa got killed last year. Still sits right here on me."

"It's hard on a boy to lose his pap. But grief's a curious thing. It'll kill you sure as the grippe. Take it one day at a time."

We listened to the buzz of the cicadas.

"I just want to stay alive to see Sally Smith again. And my ma and sister."

"Only got my ma back in Connecticut. She's pretty much blind now, but she didn't say one word against me signing up. I'd like to stay alive to eat some more of Sally Smith's spoon bread. Flapjacks, too. And find a nice girl to settle with. In just that order."

I pulled a piece of hay and chewed the sweet end. "Seems to me, soldiering is mostly waiting around."

"Until it's not and then you've never seen such a thing. When it's time, an officer back behind us'll command us to fire. And once it gets going around here, you stay back near Major Ellis."

"He told me the bugler'll sound his orders. Said it's too loud here for the drum. I learned ten drumbeats for nothing. He said I should work the ambulance."

"I call it the dead cart. Just takes a dying man to a place where he will die slower."

"Better than left here."

He shrugged. "Guess so." He pointed just uphill from us in the trees. "See that wagon with the stretchers on each side? That's the ambulance. Just stay low if you head up there."

A dark thing flew fast through the air above, the shadow passing over us, and landed uphill with a big boom and shook the earth.

Every piece of me turned to jelly. "What was that?"

Raymond knelt and yanked his gun from the earth. "You git back to Major Ellis, *now*. That was cannon fire and just the start."

All around us came the sounds of locks clicking as each man raised the hammer on his rifle, and the scrape of metal on stone as they set their rifles on the stone wall and aimed downhill.

Another bomb dropped in the woods nearby, which splintered trees and sent the smell of pine and gunpowder to us on the breeze.

I could barely move, heart pumping so hard, back stuck up against the cool stones of the wall.

Then came another boom, and another—they came slow like raindrops at the beginning of a storm and then faster, some bursting right over us, some hitting the ground and spraying dirt into the air, raining down. Soon they came so fast all you heard was one long roar as the booming earth opened with great sprays of dirt thudding down. A bomb fell just below us, and a man's rifle and knapsack, along with his arm, went flying up in a fountain of dirt and grass.

A shell exploded the ammunition wagon behind us, sending up a wall of black smoke tall as the trees, gunpowder floating down on us, fine as talc. The earth trembled as our cannon just below sent shots back, the men cheering sometimes when they hit a target, all the while so much smoke clouding everything.

Soon the smoke lifted and a quiet came over us all, for there down the hill was a sight to take the breath from anybody, Reb soldiers thick across the slope, their red flags waving overhead, marching up toward us holding their long swords bright in the sun. "There they are," Raymond said. "Here they come."

The Rebels came steady up the hill. "Hold your fire," an officer behind us called out.

My hands shook so bad I kept them in my armpits. "They're coming, Raymond. Why don't you shoot?"

"Gotta wait till they're close enough."

"Fire!" the officer behind us finally called out, and every cannon and musket went off at once.

Raymond and the other men along the wall pressed themselves against the stones, firing, and I covered my ears. I looked through a crack in the wall and saw the Rebels down the hill kept coming, falling one after another, the smell of gunpowder thick in the air.

Raymond reloaded quick while our blue troops near the trees knelt and fired. I peeked over the wall to see the Rebel line below us break apart as men fell on top of one another, piling up.

Raymond grabbed me by the arm. "Get *down*."

Just then I heard a whistling sound to my left.

"Jesus," Raymond said. He dropped next to me, his coat open, red seeping through his shirtfront. "My hat."

"I'll get it."

I searched all around him for it and then saw the brim of it up on top of the wall, snatched it quick, and tucked it into his shirt.

I put two hands under Ray's arms and pulled him along the stone wall, my head ducked, toward the ambulance. Shots whizzed overhead, some thunking into the tree trunks in the close-by woods. A runaway horse ran by, got hit, and fell kicking and crying, blood streaming from its chest so bad I could barely look. At the end of the wall I stopped, every part of me cold. Almost to the ambulance, an orderly waved for me to come on.

I stopped, afraid to come out from behind the wall.

"Come on, boy," the orderly called.

I held my breath and pulled Ray out into the open toward the ambulance.

The orderly hurried to us. "Almost there."

"He's Raymond Gleason. His ma—"

A hot rush hit my arm and knocked me clean over, face-down. I tasted grass and felt warm blood seep into the earth under my chest as the quiet closed in and I slid back slow into darkness.

Anne-May

※

I T RAINED THE DAY EUPHEMIA TOOK FERGUS TO SEE DR. WENTWORTH in Leonardtown, and Jubal arrived on horseback, soaked. I took his overcoat; his shirt was wet to his chest under his frock coat.

"No servants?" he asked.

"Only Sable's left and I had her busy herself in the kitchen so we can be alone."

"Have a big kitchen?"

"Good-sized. Not attached. Set off from the back of the house in case of fire."

He hurried to the front parlor window.

I wore my pink silk dress, the one Jubal once admired, and had perfumed the backs of my knees, and told Sable to set out Aunt Tandy Rose's Tiffany repoussé tea set, with hollyhocks and camellias covering every inch of the five pieces, the one good thing the old crab brought back from Paris.

I joined Jubal at the window and we looked out over the sloping lawn to the indigo blue river. "Well, what do you think of my little place?"

"I've never seen such a view up and down the Patuxent. Look, there's a U.S. Army ship."

"How can you tell?"

He took up Fergus's telescope and glassed the river. "That's Mr. Lincoln's *Thomas Freeborn,* sidewheel gunboat, part of the Potomac flotilla, flying the Stars and Stripes."

"What do Yankee boats want around here?"

"Six ships patrol the bay and rivers looking for smugglers. Cut Confederate telegraph wires when they can."

"Don't tell me *you* are smuggling, Jubal Smalls."

"A man has to keep his fingers in many pots these days, Anne-May." He shut the telescope with a clack. "If I bring Sheriff Whitman news of that Yankee boat, he'll be happy and that's good for our, well, arrangement. Whenever you're up here, keep an eye out for ships and tell me, won't you?"

"Don't see why not. Isn't it a nice view, Jubal?"

"Whole house is the prettiest on the river by far. I can see myself here someday."

"You mean you can see *us* here."

He turned to me and ran one finger down my cheek and continued down the front of my dress, sending a shiver down my arms. "Of course. With a whole passel of children."

"Boys or girls?"

He thought for a moment. "Equal number of each."

"Charlene Tidwell Weed says you asked at the sheriff's office about their tax situation. She was thinking you might be trying to buy Ambrosia out from under them like you did old Mr. Burns's farm."

He took my hand. "Yes, I'm in the market for properties. Sometimes that helps a family out if they're overdue on taxes. It's a service to those in need, really."

I thumbed his coat button. "We're up to date on ours. Fergus lives for paperwork."

"Of course you're current. But some folks aren't, and I offer them a mutually beneficial contract. Sheriff Whitman just helps me expedite the deals. I give him some information he needs to help our Southern troops, like what Jemma wrote in the red book, and he points me in the right direction on properties ready to foreclose, so I can help them."

"You're a good man, Jubal."

He slid a handwritten note from his trouser pocket. "I wrote you a poem."

I slid the fan from my sleeve and cooled myself. "I had no idea you were sentimental."

"Took me a week to get it right. It's called 'Love Never Dies.'" He read:

> "Love never dies—'tis as the sun
> That for boundless ages
> Ceaselessly its course has run
> Through earth's changing stages
> Firm, unchangeable, and true,
> Lives love on forever,
> And then time itself be through,
> Love shall waver never."

Jubal returned the page to his pocket and pressed the bridge of his nose between thumb and forefinger.

I touched his arm. "Don't cry, my darling."

Jubal stepped to the trophy on the side table. "Who's the dove hunter?"

"My father. We won that cup together. He's dead now."

"How'd he die?"

"I don't usually speak of it, but he and Mama, their darkies came after them in the night and he couldn't get to his gun in time. He helped Mama get away without injury, but they got him. I heard it all from my bedroom, too scared to come help."

Jubal took my hand. "He was a brave man."

"Once the marauders left, I crept to the bedroom and found him on the floor. They'd cut his throat, ear to ear, heathens. You should have seen the blood. Ruined a most precious Aubusson carpet. Mama and I had to roll it up and take it out ourselves since all ten of our servants left that night.

Took Mama's diamond brooch. Father'd always been good to them, too. Think it was Mama they wanted, to be honest."

"That's what our Confederate troops are fighting against, Anne-May, that kind of wanton butchery. But we need to find that book, Anne-May. Anyone finds out I've been supplying U.S. Army secrets to Sheriff Whitman, we could all hang."

"I *will* find it, Jubal. I'll tear this house apart."

"If you don't find it, you'll have to track Jemma down and force it out of her. Who'd Fergus sell them to?"

"A photographer in Hagerstown, along with his precious Sally Smith. That'd be my first stop."

"Thought they're your property. Why'd you let Fergus sell them?"

"You know what a wife's rights amount to around here."

"Surprised Fergus went through with it. He's always been soft on those coloreds."

"Cried like a child the day they left, but he accepted the cash money sure enough. Said all the bad things had started the night Joseph was strung up and how he'd have saved him if he'd been here."

"How'd he let old Sally go?"

"I told him she stole us blind. A little white lie to get her gone."

"And what if they've moved on from Hagerstown?"

"Jemma's friend wrote a New York address in a book with the name Woolsey, so I can check there."

"You'll need travel money. I'm afraid I have little to give."

"My ex-stepfather, Reggie Stickman, lives in Washington, so I could stay with him after Hagerstown. And then move on to New York City if need be."

"Reggie Stickman? Of Stickman Industries? He can provide funds."

"Yes. Only problem is, I've had some difficulties with him. Can be a little, well, handsy sometimes. Touches me in places that are not at all appropriate."

He pulled me to him, lifted my skirt, and caressed me between my legs. "Like this?"

"Oh, Jubal, please. I can't breathe."

He removed his hand and let my skirt fall. "You'll find that book."

I held on to the tea table and smiled my best. "Don't want anything to get in the way of you owning half of St. Mary's County."

"Why don't I just buy it all?" He took me in his arms. "And you'll be my queen."

My knees felt weak and thank goodness he was holding me or I would have fallen right there.

Jubal kissed me, long and deep.

"Let's go up to the bedroom," I said.

He smiled. "Or we could attempt things right here."

"Wicked man." I stepped out of my dress and unbuttoned the cage beneath, as he watched every move.

He stepped out of his trousers, still in his long, white flannel drawers, and stretched out on the sofa. "I like it here. Ever do this with Fergus here?"

I unlaced my corset and let it fall. "No. He's sleeping out in that tadpole shack of his mostly these days."

"What did he do to you?" he asked with a smile.

I lay next to him on the sofa. "Let's just say it was always over blessedly quick."

All at once a voice came from the entryway. "Anne-May?"

I sat bolt upright. "Don't come in here, Euphemia."

As she entered, Jubal propped himself up on one elbow.

"Anne-May—" She stopped short, took in the scene, and averted her eyes. "Dr. Wentworth was called away to a birth. I'll take Fergus down to his shack while you two get yourselves together."

THE NEXT MORNING, I tore the main house apart, hell-bent on finding Jemma's book. First I pulled out every drawer in my writing desk, then slit open the front parlor sofa cushions, sending goose feathers everywhere, and went to the kitchen and dumped out Sally Smith's drawers, ending up with a beaver dam of wooden spoons, tin cups, and silverware on the kitchen floor.

"What's all this, Anne-May?"

I turned to find Euphemia in the doorway. "If you must know, I'm looking for that crystal glass I take my water—"

"You're looking for that book."

"Don't see how it's any business of yours."

I grabbed a knife and moved on to the pantry, the shelves lined with boxes of cornstarch and cloth sacks of flour. I slit one sack and a cloud of flour poured onto the floor.

Euphemia followed. "I know you've been passing on Northern secrets to Jubal Smalls, Anne-May."

An ice pick of fear stuck me. "You been into Fergus's opium again?"

"How many times did you send Jemma to town with that book? Couldn't have been more obvious."

"Well, our brother was killed by Yankees and I happen to be avenging his death. If you loved him, you'd help me look for it."

"They hang traitors, you know."

I picked up each box and can in turn and searched its depths.

Euphemia came closer. "The whole sewing circle knows about you and Jubal—flaunting your love affair in front of his poor wife. She has a mind to take action, Anne-May. Get the sheriff involved. You might think about staying back home in New Orleans with Mother for a while."

"You might've noticed there's a war going on. May be dangerous to travel cross-country. Besides, I'd rather die."

I plucked an arrowroot can from the top shelf and pried off the top to find a neat sheaf of dollar bills nested inside. "Well, hell's bells, Euphemia. That sneaky Sally Smith."

"Her jelly money."

I pulled the bills from the can. "She stole us blind to make it, so this money is rightly mine." I slipped the bills into my skirt pocket. "And I know just how to use it."

I stepped into the dining room to Aunt Tandy Rose's picture, grasped it by the frame, lifted it off, and opened the safe. "May need to stay with Reggie up in Washington."

"Anne-May, no. After he abandoned us like he did?"

"I'd abandon Mama, too. And besides, when a person's stepfather owns most of Washington, they're nice to them. In case you haven't noticed, Euphemia, money's something we're lacking around here."

I pulled off my diamond ring, placed it in the safe, closed that up, and replaced the picture over it.

"Don't go up there, Anne-May. He swindled half of New Orleans out of their life savings and sued the other half. You'll travel alone?"

"Well, you won't come."

"You didn't ask me. But no, I need to stay here and take care of Fergus."

"Don't pretend you don't enjoy it, sister, rubbing that stump of his. Makes me queasy just thinkin' about it."

"Jeff Davis says the limping soldier should be treated as an aristocrat. As a Southern sympathizer, you should heed his words."

"And how should *I* be treated?"

"You've not been to battle, Anne-May."

"But I've lost everything just the same. Look at me, my hands all freckled. I'm a fright after Fergus had us in the fields. What man would look twice?"

"Reggie, that's who. He's the worst sort of trouble, sister. You should take Sable, and don't allow yourself to be alone with him."

"Sable would slit my throat in the night soon as look at me. But I won't stay long with Reggie. If I'm going to find that book, I need to pay Jemma a visit in Hagerstown."

"Just let it be, Anne-May. Jemma won't show that book to anyone. She's just as much to blame."

"Jubal wants it and I won't feel safe until it's in the fire. So I'll find her. You watch my cat? Joan likes you way better than me anyhow."

" 'Course I will. But what if Jemma and Sally've moved on from Hagerstown. Sold off? You willing to follow them wherever? There's a war goin' on."

"If they've moved on, gotta hunch I might know where to. The address Celeste wrote in that book. Eight Brevoort Place, New York City."

———

THE NEXT DAY, AS I prepared to leave on my trip, a letter came from Hagerstown, a curt one from the photographer's wife, replying to my inquiry, saying only that Jemma and Sally were no longer in residence there. So I had Sable pack up my valise, my new destination Washington, a stop on my way to New York.

I visited Ambrosia Plantation before I left, to see Jemma's sister, Patience, and have her write a letter to Jemma saying how much she missed her. Thought it might come in handy once I found Jemma, to get her back down to Peeler.

I wore my Stars and Bars bodice for the train ride to Washington and taunted Yankee soldiers at the train station there. They mostly just laughed and called back nasty insults about my walking unaccompanied and questioned my chastity. I did it for Harry, though my poor brother no doubt would've just smiled, smoothed one hand down my arm, and said, "Just let it go, Anne-May."

Washington was hot as blue blazes and the biting flies were out, and I held Jubal's hankie to my nose to keep out the Washington stench. I finally breathed once the coachman dropped me at the door of my stepfather's K Street home, a four-story blue stone monstrosity that took up most of the block. Carriages of every type lined the sidewalk in front. How strange to be entertaining in midsummer, when the season was usually fall and spring. The war had thrown everything into disarray.

Nighttime was descending and the lamplighters were out as I disembarked. From his perch above, the coachman threw down my leather valise, which landed in a street puddle, throwing up a splatter of mud onto my silk skirt.

The coachman whistled. "That's one fine place. Hotel?"

"Private residence," I said.

I pulled my valise out of the mud, lifted my skirt, and climbed the granite steps. The door was painted so shiny black I could see myself in it, and I admired my tiny waist and the flowerpot bonnet Jemma had made for me, with the French blue satin ribbons that matched my eyes.

I rang the bell and stood melting in the twilight haze, a lazy Union flag barely swaying over the entry.

The door opened to reveal a white manservant in a tight black coat. "May I help you?"

I nodded. "I am Anne-May Wilson Watson here to see my stepdaddy, Reginald Stickman."

"He is busy, miss. Come back tomorrow." He attempted to close the door and I swung my valise in to prevent it from closing.

"Then call his wife. Melody."

"It is Mr. Stickman's party, miss. Neither of them can be disturbed. Would you care to leave a message?"

"Here's my message. You tell her I will raise my voice to this fine neighborhood about the injustice of this if she does not come down here this minute."

The butler bowed. "Would you be so kind as to wait here?"

He closed the door as I slid a fan out of my sleeve, created my own breeze, and surveyed the neighborhood. As usual, Reggie dominated the best part of town, right on a fancy park. Stickman Industries had done well since he'd left Mama. Our own poor, dead daddy, quite a prosperous merchant, could never have rivaled this. Surely Fergus was wrong about Reggie losing all our money? The investments Reggie had made on Fergus's family's account had surely thrived?

The door opened and cool air met me as Melody stepped forward. "What do you want, Anne-May?"

Poor Melody had fallen from the ugly tree and hit every branch going down, her nose the size of a parsnip, which a center-part hairstyle only accentuated. But Melody's homeliness was something Reggie could overlook, seeing that her father owned the other half of Washington and he could seek handsome companionship elsewhere. Melody insisted on wearing dull pastel shades, which only accentuated her sallow skin, but cleverly eschewed simple cameos and the dainty, rosy-toned jewelry of the day. Twenty carats of dazzling diamonds at her throat guaranteed no one noticed her face.

I closed my fan and slid it back up my sleeve. "Well, that's a fine how-do-you-do, Melody."

She folded her hands at her waist. "You can't just present yourself at good people's doorsteps, Anne-May."

"I only need a place for one night. On my way to New York tomorrow."

She craned her neck and looked out the door, up and down the street. "Come in, then."

I followed Melody, a symphony in mauve, through the cool hall and across an acre of parquet flooring. We passed drawing rooms furnished in white and gold, upholstered with scarlet and blue satin, the curtains of fine lace. From behind the closed doors of the dining room came the sounds of glasses clinking and guests laughing.

At the back staircase she stopped and turned. "Every notable in Washington is here, save Lincoln himself. Senators. Reporters covering it all."

"It seems a six-million-dollar company amassed from war profits will win any man a great many friends."

Melody drew me close. "You're depending on the charity of that man right now, so watch your tongue, Anne-May. All the guest rooms are occupied on account of the party, but I suppose you could share with Bridget on the third floor. You'd have to wash up in the hallway."

"You're so good to me."

"Jackson will show you up there. I would appreciate it if you would take your supper upstairs in your room. And you will be gone by morning?"

I smiled. "Of course, Melody. I'd never dream of intruding."

I WAS SHOWN TO the servant's room, which featured one lumpy-looking bed and a cracked mirror above a washstand.

"Have a good sleep," Jackson said, and bowed his way out the door.

I set my valise on the bed, unpacked my things, and set to work. I had no intention of sleeping any time soon.

Georgy

I RUSHED BACK INTO THE TENT TO FIND MOTHER PUSHING PAST A line of orderlies carrying men on stretchers. Every part of me felt drained after seeing the young soldier I had thought was my brother, his face horribly mutilated. But the pocket watch in question was engraved with some other poor mother's son's initials.

Mother hurried to me.

"Oh, Georgy dear. Mr. Olmsted has left word. Seems there's been a most unfortunate mix-up. It turns out Charley was indeed wounded, but just a hand wound."

"His bad hand?"

"Yes, if it can be believed. A simple surface wound, and easily fixed. That letter from Mr. Olmsted asking if we were coming to Gettysburg was simply a question and we *assumed* our Charley's wound was severe."

Every part of me drooped with relief. "Mother, how foolish of us."

Mother leaned in closer. "But since then Charley has moved on with a new regiment, south. And now Olmsted has sent word again, inviting both of us to remain here and serve as nurses since the casualties are so numerous. With the help of Dr. Letterman, they are assembling a larger hospital across the road, up on the hill. We are to find lodging here for now and later in town. Can you even believe the strangeness of it all?"

I nodded, barely able to take in the relief that Charley was safe.

Mother linked her arm in mine. "Frank Bacon was in Washington when he heard about Charley and came as well. A guard is due soon to escort us to a tent for the night. They say we must try and sleep, since tomorrow the gates of hell are due to open once again."

THE NEXT MORNING, MOTHER and I woke at dawn to the sound of reveille and surveyed our new home. We quickly learned that the trains left our little cluster of white tents at the train depot twice daily, loaded with wounded soldiers headed for Northern hospitals. And every day, long lines of ambulances arrived bearing fresh wounded, often too late for the last train, with no army provision being made for them. Our job was to keep the poor souls overnight, feed and clothe and dose them with medicines, sweep out the cow dung when the next cars came, set down fresh straw, and board them safely off to the hospitals.

Guns boomed softly in the distance as Mother and I walked the twenty tents, arranged in rows adjacent to the makeshift train depot, an unassuming white shed next to the most basic of platforms. The smaller tents held the wounded men; in the bigger tents the surgeons lived and did emergency cutting.

Mother and I found the kitchen tent, complete with a temporary stove and cauldrons in which to make soup, the basis for each dinner, and its own set of men assigned to bread baking, soup making, the roasting of beef and vegetables.

We entered a larger tent at random, to find it jammed to suffocation, the smell of illness in the air, patients lying two or three to a cot. In the far corner, a group of wounded Rebel soldiers in their butternut-colored homespun uniforms sat on the straw-covered dirt floor.

Orderlies carried men in from the ambulances, where the injured sat atop corpses, too dazed to care, with chest and abdominal wounds, mangled and missing limbs, and every kind of horrific facial injury. It was often difficult to tell the ages of the patients, their faces blackened with gunpowder. In the tent, so many soiled newspapers, stale tobacco scraps, and dirty tin plates lay about, we didn't know where to begin.

Two doctors made their rounds, in their navy uniforms and gold-trimmed epaulets, choosing candidates for surgery with a hurried air, and I approached one from behind.

"Excuse me, Doctor. Frederick Olmsted has asked us to lend our services. I have nursed soldiers previously at—"

The man turned. "Let me guess. At the Patent Office Hospital in Washington. I've been following your career, such as it is, Miss Woolsey."

Whatever positivity I'd mustered that morning dissolved as I considered that hard face.

I stepped back. "Mother, please meet Dr. Compton. He sat on the board of physicians who examined the nursing candidates."

"Oh, the ministering angels just keep coming. Delighted to meet you, Mrs. Woolsey. I know your daughter quite well. She thought it smart to try and teach us doctors on the board some lessons about choosing the correct writing utensil for the application, I believe it was?"

Mother nodded. "Pleasure to meet you, Dr. Compton. It has been my experience that the people who can profit most from lessons seldom know they need them."

"As much as I would enjoy chatting, I have six hundred wounded men in my care alone. Make yourselves useful and see to this row of tents. Fill our nutritional orders, clean the sheets—"

"We know what to do, Doctor."

"Well then, hop to. Attend to the comforts of these poor wretches best you can. And remember, you may be called to the surgical tent at any time."

"Why are the men in the corner receiving no care?" I asked.

"Rebel prisoners," he said with a dismissive wave. "There's no time to tend Confederate troops."

"Certainly the rules of war render it necessary to give Rebel and Union soldiers equal consideration, Doctor?" I asked.

"We'll treat them after our own troops have all been attended. But most of them are too far gone anyway, like that one with the rotten leg. Advanced sepsis. Train your meager attentions on those that can be saved, Miss Woolsey. And confine your energies to your proper sphere of duties."

Dr. Compton rushed off.

"Welcome to the U.S. Army, Mother."

"Stay strong, my dear, and stick to your convictions. Because as Dr. Compton has so perfectly demonstrated, knowledge has no enemy but the ignorant."

MOTHER AND I REMOVED our bonnets and set to work. With men dying all around us, there was no time to even say a kind word as we were called from tent to tent, with urgent pleas for milk punch or ice chips, the latter of which the doctors refused us access to, saving them for their most serious cases.

Mother put great spirit into it, listened to all their stories, petted them, fed them, and distributed clothes, including handkerchiefs with cologne, and got herself called Mother. "This way, Mother." "Here's the bucket, Mother." "Isn't Mother a glorious woman?"

I made a pail of beef tea and ladled it out to waiting cups, while Mother headed to the Confederate troops, called an orderly to refresh their straw, and located some clean shirts and distributed them to the ragged Rebels.

She soon made fast friends with the young lieutenant whose wound Dr. Compton had referenced. The poor young man lay on the floor, his pant leg cut away, his leg horribly inflamed, the skin blue-black. Mother rested the back of her hand against his forehead.

"Bring me a cool towel, Georgy. He's terribly hot."

In appearance he seemed a mere boy, with a clear innocent face, bright blue eyes, and blond hair that any New England girl might have worn with pride.

"Henry Rauch, ma'am. Fourteenth South Carolina Volunteers. My father is a Lutheran pastor in South Carolina."

"And your mother?"

"Died when I was six. You sound a lot like her, though."

Mother patted his hand. "I was raised in Virginia, so perhaps I still have an accent. Can you take a little bite?"

Mother begged a pillow for him from an orderly.

I pulled Mother aside. "You mustn't dote on any one patient. And you heard the doctor. He cannot be helped. We must focus our attentions on those that can be saved."

"I appreciate the fact that you are an experienced nurse, Georgeanna, but I will do this my way." She returned to her patient.

"Thank you, ma'am," Henry repeated over and again. "That was a good supper. Would you read to me, if it isn't too much trouble? I know you have a lot of your own boys to tend to."

"You are all America's sons to me, Lieutenant Rauch. My own boy has gone off south of here to fight, and I would hope a Southern nurse would treat him fairly."

Mother helped me serve the dinner trays, and once our charges were well cared for and quiet, she returned to Henry's side at intervals to read him scenes from her personal volume of Emerson's *The Conduct of Life*. "'When there is something to be done, the world knows how to get it done.'"

"What did Emerson think of dying?" Henry asked.

"Well, he said, 'Do that which you fear to do and the fear will die.'"

Henry was quiet for a moment. "So, he meant don't fear death, just let it come?"

"I suppose."

Rain pattered the tent roof as Lieutenant Rauch slept and we made our rounds, serving the men their special diets prescribed by Dr. Compton, changing bandages, and providing our best comforts. But later that afternoon, Henry grew weaker and called out snatches of prayers one moment and military orders the next, the lessons of his childhood floating back upon him as he went deeper down in shadow.

Suddenly a Rebel soldier, arm bandaged, gray uniform splotched with rain, rushed into the tent and knelt by him.

"Henry," he said.

The man received no response and turned to Mother. "He's my older brother. I'm Jacob Rauch, ma'am, South Carolina Company B private, a prisoner in the next tent."

"Henry may not have much time left," Mother said. "Would you like to stay here with him?"

We laid fresh straw by Henry's side so that his brother could lie next to him, and Jacob remained there for the rest of the day. Toward night, Mother and I knelt near Henry, and she held his hand as he began to breathe his last.

Dr. Compton chose that unfortunate time to enter. "We need nurses in the operating tent." He waved Mother and me to him. "You two'll do as good as any."

Mother stood. "As you see, we are comforting a dying—"

Dr. Compton stepped to me. "An enemy soldier you're spending precious resources on, when U.S. Army soldiers are in need."

Mother drew herself up. "Dr. Compton. We will attend to your needs as soon as this good young man is properly cared for."

I stood and brushed the straw from my skirt. "I will assist, Doctor."

Dr. Compton rushed off and Mother turned back to Henry Rauch.

"I'm sorry, ma'am, to cause such trouble," Jacob said.

Mother smiled down at him. "The important thing is to say a proper goodbye to your brother. No doubt the great whirligig of time will someday bring its revenge to our Dr. Compton."

ONCE HENRY RAUCH DIED, we called for a coffin, laid his body upon it, and all night long the wounded brother lay close against that wooden box. Mother slept in snatches and tended every call for comfort through the evening and I assisted in the operating room much of the night, and reported back to the tent toward morning.

Neither of us had slept much as dawn approached and the cannons began to boom softly in the distance. The prisoners were called to march and the bereaved brother prepared to go away with his comrades, but first he came to Mother and me.

"Thank you for taking such good care of Henry." He pulled the palmetto ornament from his dead brother's cap and a button from his coat. "Don't have much, ma'am, but I want to show I appreciate the care."

Tears came to Mother's eyes as she accepted the tokens and held them to her breast as if they were emeralds. "I will write to your father and tell him Henry died a brave soldier. One of America's very finest."

AS THE GUNS BOOMED louder that morning our sick men stirred. Made of more enduring material than the rest of us, Mother operated perfectly well without sleep and sat on a box, under the shadow of a string of codfish, writing a note to Henry Rauch's father. I had just begun distributing bottles of corked milk punch to the waking men when Frank Bacon threw back the flap of our tent and entered.

He stepped through the cots, stopping here and there at a patient, with a good word or to loosen or right a strap or bandage. He then came to me, tall and serious, a small entourage in his wake.

As he approached it occurred to me how Mary had been so right as always—I had missed him, with his kind face and sharp eyes. He carried his black medical bag and wore a white shirt, open at the neck, sleeves rolled back to show tanned forearms. Even against that backdrop of suffering and death, he somehow brought a more optimistic feeling to it all. How had he found a way to remain clean-shaven in that terrible place?

I rushed to him and reached out. "How *very* glad I am to see you, Frank."

He took my hand briefly. "Good to see you as well. We've been working out at a field dressing station."

"I have so much to tell you. Since we last spoke I have had a great many thoughts about projects we might consider."

Nathan, whom we'd met in Washington, came to stand beside Frank.

"You remember Nathan?" Frank asked.

"Of course." I shook his hand with a cordial grasp. "Very happy to see you again."

Frank turned and gently led Bethada forward by the arm. She wore a claret-colored dress with lovely, open pagoda sleeves, the most costly to make, and a French teaspoon bonnet similar to one I'd admired in *Godey's Lady's Book*.

"And you remember Bethada?"

I nodded to her. "Of course."

Mother stepped to Frank. "Thank you for coming when you heard about Charley."

He turned to her. "Fortunately, I saw him before he left. He was delivering a message in the thick of it and received a surface wound to the wrist, but he'll be fine. Charley even remarked that he marveled upon his own immense talent to keep all injuries to that one hand."

Bethada wedged herself between Mother and Frank. "I helped as well. Several of the doctors commented upon my bandaging skill."

Frank busied himself with his medical bag. "The three of us are staying for a few days. Feels wrong to be on leave when all hell's breaking loose here."

Bethada pulled a hankie from her pocket and held it to her nose. "It all worked out splendidly; I was visiting Washington since it was Mother's birthday, so I didn't miss the party."

"We mustn't miss our cake," I said.

Mother sent me a warning look.

"Having trouble with the air, Miss Barnett?" I asked.

"Oh, no. Just a bit close in here."

Frank took Bethada's arm to steady her, and the new silver link bracelet at her wrist caught the light.

"We've been assigned this tent row," Frank said. "Expecting increased casualties today." Frank turned to Nathan. "We must set up an extra operating theater just outside."

Nathan stood straighter. "Already done, Doctor."

All at once the tent flap flew back and two orderlies hurried in bearing a man on a stretcher and Dr. Compton followed.

"Wounded from Cemetery Hill," an orderly called out. "Require immediate attention."

Frank checked the man, his face black with gunpowder and blood. "Prep him for surgery, Nathan."

More orderlies rushed in with stretchers and we transferred the wounded to the few free cots or straw beds on the floor.

Mother and I carried a young colored boy to a cot.

"Probably left on the field since yesterday," Frank said. "Who knows how long he's been unconscious. A drummer by the looks of the uniform. They get younger every time."

I ripped open the drummer's sleeve at the shoulder to expose a nasty wound. "Bad shoulder here."

Dr. Compton glanced over. "Tend white soldiers first."

"This boy will die without care," I said. "He has barely a pulse."

"Move *on*, Miss Woolsey."

Frank stepped to my side. "Compton, you take the head wound outside and I'll work here."

Dr. Compton rushed out and Mother and I prepped the boy for surgery. He was unconscious, mouth slightly agape, his closed eyes longlashed. How thin he was. I felt again for his pulse, and found it weaker still.

"We need to hurry, Frank."

Bethada stepped to the boy's side. "Perhaps Dr. Compton has a point. The soldiers should take precedence."

"You mean the white soldiers?" I asked. "This boy fought alongside the rest and deserves to live as much as any of them."

"Clear the area," Frank said. "We shall operate here. Get those dirty clothes off him. If he wakes, Bethada, you administer chloroform. Mrs. Woolsey, you keep his pulse, and Georgy, would you assist?"

"But—" Bethada started to protest.

"Of course, Frank," I said.

Nathan carried in two buckets of soapy water with which to clean the instruments in the surgical kit, as Frank had been taught to do in the French hospitals.

Frank grabbed one bucket and set it on the table. "Would you help me wash up, Georgy?"

As Nathan set up a second table on which to operate and toted in Frank's medicine pannier, a wooden box filled with bottled remedies of every type, we washed our hands and I set out a fresh towel upon which we arranged the clean blades, bullet removers, and tourniquets.

I pulled a pair of bandage scissors from Frank's bag. "Quickly, Mother, help me cut off the boy's pants."

She held the cloth tight as I cut, scissoring along the inseam. Soon the linen trousers and woolen undershorts fell away and Mother and I exchanged glances, our eyes wide.

She yanked the shawl from her shoulders and arranged it over the drummer's lower half.

I turned to Frank. "Dr. Bacon, I'm afraid the drummer boy is a drummer girl."

CHAPTER 32

Jemma

※

GETTYSBURG, PENNSYLVANIA

JULY 1863

I WOKE TO SO MUCH NOISE AND YELLING, I THOUGHT I WAS ON the battlefield still. My head hurt as I looked around the tent, men dying all around me, some quieter than others in their last moments, some crying or praying. Soldiers rushed in shouting directions, coming and going with dead and alive on stretchers. The man in the bed next to me sang church songs, loud like a preacher on Sunday, and then gurgled in mid-psalm and they took him away and brought a quiet one in his place.

As the cannons boomed far off I tried to sit up and a stab shot through my shoulder. They'd cut my sleeve off and bandaged my upper arm up stiff. If Sally'd been there, she'd have gotten me pokeweed to put on it and opium lettuce for the hurt.

Raymond. Had he come here, too?

I looked to my left, saw a dead man, eyes and mouth wide open, the flies having a party on him. Across from me was a soldier, his whole bottom leg gone—like Mister Watson's.

The mattress was soft, and even with all the noise in there I slept some more and woke to find a gray-haired white lady standing over me, giving me a fright.

She set one warm hand on mine. "What is your name, dear?"

I jerked my hand away as a jumble of worries ran through me. They'd cut the sleeve off my U.S. Army–issued shirt. Would I be hauled out for it? Would they tell the old photographer and his wife to come and get me? Anne-May? I just stayed mum.

Another lady joined us, younger, with dark hair pulled back and worn in a net.

"You've been shot in the upper arm," she said. "A serious wound, which required an operation to save the shoulder, performed by Dr. Bacon."

I smiled at that, a doctor named after pig parts, and she must've taken that as a yes to food, for she set a metal tray next to me and a tin cup with what smelled like beef soup. I turned my head.

"Not ready for food yet?" the older lady said.

The younger one set herself down on a grocer's crate next to me. "You've no cause for worry. We know your secret and it's safe with us."

Which secret? Had at least three, last time I counted.

The older lady brought another grocer's crate and set down next to the first. She leaned in closer and I caught the scent of talcum powder like Aunt Tandy Rose used to wear.

She spoke soft like someone keeping a secret. "You are a very brave girl to go into battle."

They both stared at me, hands clasped in their laps.

I looked up at the white tent ceiling.

The older lady leaned in toward me. "My name is Mrs. Charles Woolsey. Does that name mean anything to you?"

I shook my head.

She stared me down good. "Eight Brevoort Place?"

My eyes filled with water, just thinking about Celeste. "The card."

Mrs. Woolsey came and sat on the side of my bed. "My daughter Georgeanna here and I are nurses, obligated to catalog a soldier's possessions. That is how we found the card in your possession. May I ask how you came to own it?"

"My friend."

"She gave it to you?"

I nodded. "Name was Celeste. Sukey before that."

Mrs. Woolsey sat up straight as a board and looked at Georgeanna. "The girl sold in Charleston. God does work in mysterious ways."

"I didn't *steal* it. Celeste said a lady gave it to her ma. Told her she'd have a friend in New York City if she ever got there."

"Of course," Georgeanna said. "We believe you. It's just so extraordinary to see Mother's card here with you. Hard not to believe we were destined to meet."

"It was Celeste's prize possession, but she gave it to me before she died."

"Pardon the intrusion, but how did she die?" Georgeanna asked.

"LeBaron Caruthers. He killed her."

"And who is that?"

"Overseer at Peeler Plantation."

"And your name?"

I looked away.

Mrs. Woolsey covered my hand with hers, warm and soft. "You are safe with us, dear."

"Jemma, missis."

"Jemma what?"

"Just Jemma. Owned by Miss Anne-May Wilson Watson of Peeler Plantation, near Hollywood, Maryland."

"So you've been freed?"

"No, ma'am. Mister Watson sold me to Mr. Swift of Hagerstown, Maryland."

"And how are you here?"

"Got conscripted to the U.S. Army by Major Ellis of the Fourteenth Connecticut."

Mrs. Woolsey looked about to cry. "You have been through tremendous hardship."

"Came here with my grandma Sally Smith, not my blood but might as well be. Left her back at camp before we went up that hill. I need to go back and fetch her."

Georgeanna lifted my bandage and peeped under. "You are beginning to heal nicely, the benefit of youth, perhaps, but you must rest. Soon you may go and find your Sally Smith. We will send a messenger to try to find her, but for now you must rest and eat something."

Georgeanna brought me a new tray, with a soft yellow napkin and a china bowl of chicken soup, which she fed me from, each bite better than the last, and some white bread buttered on both sides, with jelly on it.

I fell back asleep and dreamed of Ma and my sister, Patience, swimming through a river with me toward Sally on the other side, her two big arms stretched out to me.

ONCE I WOKE, AFTER a while I made myself a sling from two yellow napkins and got out of bed. Mrs. Woolsey and Georgeanna fussed at me, trying to make me rest, but there was much to be done, with soldiers lying on the straw calling out for water, and I figured they could use my bed. And I wanted to go see Sally Smith and figured making myself useful was the best way to get to do that.

Miss Georgeanna came to me holding a man's shirt and a white apron folded into a nice little square. "Here is a clean shirt and the smallest apron I could find and new trousers. I am still searching for shoes your size. Let me help you change."

She reached to unbutton my shirt, but I pulled away. "No."

Miss Georgeanna smiled. "You're modest, of course. We'll hold up a sheet for you, Jemma."

She and her mother held up a big white sheet around my cot and I unbuttoned my one-armed shirt and folded it on the cot and slipped on the clean shirt, so big it slid off my shoulder if I wasn't careful. It was soft against the lashes Mrs. Swift last gave me, still tender. Then I stepped into the trousers and tied on the apron over it all.

I grabbed an oak bucket with my good hand and went to Miss Georgeanna. "I can get water."

"Only if you don't tax yourself."

A tall man about my color walked up to us, maybe five years older than me. He wore a blue uniform with bright buttons down the front like all the soldiers. Hard to see his face full on since he looked down his nose at me, but he had the prettiest eyes I'd seen on any man, colored or white, green as fall sassafras. I stared at him, trying to remember where I'd seen those eyes before.

"This is Nathan," Miss Georgeanna said to me, and then turned to him. "Would you mind escorting our Jemma to the spring?"

He barely looked at me. "Of course," he said, and set off, me following him.

"Come straight back," Georgeanna called after us. "They say there are still sharpshooters about, Rebel soldiers in the woods."

"Yes, Miss Georgeanna," I called back.

We left the tent and I breathed in the fresh air, a good change from that smelly tent. Our tent was bigger than the rest, and I looked back behind the train tracks, where so many of the smaller ones were lined up in rows.

Nathan walked away from the tracks and pointed to the edge of the woods. "Spring's over there."

I followed him through the tall grass, the wooden bucket bumping my hip, the knee-high grass thick with wild plants and flowers, butterflies going about from one to the next. What a pretty place, if not for the cries of dying men and the smell of sick in the breeze.

I looked back toward the little town in the distance, shimmering in the heat, the white steeple still standing, and hoped Sally Smith was waiting for me over that way.

"Seems like they need a bigger hospital," I said as we walked.

"Dr. Bacon says they're making one across the road there, eighty acres' worth of hospital on Wolf Farm. Saying it'll be called Camp Letterman after Dr. Letterman. He runs the show here."

I swatted away a bumblebee. "Eighty acres isn't that much. Plantation I came up on, Peeler, had ninety."

He turned and walked backward. "Peeler? I lived in Hollywood. Dr. Gardener's apprentice."

I stopped short. "You're one of those that got freed when he died?"

So that's where I knew Nathan from, seen him in church now and then, long ago.

He stopped and looked at me full on for the first time, then shrugged and kept walking. "Don't remember you."

I bent to pick a stem of pokeweed. "Me neither."

"Only lived there two years."

We walked on, sun beating down, and I stopped now and then to pick plants that might help the patients. I gathered herbs and spiny purple burdock flowers in a bouquet. Bright green Devil's Dung. Opium lettuce.

Nathan forged ahead. "Can you hurry up? I'm due in surgery soon."

"You a doctor?"

"Practically. I'm Dr. Bacon's assistant."

"Guess you're pretty smart."

He took a root beer barrel from his pocket and ate it right from the wrapper. I caught a whiff of that sassafras on the wind and it made my stomach growl.

"Smart enough to know you should stop letting those white ladies boss you."

I stood up straighter. "What do you know about it?"

"The Woolseys are good people, but you need to be careful. I hear them telling you look out for this and that, calling you '*our* Jemma.' Pretty soon, telling you to empty their slop jars and you might as well be picking cotton. They're all righteous about ending slavery but their pa made his money in sugar, I heard someone say to Dr. Bacon. That's what they call a hypocrite and you should watch out for it."

I bent and pulled a whole peppermint plant up by the roots, held it to my nose, and breathed in the peppery-fresh scent. "Easy for you to judge. You're free. Mister Watson sold me off from my ma to an old coot that took pictures of dead people, though I wasn't Mister Watson's to sell, so I guess I'm still Miss Anne-May's."

"Doesn't mean you can't have opinions. You ever in a bad temper or sad? You'd never know it, face plain as a board."

"Guess Anne-May wasn't big on anyone but her having opinions."

"Don't remember her."

"She came after you left, I suppose."

We stopped at the edge of the woods, next to a silver pipe, red pump head screwed on top.

"I'm saving up to finish school," Nathan said. "In Brooklyn. The African Free School in Williamsburg."

"That near New York City?"

"Just across the river. Gotta take a boat."

"Always wanted to go to New York. What's it like? There's no slaves, right? So is everything brokendown and decrepit, nobody to tend to things?"

Nathan smiled a rare smile, his teeth so pretty. "Why would you think that? New York City's handsomer than any city I've seen. Fine buildings. Shops and museums. You should see the school where I learn botany."

"Never heard of botany."

"Study of plants. Want to work the earth someday."

Nathan pumped, and clean water gushed out.

I knelt and stuck my bucket under the stream. "Once I'm free, I want to make hats."

He knelt next to me. "It all starts with you acting free. No more 'No, suh' or 'missis.' Speak up. Otherwise you're just another stupid slave who can't think for herself."

"Here's what I think." I cupped my hand, held it under the pump, then dumped the cool water down the back of his shirt.

He stood and laughed and dipped his hand in the water and pulled my shirt out and dumped water down my back. Then all of a sudden he stepped away like he seen the devil himself.

"What is it?" I asked.

"You know what."

I gathered the neck of my shirt. "You never seen a girl's back before?"

" 'Course I have. But not bad as that."

"Suppose Dr. Gardener never whipped you all."

"No, he did not."

I shrugged, giving me pain in my lashes and shoulder. I tore off a piece of the opium lettuce and put it under my tongue, silky sweet. "It's just the way it is. They killed my pa, too."

I started back to the lodge.

Nathan followed. "Here, let me carry that," he said as he took the bucket from me. "Why are you so accepting of that, Jemma? That's a sin what's been done to you."

"And what am I gonna do?"

"Have a say, that's what. Half of New York still favors slavery. Show the world what it's really like. I have a friend at a newspaper."

"I'm all out of angry, Nathan. I just want to get my ma and my sister and go somewhere we can have something to look forward to. A wage-paying job maybe."

"Would help others if you spoke up."

I started back down the hill. "Leave me be, Nathan, would you? Just let me disappear."

Anne-May

I FOUND MELODY'S BEDROOM, SURE TO BE HERS FOR THE LIBERAL use of pinks and mauves on the papered walls and velvet sofa. It was as far from Reggie's as possible, no doubt at his request, in order to accommodate his current lady-of-the-hour in his own chambers.

I passed the canopy bed, with its peach silk ruffled header, and holding back from stretching out onto the satin-covered featherbed, stepped to the armoire and opened it to find umpteen dresses, all with the label of *Willian,* the most elegant fashion house on Pennsylvania Avenue.

I chose Melody's cream silk dress and matched it with my own lace cuffs, which I washed in the hallway servant sink and dried outside the garret window. Melody was thicker in the middle than I, but a brown velvet band at my waist improved the dress greatly. It was not easy preparing my toilette in a servant's room, but with Bridget's help, I managed to curl my hair into two pretty banana curls to frame my face.

The party was in full swing by suppertime and all the first-floor rooms were filled with black-jacketed men and ladies in dresses, each one more lovely than the last, and I became distracted as every Paris fashion went by, emerald-green orchids on white silk, ruby roses on a cream field. I passed through conversations, mostly giddy war talk of the U.S. Army's victories at Gettysburg. But nothing could dull my elation at being in that throng of fine guests as I squeezed through the crowd, silks and velvets brushing my skin, inhaling the heady air of perfumed men and women.

I found Reggie near the hearth, surrounded by a horseshoe of handsome men and women hanging on his every word.

"And I have it on good authority old Reb General Lee miscalculated at Gettysburg," he said, waving a glass of claret. "Our boys sent Pickett packing at Cemetery Ridge."

A ruddy-faced man leaned in. "How do you know all the war news, Reggie?"

"The reporters call me first. They tell me Lincoln's practically been living in the telegraph office all through Gettysburg. They sent me a copy of his official statement on that battle even before the papers received it." Reggie pulled a paper from his vest pocket and read.

"The President announces to the country that news from the Army of the Potomac, up to ten P.M. of the third, is such as to cover that Army with the highest honor, to promise a great success to the cause of the Union, and to claim the condolence of all for the many gallant fallen."

"Finally a solid Union victory," a red-haired woman said. "Lincoln writes a flowery speech, but I hear he's hopping mad Lee's getting away so easy. We could've finished him off at Gettysburg and won the war right there."

Reggie smiled. "It'll happen." He leaned toward her and looked down the bosom of her dress. "Mark my words, that battle will change everything."

I joined the circle, pulled the décolletage of my own dress down, stood taller, and waited for Reggie's eye to fall upon me.

"Anne-May? Come here, darling. Aren't you just the jammiest bit of jam? Everyone, please meet my eldest stepdaughter. Pretty as all get-out, wouldn't you say?" He kissed my hand and allowed his lips to linger there too long.

I drew my hand away. "Good to see you, Reggie. I need a word, if I might."

"Of course you do, darlin'." He slipped one hand around my waist. "But first meet some folks. This here is the famous journalist Martin Davies. Writes for *The Washington Register.*"

I nodded. "Nice to meet you."

Reggie steered me toward the red-haired woman. "And the very wicked Mrs. Demorest, who invented the imperial dress elevator. You've heard of it?"

"Oh, yes. But never saw it."

Mrs. Demorest pulled a string at her waist and her hem lifted as if by magic.

"It is perfect for crossing over muddy streets," she said. "Your daddy has a drawerful of them I gave him—have him gift you one. Or if you are ever in New York City, come by my shop."

"I just might. And please tell me, where do the best people live?"

"Along Fifth Avenue, of course."

"Do you know Brevoort Place? I've heard it's *très charmant.*"

"Oh, it is indeed. The home of Hotel Brevoort. You will find many of the best families on that street. Lanfords. Carsons. Woolseys and Keplers."

"Woolseys, you say?"

"An *old* Boston family. Mayflower lineage."

"I'm fascinated with New England families, Boston bein' the cradle of our whole nation and all. Is it a large family?"

"Mrs. Charles Woolsey is the one living on Brevoort Place, a widow with seven daughters and one son. Staunch abolitionists. Won't even buy cloth made from slave-picked cotton."

"How admirable."

"Her brother-in-law Edward Woolsey is often here in Washington on trade business. Delightful man. With your avid interest in history, I'm sure he'd be pleased to share his family stories with you. Melody can make the introduction."

Reginald pulled me aside. "Come to my office, Anne-May."

"I was talking, Reggie. Besides, you shouldn't leave your guests."

He pulled me by the arm. "Just want to get you one of those dress elevators Mrs. Demorest told you about."

We stepped into his office and he shut the door, the thick carpet drowning out the sounds of the party. It was a large room, almost as big as the whole dining room and kitchen of Peeler Plantation, and paneled, walls and ceiling, in walnut, the one window shuttered. What went on upon that chaise lounge on the far wall?

"Reggie, could I trouble you for some snuff?"

"Since when don't you call me Daddy anymore?"

I admired the silver cups on the mantel. "Since you left Mama."

He stepped to his big desk and unlocked one drawer, pulled out a brown paper package, and handed it to me. "Open it."

I slid my hand under the paper. "Is this what you give your lady friends? How does Melody feel about that?"

"I actually bought these for her, since pink's her favorite color, but I'd like you to have them."

I lifted out a pair of impossibly smooth, pale pink bloomers, the hems edged in fine lace, open at the necessary area. My face burned at the sight. "How pretty. However, I cannot accept these, Reggie."

I handed the bloomers back, but he pushed them toward me. "You mean *Daddy*," he said.

I ran one finger along the lace. "It's been so long since I've had anything this pretty, though no one will see them."

He came to me and stroked the silk. "But I'll know they're there. I want you to wear them so I can think about them under your skirt."

I stepped away. "I need money, Reggie. An advance on Fergus's holdings you invested for him."

Reggie lit a cigar. "Oh, that's tied up in bonds."

"Can you not sell some?"

"Not now. It's all invested down South. Let's hope the war goes their way, though with the way things went at Gettysburg, you Watsons may be out of luck."

"But we need money, Reggie. Of course, you heard Harry died fighting for the South. And Fergus lost a leg in the same battle. And it's been hard keepin' up with our tobacco crop. Is there nothing to be done?"

Reggie smiled. "You put on those pretty pantalets for your old Reggie and we'll see what we can do."

I SLIPPED AWAY FROM the party around midnight, as the festivities reached a fever pitch. I went up to the third floor and picked up my valise, then returned to Melody's room, my silky pantalets brushing my thighs. I hurried to her vanity table and the silver jewelry casket, lifted its lid, which was fitted with a pastoral scene of troubadours and goats, and found its green velvet interior surprisingly sparse, holding only a few rings and a cheap bracelet. I pulled out a pink tourmaline and slipped it on one finger.

The door opened behind me and I turned. "Hello, Melody."

"It was just a matter of time before you'd be up here stealing, Anne-May. But this is a record. Pack your things immediately—*you*, with your stained teeth and dirty cuffs."

She handed me a folded stack of paper money. "I will give you this, but you must not come back again. I'll tell Reggie you were called home and had to leave at once."

I took the bills and tucked them into my pocket. "How much is here?"

"Two hundred dollars. Entirely too generous, but I advise you take it."

"That's a fair start. But you had better sit down, Melody. Things are about to change around here."

Georgy

GETTYSBURG, PENNSYLVANIA

JULY 1863

THAT NIGHT, THE SOUND OF THE BIG GUNS CEASED AND THE fighting stopped at Gettysburg. General Lee escaped back to Virginia and left one-third of his army dead or wounded and in our hands. The U.S. Army had achieved victory, but one could hardly call it winning.

Seven thousand soldiers, Union and Confederate, lay dead on the fields, and the grisly work of burying them began the next day. All of the buildings in and around the little town sheltered wounded men, and our tents became full to bursting with men experiencing the worst injuries one could imagine, many screaming in pain, even after taking the highest doses of opium, begging for relief we could not bring.

That morning, I took a hurried break and lifted the brass binoculars from the hook in the tent and surveyed the battlefield, the bodies strewn about, some dressed in Union blue, some in Confederate butternut and gray. I observed the dressing station set up under a tree, medics toting wounded there on stretchers, doctors administering remedies out of a medicine wagon, the back open and the little drawers and shelves filled with supplies. An ambulance waited nearby, the horse pawing the grass. I adjusted the focus to look beyond, to see the townspeople arranging the corpses along the sides of the roads to bury them.

Mother came to my side.

"May I read you the letter I wrote to Henry Rauch's father?"

"Of course," I said, and she began:

"Dear Sir,

"I address you at this time, fearing no word may ever yet have reached you in regard to the last hours of your son Henry— Lieutenant of the Fourteenth South Carolina Volunteers. It was the privilege for my daughter and self to be in Gettysburg during the terrible battle there early in July—the result of which battle has caused so much sorrow over our whole land. Amongst the hundreds of sick, wounded, and dying, who were at that time brought into the tents of the Sanitary Commission for care and such comforts as we could bestow, was this young lieutenant, your son.

"He was greatly exhausted, but was so revived during that first afternoon by nourishment and all care given him, we greatly hoped he would live. We attended him constantly and every thing was done for him that could be but a change came over him in the night and the next morning it was evident he was passing away.

"While Henry was lying in this condition, his brother arrived— also a prisoner wounded. I am sure it will comfort your hearts at home to know that although your son died in the hands of Union women he could not have had kinder attention amongst his own people. We were there as members of the Sanitary Commission, giving aid and comfort to our suffering soldiers, and when 'our enemies were brought to us hungry and thirsty and naked, we fed and clothed them and gave them drink.' You will feel comforted to know your son's remains were placed in a coffin and that he was buried with the church service and the grave marked by the headboard, on which was stated his name and rank. It will be a satisfaction to know you received this.

Jane Eliza Woolsey

"Do you think it will offer Reverend Rauch consolation?" Mother asked.

I nodded. What a paragon of comfort Mother was. Just days into our time there she had amassed a collection of gifts—cap emblems and jacket buttons—testaments to a talent I did not have—her ability to provide such loving consolation to dying and grateful men.

"I think he'll take comfort in it, Mother. Yes. How many more do you intend to write?"

"Every one of our fallen boys in this tent shall have one. North and South."

THAT NIGHT, AS EVERY night, beds were at a premium in and around Gettysburg, and we slept when we could. While Frank, Nathan, and Bethada stayed at her cousin's home, Mother and Jemma found beds at a farmhouse recently vacated by Confederate soldiers, offered to us by a generous local woman. I volunteered to take the lone bed at an elderly widow's boardinghouse, where nurses and visiting families looking for their husbands and sons found rest.

"Can I pay you?" I asked the widow.

"I should not like that sin on my soul when I die," she said. "Just don't bring men around at all hours. I'm a light sleeper."

I had just settled into my bed on the second floor in a room no more spacious than a broom closet, when an odd noise, a muffled bump, came at the window. I chalked it up to a confused bird, until the sound repeated. I went to the window and threw up the sash and hung myself out the window. There in the dark stood Dr. Compton, readying himself to throw again, arm cocked, holding a roll of bandages.

"Stop that immediately, Dr. Compton."

He raised one finger to his lips. "Quiet now. I have a message for you."

I hurried down the narrow stairs to find Dr. Compton in the side garden pulling up a white carnation plant by the root.

"You probably hate carnations," he said.

"You have men to attend to tomorrow."

He handed me the flower. "It is a symbol of fresh starts."

"It's time you left, Doctor."

"Do you even know my first name?"

I stood silent.

He stumbled a bit and almost fell.

"Come into the kitchen. You reek of whiskey."

"Not the medicinal stores, Nurse, I promise, cross my heart."

"I'll find you a cool drink, but then you must go. There are twenty people sleeping here and one very particular widow."

I sat him on a chair in the kitchen and found lemonade in the icebox.

"Leonard."

"Leonard who?"

"That's my name."

I smiled. "That's the last name I would have predicted. I saw you more as a Harold."

"As a vile bastard, you mean. That's a vile bastard name."

He rested his head in his hands and I knelt beside him and handed him his lemonade. "Drink this. You need to sober up and then get back to the camp. You have an early morning ahead."

"Where is your mother?"

"Staying with Jemma in town."

"She's a good woman, Mrs. Woolsey. The men esteem her greatly."

"She has quite a collection of soldiers' tokens of their gratitude."

"But not you. You barely touch the men. They say you only scrub their faces, and none too gently. Why is that, Georgeanna? You are quite a puzzle." He ran his fingers through his hair. "I marvel at you, really. You're everywhere, putting rights to wrongs. You spring from the ground to the floor of a freight car, in one hand a flask, in the other a can of beef tea, recording it all in your little book, to relay bad news to families."

Dr. Compton got a queer look on his face and lifted my hand and kissed it, his lips lingering there.

"You need to go, Dr. Compton."

He hung his head and cried. "I must tell you it is painful to look at you."

"And why is that?"

He shook his head. "No. I can't."

"It may help you to speak of it."

"My wife, Lucy . . ."

"What about her, Doctor?"

He brought his gaze to my face. "She was seventeen when she died. You could be her sister. Our daughter Bess followed her. Six months old. Lost myself in my work."

"I'm terribly sorry, Leonard," I said, and led him to the sofa in the parlor.

"Doesn't help that Dr. Bacon is always around so high and mighty. Challenging my competence."

I helped him sit down on the sofa. "Dr. Bacon has a tendency to do that."

"And a tendency to not keep his eyes off of you."

"Please, Dr. Compton. You must rest."

"It's true. Despite the lady assistant. It's you he esteems. And you obviously return that sentiment."

Dr. Compton rested his head on the sofa arm and I rolled my shawl and tucked it under his head. "Sleep now."

"You two are damned fools." He closed his eyes and drifted off. "A real love only comes once in a life."

I watched over him as he slept, poor man, as much in need of care as the patients. And considered his thoughts about Frank and me.

THE FOLLOWING DAY, THOUGH the battles ended, the wounded kept coming to our little lodge. Outside the surgical tent, the piles of arms and legs grew taller every day.

As we walked the wards, serving three shifts of hot meals prescribed by doctor's order daily, Jemma joined Mother and me so naturally. Her arm wound was healing well, thanks to Frank's good surgery and Mother feeding her like the favorite parson, with milk punches and custards.

Quiet but never silent, kind and gentle with the patients and always quick to help, Jemma somehow sensed our medical problems before we had them and invented ingenious solutions. She rarely spoke of her past, but would talk of her ma and sister every so often, and the idea of returning to Maryland to bring them north someday.

While sharing a farmhouse room with Jemma, Mother told me she found her sleeping at the end of her bed one morning, and when pressed, Jemma said she must have gone to rest there from habit, for she'd been made to sleep at the end of her mistress's bed in Maryland. Mother and I, although exceedingly nosy by nature, did not press Jemma for details, but grew terribly fond of her and hoped she would return with us to New York City when we left Gettysburg. Still so young, she needed assistance retrieving her mother and sister, and in the meantime required the companionship of energetic and well-meaning women, and that was one thing we had an overabundance of at Brevoort Place.

That afternoon Dr. Compton had only gruff words for all, perhaps feeling the previous night's drink, but I was determined to raise him from his funk as we filled out the meal requests.

I tucked his flower from the night before up my sleeve. "I will wear your carnation, Leonard, with simple affection and collegiality."

He smiled. "Kind of you, Georgy. Perhaps we can check the medication lists together this afternoon?"

Frank stepped into the tent, Nathan in his wake. "Dr. Compton, we need to go out to the dressing station and make sure savable men have not been left behind."

"You can't be serious, Bacon. We have more than we can handle here. And there're sharpshooters in the woods. They just caught one up on the ridge, a right good shot—might be deserters. Let the orderlies fetch the last of the wounded."

Dr. Compton hurried out of the tent and Frank came to me. "You've been assisting him in surgery. Bethada told me."

"Glad to know she's reporting on me."

"The flirtation. That carnation. All to spite me."

"Have you had enough sleep, Dr. Bacon?"

"You're doing it again. Calling me Dr. Bacon, while you call him Leonard."

"Have you completed your meal requests? The private with the wired jaw is refusing the milk punch. Says it reminds him of his ex-wife."

"You loathed Dr. Compton and now you're suddenly laughing like a simpleton at his put-ons. And checking medications together."

"I simply understand him better now, Frank. He's suffered terribly in his private affairs."

"A good storyteller, no doubt."

"Frank, I know our affections for each other have not always matched up. At Newport I was willing to reconsider our association, but you had already forged another relationship. And now here you are with your new *colleague*. Dr. Compton and I are simply good friends, but you cannot blame me for seeking companionship, when you have imported your own."

"Who is to say Bethada and I are not simply friends?"

"The love token. The way she clings to you."

"And so you seek that man's companionship to spite me? You barely know your own heart one day to the next. At least Bethada is constant."

Frank packed up his bag.

"Don't go off with a hot head, Frank."

"I'm going to do my job and make sure, if there is one more soldier alive out there, that he be saved."

"Wait, Frank. You heard Dr. Compton. Stay here until it's safer."

"Prepare my surgical tools in the operating tent. And when I return, if you're not too busy seeking companionship, I request you assist."

BETHADA JOINED JEMMA AND ME during afternoon rounds, somehow managing to slow our progress at every turn, making pronouncements like "This milk punch is sour," and when asked to retrieve a tray or cup, always taking the long way, a perfect snail.

The heat in the tents sent the men's wounds putrid and tempers short.

Jemma and I brought fresh water around in a bucket, and with extreme gentleness she applied cool compresses to the grateful men's foreheads.

With our rounds completed, I lifted the binoculars from the hook and stepped outside. I surveyed the woods upon the gentle rise above the camp, and finding no sign of sharpshooters, returned to the tent.

I dug through the reuse bin and found some boots I recognized as belonging to a young Georgia boy who'd died the day before. The soles were worn rag thin, but the boots seemed like perfectly serviceable temporary footwear so I offered them to Jemma. "They're close to your size."

She took them and hugged them to her chest. "Hate to benefit from another's bad luck, but happy to have them."

Once the heat sent most of our patients to blessed sleep, the afternoon wore on and I paced, waiting for Frank, as Bethada sat darning a sock, using her skirt as a worktable.

"Why did you not go with Dr. Bacon to the field?" I asked.

"He said it was too dangerous to accompany him. That's what I like the most about Frank. His considerate nature. But it's no wonder he esteems me. I do supply a certain ease to his rounds, producing the exact instrument he needs at the moment he needs it."

"What a gift you have, Bethada. Perhaps you should pursue a career in carnival fortune-telling."

Jemma smiled.

"You *are* funny, Georgy," Bethada said. "No wonder Frank admires you so. Don't look so surprised. He considers you like a beloved sister. He didn't have to tell me—I can tell people's slightest emotions. It's a gift."

Bethada held up her darning egg and examined the sock for holes, turning it this way and that, until it occurred to me she was calling attention to the silver bracelet at her wrist, from which a tiny silver coin dangled.

I stepped to her and slid two fingers under the coin. "Frank's token."

"Oh, this? He insisted I accept it. It means a great deal to him, for he considers such tokens true symbols of deep affection."

"Isn't that lovely?" I said.

"Would you care for a closer look? The engraving is well done."

Ignoring her, I again lifted the binoculars from the hook, and stepped out of the tent, over to the rise across the road from the camp. I kicked a stone onto the grass. *Why shouldn't Frank bestow his love token on whomever he pleases? I refused it, after all.*

I trained the glasses to the distance, past lines of ambulances choking the road toward us. I searched the battlefield until I found Frank and Nathan at the dressing station, seeing off an ambulance. I turned the ridged focus wheel on the glasses to bring the two men into sharp focus.

Jemma came and stood next to me. "What do you see?"

"Frank and Nathan at the dressing station. Looks like an ambulance just left them."

"How far is it?"

"At least half a mile."

I trained my gaze upon the nearby ridge, slowly panning the forest floor, alert for sharpshooters, searching down the row of hemlock and spruce.

"Just woods now," I said.

I moved my watch up into the trees and scanned along the row as before. A shiver went through me as my eye caught a movement, and I returned to that spot. I adjusted the focus and trained in on a young man, a boy almost, wearing a slouch hat common to the Confederates, sitting on the branch of a pine tree, back to the trunk, his rifle trained in the direction of the dressing station.

I reached one hand for Jemma. "In the tree."

A puff of gray smoke came from the boy's rifle and a few seconds later we heard a shot ring out and I turned the glasses again to the dressing station to find Frank standing over Nathan.

"God in heaven, Nathan's been shot," I said.

I dropped the glasses and Jemma and I started running toward the spot, along the road, across a field, and then to the battlefield, past piles of bodies and dead horses. Another shot rang out from the same area of the woods and the cavalry rode toward the puffs of smoke.

After what seemed like an eternity of running, we came to the dressing station to find Frank stretched out on the ground, atop a rubber blanket, his bloodied white shirt unbuttoned and splayed out. Nathan crouched over him, his own hand loosely bandaged, pressing a thick lint square to Frank's side.

A horrid chill went through me. "Frank!"

"What are you doing out here, Miss Woolsey?" Nathan asked.

I bent, short of breath. "I saw it happen. It was you they shot."

"Just grazed my hand. Same Reb got Dr. Bacon in the side. He's conscious. But thready pulse, cold extremities."

"Where is the ambulance?"

"Gone. Roads are clogged, anyway. We'll never make it back."

"My bag," Frank said.

His face was terribly gray, the color draining as I watched. Nathan removed the lint pad to display a nasty-looking entry wound, which he'd washed with iodine. He hurried toward Frank's bag.

I knelt and kept the lint pressed to the wound, just below his ribs. "Frank, you cannot leave me."

Seeing him there so helpless knocked something loose in me.

Frank looked up, his gaze unfocused. "Georgy. Good you came."

I smoothed his hair back from his forehead. "Of course I came, Frank. How can I help you?"

Frank closed his eyes.

"Stay with me, Frank." I rubbed his cheek. "You cannot sleep now, Frank. Listen to me."

Jemma took Frank's canteen, splashed her apron hem in water, and applied it to Frank's forehead.

He opened his eyes and looked up at me.

"Frank, darling, remember when we were so young and you fell out of that big elm at camp and you knocked yourself out cold? And I poured lemonade on your face to wake you and you grew so mad because your neck got so sticky and you drew ants?"

Frank managed a weak smile.

I checked the lint, now thick with blood. Every part of me grew cold. "What should I do, Frank? The blood . . ."

"Nathan says there's an exit wound," Frank said softly, trying to raise his head. "Ball passed right through. Thinks it nicked a rib, but not the lung, obviously." Frank set his head back, closed his eyes, and lay quiet for a long moment. "You must remove the bone fragments in the wound to prevent puncture of the lung and then continue to apply pressure."

"But, Frank—"

"Finish with a cross suture. You've seen this done one hundred times, Georgy."

"I would never forgive myself if I lost you this way. Perhaps we should wait for the bleeding to stop."

Nathan returned with Frank's black bag. "We must prepare the chloroform."

"His pupils are dilated," I said. "Should he take brandy first?"

"There's no time. I'd operate, but my hand's not useful."

"Where are the other assistant surgeons?" I asked.

"Left with the ambulance," Nathan said.

Frank nodded toward his bag. "Find the finger knife and probe the wound."

"No, Frank. You need some opium at least."

"Wipe it with brandy. And find the collodion syrup. Use the small retractor first and the plain artery forceps to extract the bone . . ."

With shaking hands I searched Frank's red-velvet-lined doctor's bag for the finger knife, inhaled sharply, and then probed the wound as gently as I could.

Frank cried out in pain. "Dear Jesus."

I sat back. "Please, Frank, I cannot hurt you this way. Take the opium."

Frank waved that idea away. "No. Please proceed."

I probed the wound once more, and Frank again cried out.

"Chloroform, Jemma," I said. "The white bottle. Fit the white cone over his nose and mouth and drip it in slowly. Just two drops at first."

Frank tried to grab Nathan's arm. "Use the silk thread, not the horse-hair."

Nathan knelt near Jemma as she administered the chloroform, removed the cone, and Frank sank into deep slumber. How young he looked in sleep, lips lightly parted; he seemed the boy I'd known at summer camp so long ago. How could I not live the rest of my life with him?

I worked swiftly and removed seven bone fragments and, with Nathan's help, stitched the wound with a cross suture and finished with collodion syrup. As we waited for another ambulance, I stitched Nathan's hand wound and then returned to Frank's side and monitored his labored breathing.

Frank woke and raised his gaze to mine. "Stay, my angel," he said, and sank back into blessed sleep.

I stood and felt for Frank's pulse. *Please,* I prayed. *I will ask for nothing else in my life if you let him see morning.*

Jemma

GETTYSBURG, PENNSYLVANIA
JULY 1863

THE DAY AFTER GEORGY SEWED UP DR. BACON, BY AFTERNOON rounds he was getting worse. Even with half the spiderwebs Nathan and I found in Gettysburg that we packed on that wound, Sally's favorite remedy, he lay there in the lodge tent gray as dirty snow, bad pain on his face now and then. He was too sick to be moved home on the transport trains, and it was hard to see such a nice man who did for others suffer like that. Much as I wanted to go back and see Sally Smith, I couldn't leave with Dr. Bacon so sick.

Dr. Compton came and looked at the wound, and said it was a good sign the pus was yellow, but anyone with two eyes could see Dr. Bacon was dying.

I went to Georgy, who was keeping watch at the bedside. Bethada was on Dr. Bacon's other side, sleeping sitting up, as most of us did, one fist under her chin.

"Miss Georgy, you haven't slept all night," I said.

I'd only seen a few women in love, like my ma and Delly, but it was plain as day on her face that Georgy had it bad when she looked at Dr. Bacon.

"Nor have you, Jemma. Can you find a pulse?" she asked, her eyes fixed on Dr. Bacon's face. "Just feel for his heartbeat with two fingers, like this." She touched him gentle on the side of his neck. "I've had no success finding one."

I pressed two fingers to the side of his neck. "Think I feel it. Weak, but it's there, ma'am. I hope you don't mind me suggesting we might try some old cures my folks in Maryland used."

Georgy looked up at me, purple smudges under her eyes. "He's far gone, I'm afraid, Jemma."

"Worked when my pa slit his arm cutting slats for a chair. Sally swore by burdock root. Devil's Dung, too."

She rubbed her eyes. "What kind of dung?"

I shrugged. "Just plants. Sally said we don't need doctor's medicine at all. The garden heals us. I put pokeweed on my own shoulder and you saw how quick that healed."

Bethada woke and sat up straighter. "Plants? Nonsense. Besides, what works for colored folk may not work for us. Dr. Compton will be—"

Georgy stood. "There's nothing further Dr. Compton can do for him, Bethada." She turned to me. "Jemma, can you go find some of those plants?"

I waved toward the pitcher on the check-in table. "Reckon they're all right there. Have any turpentine?"

"Turpentine?" Bethada asked.

Georgy stepped to the table. "If you took a nursing course, you'd know it has many uses. We can find some, certainly."

I fetched the pitcher and set it on the table next to Dr. Bacon. "Mix the juice of this green plant with turpentine and hang it in a cloth sack at his chest. Put a necklace of the foxglove and peppermint around his neck, and set some minced opium lettuce under his tongue for the pain. Then put wet pokeweed on the wound. That's Sally's best cure. Takes the poisons right out."

Bethada stood. "This is ridiculous and could right well kill him." She started off. "I will call Dr. Compton."

Georgy grabbed her arm and squeezed it good. "He's operating. Asked not to be disturbed."

"Your mother, then. Certainly she would see the foolish—"

"My mother's assisting him."

Bethada yanked herself away. "I will not stand by and see my future husband treated in such a reckless way."

"Feel free to take your leave, Bethada."

Miss Georgy turned to me. "If you prepare the foxglove and peppermint, Jemma, I'll fetch the turpentine. Let us get to work."

ONCE WE GOT DR. BACON fixed up, turpentine and Devil's Dung at his chest, a pretty ring of flowers and mint wrapped around his neck, I waited with Georgy. She had to fight off Bethada, but she watched him, all nervous, eyes on his face for any little sign.

It took some time, but when he finally woke and took a little more opium lettuce, I knew he was on his way to better, and I would soon be on my way to meet Sally.

I COULD BARELY SIT still up on the box of the wagon as one of the lodge drivers, a skinny man with a long, yellow beard that flew over his shoulder in the wind, gave me a ride by carriage close to where I last saw Sally. I wore a homespun shift Mrs. Woolsey found me, a nice change from trousers, for the breeze traveled up my skirt, nice and cool. The fighting had stopped by then, and the troops moved off like a carnival leaving town, but I still jumped at every little noise, on account of Dr. Bacon being shot by that sharpshooter.

As we passed fields of dead men, horse carcasses steaming in the sun, the driver held a handkerchief to his nose and handed me one, too, soaked with sweet peppermint oil.

"I'm going to see Sally Smith," I said, through the handkerchief, while he stayed mum. "My grandma. You should taste her cornbread kush. Once I meet up with her, we're going back down to Hollywood, Maryland, and get my ma and sister."

Far out in the field, we passed rough-looking sorts searching the bodies of the slain soldiers, even those who looked to be still living, stripping them of their boots and trinkets of value, while ignoring their pleas for help.

"Who's that out there?" I asked.

The driver waved one hand toward them. "Battlefield robbers. Been at it two days now, plundering. No respect for the dead."

The driver finally let me off, at the base of the mountain where Raymond and I went up, and seemed relieved he could have his quiet back. I stood in the dirt road, sun hot as a waffle iron on my head and back of my neck, cicadas buzzing loud. I shielded my eyes with one hand and looked up the hill, dead horses and soldiers all over that rise, like God just tossed them there.

It was a queer kind of quiet, no more cannons booming, just some children playing near the creek. I walked closer and saw it full with bloated dead horses and turned away. All around on the ground were soldiers' belongings, thickly strewn. Canteens, tin cartridge boxes, belt clasps. God's book, open and wet and fairly soiled.

Three men with green armbands tied around their sleeves wandered through the piles of bodies, crouching near one every now and then to check for life and say a prayer.

I found the place where we'd met Mag Palm a few days before, most of the tents gone except for hers, paper cartons and trash all over the field. She stood, packing up her pots and pans.

"Can I help with that?" I asked.

"Best you can with one arm."

We worked in silence, loading dishes and cups into grocer's crates, sweat trickling down my back and pooling under my sling.

Mag stopped her packing, ran the back of her hand cross her forehead, and squinted at me. "You been in these parts before?"

"Name's Jemma. Came through on our way up that hill back there. With Sally Smith."

"You the little drummer? I said you were a girl, didn't I? She told me about you."

My whole body quickened. "She's here still?"

"No. Long gone now. Told me you might be back, though."

Tears pricked my eyes. "She didn't wait?"

"Couldn't. Saw her chance to go and had to take it." Mag looked about. "Dangerous to hang around here."

I helped her load a crate onto the wagon. "Where'd she go?"

Mag stepped back, hands on her hips, a dark circle of sweat under each arm. "Can't tell you that, sorry."

"She's not my blood, but all I have in the world right now."

"Them that took her's good people, but got strict rules. Not that they tell me much. Less I know, the better." Mag climbed up on her cart and her mule just started up walking. "Hop up. You can come live with me."

"Can't. Got to go get my ma and sister."

"Don't go alone, though." Mag started humming a little song. "You take care now."

"There's no way I can see Sally?" I called after her.

Mag went off without even a wave back and I watched her go. All at once my arm hurt worse and every care in the world came down on me.

A piece down the road Mag stopped and turned in her seat and called back. "Hey, Jemma."

I raised one hand to shield my eyes from the sun. "What?"

"Sally told me you were her blood kin. Said she was your granny." She sat silent for a second. "Thought you'd like to know."

Mag slapped her mule with the reins and headed off as I stood in the road, the heat bearing down, missing Sally Smith so much, wished I'd die.

Anne-May

MELODY HELD ON TO THE POST OF HER CANOPY BED. "I WILL not sit down, and you put my ring back this instant or I will call Jackson."

I opened her armoire and considered the contents. "I wouldn't do that, Melody."

"What makes you so bold?"

"Something your dear husband gave me."

"Tell me this instant."

I stepped back to her. "Well, let me just say they are made of satin and lace and the private area is completely open to the elements."

Melody pressed two hands to her belly. "My husband would never. You are his former stepdaughter, for heaven's sake."

I moved to the jewelry casket and poked one finger through the remaining pieces. "I will, of course, need the key to your jewelry safe."

"You must be insane to suggest—"

"I met a wonderful journalist tonight. Wouldn't he love to spread this all over *The Washington Register*'s front page?" I lifted my skirt. "'Reginald Stickman Gifts Ex-Stepdaughter Wife's Naughty Knickers.' That's the kind of headline that sells newspapers, don't you think? I might even have him add 'And Watches with Great Interest as She Lifts Her Skirt and Slips Them On.'"

"You bought those yourself, you horrible girl."

I dropped my skirt. "Oh, no, Melody. Reggie said they were intended for you, purchased at your favorite shop right here in Washington. The salesperson even wrote you a sweet note on the sales check. They suggested you'd like them, with your love of pink and all. But Reggie gave them to me, generous man. Said he wanted to think about me wearing them. Once *that* gets out, who knows, you may need to sell some of these nice things."

"What do you want, Anne-May?"

"I want you to tell Reggie you've had a sudden change of heart, that you want me to stay here in this house as long as I like, and you'd like to give me this very room, since I deserve every comfort, on account of our sudden unfortunate change of circumstances on Peeler Plantation and all, and you will move out to a guest room. I want a reasonable allowance, an account at your dressmaker, and I want you to pretend you like me. And the first time I feel the least bit of chilly attitude, these pantalets will be the next morning's breakfast reading."

Melody moved toward the door. "One week."

I smiled. "We'll see about that."

Melody left the room and closed the door with a little slam.

I unpacked my valise, removed my skirt and shirtwaist, and stepped out of my hoop cage, leaving me in a corset and the pink pantalets. I poured a glass of port, set my New York City map on the bedside table, and reclined on the bed, descending into a cloud of feathers.

I sipped my port and unfolded the map. I squinted and then couldn't help smiling when I found it. Such a nice-sounding little street. Brevoort Place.

THE NEXT FEW DAYS were perfect. Each one included luncheon with my new friend, Chauncey Bainbridge, a client of Reggie's who was even richer than him, though twice as fat. I felt like the queen of Washington, for

Chauncey brought me surprises, like tiny leather boxes holding a gaudy sapphire ring or a seed pearl pin, often not to my liking, which I promptly pawned, using some of the proceeds to buy all the Golden-Banded Oco snuff I wanted.

Chauncy introduced me to Washington society. He never seemed to mind I was married and he didn't touch me in any amorous way, the perfect situation for me. It also kept Melody tied to our arrangement, though she clearly hated every second of it.

Melody came to see me one day, while I waited at a restaurant in the Ebbitt House hotel.

"I hope you've not been waiting for Chauncey too long, dear. He sends his deepest regrets."

"He's not coming? I've already ordered the lamb."

"Seems he won't be coming today, or any day, really."

I shrugged. "That's fine with me."

"You see, I saw his wife at tea yesterday. She'd heard from her maid that Chauncey'd been seen dining with a married woman."

"What's wrong with that? Half of Washington does it."

"Funny enough, that's what he said. His wife didn't object, really. Seemed quite happy another woman was putting up with old Chauncey."

"What was it, then, that spooked him?"

"Well, I felt obliged to share with her that *this* particular married woman is being investigated by federal detectives. Jackson tells me they were at the house again today, much more insistent they know your whereabouts, so I'm sure you understand I had to share that with Mrs. Bainbridge. The detectives mentioned the word *spying*. Know anything about that?"

My rack of lamb arrived, not that I could eat, my whole being shaken by the prospect of imminent incarceration. I waved Melody off.

She leaned down, her bonnet ribbon perilously close to my plate. "You can't hide in your armoire every day the law comes, dear Anne-May. Next time, I'll be there to tell them just where you are."

Georgy

GETTYSBURG, PENNSYLVANIA
JULY 1863

OR DAYS AFTER THE BATTLES ENDED, THE PARADE OF WOUNDED continued and the tents resounded with anguished cries as the men waited for the trains to Baltimore.

Just when we thought we'd witnessed the very worst, a new dear man would arrive on a stretcher, half his face shot away or his bowels exposed, trying his best to be stoic and not cry out. Chronic dysentery and diarrhea were the meanest killers, taking the most men by far.

Once the railroad bridge was repaired, Mother and I worked to establish a new Sanitary Commission lodge closer to town near the Gettysburg train depot. We lugged cauldrons and stoves to the new site on our breaks, but I stayed close to our original site, to make sure Frank was well bandaged. Bethada attached herself so barnacle-tight to him it was impossible to have a private word with him, but one morning he woke and I rushed to his side, hoping he'd remember our tender moments at the dressing station.

I took his hand with a smile. "I hope this puts an end to the idea that medical officers are not exposed to fire, Frank."

Frank averted his gaze. "Good to see you, Georgy." It was clear from his cool manner that whatever he'd felt at the dressing station had dissolved into thin air.

"Jemma saved your life, Frank. We were about to lose you when she suggested plant medicines and herbs."

"I'm immensely grateful and will tell her so. You helped as well. Thank you."

Frank held one end of his bandage taught while I rewrapped the other. "Frank, now that you are recovering, I thought I might introduce an idea to you—a project I'm considering, a rather large one."

Bethada smoothed Frank's bedcovers. "Dr. Bacon is too weak to be engaged in such conversation."

I looked deep into her eyes. "The bullet struck his abdomen, not his mouth."

Frank produced a gentle wave. "Please continue."

"With the severe shortage of good nurses, well-trained women of substance, I believe we need a school for nurses."

Frank tipped his head and studied me. "On what model?"

"I'd base it on Florence Nightingale's British school, and teach a version of Dr. Blackwell's curriculum, stressing the value of cleanliness, good diet, and ventilation."

"But you already see to all that."

"These nurses would learn not just to clean up after patients and see to their lunches and kowtow to doctors, but to *themselves* heal patients."

Bethada felt Frank's forehead. "Women do the healing? Only the doctors can do that, isn't that right, Frank?"

Frank pushed her hand away. "Clearly women heal as well as men do. But such a school would require considerable funds."

"Here is the good news, Frank. Mrs. Peabody of the New York Orphan Asylum gifted me a good sum to—"

Bethada waved me away from Frank's cot. "Dr. Bacon must sleep now. I don't need a nursing course to know the best way to revive a man."

"I'll not be shooed off by anyone, particularly the untrained."

Bethada pulled me by the arm, away from the bed. "You can stop trying to impress Frank with your talk of a school, Georgy. He's not taken in by it."

"Step away, Bethada."

"My aunt has written me that she feels Frank's health is suffering here and she has contacted his mother and told Mrs. Bacon her personal train car carrying her team of physicians is on the way to bring him back to his parents in New Haven. She's coming down to personally direct his relocation."

I glanced toward Frank's bed. "And has Frank been informed?"

"He is grateful for it, actually."

I stepped to Frank's side. "Is it true, Frank? You've consented to Mrs. Barnett's plan?"

He nodded. "She has arranged a surgical tutorial for Nathan in New York, and I'll heal and get back to work faster this way."

"You could at least ask them to allow Jemma along, back to New York. She won't say it, but I can tell she's still in pain. Working here won't alleviate that any time soon."

Bethada stepped back to Frank's bedside. "I'm sure Auntie would allow that. She can ride in the back car with Nathan."

I leaned down closer to Frank. "Mother and I could accompany you instead, Frank. You will owe Mrs. Barnett for this and she'll want big favors."

"No need to take pity on me, Georgy. I know all too well where your sentiments lie. If you would be so kind, just leave me be."

MOTHER, JEMMA, AND I shopped at the Fahnestock House mercantile, looking to purchase a few sundries for Jemma's trip and silk for a flag for our new medical lodge at the depot. The store's meager offerings were shown to the best advantage to make them seem robust, the notions case piled with spools of Carter's fine white, black, and red thread and Milward needles. Several silver thimbles were offered, each one prettier than the last: one edged in Greek key design, another growing sunflowers along the edge.

Mother bent to examine them. "Imagine, so many designs for something that helps one push a needle through cloth."

Jemma turned to me. "Must I go up to New York City with the others? I need to go back and get Ma and my sister."

I linked my arm in Jemma's. "We'll all figure out how to get them soon, but you must get *well* first, up in New York. We shall miss you terribly, you know. And you're so helpful to us here, but that's the point. You're working every day, delaying your full recovery. Plus, it's still dangerous here for you, with rogues snatching anyone of color and taking them south."

Mother came to us. "And we would like you to know that if you so desire, you may use our name as your own."

"No, I couldn't do that, Mrs. Woolsey."

"It would be a good idea for you to have a full legal name," I said. "We can instruct our lawyer to make it official."

"It's not that. I want my own name—of my own choosing. Not that I don't appreciate the offer. I'll just stay plain Jemma for now."

"You're smart to make the choice carefully," I said. "Your name will be with you forever."

"I want to ask my ma and my sister before I decide. They'll have opinions."

Soon Nathan appeared and spirited Jemma away, and Mother and I continued to the fabric counter and considered the bolts piled high on display. Our attention soon became drawn to the front of the shop and a familiar voice—unmistakable—that of Bethada's aunt, Mrs. Barnett.

"Have twenty of those brought to my train car. We are leaving tomorrow morning at ten sharp."

Mrs. Barnett swept toward us, a man following, notebook and pencil stub in hand.

She stopped near us. "Oh. Miss Woolsey."

"This is my mother, Mrs. Charles Woolsey."

Mother nodded.

"So you *are* taking Dr. Bacon back up to New Haven," I said.

Mrs. Barnett leaned closer to Mother. "That cotton is Barnett cotton," she said, pointing to the bolts on the counter. "Cannot find a finer hand. I'm happy to have the clerk cut you however many yards you'd like."

"We were considering the silk, Mrs. Barnett," Mother said. "We don't purchase the fruits of slavery."

"Oh, yes. Of course. I've read about you Woolseys. Doing good deeds, attending abolitionist lectures, and parading your Negro friends about. You're acquainted with the two that just left?"

Mother squared her shoulders. "We parade nothing, Mrs. Barnett. And if you will excuse us—"

Mrs. Barnett stepped back, eyes wide. "It's all just a charade, isn't it? To secure decent marriages for your daughters."

Mother laughed and stepped along.

Mrs. Barnett blocked our way. "Oh, let's be honest. All of this nursing and dealing with men is to get your daughters noticed. There are so few eligible prospects left after this terrible war, I can understand, but leave Dr. Bacon alone. He's told me he loves my niece quite dearly and intends to marry her—soon in fact. We're going to do great research together, world-changing, and he doesn't need you ladies cocking it up."

Mother drew herself up. "If and when my daughters marry is none of my concern. I shall encourage my children to love whom they choose."

"What would it cost me for you to cease all interaction with Dr. Bacon? To allow him to heal and focus on his work? You're a widow after all, you must have limited means."

Mother stepped closer to Mrs. Barnett. "You can use your money to buy doctors and train cars and even people, Mrs. Barnett, but you, madam, will never buy a Woolsey."

THE NEXT DAY, JUST as dawn broke, a grizzled army lieutenant delivered Mother and me by supply wagon to our new makeshift hospital for our first day of work there. Once the railroad bridge was fully repaired we'd set up our lodge at a first-rate camping ground with an unlimited supply of pure, cool water, in a large field directly across the tracks from the Italian-ate Gettysburg train depot. But as excited as I was to move in, I couldn't help thinking of Frank Bacon leaving that day, and planned on intercepting him, away from Bethada, to convince him Mother and I should accompany him home instead.

"Hear that?" Mother asked as we drew closer to the site and the sound of hammers pounding iron stakes met our ears. "That's the sound of progress," she said. "Our work will be immensely easier here closer to town."

I linked arms with her. "And with our very own kitchen tent."

I helped Mother down from the wagon and we toured the tents, wounded men already comfortably resting there.

We'd worked for days getting things in perfect order there, our barrels full of clean shirts and dressing gowns, socks and bandages lined up along the tent walls. In the kitchen tent we'd set up two stoves with four large boiling pots always kept full of soup and coffee, watched by four colored men who did the cooking and sang at the top of their voices all day.

Donations had arrived from every Union state. Abby sent us House of Industry cartons of soft shirts and clean sheets, and Canandaigua sent bottles of cologne, which went right to the noses and hearts of the men.

Mother and I prepared the breakfast trays.

"Don't you think it wise to keep Frank here for another week or so, to heal?" I asked. "We could accompany him back to New Haven, where his mother can resume care."

Mother set a tin cup on a tray. "You haven't always been so considerate of him, Georgeanna. I suppose it is Frank's decision."

"If I can wrench him from Bethada for one minute."

"You're entitled to present your idea, Georgeanna, but Frank seems to have made his choice."

Mother and I stepped around the tents, tipping the cologne bottles up on clean handkerchiefs and leaving each man with a last token. Mother approached a lieutenant from Vermont who'd lost both arms and gently held a hankie to his face. He breathed deep and smiled up at her. "That's worth a penny a sniff. And many thanks for writing home for me, Mother."

She tucked the handkerchief into the neck of his shirt. "I'm proud to have known you, son."

At the sound of the train pulling up to the station, Mother and I hurried out to see it come to rest at the end of the line, the engine above us, gleaming black in the sun, light bouncing off the silver cowcatcher. Three U.S. Army train cars stood hitched behind the engine, former cattle cars. Next came Mrs. Barnett's two personal train cars bringing up the rear, painted a gaudy emerald green, finely upholstered seats visible through the lace curtained windows.

Steam billowed from the engine's stack and she heaved the usual sighs trains do as they settle in, and we quickly swept the dung out of the cars, set down fresh straw, and helped the medics situate our patients there, easing them down onto their new beds.

Mother bent to a young soldier who'd lost a leg and offered her own handkerchief, which she'd scented with cologne. "Keep that to your nose, Private, and it should help with that manure smell."

He held it and breathed in. "That kinda gives one life. Many thanks, Mother."

We stepped down from the train car as an ambulance arrived, the horses kicking up a cloud of dust, the canvas flaps tied up. How good to see Jemma looking so rested and well, sitting next to the driver, arm suspended in her yellow sling. Though Jemma's trip north to recuperate would help her immeasurably, having her leave along with Frank felt like a doubly difficult loss.

Nathan and Bethada sat behind them, below in the wagon bed, flanking the recumbent Frank Bacon. As the ambulance neared the train, orderlies and Mrs. Barnett's phalanx of personal physicians came at a trot from the front Barnett train car to assist them.

"Georgy," Jemma called out. "Mrs. Woolsey."

I stepped to the ambulance and helped her down. "We shall miss you terribly, Jemma." I handed her an envelope. "In here you will find sufficient means to see you through until we return."

She waved it away. "Oh no, I can't take a handout. I'll find a paying job."

"You'll secure one soon but this will keep you until then. You will also find in the envelope the address of our friend Dr. Smith, director of the Colored Orphan Asylum, which houses over two hundred little ones. A true and brilliant gentleman. See him for the liniment prescribed by Dr. Bacon for your shoulder."

Jemma tucked the envelope in her pocket. "Can he give me a job?"

"He owns an apothecary and several other businesses, so all you need do is ask."

Mother took Jemma's hands in hers. "Beware pickpockets in New York, my dear. We've sent Margaret word—she takes care of things at Brevoort Place—and she will take you under her wing."

Mrs. Barnett, dressed in nurse's costume, appeared at the Barnett car door, and called to the orderlies. "Bring Dr. Bacon this way. Gently, now."

Orderlies lifted Frank by his stretcher down from the wagon and headed toward the train, Bethada close behind.

I stepped to him. "Frank—"

The orderlies halted and Bethada stepped between Frank and me. "We're late and have little time for goodbyes."

I drew myself taller and laced my fingers to prevent one hand from finding her face in the form of a slap. "I have a private matter to discuss with Dr. Bacon."

"What is it, Georgy?" Frank asked, and Bethada stood aside.

I stepped closer to Frank. "I propose you stay here and heal a week more at least and then Mother and I can see that you get home to New Haven."

Frank looked toward the train cars. "I wouldn't burden you with that, Georgy."

Mrs. Barnett called from her train car window. "Hurry, now."

I took Frank's hand. "You don't need to go with that woman, Frank."

He slid his hand from mine. "As you can imagine, my new role as patient is not one I relish, but I need to recover and get back to the fight. Mrs. Barnett has shown great consideration and kindness to me, Georgy."

"Are you saying I have not? I've tried, Frank. That day at the field hospital—"

"I'm tired of it all, Georgy. We need to go."

"You've stopped listening, Frank. It's as if you're wishing yourself dead."

"I might not make it to Connecticut, so I may get that wish."

The orderlies moved on, the stretcher between them.

"Please reconsider, Frank," I called after him, but he barely glanced back.

Bethada turned and shouted back to me from Frank's side. "There will be no need for any further concern on your part. These are the finest specialists in the country."

We helped Jemma up to join Nathan on the last train car and assisted the orderlies with our additional wounded. I then stood with Mother as the train moved backward out of the station.

Jemma waved to us from the window and our wounded men held up the handkerchiefs we'd gifted them, and called back "God bless you" to Mother and me.

How good it was to hear the joyful thanks of our men, washed, fed, and dressed, and on their way home. But hard as I tried, I couldn't shake the anger watching Mrs. Barnett steal Frank from us.

Mother and I waved to all, the heat of the day rising there on the platform. "Perhaps it's best Bethada and her aunt are leaving," she said. "I may have committed murder, and we *are* here to heal."

I linked my arm into hers. "Bethada has poisoned Frank against me. He refused to consider my plan to keep him here. He no longer esteems me at all."

"Seems you regret declining his proposals, Georgy, but he has every right to move on. He's not getting any younger and, as tactless and snobbish as I find her, in Bethada, Frank has clearly found a companion willing to pledge herself."

"But she—"

"Are you finding fault with her to cover your own stumbles? She's simply taken action when you have not."

"I'm sorry I mentioned it, Mother."

She pulled me closer. "But one thing is certain, my darling. With people like the Barnetts in this world, you may never find love if you wait for it to come to you."

Jemma

❋

NEW YORK CITY
JULY 1863

MRS. BARNETT ORDERED A CARRIAGE FOR NATHAN AND ME once they dropped us in New York City from the train. I kept picking up my bottom lip as we drove by all the sights, down streets so crowded we could barely move. I stuck my head out the carriage window like a turtle peeping its head out of its shell after a long winter, everything new, the colors so bright.

Nathan was right about the buildings being so trim and fixed up nice. There were tall ones everywhere and restaurants that fed people at outside tables along the road, since it was so hot inside, people eating and talking and fighting. There were folks of all shades, but mostly white, fanning themselves with paper fans, some with patriotic colors, like butterflies all over the crowds. Across the side roads folks'd strung so many Union flags it looked like red, white, and blue laundry day, them gently swaying in what little breeze there was. Signs hung everywhere. WALLACE AND REED BILLIARD ROOMS. VAN BUREN GENTS FURNISHINGS. The one for CHEAP BOOKS looked best to me. You've never seen so many kinds of carriages, from fine to broken down, people with things to do going every which way, the horses sometimes spooked by this or that rearing up.

Best thing was, it was all real. Patience wouldn't believe her eyes. Ma too.

"Look at that ambulance with the folks sitting on top," I said, and pointed out what looked like a smaller train car with stairs going up the back, folks sitting on top of it under umbrellas to shade the sun. Each one had a different name painted along the top. 6 CENTS 5TH AVENUE. CENTRAL PARK.

Nathan leaned toward me. "That is an omnibus, Jemma. Transportation for those who can't afford their own carriage. I thought the same when I saw my first one in the street, last year when I first came here. They're very similar."

"Never seen so many fine-looking people. Where do they all sleep at night?"

Nathan tried to hide his smile. "In tall buildings with apartments in them, rooms where they live and cook."

"What do they do? Hope I can get a job that pays."

"There's all kinds of jobs. Some have two and three sometimes. People come here to seek a fortune. There's something like one hundred and fifteen millionaires in residence in New York City."

I considered the folks dark as me in the crowds, some dressed pretty fine. "Are all the colored people free?"

He turned toward me. "New York freed their slaves in 1827. So most here are free. Except fugitives."

"Guess that's me."

Nathan looked out the carriage window. "Most colored folks here live west of Broadway. 'Course, this is nothing like where I live. Over in Brooklyn. Weeksville. More small-town. We have everything our own. Churches. Schools. You can be buried in any graveyard you want."

"Where's that from here?"

"Across the river. Need to take a boat to get there."

We passed a sky-high white building, BARNUM'S AMERICAN MUSEUM written across the top; red, white, and blue flags flying all over it; a big piece of cloth hanging from the roof, wafting in the breeze, with a picture of Ned the talking seal painted on it, his whiskers like broom straw. Along the sidewalk in front of it, ten or twelve white men walked together, some with clubs.

"And why are there so many people out looking for trouble?"

Nathan leaned past me and looked out my window. "Irish roughs. Stay clear of them. Look to be demonstrators. Papers say they've been having their say on streets north of here. Some Irish object to the new Conscription Act passed, made single men of age subject to a draft lottery."

"Never heard of a draft lottery."

"Up at the recruitment office they have what's called a draft wheel, a big wooden barrel with every eligible man's name in it. They roll it with a crank and pick out cards with names of citizens and force 'em to fight in the war for three years."

"Why're they upset?"

"Because as you've seen, the war's no walk in the park. Rich people can avoid fighting by paying someone to take their place or by paying three hundred dollars."

My shoulder started to ache something bad and I rubbed it through the sling. "So rich people don't fight?"

"Lots do if they sign up but they don't *have* to. And colored freedmen like me aren't citizens, so we can't be drafted. So the Irish think they alone'll be dying for the country. And some think freed slaves are taking their jobs, and hate us for it."

We passed a furniture shop. "My pa would've liked it here."

"Offer's still open to have my friend write that story 'bout your pa. Tell everyone. Out in Weeksville we got a paper called *Freedman's Torchlight*. We speak out about—"

We stopped out front of 8 Brevoort Place. "Glad we're here. I better get inside."

"You gotta talk about things sometime."

Nathan walked me up the steps to the door.

"And can you mail this for me?" I handed him the letter I'd written on the train. It was to Patience, in my favorite code:

My dearest Patience,

I am most interested now, not exactly when you offered, regarding keeping including wildflowers in lovely letters. Carnations or marigolds, even foxglove or roses, yonder overflowing, urge several others on nature.

> *With tender love,*
> *Your sunflower sister*

I had included in the folds of the letter a little orange felt sunflower I'd made at Gettysburg, with the center made from the perfect shade of brown wool Miss Georgy had given me, a scrap from her making undershorts for the men. Patience would know to read every first letter of each word to reveal my true intention of the letter and Anne-May, not the best reader, should she open it, would never suspect our game:

I am in New York. I will come for you soon.

"Happy to, for a price. First you must accept this." He took from his sleeve a brown paper package the size of my thumb and handed it to me.

"What's this?" I asked. I opened the paper to find a silver thimble, the one I'd fancied at the store, sunflowers running along the bottom.

He shrugged. "Thought you'd like it. Bought it at the mercantile."

All at once I got shy and stuffed the whole thing in my pocket.

"Thanks, Nathan," I said.

He twisted a key that made a bell sound. "Hurry and get in," he said, and started back down the steps.

The door opened and a skinny girl in a gray dress stood there and Nathan hurried back to the carriage.

"So long," I said to his back as I stepped into the house.

"He's cute," the girl said. "He your fella?"

"Not sure," I said, watching the carriage drive away. "He just gave me a thimble, though."

"Lucky you. To some men that's an engagement. Cut the bottom off before the wedding and wear it as a ring."

"No. Bet this man thinks it's just a thimble."

I walked into the house and ogled all the pretty things in that front parlor, the fat sofas covered in good velvet and a gold-painted mirror over a table with carved duck feet, like one Pa made once. Pa would've liked it there, not all done up with crystal and frills, but fine just the same, with fine carpets and thick drapes on the windows.

I'd heard the girl's kind of accent in Leonardtown before and knew it's what's known as Irish, and felt certain she was what Charlotte Brontë called in Tandy Rose's favorite book, *Shirley,* "a native of the land of shamrocks and potatoes."

What you noticed first about Margaret was her blue eyes, not pale like some people's, but bright as the Patuxent on a June day. Next you noticed the freckles. Never seen so many freckles on a person.

She nodded to me. "I'm Margaret Lynch, the Woolseys' day maid. Mary, the other, is home for a spell, took sick last week, but she'll be back, won't she, God willing. Heard all about you, mostly good things, o' course."

She tried to take my bag, but I held it tighter.

Margaret shrugged. "Suit yourself. Just trying to be hospitable and carry it for you."

She started toward the stairs and then turned. "Well, what are you waiting for? Had word from Miss Georgeanna she wants you put in her bedroom, second floor. I'm in the basement."

"Where's all the sisters?"

"Eliza, the wealthiest one, is up at her estate in Fishkill with her wounded war-hero husband, Joseph Howland, along with Abby, the oldest, who's visiting them. Miss Mary lives out in Astoria, across the river, with her clergyman husband, also named Howland, think they're cousins, and Carry and Hatty went out to Astoria to their uncle Edward's just an hour ago, run off shouting something about the Irish being up in arms. 'Since when are they not?' I said to them. Their uncle sent his carriage around for them and they ran off shouting, 'Close the house up early and be very particular about fastening the windows and doors,' which I have been, of course, but doubt there's much to worry about."

"Hate to interrupt your talking, but can you tell me if it's safe out there?

I need to get my medicine at the colored orphanage. My shoulder hurts real bad."

"It's some walk. Fifth Avenue all the way up to Forty-fourth Street. Over thirty blocks. Miss Carry and Jane work there sometimes but they take the carriage, which is gone off with them. But I wouldn't go there now if I were you. Clearly the Woolseys are scared of something since they hightailed it out of here. But if you must, I'd take the omnibus. Just walk over to Fifth Avenue and catch it."

"I need a pass?"

"A *pass*? To step about the city? That'll be the day." She slid two coins into my hand. "For there and back. You got to sit in the back, but it'll get you there in two shakes."

I FOUND MY WAY to the crowded omnibus, careful to sit in back with the other people my color, and we started up Fifth Avenue past houses bigger than the whole town of Hollywood. On my way, I heard clusters of angry voices here and there, off in the distance, but saw only a few small groups of what looked like ruffians.

I got out at the Colored Orphan Asylum, Forty-fourth Street, just as the sun was dropping in the sky. It was the biggest snow white building, what I imagined President Lincoln's house looked like, four windows high, a neat black gate surrounding the whole place.

The heat caused the manure smell from the stockyards next door to rise and I hurried in the front door to the cool stone-floored room inside. Groups of colored children of all ages, from those just walking to some almost my age, coming and going, up and down the prettiest wide stone stairs, led in little groups by colored ladies in black dresses with white aprons and collars. I followed a sign to Dr. Smith's office, up the steps.

Along the way I passed room after room of colored children, tended to by matrons, in schoolrooms, sleeping rooms, nurseries full of cribs. I peeked in one room to find what looked like twenty little Tobys, fine healthy little toddler boys in light blue smocks worn over their clothes, riding wooden toy horses. I knew there was a kitchen somewhere from the fine scent of roast chicken in the air.

Once I arrived at the room with the sign saying DR. SMITH, an office much like Mister Watson's back at Peeler, filled with curiosities like a stuffed duck on his desk and a cabinet long as it was tall, filled with medicine bottles, an older man standing near a tall window waved me in. He was dark-skinned, with a black mustache and white hair, which curled around his ears.

"You Dr. Smith? Followed the signs here."

"What brings you in?" he asked in a nice way. He stood and opened his humidor, like the one Mister Watson had on his desk.

I handed him my paper the Woolseys gave me.

"You are Jemma, for whom this prescription is written?"

I nodded. "Yes, suh. Jemma, owned by Anne-May Wilson Watson of Peeler Plantation, Hollywood, Maryland."

"This prescription is written by Dr. Frank Bacon of the U.S. Army."

"He's a friend of the Woolseys."

"And where do you currently reside?"

"Eight Brevoort Place. Miss Carry and Jane Woolsey both work here."

"Good women, both."

"They say you got more than two hundred little ones here."

"Two hundred and thirty-three to be exact. So, you came for liniment? And how do you know the Woolseys?"

I glanced down at my arm in the sling. "From Gettysburg. They found me in the hospital there."

Dr. Smith pulled a cigar from the box. "Mind if I smoke?"

I shrugged. "Don't mind me."

He lit his cigar and the smoke curled up.

"I right like the aroma," I said. "That's a Cuban, I think, from the smell of it. Mister Watson, he liked Oriental Orange Blossom in his pipe."

Dr. Smith looked again at the piece of paper. "May I inquire as to how you became injured, Jemma?"

"Fighting a battle. At Gettysburg."

He took a step back. "My word. You don't see that every day with a young lady. You need to write a book, don't you?"

He held out his hand and shook mine. "I'm Dr. James McCune Smith. Dr. Bacon knows his medicine. I often recommend this liniment myself."

Dr. Smith turned to the cabinets, pulled down a bottle, and handed it to me.

"This will help the pain right away. And no charge. You get home quick, now. There's some unrest happening around town."

"No worries about me. But I did want to ask, Dr. Smith, if you knew of any work here at the orphanage."

"I'm afraid we are fully staffed at the moment. Just hired a new assistant."

"I see. Thank you anyway." I turned to leave.

"But wait, Jemma. You seem to know your tobacco."

"I came up on a plantation full of it. Plug. Twist." I sniffed the back of my hand. "Surprised I don't still stink of it."

Dr. Smith smiled. "I have an interest in a tobacco shop over west of here, other side of Fifth Avenue a ways, owned by a friend. Called Superior Cigars, but they sell every kind of leaf. He's always looking for good, honest help. Just sweeping up and keeping the jars full, but business is good and a smart girl can move up."

"Oh, I'm not smart."

"Let me be the judge, Miss Jemma, won't you? It appears you can read, since you followed the signs here to find me. And your vocabulary is quite good. Many who consider themselves literate cannot use the word *aroma* as well as you do. So do keep the word *stupid* out of your lexicon and feel free to visit Superior once the streets are safe and use me as a reference. But for now, let my assistant escort you home."

"I can take care of myself, Dr. Smith."

"I insist, Jemma. It's the least I can do for a wounded veteran. My new assistant is on his way up. Tell him I said he should accompany you."

I tucked the bottle in my pocket and I hurried back down the wide marble steps, so happy I had that medicine and a paying job soon.

Halfway down the stairs I passed a man coming up and stopped in my tracks. "Carter?"

He stopped, too, and turned.

"Yes?"

"It's me. Jemma. From Peeler."

You have never seen a man smile so big, with all the joy of the heavens. He came to me, hugged my middle, lifted me up, and twirled me about, right there on those stairs.

"Tell me this is real, Jemma? I wished for it every day."

"Not sure myself. Been here only one day."

I just about melted with happiness to see his handsome face, those slanted brown eyes and wide smile and just a hint of beard on his fine chin.

He took my hands and blew warm breath on them. "Your hands are freezin' cold."

"Just thunderstruck, that's all."

"Anne-May free you?"

I looked around to make sure nobody was listening. "No. Got conscripted by the U.S. Army. She still holds my paper, though."

"I'm on the run, too. Just started working for Dr. Smith but it's still not safe anywhere up here. Friend of mine just got took from his bed the other night by slave catchers and taken off, probably to parts south."

"No one knows I'm here."

"You can't be sure. So you gotta come with me to Canada, soon as I save up some money."

I took a step back. "Don't know, Carter. Need to get back'n get my ma and Patience."

"They're still there? Not like you can go back without gettin' caught yourself. They can come to Canada once the war's won."

"Think I'm to have a job, too. Can't leave that."

All at once a terrible chorus of voices could be heard outside. The front door burst open and the biggest crowd of white women and children burst in and in a most excited and violent manner ran about pillaging from cellar to garret. We rushed to hide in a draped hallway window as they overran the place. They ran into rooms and threw furnishings from the windows, into waiting hands below, stripping the place of school desks and sofas, child-sized beds, clouds of white bedding falling past the windows like heavy snow.

Dr. Smith came to the balcony above the stairs, hung the white flag of truce over the rail, and made an appeal to the mob.

"Please. You have legitimate concerns that need to be addressed, but these are innocent children. Do nothing so disgraceful to humanity as to molest a benevolent institution, which has for its object nothing but good. This will be a lasting disgrace to this city."

His remarks had little sway with the mob and they pushed past the doctor, minds on looting. As the matrons came from all points in the house and ran the children, still in their blue play smocks, down the stairs by us, Dr. Smith joined them and Carter and I took the hand of a girl who looked up at me, eyes wide, as the mob stomped past us, carrying out framed pictures and the stuffed bird from Dr. Smith's office, even armfuls and dresser drawers full of the little garments for the orphans.

A stout woman, pipe in her mouth and carrying a small table, pushed by me, causing me to fall against the metal railing and I felt something pop in my leg. I set myself down on a stair, the pain too much.

Carter came to me and held out one hand. "Hurry, Jemma."

"Can't walk. Go without me."

A pane of glass next to the front door shattered and someone tossed a flaming bundle in. Right quick the wall and draperies caught fire, flames scurrying up to the ceiling. Carter ran to the window and yanked down the drapes, tried to put out the fire with his own hands until a second window shattered and another fiery bundle came in and then another. Soon, after great labor on the part of the mob, the whole wall was in flames.

He came back to me on the stairs. "Jemma you have to walk. There must be two thousand out front, half drunk. We'll go out the back. Follow the children."

The flames climbed the wall behind me, so like the fire in the tobacco barn all those years before. I froze in place and breathed in the same terrible smell of burning pine. Just like when I couldn't go back in and get little

Toby. I pressed the edge of my apron to my nose and mouth to keep out the smoke.

"Go on, Carter," I called to him.

Carter picked me up in his arms and carried me down the stairs to the back door. I hid my face in his chest as the crowd of ruffians parted when we came out of the building. As the frightened children ran ahead of us with the matrons, men and women shook their sticks and bats and shouted, "Wring the necks of the damned Lincolnites!"

After he helped get more children out, Carter carried me all the way back to Brevoort Place and set me down on the front parlor sofa like I was made of cut glass. He and Margaret barricaded the door with every piece of furniture in the front parlor except the sofa, and we heard terrible fighting and what sounded like more looting going on in the streets.

Once the sounds quieted and Margaret went down to bed, Carter and I sat on the sofa and talked, my foot propped on his lap.

"Remember when Tandy Rose caught you hiding that ear trumpet of hers? She was so mad."

"That woman hated me. Every time I came near she'd shield her eyes like she was seeing a monster. 'Don't come near me, you,'" he said in his high-up Tandy voice.

"You know it's just because you looked just like her brother."

"Hate that he's my pa. Though he gave me a licorice whip once. Still can taste how good that was."

"He died, you know. Remember how Tandy Rose used to mix up flour and poison and molasses water to set out to kill flies? He drank that by mistake and I found him stiff as a board when he didn't come down for church one day. Still in his Sunday clothes."

"Nobody ever said he was smart."

"Could be worse. Wilfred got the looks in that family. You coulda come out looking like Tandy Rose."

He smiled. "Oh, no. With those beady eyes and a mouth like a chicken's behind?"

"Hard to think about Ma and Patience still there."

"You're a grown woman, Jemma. They don't expect you to come rescue them. Your ma's a practical sort. She knows you gotta protect your own self."

"Guess so."

WE CAUGHT A FEW winks and woke at dawn on the sofa, me in his arms, his feet hanging off. I watched him as he slept, snorin' a little, his beautiful rose-petal pink lips open a crack. At rest, he brought back the Carter I knew coming up, when we all slept together with Sally Smith, before he moved to the beet farm.

When we were six, Carter, Patience, and me, we'd spend all day runnin' wild through the sunflower fields and stealing snap peas and carrots from Sally's garden. We didn't even know we were slaves that young. Not until the summer after that and we were all in the tobacco fields.

His was a fine face. Just like the picture in *Villette* of John Bretton, the handsome doctor Lucy loves so much but can't have, a wide brow and eyelashes a girl would be proud to have and a good firm jaw.

I leaned over and kissed his pretty pink lips, long and slow, and Carter woke.

"Well, that's a good way to wake up. They got any coffee here?"

"I kiss you and that's all you can think about?"

He tried to go back to sleep. "It's early, Jemma."

"You may need a while to save some money. You got a girl?"

"I like to talk once I'm awake." He turned onto his back. "But no. How 'bout you?"

"Just this one named Nathan. More pals."

He sat up and rubbed the sleep out of one eye. "Well, you two won't have a chance to be any more than pals, since we're getting out of here. You thought about coming with me? You saw last night. It's not safe here."

"Sure is fun to think about," I said, smoothing my hand down his cheek. "I just need some time."

Anne-May

WASHINGTON, D.C.

JULY 1863

LATER ON IN JULY, I MANAGED TO TURN EVADING THE PINKERTONS into an art, after giving Melody's opal ring to a man that kept watch for me from the park. He showered my sitting room window with pebbles whenever the men in their signature bowler hats arrived at Reggie's front door. Never particularly creative, the detectives consistently appeared around the noon hour.

One morning at breakfast I approached Melody before she'd had her sixth cup of coffee, a dangerous move.

"What exactly do the Pinkertons want to discuss with you?" she asked. "You'll get us all hung."

I broke off a piece of scone. "I'd like you to invite Edward Woolsey here to the house for tea."

Melody waved the idea away. "What for?"

"Tell him I've become terribly interested in the genealogy of old New England families, Boston in particular."

"He's very happily married to a woman of great substance, if you are thinking of trapping him for his money. He'd never look twice at you."

"Send the butler round to his place with your card."

"He won't come. We barely know him."

I shrugged. "Men love lecturing women about themselves. Do me this one favor and I will go on to New York, I promise."

EDWARD WOOLSEY CAME TO tea the following Friday, contrary to Melody's prediction, and I had my questions ready, determined to discover more about Jemma's possible whereabouts in New York City. In the drawing room Melody presented a grand spread of scones, strawberries big as your fist, clotted cream, and peach biscuits, all on a silver tiered tray, the kind of thing men pretend they don't like but secretly adore. I wore a pretty peach-colored silk with my widest hoop yet, which presented my figure well. Not that I wasn't generally slim all over, but the genius of the hoop was to keep secret any slight disparities that might lie between waist and ankles.

Mr. Woolsey turned out to be an amiable, handsome man for his advanced years, and after a tedious lecture on the virtues of Boston, proved easier than a dead oyster to pry open.

I leaned forward in my chair, wide-eyed. "And where do you live in New York, Mr. Woolsey? Is it very grand?"

He buttered a scone. "Astoria, Queens. Not what you might call *grand,* but it has no equal for pastoral beauty."

"I long to see New York City."

"It's worth the trip. But mind your valuables; there are thieves about. New York has a prejudice against hanging its greatest scoundrels."

"And where do you recommend she stay?" Melody asked. "She would like to leave immediately."

"Why, New York is known for the finest hotels." He pursed his lips and gazed up at the ceiling. "Well, you might consider Astor House. President Lincoln stayed there once. Or the Hotel Brevoort is top of the line." He plucked a strawberry from the tray. "My sister-in-law, Mrs. Charles Woolsey, lives a stone's throw from the front door."

"Can you show me Hotel Brevoort on this map?" I asked.

He tapped the map with one handsome finger. "Right here at Fifth Avenue and Eighth Street."

"How terribly fancy."

Mr. Woolsey sipped his tea. "I must warn you, Mrs. Watson, the Brevoort is on the snobbish side."

"I actually prefer an air of snobbery—to experience the true Northern experience. Not like Southern hospitality."

"Our attitude is at least sincere. Sometimes I detect a bit of fakery in the Southern attitude."

"Not on my part, I hope, me being from Louisiana originally and all."

"Leaving soon for New York, Mrs. Watson?" he asked.

Melody sipped her claret. "*Very* soon, isn't that right, Anne-May?"

"Do you know any ladies my age who are open to new acquaintances, Mr. Woolsey?"

"My seven nieces are all so busy with war relief—everything from working in the service of our troops to running war supply depots. One is actually finishing up at Gettysburg, with Mrs. Woolsey nursing soldiers."

"What industrious women. Are they amiable?"

"They are indeed. Their home is always open to people of any color or creed." He leaned in and waved his butter knife at me. "Staunch abolitionists."

I forced a sweet smile. "Truly *admirable.*"

"Back a few years, they stumbled on a slave auction in South Carolina. Terrible business."

I bit into a peach biscuit. "I can only imagine."

"Once Mrs. Woolsey talked to some of the people being sold there, she and her daughters became abolitionists for life. Always in the front row at the lectures at the Cooper Institute, for the likes of Wendell Phillips and Dr. Cheever, singing, 'Am I a Soldier of the Cross?'"

"I suppose the Woolseys extend a proper Christian hand to our colored sisters and brothers?"

"Oh, certainly. Abigail sets up colored girls with sewing at the House of Industry. The youngest, Carry, works at orphanages all over the city, but is particularly invested in the Colored Orphan Asylum. Jane keeps the books there."

"Do they take the needy into their home?"

"Wouldn't put it past them. Good people of every sort go in and out, colored and white, every day. Colbert, the son of General Robert E. Lee's slaves, has lived with their Quaker friend Mrs. Gibbons for months now. Brings him around often."

"Such fascinating ladies. I do long to meet them."

Melody leaned in. "Anne-May, Mr. Woolsey can't be bothered with your social calendar."

"You might try the Newcomers Club on Broadway. They help those new to town with introductions. It's right down the block from their town house."

"And what is their address?"

"Eight Brevoort Place. You'd think it was a U.S. Army quartermaster's headquarters, so many war supplies coming and going from there."

I swallowed hard. "Number eight, you say?"

Mr. Woolsey took the napkin from his knee. "I do apologize I cannot be of more assistance."

"On the contrary, Mr. Woolsey," I said with a smile. "You have helped me very much, indeed. I simply cannot wait to arrive in New York City. I'm going to see if I can find an old friend."

PART

THREE

..

Jemma

❋

POINT LOOKOUT, MARYLAND
SEPTEMBER 1863

MRS. WOOLSEY AND GEORGEANNA RETURNED FROM
Gettysburg after the Draft Riots and tucked me into bed upstairs, propping up my foot with pillows and ice bags. Eliza's servant Moritz even sent me down a little crutch he'd carved for me with a pillowy armrest covered in red gingham check. Not being able to walk like usual was a hardship, but reliving that night at the orphanage was the worst, the whole place burning, the children crying and screaming. Brought back that night in the barn when Toby died and the beam fell on Patience.

Turns out the mobs did more than burn the orphans' home to the ground, they sacked the whole city. They cast paving stones through shop windows, cut telegraph lines, killed the horses that pulled streetcars, and ruined the cars. Georgeanna read me the papers that said the ruffians hunted colored people on the streets and viciously beat and murdered them. They burned the mayor's home, hotels, and newspaper offices, and when the rioters approached the offices of *The New York Times,* the staff turned Gatling guns on the mob, dispersing them. They kept at it for days, until over one hundred colored folks died, eleven of them murdered by hanging.

But it was like a miracle to find Carter again and I replayed that in my mind, lingering on his smile and the two of us on the sofa together, his whole body snug around me.

Carter, Margaret, and I had kept the Woolseys' house from getting sacked, though their friend Mrs. Gibbons was not so lucky. The mobs looted her house, carried off all her worldly goods, and tried to set it afire. After that Mrs. Gibbons asked Jane, Georgeanna, and me to go down to Maryland to take over for her while she came back to New York to tend her home.

I was happy for a chance to get away from the city and back down so close to Ma and Patience. Just the thought of being nearer to them made me smile, though we all agreed the chances of a meeting were slim.

GEORGY, JANE, AND I arrived in Maryland by steamer that September to spell Mrs. Gibbons. Only white folks were allowed on the lower decks, so we stood up on the top deck as the boat arrived and looked over our new home, Point Lookout Camp, a big U.S. Army camp at the very end of the peninsula close to Peeler, a half hour away by carriage. Folks all over the boat that day were talking about the Union defeat at the battle at Chicka-mauga, somewhere on the border of Georgia and Tennessee, the dead counts big on both sides, second only to Gettysburg.

We brought our bags to Hammond Hospital and Mrs. Gibbons took us on a tour of the camp, including a trip up into a guard tower for a quick look-see of the place, quite a feat climbing that high in our long skirts and my bandaged-up ankle.

Up there we got a bird's-eye view of the point, stretched out long, low, and windswept, a lighthouse the tallest thing around, the trees in the dis-tant woods just starting their fall turn. First thing I looked for was Peeler Plantation, up north a ways, the sun shinin' on just a bit of the roof show-ing through the trees. Water came to my eyes picturing Ma out in the field, Patience down the road at Ambrosia, not knowing I was so close.

I cast an eye around the place, Hammond Hospital, built in a circle like the spokes of a wheel. Near the water, the wide wharf was busy, white men all over. Some sat fishing off it, some bathed naked in the sea, some rolled barrels down a plank from a boat tied up there, and others carried off wounded soldiers toward the wards.

Mrs. Gibbons swept one arm across the landscape. She was a Quaker and talked just like the others I'd heard in Leonardtown. Spoke more proper than the Woolseys, but without the "thee" and "thou."

"Point Lookout. Your new home, such as it is. Hammond Hospital, of course, a fourteen-hundred-bed complex. Beyond that you will find store-houses, stables, and additional quarters for officers, doctors, and U.S. Army troops. A small number of Rebel prisoners can be found in the barbed-wire area just beyond, traitors to the cause, spies; however that number is expected to grow."

"And the barracks adjacent to the hospital?" Georgy asked.

"That is the contraband camp where fugitive slaves have been coming in great numbers for protection. Unfortunately, of late many masters are arriving to retrieve the enslaved seeking refuge here."

"But are they not protected?" Jane asked.

"The general says they should be, but unfortunately the Union soldiers who've pledged to protect them sometimes accept bribery and surrender them back to their masters."

"Such a wicked game," Jane said.

"As you can imagine, I try to protect against that at all costs. Northern spirits may be at an all-time low, but even if we don't win the war we can help get as many as we can to freedom."

"How can we help?" Georgy asked.

"Please stay alert to runaway slaves seeking refuge. I consider it one of our most important roles here. For many, we are their only hope."

We got our wards cleaned up, the beds full with sick and wounded troops, and Jane rolled out molasses cookies, a special treat for the troops, with a table leg, having no rolling pin, but they still tasted good.

I washed plenty of dishes from my chair at the sink and pressed every-thing in that place at my lowered ironing board. Then we went next door and cleaned up the contraband quarters. They were regular soldier barracks, low huts with only cots inside, filled to the brim with colored folks, mostly women and children fleeing from miles around from whatever masters they'd had. Before we washed the sheets, Jane, Georgy, and I doused them with kerosene, to kill the lice. It felt strange to be on the other end of things, helping colored folk with their new lives, me not officially free either.

I felt bad walking around in my nursing outfit while so many women there wore practically rags, but to make up for it I'd remade six dresses the Woolseys had begged from nearby houses on their door-to-door donation trips.

One day I was stepping up and down the rows of cots, handing out those dresses and passing out cold water from a bucket, when someone called my name.

"Jemma? That you?"

I turned to find a face I knew real well, Sybil, Miss Charlene's skinny little house girl from Ambrosia. She lay on a cot near a window, sweat beaded up on her forehead.

"Thought it was you, with that uppity way of talkin' a yours." She held up one palm. "Don't come too close. May have the typhus. Think they got every bedbug in St. Mary's County here." She tried to sit up. "What's wrong with your foot? Look like a right cripple."

"How'd you get here, Sybil?"

"Just up and left Ambrosia one morning and walked all the way here." She looked around like seeing it for the first time. "Not sure if I wasn't better off back combin' Miss Charlene's hair."

"Nobody caught you?"

"Never even noticed I was gone, at least in time to call out the dogs. Miss Charlene's some sorta mess now. 'Bout ready to lose the house, if you ask me."

"How's my ma? Patience?"

Sybil leaned in. "Haven't been to Peeler in a long while so don't know 'bout yer ma, but Patience's good enough, I guess. Hate to tell you, but LeBaron's been over Ambrosia a lot, teachin' her this and that. Like how to clean his boots and guns. She don't seem to mind."

"She does mind. Hates him worse than anything."

"Aren't you all fancy in that getup."

"It's a nurse costume. I'm at work with the Sanitary Commission. I'm here nursing wounded soldiers."

"Then maybe you can help Doreen. What's owned by Jubal Smalls? She's here with her four little ones, out in the woods too skeered to come in here, her oldest boy not fourteen, hit in the head."

"Terrence?" Tears stung my eyes. "He's a good boy."

"Hit over the head by Masta Smalls with a carpetbag, and the metal rod in the bottom hit his poor head, if you can believe it, and gave him a hole above one ear so bad you can see brains. Masta Smalls piled it on with hot tar to make it worse, so Doreen took all four and ran. I met up with them on the way."

"Where's she in the woods?"

She pointed through the glass. "A few rods in, just there. You better make it quick. Poor boy's at death's door."

I TOLD GEORGY AND JANE about Doreen and they went for a stretcher. We found Mrs. Gibbons, got help with our patients, and were out the door like a shot, though it was getting dark. It was still warm that time in September, but getting cool at night, the fireflies out all over, helping light the way.

We followed Mrs. Gibbons toward the woods, a lantern in her hand, frogs starting up their night talk. "Hate to ask you to come out here, lame as you are, Jemma, but can you show us where your friend said Doreen's camped?"

I took the lead, my crutch making it a world easier to step, and led to a piece of the woods Sybil had pointed to. We looked for a good long time and almost gave up when we heard a soft voice.

"Jemma. That you?"

"Doreen?"

She stepped out of the brush, holding Terrence at her chest. "My boy's in a bad way."

Even in the near dark I could see the hurt in her eyes. "He's not talkin' anymore, Jemma."

Georgy stepped up to us. "May we help you set him on the stretcher here? And back to the hospital. Jemma and Mrs. Gibbons can help you with the other children."

Mrs. Gibbons took the hands of the twins and I took little Sam as Doreen set Terrence down on the stretcher with great care. Georgy and Jane took it up, lifted the boy gently, and we started back the way we came. Then, just at the edge of the woods, the sound of men's voices came from nearby, both as familiar as my own.

"They've found us, ladies," Mrs. Gibbons said in a low voice. "Stand still and let them course by."

Two men started toward us in the near dark.

"They're here somewhere," one said.

"I can smell 'em," said the other with a laugh, as Jubal Smalls and Sheriff Whitman came straight at us from the woods.

CHAPTER
41

Jemma

✦

POINT LOOKOUT, MARYLAND
SEPTEMBER 1863

I PRESSED MYSELF UP AGAINST A TREE, THE GRAIN OF THE BARK
cutting my back, as Jubal Smalls ran by me and little Sam.

"Quiet, now," I whispered to him, and kept my hand tight over his
mouth, as he shook like he'd been doused. My heart went solid as Jubal
passed by, so close I could see his snaky eyes flash in the dark. He and the
sheriff headed for Mrs. Gibbons, Jane, and Georgy, who'd all linked arms
to hide Doreen and the stretcher.

"Where's my slave goes by the name of Doreen?" Jubal asked. "I know
she's in these woods."

Georgy turned to him cool as can be. "We are Sanitary Commission
nurses, gentlemen, gathering medicinal herbs."

Jubal turned to the sheriff. "We need the dogs."

I'd never laid eyes on white-haired Sheriff Whitman up close before
and could only see the general shape of him from where I hid behind the
tree, but from his paunch I could tell he was a bacon eater for sure.

"I'm warnin' you ladies. You're Northern by the sound of it and you
don't know the ways of these parts. But this man's property is known to be
hidin' in these woods, and if you know anything about their whereabouts
you'd be smart to 'fess up."

"I believe a private from Barracks B found a family meeting that description," Jane said.

Mrs. Gibbons nodded. "Brought them over there for processing."

The two ran off toward Barracks B and we waited for them to be well inside before we hurried ourselves to the hospital.

THE DOCTORS WORKED ON Terrence most the night but they called his ma in to say goodbye just after dawn. Jane and I looked after her other boys while she cried over him nigh an hour like her heart would break, and mine did, too. We made him a nice funeral with a stone I picked out special. And the next day we worked with Mrs. Gibbons to get Doreen and her three babies snuck on the next boat up to Boston and took her name off the roles so Jubal Smalls'd never know where she went.

But once that boy died, something turned over in me. Everything irked me, even things that never had bothered me one bit. But it was Jane and Georgy Woolsey bothered me most. While once I hadn't minded their bossing me about on every little thing, suddenly it bugged me fierce. Something bad was brewing in me and it wanted to get out and it picked that next night in the library.

"Elevate that foot, Jemma," Georgy said as Jane and I joined her in the library and she settled in with some sewing in her lap.

"I'm fine, Georgy," I said as I sat in a soft chair, wishing for some quiet time to myself, to mourn little Terrence and to think about Carter and Nathan and which one I liked best, the only good thing I had left to fix on.

Jane set my foot on the hassock. "You really should talk to us more about what's inside you, Jemma."

"Rather stay quiet, I guess."

Georgy snipped off a stitch. "Are you happy? Sad? Angry? We can never tell. Jane and I have each other to confide in, while you don't have anyone close."

"Now that you mention it, yes, ma'am, I am angry about that. Wish I had my own sister, but she's otherwise engaged as a slave picking indigo."

"You must be happy about your bonnets," Jane said. "Two more nurses have expressed interest in owning one. You could charge a fee for your work and have a good business."

I crossed my arms over my chest. "I like giving them away."

Jane went to the bookshelf. "Let me fetch you a book. Perhaps *Little Dorrit*? How lucky you were taught to read."

"Think I'll read *Oliver Twist*. I started that at Peeler and—"

"That might induce nightmares, Jemma." Jane handed me *Little Dorrit*.

I set the book on the side table. "I went up on the roof today and stood on an apple crate to see if I could catch another sight of Peeler."

Georgy kept her gaze on her sewing. "I hope you were careful of your ankle."

"Hard to think about Ma and Patience so close by here, with me sitting warm by the fire."

Georgy tied off a thread. "Jane checked the contraband list and did not see anyone from Peeler. At least you've been saved from that dreadful place. Perhaps write them a letter?"

"Already sent one from New York." I held the arms of the chair, in order to stand. "But I'll write her another before it gets too late."

Jane waved me back into my chair. "Not just yet."

"Would you two please stop?" I asked, a little too loud.

Both sisters sat up straighter.

"What is it, Jemma?" Georgy asked.

I paced the floor. "Never mind. I'm fine."

"Perhaps you could address how you feel? A person has to face things or you just get stuck."

"You want to know how I feel? Like a squirrel on a leash. And let me just say, no one has saved me. I saved myself. I don't need you folks to protect me, saying 'my Jemma' and making my decisions for me. Can't you see how claimin' ownership of me hurts?"

Georgy put aside her sewing. "Jemma, please."

I stepped to the bookshelf. "I want to read as I please."

Jane laced her fingers tight. "Some would be grateful for such caring attentions."

"Thank you for the concern. It's kind of you. But I want say in my own affairs. And I want to read what I like. I've seen things far worse than anything in *Oliver Twist,* so let me decide. So what if I want nightmares? And another thing, I'm not *lucky* I was taught to read. Tandy Rose taught me for her own selfish reasons, so I could read the Bible to her half the day. So, no, I'm not grateful that the woman who *owned* me, and worked me senseless and rapped me on the head with her thimble six times a day taught me to read. Isn't that my right, just as it is yours? You took me in and I'm grateful, but you all say one thing and do another. You talk about protecting the less fortunate, then your sisters and uncle leave Margaret and me to fend for ourselves when they knew those riots were coming. You won't buy cotton but your father made his money in sugar."

"Our father was a good man," Georgy said.

"But the money he made was off the backs of *us.*"

"We've tried to make amends for that," Jane said.

"But what do you really do? With your *Is this not a Woman* tokens and your visits to the colored orphans and lecture halls? What really matters is freedom."

"I'm sorry, Jemma," Georgy said. "We've tried to help."

"You've done everything good for *me.* But the ones who really need help are my ma and Patience. Getting them out of that place. Now, that would be helping."

THE NEXT MORNING, MY boiling anger spent, and feeling good as I could, Jane, Georgy, and I took the Hammond Hospital ambulance out to seek donations in Leonardtown. I sat in the back with all the canvas side flaps down to make sure I was not recognized, with the flaps front and back open for air.

Turns out my telling what was inside me had been more than they bargained for, since their feelings seemed hurt, especially Jane, but Georgy told me she was glad I didn't play it mild for her sake and the next day we set off, back friends.

By early afternoon we'd stopped at our last house, and after taking a carton of shirts from a woman whose son died at Gettysburg, we were headed back south to Camp Lookout.

Georgy turned in her seat on the buckboard. "Where's Peeler Plantation from here, Jemma?"

"Not far. Go through Hollywood and it's down Moneysunk Road a good long way."

Jane and Georgy looked at each other.

"What?" I asked, something aflutter in my belly. "Are you thinkin' we could just go by and take Ma and Patience?"

Jane slowed the horses. "We could just drive down there and assess the situation."

I peeked out the crack in the canvas flaps. "I'd have to stay outta sight back here."

"Isn't there an overseer on the premises?" Georgy asked.

"He's in charge of both Peeler and Ambrosia. Out in the woods doing who knows what most days. We could stop by Ambrosia first and see if Patience is out working."

"But what if Anne-May were to see you?" Jane asked.

"She'd have LeBaron take me back for sure. I'm her property after all." I was quiet for a minute. "But I'd like to try."

"If we succeed, your ma and Patience would be considered contraband at Point Lookout," Georgy said. "Perfectly legal."

"I'd be forever indebted," I said.

With mixed fear and hope, Jane turned the carriage around and we headed for Peeler Plantation.

AS WE BUMPED ALONG Moneysunk Road I tied down the canvas flaps along the front and back of the ambulance, careful not to be seen.

LeBaron. Anne-May. Jubal Smalls. Wouldn't they jump with joy to get me back?

I folded the donations back there, to keep my mind off going to get Ma and Patience. By the looks of the skimpy contributions, things had sure gone downhill in that part of Maryland since I'd left. I set to thinking about my most favorite thing, Carter and what it'd be like to go off to Canada with him. I tried making a picture of him in my mind, that sweet smile, his body wrapped around mine on the sofa that night. But who knew if his offer to go away was even still good? Hadn't heard from him since July.

I brought my head back to folding the four homespun shirts some poor lady gave up after her son died in the war. Pa had shirts like those.

Pa.

After letting go the night before, it was a little easier to think of him without wanting to punch something. What was Ma doing right now? In the Peeler fields, no doubt. Patience was most likely at Ambrosia, back at the shack after noon meal in the fields. The plan we'd cooked up was a good one, but just thinking about it made my mouth go dry as dust.

It was hot enough to make bread rise, closed up there in the ambulance with the canvas curtains down. I wiped the palms of my hands on my skirt as Miss Jane drove, Georgy beside her up front on the box. The ambulance was just like the ones at Gettysburg, with room to fit two wounded stretched out on the floor, though I don't remember riding in one after I was shot.

I pulled back the canvas up front and listened to Georgy go over the plan we cooked up.

"Jane will drive to the back door of Ambrosia, where I'll engage the mistress of the house in conversation, under the guise of seeking donations for the hospital, and persuade her to invite me into the house. Jane will ask to water the horses and drive around to the shacks. Once there's no sign of danger, she will give the sign for you to disembark and find Patience. Once she has you both, you will pick me up. Having Patience safely aboard, we'll do the same for your ma and be off back to Point Lookout before dark. Is that exactly what we agreed upon?"

I nodded, shaking all over just thinking about it all, half excited to see Ma and Patience, half just plain scared.

"What if Miss Charlene has the dogs out already? They can smell me a mile away."

Georgy swatted away a horsefly. "Jane will make sure it's safe before you exit the back to get Patience."

"What if Miss Charlene won't invite you in? She has a husband. Maybe offer to tend to him?"

"Good idea, Jemma. Our plan is solid, but we must leave room for spontaneity. Now, shut the flaps and tie them tight."

Miss Jane urged the horses on, but it took the longest time to get to Ambrosia Plantation and that ambulance was a rough ride for something supposed to cart sick people.

As we drove I peeked out at everything, through a slit where the canvas didn't quite meet the wood, and once we passed through Hollywood and I saw Smalls and Sons store I started to shake worse. We drove past the turnoff for Peeler and on to Ambrosia, past the gate to old Mr. Burns's farm, and I was glad I didn't have full view of that spider tree where Pa died.

We pulled up to Ambrosia and the dogs started up barking, sending a new shiver down my back. I barely breathed as Miss Charlene came out the kitchen door, screen door slamming behind her, wearing an apron over her dress, holding a black fry pan. Where she always used to have Sybil comb her hair nice, it was ratty and only half pinned up, and her usual camel hair shawl was missing.

"What you want?" Miss Charlene said, one eye squinted shut.

Georgy stepped down from the ambulance and I could just see the back of her. "We're here from Hammond Hospital."

"Down at Point Lookout? You got contraband there? Probably some of my slaves, while I'm forced to do my own washing up."

"We're here soliciting donations—gently used clothing, perhaps—"

"I have nothing. Times are bad, not that you'd know, with your fancy shawls."

"Even the humblest donation could help our wounded men at the hospital."

"Our men? Yankees, you mean. They started this war."

"No, actually, ma'am—"

"And here I am with a sick husband. He didn't even get a chance to fight."

"I am trained as a nurse. Happy to examine him."

"You a nurse? You look too fancy for that kind of work."

"I've been serving on board the hospital ships. And at Gettysburg. Now Point Lookout."

"You know about croup?"

"I do."

"Mr. Weed's got it bad."

"Perhaps I can come in and take a look?"

Miss Charlene stood looking at Georgy for a long minute, slack-jawed and gently swinging the fry pan at her side. "C'mon inside."

"May my sister water our horses? Poor beasts are thirsty."

Miss Charlene waved in the direction of the shacks. "Pump's behind the barn."

Georgy followed Miss Charlene through the kitchen door and the ambulance started moving. I tried to see more of Georgy, but we soon passed the dogs in their pen, who didn't bark one bit, and then turned the bend around the barn. I held my own hands so tight the blood got cut off and they tingled.

I was going to see *Patience*—Ma too.

Jane stopped the ambulance in front of the shacks and I raised the canvas, opened the wooden door, and hopped out. Miss Jane sent me a worried look and I stepped inside the shack, limping a bit.

I found Patience there sweeping out the room and held my breath, puffed up with happiness, and waited for her to see me. When she finally did, she bit her fist and rushed to me, quick as she could on her bad leg, a look of real fear on her face.

"Jemma. What are you doing here? What happened to your foot?"

"Hurt it in New York City." I held her hands. "I have so much to tell. I'm at Point Lookout, nursing soldiers. We're here for you and Ma."

"You need to leave. Now."

"What's wrong?"

"Who are those women?"

"My friends are pretending to ask for donations—"

"Take your friends and go. LeBaron's here today. Out in the field now, but he's due back anytime. Came to talk to Miss Charlene about a transaction."

"What kind?"

She dropped my hands and turned away. "Me, I suppose."

"*Patience.* Why Miss Charlene? Anne-May holds your paper."

"Anne-May won't sell me without her say-so."

I took her by the arm. "You gotta come quick."

She pulled away. "No, Jemma."

"You stay here, LeBaron will do just what he did to Celeste."

"He don't give me a second look. Besides, Miss Charlene keeps an eye out. Told me she'll never stop renting me."

Jane called softly from the ambulance. "Ready, Jemma?"

Patience went to the door and looked out. "You go on. This is my life now. Get back to yours or you'll be stuck back here again."

"I won't leave here without you. We're going to New York City."

Patience looked at me long and hard. "You'll never give up." And then she let out a big sigh and held out one hand. "Okay, then."

I couldn't wipe the smile from my face as I pulled her outside, helped her into the ambulance, and Miss Jane set off, medium slow. We picked up Georgy, and Patience and I sat back there, me squeezing her hand so tight, heartbeat pounding in my ears.

"We're going back to Camp Lookout, close by," I said.

"LeBaron is out here with his dogs. If he finds us, I'm jumping."

"We'll outrun him. Miss Jane drives like a house on fire."

"You know how that'd end. I'm not pulling you back into this, Jemma. Look at you with your fine nursing dress and white friends. You have a chance now. I can come to New York another day, once this war's over."

"And what if the South wins? This is our only chance."

We got to the Moneysunk Road turnoff and slowed down a bit and I could tell Miss Jane'd lost her way.

That's when Patience and I heard the sound, far off, but it was coming closer. She looked at me in the growing dark, and pressed her arms across her middle.

The dogs.

"Go right, Jane," I said. "Back to Point Lookout. We'll get Ma another day. LeBaron's coming."

She went right and we got up speed, bumping along pretty well, when we heard LeBaron's voice up front of the ambulance and we stopped fast. Patience and I crept forward and peeped through the canvas crack.

He and Clem had come from the opposite direction, driving a ramshackle wagon, blocking our way. I barely breathed as LeBaron jumped down, his blacksnake whip coiled in one hand, his two favorite dogs by his side. They yapped at the ambulance, running up and down the length of it.

"Where you ladies headed?" LeBaron asked.

"Back to Hammond Hospital," Georgy said, voice steady.

"What you got in the back there? My dogs are pretty interested."

"Nothing but used apparel, sir."

"Let's take a look. I like used apparel. You like used apparel, Clem?"

Jane urged the horses on, but LeBaron stood his ground and unfurled his whip. "See, we don't take kindly to outsiders coming in here and disrupting the natural order of things."

"Let us pass, sir," Georgy said.

"Once I get a good look back there. See, this is private land you're trespassin' on."

The horses stamped the ground and the ambulance rocked. "We are U.S. Army nurses, sir," Jane said.

"Since your Point Lookout's been around, we suspect a good many of our slaves run off to the contraband camp there. That's a sizable investment lost."

Patience whispered in my ear, "I'm jumping."

I held her tight by the hand.

Georgy raised her voice. "This is a U.S. Army conveyance, and comes with a two-hundred-dollar penalty for defiling it. Excuse my frankness, but you do not appear to be the kind of gentleman who has an extra two hundred to spare."

My heart beat out of my chest as LeBaron left Clem and moseyed toward the ambulance, dragging the tail of his whip through the dust of the road.

"These dogs are mighty wound up. Curious what you got in there."

Patience whispered, "He'll find you. I'm gonna show myself. Otherwise he'll find you, too."

"No—"

"He'll keep you and then we're worse off."

LeBaron's voice came louder. "How 'bout we take a look?"

Patience pulled me so close I could feel the thump in her chest, and then she stepped quiet to the back of the ambulance.

I held out one hand.

She turned to me and whispered, "I'm gonna do something. You love me, you'll stay put." She pushed open the little door, stepped out, and closed it fast.

"I knew it!" LeBaron called. "Get back here, you."

I pressed one eye to the gap in the canvas, both hands covering my mouth, as Patience ran best she could for the woods.

LeBaron took off after her and at the edge of the road jumped on her like the butcher takes down his hogs.

He pulled her up by one arm and dragged her back to the cart. She was covered in leaves, had twigs stuck in her hair.

"Well, lookee here," he said.

Patience pulled away from him.

Tears stung my eyes and I slid down closer to the end of the ambulance. What if I just ran out and yanked her from him? The dogs'd be on me quick.

He waved his whip handle in Jane's direction. "I knew you two were up to no good."

"Weren't their fault," Patience said. "Climbed in there without them knowing."

"So you'd run off and leave Miss Charlene with no one to finish the indigo? You do know what we do to runaways?" LeBaron took a rope from his wagon and tied her hands, then shoved her up into the back of the wagon. "Gotta get you back before you run off again."

"The poor child is bone thin, obviously mistreated here," Georgy called to him. "No wonder she was so desperate to escape."

LeBaron climbed up onto his wagon and took the reins. "She's the personal property of the mistress here, and what you ladies don't understand is, her kind don't feel pain and hunger like other folks do."

"You'll be hearing from the authorities," Georgy said.

LeBaron smiled. "Have 'em contact Sheriff Whitman. He'll handle things. Clem, let them pass. Now, I suggest you two ladies get off this property."

Clem yelled "Get!" to our horses and we lurched off.

From my crack in the canvas I watched Patience ride off in the back of LeBaron's wagon, head held high. I'd saved myself, but the rip of losing her again sent me back down a dark hole, as we sped off back to Point Lookout, leaving my beloved sister behind.

Anne-May

I WAS IN NO HURRY TO LEAVE WASHINGTON. YES, I WANTED TO find Jemma and make nice with Jubal, but it was intoxicating living in that lap of luxury. I tried to keep my distance from my ex-stepfather, Reggie, whose taste, thankfully, ran to those much younger than I, as he ferried a constant stream of nubile maidens to his chambers each night, sometimes several at one time.

Melody's patience for our little arrangement was growing thin, so I was suspicious one spring afternoon when she invited me to tea at the fanciest hotel in Washington, the Willard. Everyone knew the Willard had the best dining, since Abraham Lincoln ordered whole prepared dinners from there. It had all the latest conveniences: running water, gaslights, and toilets—to some, more awe-inspiring than Lincoln's White House.

Melody and I took our seats in the dining room, a bright room anchored by massive potted palms, the ceiling open to an atrium, conversations echoing off the tile floor. Groups of men and women sat clustered about tables topped with tiered silver trays filled with every type of tea cake and delicacy. Women paraded about the room visiting different tables, stopping to greet Melody with a "How do you do"—the same Washington society ladies that routinely snubbed Mary Lincoln.

Suddenly there arose a great commotion in the restaurant vestibule: the waiters were trying to restrain a patron from entering, but I soon saw her approach us, weaving her way through the linen-draped tables.

Mama.

Melody looked up. "Oh, Zoretha. Right on time."

Mama stepped, calm as can be, straight to me. "How *could* you double-cross me, Anne-May?"

"She's been taught by the best," Melody said, and waved the waiter over to pour more tea.

Mama unbuttoned her cape with shaking hands. "The very day I arrived back in New Orleans they came for me. Nasty Yankee soldiers dragged me down Elm Street, tossed me in jail with no change of clothes or breakfast, and kept me there for *two* weeks."

On closer inspection Mama was a sad sight to see, for a moth'd laid waste to her cape, and her cuffs'd grown grimy at the edges. "I'm sorry, Mama, but I had to—"

"My friend Belinda-Jean from Baton Rouge knows people and came and got me out, but soon more soldiers arrived at my door and took me back. At first I stayed mum, you being my flesh and blood and all, but when they told me you described me as *advanced in age* and the perpetrator of such gross alleged acts, and suggested I might *hang,* I finally told them the truth. Took a while for them to believe me, but they finally let me out and kept me months under house arrest, couldn't even take a turn in the park. They sure wrote down every detail I told 'em about that red book of yours."

"Damn you, Mama." My temple throbbed.

"So, now you're cussing? The North has ruined you."

"I'm an adult. I'll do as I please."

"It took me an absolute eternity to get here, after endless train delays on account of this wretched war. Was forced to travel second class due to my limited means."

"You could've sent a letter."

"I wanted to see your face when I told you how deep you've hurt your own kin."

If our fellow diners were listening, they had the good manners not to turn and gape, though at many tables conversation had abruptly ceased.

"It felt good to tell those soldiers everything, dear daughter. Like how it was you who passed on that information about the troop addresses."

"Hush, *please*."

"How you have a little red book in which you write every word."

"Could you keep your voice down, Mama? Hope you didn't mention Jubal."

"I told them *every* little bitty thing. They took notes, Anne-May, asked ten questions about that book. Said they'd send U.S. Army soldiers to come interrogate you. Any day now, in fact."

"I'll just deny it all. Besides, living here with Reggie affords me protection."

"You won't be here forever, evil child. I consider you dead from this day forward."

"Well, I guess that leaves you with Euphemia."

"She wouldn't turn in her own mother just to save herself."

"No wonder Father took so many trips abroad. Could barely live with you."

She leaned in, eyes flashing. "That man had a wishbone for a backbone, but at least he was *good*. Wouldn't he be repulsed by what you've become?"

I stood. "As Father was repulsed by you? How could anyone love you?"

I started toward the entrance.

Mama called after me. "I was wrong that day when I told you you'd make a passable parent. A *cat* would make a better mother."

Every head in that restaurant turned toward her but I kept walking.

"Is that a fact?" I called back over my shoulder.

"Here's another," Mama said, her voice clear and strong. "That father that you defend wasn't your father at all."

I stopped and turned back to her.

"That's right. Your real daddy was a dirty rice merchant from Philadelphia, whom I slept with in his filthy hotel room just to spite my own mama."

"That is a *lie*."

"When I learned I was with child, I couldn't wait to rid myself of you, but a quart of brandy a night didn't do it. You stayed in me like a sickness and I shook like a leaf when you finally came out, with the same yellow hair as that filthy rice man. John Wilson took pity on me and raised you as his own, but never loved you as his."

"So why'd Aunt Tandy Rose leave me Peeler?"

"Think I'd give her the satisfaction of knowing you're illegitimate? Only had you three to consider leavin' it to. She said you were the strong one. Didn't think Harry could keep it up. Clearly you don't deserve it."

I straightened my cuffs. "That's your opinion."

"You can act rich and cultured all you want, Anne-May, dining fine here with the best of the best, but the truth is, you come from Yankee trash. You think about that as the Pinkertons come and drag you off in search of that vile book."

I strode out of the restaurant, vibrating with anger, and when I hit the sidewalk I dipped some snuff. I looked both ways for Pinkertons and, finding none, walked back to Reggie's house.

It was time to move on to New York City and find Jemma.

And that damned book.

SPRING IN NEW YORK CITY was glorious, and walking in Central Park, I drew the admiration of male and female strollers alike. The park was a sight to behold, the drives thronged with carriages, the waters of the lake studded with gaily colored boats. One hansom cab driver confessed there must have been over a hundred thousand people in the park that day. It was the perfect place to reflect on Mama's news about my unfortunate parentage, a desperate attempt of hers to hurt me.

I sat and pulled a letter from my pocket, the one I'd had Patience pen to Jemma way back at Peeler. I'd even had her address the envelope. Seemed the right time to send it, to remind Jemma her sister missed her so.

Next, I retrieved Jubal's handkerchief from that same pocket, the words from the poem he'd penned for me I'd had embroidered there. *Love never dies.*

Was his cologne still there in the cotton? I held it to my nose and inhaled his fading scent, of hemlocks and spice.

I strolled the wide mall, along rows of American elms, my silver snuff vial hanging around my neck by a chain and bouncing at my chest. Even with the terrible war going on, how many well-to-do Yankee ladies gathered there, in their carriage cloaks of moiré and amber velvet, mink furs, and gowns of brocade silks in deep and brilliant magenta, gold, or rosy pink. How smug those women looked, while the papers were full of reports of Southern ladies reduced to drinking chicory coffee and wearing their old dresses inside out.

After months of enjoying Reggie and Melody's hospitality in Washington, I'd amassed quite a wardrobe, and wore it well, fitting in nicely with the fashionable Yankees in my emerald silk dress and black velvet, sable-lined driving cloak made by Melody's favorite French furrier. I wore my new imperial dress elevator, and fellow strollers stopped and stared as I raised and lowered my skirt at the sight of a puddle or any little ditch in my path.

By the time I'd left Washington, with Melody's six new gray canvas Louis Vuitton trunks packed with couture and a pretty stack of U.S. currency tucked in the silk pocket of the hat trunk, she seemed positively overjoyed to see me ride off in their carriage, bound for the Brevoort hotel in New York City.

Upon arrival there earlier that day, even with my six French trunks, the hotel desk clerk had looked down his nose at me. "Have you the means to pay one hundred dollars a night?"

"More than the means, sir. I am the daughter of Reginald Stickman of Washington."

"From the sound of it, you're Southern," the clerk said. "Have you sworn your oath to the United States, madam?"

"I was born and raised in New Orleans, but I presently live in Maryland. Last time I checked, sir, that was a Union state."

His mouth tightened.

I looked about the wide lobby, at the polished marble floors and velvet drapes. "Of course, I am fussy with my standards, being from New Orleans originally. There's no city more filled with every description of amusement."

The clerk busied himself, shuffling papers about. "You don't say?"

"Don't know if you're a devotee of Bacchus, sir, but forty-five establishments there sell liquor. And the hotels are beyond compare. So, of course, I'm used to a better class of accommodations."

The clerk was markedly unimpressed, but the staff were much kinder to me once I started pulling out my silver chain *porte-monnaie* and dispensing gold eagle five-dollar coins. A lady's maid unpacked my things in the three-room suite, and I ordered luncheon for two, ate only the choicest parts and left the rest, tried on every assemblage I had and dropped my clothes wherever I liked, and opened the windows wide to air out the room.

When I tired of strolling the Central Park, I found an address I'd seen in an advertisement in the newspaper for Bigelow's National Detective Agency, with the line "We never sleep" printed under a vaguely disturbing etching of a single staring eye.

I climbed a mile of stairs and entered a shabby office, S. M. BIGELOW, PRIVATE DETECTIVE and that same unsettling eye painted in gold leaf on the glass door. I found a sweaty, overgrown tadpole of a man sitting behind a desk eating a bowl of custard.

"What's your business?" he asked, barely glancing up.

"I am Anne-May Wilson Watson, here to find a missing person."

"You a Southerner? I take payment up front. *Union* money."

"From Louisiana, but I now reside in Maryland, sir. On Peeler Plantation. You may've heard of it."

Mr. Bigelow dropped his spoon in his bowl with a clatter and gave me his full attention. "You a soiled dove?"

"Beg your pardon?"

"You appear to have been walking by yourself on the street. No good lady does that."

"If you must know, I caught many admiring glances in the Central Park."

"Admiring, or gawking at the Southern lady all got up in her fancies, out by herself? That'll get more looks than that Barnum seal exhibit."

I pressed one net-gloved hand to my cheek and felt it, hot. "If we could keep to what I'm here to pay you for, Mr. Bigelow."

"Black or white?"

"Beg your pardon?"

"The person you're looking for. Colored or white?"

"Colored, actually. A girl named Jemma. My property. My husband sold her, but she's actually mine by law."

"Here we go. Another slave runaway. What I wouldn't give for one good jilted lover."

"Last known to be living in Hagerstown, Maryland, but I've good reason to think she might be here in New York City with a family named Woolsey. At eight Brevoort Place."

"Heard of the Woolseys—in the papers all the time. That's some fancy address. Jemma working there?"

"Must I do your entire job for you? That's what I need to know—if she is indeed there, and if not there, where. What she's doing. Et cetera. I stood outside the town house at that address in an attempt to see Jemma, trying to assume the role of a passerby, and was accosted by a colored man."

"Is this a grab-and-go?"

"I don't—"

"You want her taken back to your plantation?"

"You can do that?"

"Can do anything for Uncle Sam's dollars."

"I hate even the touch of Union money."

"Ah, I suspected you were a copperhead, being from Louisiana and all."

"The Yankees killed my brother, Mr. Bigelow. I will never support them. If that makes me what you call a copperhead, so be it."

The detective patted my hand. "There, there. I hate them, too. This war will ruin our great country, bringing all those freed slaves up here." He smiled, revealing a pond-water-brown jumble of teeth. "No need for you to touch Union money, if you'd like to pay in another way."

"Don't be ridiculous, sir. How could you ever imagine I'd stoop so low?" I reached into my *porte-monnaie,* pulled out a gold eagle coin, and tossed it onto his desk blotter.

He snatched the coin and dropped it in his vest pocket. "That's a good start, but it'll cost you fifty more dollars."

"That's robbery."

"That's New York City, Mrs. Watson. But just because I like you, here's some free information. Eldest Woolsey daughter is Abigail. In the newspapers practically every day, do-gooding at the Ladies' House of Industry. Takes in indigent females, teaches them moneymaking skills. You being a woman, she'll drop information she wouldn't tell me."

"Where is it?"

"Sixteenth Street. Just get her to take pity on you and you'll get into that town house, get more information. After that, if you want some muscle to get that slave back, I'm available. All we gotta do is make some charge stick, like espionage or treason. Meantime, I'll start gathering information on her from my sources, and you make the call if you want to blackbird that slave of yours back down to Maryland."

Georgy

WE RETURNED TO POINT LOOKOUT AFTER OUR DISASTROUS attempt to rescue Patience. Jemma sat in silence and would accept little solace, blaming herself for her sister's dire situation. Mother dispatched an urgent letter to her cousin in the Maryland courthouse, begging intervention in the situation, but received no reply. I sent a letter to Mrs. Gibbons begging help with Jemma's mother and sister and received a prompt, if cryptic, reply saying she may already be familiar with the case and would do her best, but if she was successful no word would come to us and she expected me to keep our exchange confidential.

After that, life at Point Lookout went on without incident until we received a letter from the surgeon general's office:

Surgeon Heger, U.S.A.

Sir: The Secretary of War has directed the transfer of seven hundred wounded prisoners from Chester, Pa., to Point Lookout General Hospital.

Upon arrival you will discharge the female nurses, reserving only one suitable person in the low-diet kitchen and one in the linen room. By order,

> C. H. Crane, Surgeon,
> U.S.A.

It was yet another dismissal from the nursing world and the indignity of it was profound; just as we had settled ourselves and started to make real headway with our patients, we were being replaced by male nurses once again.

We'd become expert at packing our trunks and prepared to remove ourselves back to Brevoort Place, with me more convinced than ever America needed a school to train a multitude of female nurses. We would prove expert and indispensable, and never be replaced again.

THE FIRST THING I DID once I landed back at Brevoort Place was visit Mother's bank manager friend, Mr. Tempy Green, to ask for a loan to establish a home for my nursing school. I could never ask Mother for funds since she was on a fixed income derived from the investments Father left her, I was too proud to ask Eliza, and Uncle Edward could offer only a small advance, his assets being tied up in war-related funds. As a result I sat across from Mr. Green's oak desk in a short-legged, down-seated chair, possibly designed to make his clients feel small and put them at a disadvantage. A spare, goggle-eyed snapping turtle of a man, with the look many bank managers possess of a great deal of self-importance and forced affability, he leaned forward, hands folded over his blotter.

"Miss Georgeanna. How enterprising of you to imagine opening a school for female nurses. You understand your mother's funds are tied up in bonds? But I'm happy to grant you the one thousand dollars you request."

I placed one hand to my chest. "I am terribly grateful, Mr. Green."

"The loan would use her accounts as collateral."

"Oh, no. I couldn't do that."

"Then of course I cannot lend you money as a single woman. Have you a male to countersign? Are you engaged?"

"Well, no, Mr. Green."

"What? A woman like you in your, well, not far past your prime? Any number of men would be willing to snap you up."

"My uncle Edward offered to co-sign once the war ends."

He nodded toward a tall gentleman near the check counter. "What you need is a fine man like Mr. Burpee over there. No doubt preparing to invest in yet another property in our great city. Do you find the whiff of commerce distasteful, Miss Woolsey?"

"My father was a merchant, Mr. Green. But Mr. Burpee is not in uniform."

"Great men like Mr. Burpee cannot be sacrificed to war, Miss Woolsey. His projects keep the Union economy afloat. I'm happy to introduce you, but I warn you, many a fine lady has set her cap for him and none has succeeded."

"Please do not, Mr. Green. It would seem too forward."

"I've made three matches for clients who sat right where you sit. Now, Mr. Burpee belongs to your uncle's club, comes from a good family. You know what they say, it takes three generations to make a gentleman, but the Burpees have done it in *one*. Gone from steerage to peerage in no time at all. Not as distinguished as your family, coming off the *Mayflower* and all, but quite a fine match nonetheless. A little bird might suggest he come over for a meet?"

"Absolutely not, Mr. Green."

"Well, it won't do to get testy, Miss Woolsey, unless you'd like to stay 'Miss' for good, like Abigail and Jane, poor creatures."

Mr. Green raised one arm and waved Mr. Burpee over, as if hailing an omnibus on Broadway. "Archie. Come here, good man, for an introduction."

I tried to sink farther into my down-filled hole.

Mr. Burpee ambled over, telegraph-pole tall, spotlessly neat and sandy-haired, the kind of man who assumes he's always welcome. "What is it,

Tempy? I hope you've called me here to meet this charming lady. Miss Woolsey?"

He nodded to me, a smile in his pale blue eyes, his cheeks lightly pockmarked.

"You know each other?" Mr. Green asked.

"I've seen the newspaper article about Miss Woolsey's time spent at Gettysburg with her mother, in the service of our troops. The illustration was remarkably truthful."

"Thank you, Mr. Burpee. I'm writing a book about my three weeks there."

He turned his full attention to me. "You have quite a distinguished family, if the article can be believed. Your father is descended from Howlands? They have owned some of the most impressive properties in New England. And your uncle holds half of Astoria."

I glanced at Mr. Green and he raised his eyebrows as if to say *This is going quite well.*

"And you currently reside at Brevoort Place? Fine address."

"You enjoy discussing real estate, Mr. Burpee?"

He removed his gloves. "My apologies, Miss Woolsey. I'm a man possessed by my work, I'm afraid. Houses and horses, those two things consume me."

"I must admit, sometimes I like horses better than some humans."

Mr. Burpee tilted his head to one side. "How remarkably candid of you, Miss Woolsey."

I turned to Mr. Green. "I must be going."

"Please, Miss Woolsey, might I come and call on you at Brevoort?" Mr. Burpee asked. "I drive a Brewster wagon with a premium matched set— two of the finest mounts in the city. Many people come to our farm out in Lancaster just to admire them."

"I don't think it would be—"

"Please do me the honor, Miss Woolsey. I've had a terrible day and it would reverse my bad luck, at least for the moment."

"I suppose I might accept one call."

"Well done," Mr. Green said, slapping his palms on his desk.

Mr. Burpee nodded to me and strode toward the door. "My man will be in touch, Miss Woolsey," he said over his shoulder. "You'll be most happy you said yes."

IT SOON BECAME CLEAR why Mr. Burpee was a success in the real estate world, because it was impossible to decline his attentions. I ended up accompanying him in his fine carriage to Central Park, where we risked death at breakneck speeds along the reservoir, and to a splendid dinner at Hotel Brevoort, where he presented remarks to his fellow real estate tycoons and we dined on *pigeons en compote* and roast woodcocks. He was a well-mannered companion and could tell a fine story at times, but drank wine while I stayed mostly to water, and though I tried to steer the conversation toward politics and the high-stakes chess match between Generals Lee and Grant that would decide the fate of our republic, he spoke mostly of the endless qualities of his myriad houses and horses.

It was not a love match, but I consoled myself with the fact that Mr. Green at the bank was thrilled with this product of his matchmaking skills and sent me congratulatory smiles when I saw him now and then on the street.

THAT SPRING, JEMMA'S ANKLE was still troubling her, and one morning Mother declared, "We all need a restorative trip to the country." She, Abby, Carry, and Hatty packed up and set off for Litchfield, Connecticut, to visit friends, and Jemma and I headed off on the train to upstate New York, to Eliza and Joe's country house, Tioronda.

Jemma and I sat together on the train and watched the budding trees pass by in an emerald blur. We toasted each other with a glass of claret, to the good news that the U.S. Senate had finally passed a resolution proposing a constitutional amendment abolishing slavery. Though the resolution did not include border states like Maryland, and slaves there were still far from free, it still felt good to celebrate what victories we could.

Her family being left in Maryland was a constant source of worry to

Jemma and for much of the ride we strategized like war generals about how to deliver her mother and sister from Maryland.

"I could ask Nathan to travel down there with me, though even having all the correct papers would not guarantee his safety."

"Perhaps our next step should be a letter-writing campaign?" I asked. "Mother knows half the lawyers in Maryland."

After a while Jemma stared out the window, lost in thought. I hadn't the heart to tell her that I'd just seen a sickening account in the newspaper, of Confederate troops in Fort Pillow, Tennessee, that had just massacred a large group of captured colored soldiers, even as they begged for mercy. After every victory for abolition, we seemed to take a step back.

ELIZA AND MORITZ MET Jemma and me at the train station and we piled into the Howlands' enclosed carriage, Moritz riding up with the driver.

It was as if spring had wrapped all of Fishkill in her arms that glorious April day as we drove through the countryside to the estate. Soon we saw Tioronda in the distance, spread out at the base of Mount Beacon, that great foothill green with the first tender buds, and Fishkill Creek down the hill beyond, a ribbon of silver through the spring grass. What a tremendous patriot Joseph Howland had been to leave that heavenly place in the service of his country.

We turned in to the long driveway and soon the handsome brown sandstone estate rose up above us. I exited the carriage to admire the house, a fearsome large place with a gabled roof, the Union flag swaying atop it in the breeze.

Eliza met us as we entered the cool vestibule with its silk-upholstered settee and japanned mirror. Mother had sent up little Pico to the estate and he greeted us by alternately jumping straight up in the air and chasing his stubby tail.

"What a lovely place to come home to," I said.

Jemma admired the blue-and-white vases on the hall table.

"Those belonged to our mother's mother, brought all the way from China," Eliza said.

I handed our gloves to Moritz as Joe descended the carpeted stairs, leaning on his cane.

I lifted my skirts, hurried up the steps, and threw my arms about him.

He smiled. "I usually only get such a fine reception from Pico."

"I missed you so terribly much, Joe. It's a pleasure to see you looking so fine. And to see practically every municipal building in town has the Howland name on it now."

How restored he looked, after so much war and misery.

"And may I introduce our good friend Jemma?" I asked.

"Joseph Howland," he said with an outstretched hand.

Jemma limped to him, took his hand, and nodded in return. "What a pretty house you have."

"I hope you have a chance to enjoy it, with that bad foot of yours. Seems you're the one in need of the cane. We'll get you fixed up."

As Eliza directed Moritz with our trunks and showed Jemma to the study to rest and elevate her injured foot, Joe stepped to the doorway, breathing deep the fresh country air.

"Georgy, I hope you don't mind that Frank Bacon is stopping by to have a look at Jemma's ankle on his way to New Haven."

I joined Joe at the door as Frank rode toward us down the drive on horseback, his medical saddlebags flapping up and down behind him.

"Since he's arriving as we speak, I'm not sure what difference my opinion makes, Joe."

Frank rode to the block near the entry and dismounted, a groom holding his horse by the bridle. He wore what appeared to be a new uniform, still double-breasted but with finer brass buttons and pretty gold-trimmed shoulder straps, and a handsome new black felt Hardee hat, complete with gray plume. Had the benevolent Mrs. Barnett provided it all?

He looked up at us, unsmiling. "I hope I'm not intruding."

Eliza joined us at the door. "Come in, Frank."

Frank slid his saddlebags of pretty new white leather down off the horse's back. He hurried up the steps, walked into the entryway, and removed his hat. "You're looking well, Miss Georgy," he said, meeting my gaze with no trace of fellowship in his smile.

I took his hat and handed it to Moritz. "How could one not thrive in this setting? And you look to have recovered nicely. How long has it been?"

"I guess, since Gettysburg, more than a year." Frank dusted off his trousers.

Joe extended a hand to his friend. "Any war news? The papers practically crawl up here on their own."

"They say General Sherman has the Rebels on the run. And I've heard news of bread riots in Savannah."

Eliza shook Frank's hand. "Perhaps the Confederates are giving up?"

Frank shook his head. "Not a chance."

"How good to see you, Frank," I said. "What perfect timing. Jemma and I have only just arrived."

He took up his saddlebags. "I cannot stay long."

Eliza linked her arm in his and led him toward the study. "Thank you for coming, Frank."

"Nathan tells me Jemma's still suffering from her sprain of last summer."

We entered the study, where Jemma sat sewing, her right foot upon a hassock.

I arranged the pillow more firmly under her foot. "We've kept it elevated, hoping the swelling would finally come down."

Frank shook Jemma's hand. "It seems last time we met, you were doing the healing on my account."

Jemma smiled. "I've tried all my usual remedies. But nothing works."

"Still painful to put pressure on this foot?"

"Yes."

Frank squatted down next to her foot and with both hands felt her ankle.

She winced.

He looked up at her. "I hate to ask you to relive that painful day, but how did the injury occur?"

"We were caught in a great crowd, and someone fell on me, causing my ankle to turn. I heard a popping sound. I limped home on it perfectly well, but the next day the pain was much worse. Margaret kept it packed with ice, but it still hurt."

"I see. How about up here?" Frank felt farther up her calf.

Jemma called out in pain. "Please, no, Dr. Bacon. It's worse there."

I stood behind Jemma's chair. "It is her ankle, Frank."

"I understand why you might think so, Georgy." He stepped to the table, opened one of the saddlebags, and removed two carved hardwood splints and a variety of bandages. "But actually, it's not."

He sat next to Jemma's foot on the hassock and set one splint on each side of her calf, and, to secure it, began winding a length of rolled bandage around both.

"What is it, then?" Eliza asked.

"Jemma will wear this splint for at least two weeks, and then she may begin therapeutic exercises."

"I don't understand," I said.

"She has suffered a terribly painful break, a Maisonneuve fracture, a spiral fracture of the fibula."

"So, it's not sprained?" Jemma asked.

"No, a sprain would have healed months ago. You did turn your ankle, Jemma, but in a traumatic manner, which actually broke your fibula, this bone farther up in your leg. Walking on the injury all these months didn't allow it to heal."

Frank clasped Jemma's hand. "You are a very brave girl to suffer that pain every day. It will not heal without rest. Will you stay off it?"

Jemma nodded.

Frank waved me over. "Would you work with me here, Georgy?"

He directed me to sit in front of him on the hassock. With my back to him, he wrapped his arms around me and took my hands in his.

"Put your hands here so you can get a feel for it." He placed my hands on either side of the splints as he continued winding the bandage. "Keep the tension snug, but not tight. Immobilize the fibula, but keep the blood supply. Here, you finish."

I wound the bandage up to Jemma's knee, tucked it, and Frank stood.

At once, I missed the warmth of him.

"How does that feel?" Frank asked Jemma.

She released a grand sigh. "No pain—for the first time in so long."

Frank packed up his saddlebags. "First sign of numb toes it must be loosened."

Eliza poured a cordial glass of brandy. "May she have a bit, Dr. Bacon?"

"Yes, indeed, Jemma deserves it. A glass of brandy and the Woolsey sisters, two of the best nurses of the Sanitary Commission—what more could a patient want?"

FRANK STAYED FOR LUNCH and Eliza's cook outdid himself, with stuffed partridges, fiddlehead ferns, spring greens, and a magnificent custard. How good it was to see Jemma feeling better at last and to have Frank Bacon in such a splendid mood.

Eliza passed Frank a bowl of whipped cream for the custard. "I must say, it's a fine treat to have you all to ourselves, Frank. Where is Bethada tonight? She is usually so, well, ever present."

"She's visiting her parents in Poughkeepsie and I'm on my way to Danbury. Once we see my mother in New Haven I report back."

Eliza leaned toward Frank, at her left. "It's such a nice day, perhaps you and Georgy could walk down to the icehouse. We're all out of ice up here, I'm afraid."

"I do need to ride on to make Danbury tonight. I'm meeting one of my old professors for dinner."

"It will only take a few minutes, and then you can be on your way."

Frank stood. "I cannot deny any of you Woolsey sisters a request. And besides, I could use the air."

FRANK AND I WALKED down from the back of the house to Fishkill Creek and along its newly green banks, heading toward the wooden icehouse in the distance, each of us carrying an oaken bucket.

"Remember when you and Joe floated down the river on your backs and Mother ran after you, thinking you were caught in the current?"

"Look, Georgy, please don't feel you need to patronize me. I know this must be awkward, being alone with me like this when we are simply friends. It's clear Eliza is trying to encourage a match. Anyone could've run for ice."

"It's not awkward in the least, Frank; in fact I've thought quite a lot about the things I said to you in Washington. It was, well, a difficult time back then."

"You're right, Georgy. But everything happens for a reason."

We reached the icehouse and he opened the door, held it for me, and we entered the cool, dark room where a wall of ice stood in crystalline blue blocks.

"I've been thinking, Frank. About that project I told you about at Gettysburg."

Frank picked up the ice pick and chipped off ice into his bucket. "I don't remember much from that time."

"I told you I wanted to start a teaching hospital—for nurses. And I've thought long and hard about how I could raise the money, to add to the five hundred from Mrs. Peabody. That should help secure a place to hold classes."

"What do you want from me?"

"Your partnership."

He turned to me. "You cannot be serious."

"We would be equal partners. I suggest we have a board of advisors, for only with the female point of view properly represented will women nurses truly be heard. I'm suggesting New Haven as a home for the school. Property is less expensive there than in New York."

"You seem to forget there's a war going on."

"*After* the war. I can feel it, Frank, this is all going to be over soon, and if we arrange things now we will be ready right as the war concludes. We'll certainly need female nurses in this country. Families in time of serious illness have great difficulty in finding competent attendants. Epidemics may, at any time, visit us. Who would then care for our sick and helpless poor?"

"That is what family is for."

"Not everyone *has* family, Frank. And how often a woman is called upon to dedicate her life to an ill relative, when she has no training. We would school an army of women who are always ready. *Semper paratus,* as you say. A yearlong, thorough course of instruction and experience at the bedside of the sick, creating a corps of disciplined nurses, colored and white, to meet the wants of families of all classes of society."

Frank cut his ice in silence.

"Well? I request the favor of a reply, Dr. Bacon. Will you be my partner?"

He turned to me and tossed his pick in the bucket. "Once, yes. There was a time when I would have followed you anywhere."

"This is a business proposition, Frank."

"Yes and no. I cannot be with you on a consistent basis, Georgy, and not feel the pain of our past. I must say this suggestion of a business partnership feels insensitive, given your refusals of me."

I set down my bucket and stepped to Frank. "I was unfair to you back in Washington."

He met my gaze, there in the cool darkness. He reached out, stroked my cheek, and a chill ran through me.

"You're cold." He turned, grabbed his bucket, and stepped toward the door. "We should get back."

"But, Frank—"

"Georgy, my affections lie elsewhere. I must consider what Bethada might say to such a proposition. She has been a devoted companion and I must return that loyalty."

I followed him out. The sun had clouded over and did little to warm us.

"And besides, Bethada has made a similar request of me."

I stopped. "Similar? In what way, Frank?"

He started back up the hill toward the house. "She has a mind to open a nursing school herself."

I pulled Frank back by the arm. "Tell me this is not true, Frank."

He continued walking.

I gathered up my skirt and hurried after him.

"This was my project from the start. How could you let her take it from me?"

"She has a mind of her own. I'm about to rejoin my regiment. I have no time for bickering."

"Talk about a lack of loyalty. You side with that woman over me?"

"I have no contract with you, Georgeanna. You only come to me when it suits you. After all, you're going about with Archie Burpee."

"Am I to join the convent after you pledged yourself to Bethada? I am simply trying to continue a friendship with Archie."

"Let's be honest, Georgy. You like stringing me along. Here you are, practically engaged, and still hoping to keep me tethered."

"I certainly came to the wrong person for help, Frank Bacon. Seems you've been blinded by the Barnetts' money. With such fine gifts, like that smart new uniform and white leather saddlebags."

He stopped and turned. "Bethada may have suggested I upgrade my attire, but I have never accepted one pin from that family, though you could take a lesson in consideration from them."

"Is it so wrong to ask for your help with such an honest endeavor, Frank?"

He continued on up the hill. "Perhaps ask your *Archie*. He seems happy to supply his attentions."

We arrived back at the house and Eliza met us in the front hall. Frank bid a hasty goodbye and called for the groom.

As we watched Frank trot down the drive, a cloud of dust in his wake, Eliza asked, "Why don't you tell him, Georgy?"

"Tell him what?"

"How much you care for him. You certainly are never so restrained with your opinions in other aspects of life."

"Next time, perhaps."

"There may not be a next time, Georgy. Frank asked my estimation of Bethada. Said that he was considering asking for her hand."

"And?"

"I told him she was an admirable woman, but there was someone better suited to him."

"Eliza."

"He understood my meaning entirely: said you refused him, a second time, and he promised not to pursue the matter further."

"He's right."

"From the moment you two met, you were drawn to each other. That is a rare thing in a person's life."

"Is it?"

"You certainly don't speak of poor Mr. Burpee the same way." Eliza smoothed back my hair. "But you do get in your own way sometimes, Georgy. Why on earth can you not meet him halfway?"

Arm in arm, we watched Frank disappear in the distance, leaving a cloud of dust.

"If only I knew."

Jemma

ONCE WE CAME BACK FROM TIORONDA, MY ANKLE FELT SO much better I could walk with no pain. I also took care to rest it. The morning after our return, I was sitting at the Woolsey kitchen table finishing my trash bonnets, three drying on flowerpots, while I fashioned more buds out of scraps.

I liked sitting in that big kitchen. It took my mind off of the terrible way I'd botched our rescue of Patience to watch all the goings-on, clear through the whole house. Working with my hands gave my brain a chance to think over all the ways to get Ma and Patience back. Went through every scene in my head. Going down there myself and drugging LeBaron and his dogs. Having Nathan hire out a boat to pull up to the dock near Peeler. It about drove me crazy, all the plans.

I sewed a dotted Swiss jonquil to the face frame of one bonnet. It had been Ma that named them trash bonnets. She'd be proud every nurse at Point Lookout had wanted one, and I'd made ten dollars in Union money I put away to fund my trip back to get her and Patience.

Georgy came through the kitchen. "Jemma, have you seen my camel hair?"

"On the piano, last I saw it."

Once they stopped bossing me around, those Woolsey women were nice to be around. They showed every kindness to me that day, all seven of those sisters, as they ran about helping their ma. It felt wrong to be so happy when Ma and Patience were in such dire straits, but I never laughed so much in my life.

At first it was hard to tell which sister was which, but I managed a system, wrote all the names on paper and fastened a little fabric flower next to each.

Abigail hurried by, toting a pile of men's drawers. Even sick that day with the grippe, she still worked through it, she and Moritz dragging crates of ink for the troops across the front parlor. She was the oldest, solid-built, and maybe the most book smart, though that was a contest in that house. She always had her nose in a book and worked at the Ladies' House of Industry, a poorhouse-type place, and nearly ran it, by the sound of her talk at dinner. I gave her a pretty black silk flower since she only wore her old black dresses to death and back, even when every sister harped at her to make herself a new one.

Jane, second oldest, was the most excitable, always exercised by this or that, that day running about the front parlor flapping like a trapped bird at the mention of a bad war report. I gave her a light pink homespun flower, on account of how handsome she looked in her dress of that color, with her red hair with a kinky wave like Sally Smith's. She dressed the best of all of them, hands down, always putting herself together in just the right way.

Everything about Mary Woolsey Howland was pretty. As she sat across from me in that big white smock she wore when she painted, all covered every which way with dabs of color, drawing flowers on her bonnet ribbons, baby on her lap, her smile and kind way brought to my mind a baby deer. She wrote famous poems that were secretly hers, and her husband, Reverend Howland, always brought an extra lemon drop for me, and their four little girls were sweet as their ma. I gave Mary a sky-blue morning glory, on account of that being her favorite flower to paint and since that was the color of her eyes.

Eliza, the sister next youngest to Georgy, sat playing piano pretty well, but she had to look at the music. For such a rich lady she was nice as can be and Georgy's bosom friend and had a French servant named Moritz who knew what we all wanted before we knew ourselves. I made her a purple flower since that's the color of royalty and she seemed like a kind queen to me.

Georgeanna was the funniest of all of them and once got Miss Jane laughing so hard she had to have her ribs taped. She had her parlor skates on, rolling around the place, toting her books she wrote about the time at Gettysburg. She rolled to the piano and turned the page for Eliza, and then skated away. She was maybe my favorite since she and her ma came upon me and showed me a home, but she might have been my favorite anyways since she really listens to a person when they talk, good thing for her beau, Mr. Burpee, who only talks about himself day and night. Georgy got a yellow silk rose since yellow means friendship and she was a good friend.

Next oldest, Hatty sat with Mrs. Woolsey in her favorite big old chair, holding bits of dried liver in the air, making their dog Pico stand on his back legs. She was always with Mrs. Woolsey, like her little shadow, waiting on her hand and foot and maybe the most generous of all. If you needed something, Hatty would tire herself out making sure you got it. I gave her a white muslin rosette, pure and good as she was.

Carry was the youngest and tallest and stood with Margaret in the kitchen pulling pink taffy, twisting and drawing it out, near the open window. Carry was sure smart about every little thing. She didn't like being youngest, you could tell, and she'd sometimes complain about things, but the older girls wouldn't give her the time of day. She got especially mad when their brother kept sending cannonballs and mortar shells back home from the battlefield as souvenirs and their ma kept them at the bottom of the stairs on display.

"I live in mortal fear," Carry said. "What if the projectiles go off, the grapeshot explodes, and the cannonballs do something equally unpleasant?"

I helped her tote them out to the backyard, afraid myself they'd explode there in the house. For Carry I made a bright red rose, since it seemed like her mind was on fire.

Mary came to me and leaned in over the kitchen table. "Ready for your second week at Sharp's?" she whispered.

I stood, worried I was late for my job. Mary had kept it hid from her ma, since Mrs. Woolsey wouldn't have approved of me working for a tobacco store, seeing as her church frowned on what she called *intoxicants of any kind*.

"You better go now. I can finish those."

"Can't trouble you with my work." With all her running around after her babies and painting pictures for the upcoming Sanitary Fair, Mary'd worn herself out and grown purple circles under her eyes.

She gently pulled me out of my seat and sat down in it. "You can't be late this morning, Jemma. Besides, I enjoy assisting with these. Every one sold helps a soldier."

I HURRIED ACROSS FIRST Avenue and along West Broadway, and the shops changed from fancy to plainer, with a few schools and Dutch groceries on the bottom floors of the houses. Above the doorway of a crinoline shop, hoop cages and petticoats hung like bells, and swayed in the breeze.

Somewhere someone played the drums like Ma used to, and the scent of frying onions filled the air, and best of all, there were dark faces everywhere. Coming and going from shops and restaurants, everywhere I looked were people my color. I had to stop myself from smiling too much, since most real New Yorkers didn't put much stock in a grin. But my life was good. Except for missing my family, I was on top of the world, with two men vying for my affections. I carried the little bone cross Pa gave me, rubbing it in my fingers, asking him to help me decide.

I'd loved Carter since I could remember, and we were practically sister and brother. He was funny and smart and wanted more out of life, no sin in that. But what about family? Carter esteemed Ma and Patience but wanted to start our life without them. I pictured Carter, his sweet brown eyes and smooth cocoa skin and pretty smile. He was prettier than me for sure.

Nathan, on the second hand, was older than me and there was a lot that was nice about that. He knew the world better and had handsome manners. Some bit taller, too, but more serious. Maybe not as handsome as Carter but a fine face, with those green eyes. He was a soldier, too, which gave him extra points for the blue uniform, so nice across his wide shoulders. He also cared about Ma and Patience a lot. Would talk with me for days about it if I wanted.

Having made no decision by the time I got to 93 West Broadway, I kissed Pa's cross and slipped it in my pocket. He'd help me decide.

I was excited to start my second week, and looked in the big front window. "A real fine concern," Nathan had called it when he'd walked me there my first day. I hurried in the door under the sign with the cigar swinging from it, so big a giant could smoke it, SUPERIOR CIGARS writ across the middle. We sold every kind of tobacco product and that place was thick with good smells, the hundred glass jars that lined two walls to the ceiling full of the licorice, rum, and honey they used to make the chew taste good.

The war had done a lot to spread the tobacco habit and business was busy at Superior, with men sometimes two deep at the long oak counter, especially when a whole regiment came in. Dr. Smith's friend Mr. Sharp got what he called *a mixed clientele,* black and white, men mostly. Mr. Edward Woolsey bought his cigars there since he thought they were *The best this side of Havana.* Even the mayor sent his people in for his.

I'd already done well, coming up from sweeper to counter help in one day, since, being around tobacco my whole life, I knew a lot about it. Mister Watson alone had fifty kinds in his office, always looking to better his own, and Anne-May liked her snuff. Already knew pipe tobacco was called plug and chew was twist. I could tell a man's choice before he could.

"You look like a Lone Jack sort of man," I told a soldier from Boston. He ended up buying a bag and that's when Mr. Sharp put me on the counter for good.

Mr. Sharp was a kind man, old as Dr. Smith and black as Pa but free his whole life, he told me. That morning he paid me for the previous week.

"This is more than any new employee's ever earned in just five days," he said and handed me a big, beautiful dollar, fifty cents of it just from tips.

I slipped it in my pocket, smiling ear to ear, and wished Ma could see that. Mr. Sharp made my eyes well up when he said I was already *a valued member of the staff* and he looked puzzled at why I'd cry at that, but he'd never been owned by anybody, never mind Miss Anne-May Wilson Watson.

What Mr. Sharp didn't know was I had the advantage of my Aunt Tandy Rose White People Manners and pulled them out whenever those little bells up on the door rang and a customer stepped in.

Right away I'd say, "How do you do," never "Suh" or "Missis." When they asked for a certain leaf, I'd say, "Why certainly we have that, let me take a look for you, sir," always with a smile and a tip of the head at the end. "The fragrance is rather agreeable to the ladies" was a good line, too.

The better a customer dressed, the more they liked snuff and cigars. Plain soldiers and the ruffian types got chew mostly, and a pipe was the officers' choice.

I even made some tobacco jokes. "Better than smoking coffee," I'd say, and that always got a laugh.

They liked hearing how I came up on a tobacco plantation but I was careful not to say which one. "Packed twists in hogsheads myself," I'd say.

That always got me an extra half-penny.

Since I'd never touched money before I came to New York I had to learn about it right quick. I knew I was what Nathan would call a *hypocrite,* me there making money from a crop made off the backs of black folks, maybe even off my own ma's leaf. But I figured I had just as much right to have that money in my pocket as anyone.

Carter came by that morning, as he had many times that week, when I was busy, like the day a whole regiment was three deep at the counter, on their way to fight. They wanted to stock up before they left and had me up and down the ladder getting them a bit of this and that. Least I could do for boys going off to fight for my freedom, which I still didn't have.

Carter waved to me over the crowd. "Hey, Jemma!"

I hurried down to the end of the counter. It was so good to see him, rucksack over one shoulder.

"I'm leaving. For Ottawa. You coming?"

I crossed my arms over my belly. "Still don't know."

"Think you do, hate to say it. Saw you walking with a soldier the other night when I came by at closing."

"That's just Nathan."

"Just Nathan looked pretty happy to be holding your arm."

"It's not so much that, Carter." I set one hand over my heart. "You know you'll always be right here for me. But I'm serious about getting my ma and Patience. You never had a family. Don't value it like I do."

"You're my family."

"Once, maybe, but things have changed for both of us. I know more what I want. I like it here. Have a job and got paid more money today than I've ever had in my life. And friends."

"Those holy New England women? Snug and smug in that house."

"They gave me a home and cash money. I won't run off before I pay them back."

"You're gonna need that money. New York's expensive. Not like Canada."

I took the dollar from my pocket. "Here. I want you to have this. It'll go a lot further in Canada, I guess. Get yourself some licorice whips."

Carter hesitated, then took the bill and stuffed it in his pocket. "But you gotta be careful. Anne-May's not gonna stop—"

"I'll take my chances, Carter."

I squinted one eye and made a picture of him in my mind, standing there, knowing it would have to last me the rest of my life. "Write me when you get there?"

He wiped a tear with the back of his sleeve. "I will. Send you some maple candy."

"You do that, now, Carter."

He walked out without a look back and I watched him go and thanked Pa for helping me decide.

I went back to work, wondering if I'd made the right decision. Just warm all over at the thought that I finally could make my own choice.

———

NATHAN CAME BY TO walk me home and from the way I was so happy to see him, I knew I'd been right to tell Carter I was staying put in New York. He held out his arm for me to take and we walked along like a proper couple.

Almost home, he stopped me on the sidewalk. "Wish I'd had a chance to come by earlier to see you."

"About what?"

"Dr. Bacon saw a patient last night at Hotel Brevoort and I went out to get more quinine and passed by here. That's when I saw a woman standing just across the street."

"Black or white?" I asked as we started walking again.

"White. There was something about her I didn't like, and I approached her. 'Do you have some sort of business with the Woolseys?' I asked. She stepped back and let into me, shouting something awful. 'Well, I have *never* been talked to in such a way by a darkie. How dare you question *me*. I am just takin' some air.'"

My whole body went cold. "What did she look like?"

"Well, that's what I wanted to say. Thought she might be that Anne-May you told me about."

"Skinny?"

"From what I could tell. It was dark."

"What color hair?"

"Brown, far as I could see under the bonnet."

"You'd make a terrible detective, Nathan."

"Southern accent for sure."

"Louisiana?"

"All I know is she was pure nasty."

A shudder shivered through me. "That's Anne-May for sure. Come to take me back."

"Don't know, but I'm going to stay closer from now on."

"Thank you, Nathan, for telling me." He saw me in and I looked both ways down Brevoort Place before closing the door, the slam of it good and strong. That house had been my fortress.

I drew a curtain aside and watched him walk away, down the street. Had I been wrong to turn Carter away? He was probably halfway to Ottawa. Would Anne-May come at night? She'd hire some slave trader to haul me back there and take my new clothes, get me back in calico, scrubbing her feet. I held my hands to my face—cold.

I turned the key in the lock and climbed the stairs toward bed.

How stupid I'd been, ever thinking I could live safe for long.

Anne-May

NEW YORK CITY
APRIL 1864

ONE AFTERNOON, AFTER AN INVIGORATING WALK IN CENTRAL
Park, I arrived back at Hotel Brevoort to freshen up, handing the bellman
a five-dollar gold piece to ensure his continued fawning, and the desk clerk
presented an envelope to me. I recognized Jubal's pale lavender stationery
with the fawn-brown return address printed on the envelope flap, colors
that no other man I knew could make work so nicely.

SMALLS AND SONS
MERCANTILE,
HOLLYWOOD, MARYLAND

Dear Anne-May,

*Since I have not had the pleasure of a reply to my last letter sent to
you in Washington, here I pen another, for I grow more concerned
by the day. You may have heard that Maryland is rife with talk of
what they call Copperheads, Confederate spies in the midst of Yankee supporters. This morning's paper held an opinion piece stating
there are spies in Maryland, delivering U.S. Army information to*

powerful Southern forces. To make matters worse, Harriet tells me a gentleman calling himself a Pinkerton has opened a suspicious line of questioning in Leonardtown. I impress upon you the dire consequences of the material we are both familiar with turning up and implicating us both. I beseech you to locate it in a most timely manner and deliver it here to me so we can make sure it does not fall into the wrong hands.

> *Most affectionately*
> *yours,*
> *Jubal*

Most affectionately yours. He'd not written *love,* as he usually signed off.

As I slid the note back into the envelope the desk clerk cleared his throat. "Have you forgotten you owe two more days of payment, Mrs. Watson?"

"How could I forget that, now?" I smiled. "I'll be right back with it."

I repaired to my room to retrieve payment from my hat trunk, only to find my money missing.

Had I not left it tucked behind the lining?

My blood went cold as I ripped the linings from each trunk and dumped every piece of clothing, to no avail. I returned to the front desk upon shaky knees.

"Something most egregious has happened, sir. My entire means of payment has been stolen from my room. One of your employees has taken it, I'm sure."

"So, you cannot pay your bill?" The clerk opened his leather ledger. "Your restaurant charges alone come to one hundred dollars."

"I just need a bit more time, that's all."

The clerk rang his bell. "Bellman, accompany Mrs. Watson to her room and remove her trunks to the storage locker."

"How can you? Where am I to go at this hour?" I pulled out my reticule and found it empty.

"It is more than just lack of payment. First, the Pinkertons come here inquiring about you."

"So, what's a little inquiry?"

"Plus, the housekeeper has reported the suite is damaged because you left the windows open and the room service tray lying about and crows came in and have flung uneaten food around the room."

"I'll find someone to clean it up."

"The strawberries alone have permanently stained our Aubusson carpet. Perhaps you will be more comfortable in a better class of accommodations, being from New Orleans and all. We will keep your trunks in lieu of payment. Perhaps the Pinkertons would like to examine them more closely."

I leaned in over the counter. "My dear man, I cannot be more sorry for the way circumstances have left me. Will a promissory note not suffice for the time bein'?"

He slid a card across the counter toward me. *Mr. Gerald Minkman, Pawnshop.* "This establishment may be of interest to you. In the meantime, bellman, escort Mrs. Watson out. We need that room for an incoming guest."

I ARRIVED AT THE ADDRESS Mr. Bigelow had provided for the Ladies' House of Industry, a dank-looking place that took in women of questionable moral quality and kept them from the poorhouse. A layer of dark clouds overhead did little to brighten the scene.

I pinched my cheeks, lifted one arm, and sniffed under there. Did I smell as if I'd slept on the street? I would keep my distance.

As I walked in, I held the door for a woman on the way out, a paper box in her arms.

"May I help?" I asked, adopting my best Yankee accent.

"I'm much obliged," the woman said. She deposited her box in the waiting carriage, returned, and I held the door open for her again.

"Now, are you by any chance the Abigail Woolsey I've read about in the newspapers?" I asked.

"I am," she said.

"Allow me to introduce myself. Lucretia Frick, from the great state of Vermont."

"Happy to meet you, Mrs. Frick. What an unusual accent you have. I've never heard a Vermont accent such as yours."

My heart skipped a beat. "Oh, I grew up in Canada."

"I'm sorry to be abrupt, but I'm on my way to my home to drop some donations for the Sanitary Fair." She looked to the gray sky. "Before the rain comes."

A solidly built woman, not wearing a wedding ring, and well past thirty, she appeared to have no intention of attracting the opposite sex, dressed in her plain black dress and not even a dab of rouge or an earbob.

"Do allow me to help. How grateful I would be to assist the cause of good Mr. Lincoln."

"I could use the help. All of the porters are otherwise employed. Come with me to the office and we'll each take a box."

I followed her to a room, where the walls were covered floor to ceiling in bookshelves stuffed with dusty leather-bound volumes, clearly untouched for years, and a gargantuan desk sat in the middle of it all, stacked with papers and ledger books. An envelope lay upon one ledger, the color of Union money showing through the paper, *Treasury* written on the front in a looping hand.

She handed me a box. "Hope this isn't too heavy?"

As she bent to reach for another box, I plucked the envelope from the desk and stashed it in my dress pocket. "Not heavy at all."

We loaded our cartons onto the carriage. She thanked me, then asked, "You don't mind helping me unpack these at my home? It's a short distance from here. We're using it as a staging area for the fair. And every servant we have is offering their service there today."

"It's no trouble at all," I said, climbing up next to her on the carriage seat. "I'm just thrilled to help."

WE CARRIED OUR CARTONS into the town house at 8 Brevoort Place, a nice enough brownstone a stone's throw from my former home, Hotel Brevoort. I followed her into a front parlor, the edges of which were packed floor to ceiling with crates and boxes. If not for a slight musty smell and some very tired dark sofas, it was a passably habitable place. I stepped to the map above the sofa, a patchwork of pink and green squares that showed the seat of the Confederacy. "Oh, the state of Virginia. I just can't abide those Rebels."

"My mother was actually born and bred from that great state, Mrs. Frick."

"Lovely place, Virginia."

I ran one finger across the map's frame, real gold leaf it looked like. "Does my heart good to meet God-fearing people in this big city. I assume you support the abolition of slavery, as all we good Christians do."

"Absolutely, Mrs. Frick." Abigail opened one carton and pulled out a stack of ladies' kid gloves. "They've asked me to bring over to the fair all the gloves we have. Seems they've sold every pair."

I plunged my hand into the carton. "Here, let me help you."

"How did you come to New York City?"

"I was on the farm in Nashua and—"

"But Nashua is in New Hampshire, not Vermont."

"Did I say Nashua? I meant—what's that town?—*Montpelier.* That is when I heard about the Sanitary Fair and thought I would come to assist. In fact . . ." I reached into the envelope in my pocket and withdrew a bill. "I would like to donate to the cause."

Abigail took the bill. "Twenty dollars? My goodness, Mrs. Frick. You are quite a patriot. My brother thanks you. He's a soldier stationed at Fort Monroe."

"Your only sibling in this big house?"

"Six sisters as well."

"Do they all work for war relief? Think I read in the paper about your sister Georgeanna?"

"We are proud of her. She nursed soldiers at Gettysburg last July with my mother. She's just returned from a few days upstate."

"That must have been so rewarding, to be right there in the front row of battle, helping so many of our boys in need. We must end the scourge of slavery, don't you agree, Miss Woolsey?"

"Fully, Mrs. Frick. In fact, my mother and sister have become tremen-dously good friends with a young woman who once was enslaved."

I straightened. "You don't say? How kind of them. And how did they meet?"

Abigail wrapped a stack of gloves in waxed paper and tied it off with twine. "The young woman had been wounded in battle, if you can imag-ine. Conscripted by the U.S. Army from a slave owner in Maryland."

I raised two fingers to my lips. "Hagerstown?"

Abigail turned to me, a deep crease betwixt her brows. "How did you know?"

My heart raced. "Oh, I just assumed. It is one of the biggest cities close by there."

Her gaze lingered on me. "Yes, indeed."

"And what is this former slave named?" I asked.

Abigail turned to me. "I'm afraid I have to leave now, Mrs. Frick. Thank you for your help. I believe I've taken up too much of your time already."

"Could I trouble you for a glass of water and a necessary room?"

Abigail sighed. "Please be quick as you can. You will find a necessary room on the second floor. I will fetch your water, but then I must be off."

"If you have ice on hand, I would be most appreciative, Abigail. I've worked up quite a thirst toting those cartons."

ABIGAIL RUSHED OFF TOWARD the back of the house in pursuit of water, and I lifted my skirts and climbed the stairs at breakneck speed. I hurried from room to room, opening armoires and running my foot under beds in search of Jemma's flowered carpetbag. I'd almost given up the search when I entered the last room, a small bedroom at the front of the house, and spied Jemma's floral bag on a chair.

"Mrs. Frick?" Abigail called up from the first floor.

"Just one moment," I called down.

I opened Jemma's bag and searched through the shirtwaists and fabric scraps. I dumped out the contents onto one of the two beds and rifled through it all but found no red Moroccan leather book. I opened a dresser drawer and pawed through cards of needles and spools of thread, casting them to the floor.

"What are you doing up here?"

I turned to find Abigail Woolsey in the doorway.

"Mrs. Frick, if that is your true name, I must ask you to leave immediately."

Georgy

NEW YORK CITY
APRIL 1864

BREVOORT PLACE, N.Y.C.

My dear Edward,

I am glad you are returning just in time for the Sanitary Fair, for it promises to be the supreme social event of the decade. Your nieces are all employed in service to the fair. Mary is very much engaged in her arrangements for the floral department and all the ladies are agog for novelties. Abby is getting quite warmed up about the fair and is making a beautiful silk flag and lots of other little matters and Georgy will sell her books. Mary's idea of having garden hats of white straw with broad ribbons with their ends painted in flowers is a pretty one, to be hung in her arbor of flowers. Everything of hers is to be of the garden style. . . .

With true affection,
Jane Eliza

Jemma and I came back to New York City from our visit to Eliza to find every floor of Mother's town house alive with preparations for the Sanitary

Commission Fair. The war had entered its fourth year, with General Grant appointed commander in chief of the entire U.S. Army. Skirmishes in the Southwest enlivened the military outlook for the North, and we began to hope the end of the war was not far off.

In New York City, striking evidences of prosperity abounded. The pleasant spring weather found hotels and boardinghouses full to bursting, and one could not escape talk of the approaching fair, which would benefit our troops.

The house echoed with the frenzy of critical tasks, and all of us, save Jane and Eliza, rushed about the attic packing up old chairs and washbasins for donation. We had each committed to a duty for the fair, and mine was to sell copies of my book, *Three Weeks at Gettysburg*, in the Author's Room. Jemma's fracture was healing nicely and she chose to sell her bonnets, which had become exceptionally popular with the Point Lookout nursing staff, and we all searched the attic trunks for more fabric scraps for her use, grabbing any ancestral fabric treasures not already turned to lint for the troops.

Carry held up a flattened calico bonnet. "Once the fair is over, I'll lie prostrate on the sofa and do little more than fan myself."

"I will join you," Hatty said. "With one end of my straw in a sherry cobbler."

As the two youngest, Hatty and Carry had been forced to grow up quickly during this terrible war. Once known only as the most noted gigglers, overnight they had become very accomplished women, both nursing long hours at Bellevue. They were rapidly approaching the age of thirty, that vast Rubicon. Would there be any men left alive for them to settle down with once this was all over?

I never tired of spending time in that attic, for all cares melted away up there under the raw wood eaves, above the elms. As Mary and Abby directed us to open certain trunks, dust danced in the one beam of light slanting through the high oval window. We pulled out camphor-scented stores of satin slippers, robes, and calico dresses.

Hatty pulled out an ancient pink satin snood and Jemma took it in two hands.

"I can make six roses with this."

How Father would have enjoyed that little tableau.

Quick as we set out the scraps, Jemma, sitting with a board upon her lap, fashioned each one into a little flower or bud. We stood transfixed by the deftness of her touch and how quickly she rolled up and fluffed out each perfect little flower.

Carry reached for one little nosegay. "And to think that you make them out of things no longer necessary. But I think 'trash bonnet' is a loathsome name for such lovely creations."

I held a muslin flower for Jemma as she tied it off at the base. "Jemma and I are going over to Uncle Edward's today, to collect quahog shells from which to make buttons for the center of each flower."

Carry glanced at Hatty. "Father's Beach? All the way to Queens? You gave up going to that beach for good reason, Georgy—"

"I am *quite* fine, if you don't mind. Completely over it. I was seven when it happened, for goodness' sakes."

"It's terribly desolate out there," Hatty said. "Maybe ask Mr. Burpee to accompany you. Or what about trusty Frank Bacon?"

Carry pulled a pile of oatmeal-colored homespun squares from the trunk. "He's busy with his lady friend. Heard they were doing the bear in Washington Square Park."

"Frank can embrace whomever he pleases," I said.

"Still no engagement, though," Carry said.

I handed a woolen scrap to Jemma. "I prefer to discuss which of our furnishings to donate to the fair."

"Skillful subject change," Carry said.

"Perhaps the chinoiserie vases," Hatty said.

"Mother's pride?" Abby asked. "Don't even mention it."

Hatty nodded toward the china cabinet. "There's always the lavender transferware."

"How would we eat?" Carry asked.

"And what of that fan down on the mantel?" Jemma asked.

We sat silent for a moment.

"Did I say the wrong thing?" Jemma asked.

Carry reached out to me with one hand. "Please don't go out there to that beach again, Georgy."

A knock came upon the attic door and Margaret entered.

"Miss Georgy, Mr. Burpee is here."

A piece of me deflated at the thought of leaving that pretty scene.

"I'll be down soon, Margaret. Has he shared the reason for his visit?"

"He's asked to see your mother, miss. They're in the library."

All business halted and every sisterly face turned to me.

Abby tossed a skirt into the trunk. "From the look on your face, you'd think the executioner has arrived."

WITH AS DIGNIFIED A scramble as we could produce, we assembled at the library, where all momentous events occurred at Brevoort Place. Jemma linked one arm in mine, while Hatty ran for my nurse's bag, grabbed the stethoscope, and held it to the door, listening for murmurings, and Carry employed the glass-to-the-ear method.

"Nothing," Hatty said.

Mary held my hand as Abby pushed them both aside and set one ear to the door. "It's Mother," Abby whispered. "She's saying . . . Georgy has always known her own mind." She turned to me. "She's saying you're not an easy person to live with."

"Thank you, Mother," I said.

Abby pressed her ear back to the door. "I think they're concluding their meeting."

The door opened to reveal Mother and Mr. Burpee behind her, averting his gaze, in his best cravat and waistcoat, beads of perspiration shining on his forehead.

Mother's solemn gaze met mine. "Georgeanna, Mr. Burpee has come here today to ask you a serious question."

Mary squeezed my hand and trained her serious gaze upon me. "You don't have to go if you don't want to."

"I'm fine," I said, and stepped into the library, the heavily draped and carpeted inner sanctum where Father's old oak desk stood, as always, in front of the window. My sisters and Jemma filled the doorway, watching.

"Good day, Miss Woolsey," Mr. Burpee said. "Though my conversation with your mother proved quite amicable, it has been taxing on my spirits."

He pulled a dime from his vest pocket and flipped it to Jemma. "You there, run out for a nerve tonic."

Jemma caught the coin.

Mary seized the coin from Jemma and handed it back to Mr. Burpee. "Jemma is our guest, Mr. Burpee."

"Oh." Mr. Burpee slid the coin back in his vest pocket. "How is a person to know such a thing?"

I stepped to the door and closed it, knowing the conversation would be monitored and memorized to the word.

Mr. Burpee stepped to me. "I trust you know what I am here to ask."

"Perhaps."

"Your mother tells me it is your decision whom you should wed, and I accede to her. You must know I hold deep affection for you. In these months together I have found you to be an amiable, forthright companion, modest, with a facile mind, and possessed of all the necessary qualities on my checklist. I believe we would make a good match and after much consideration have decided that, once we are married, you may have the house of your choosing for your nursing school, until children come, of course."

I placed one hand on Father's desk to steady myself. "That is terribly generous, Archie."

He pulled a leather box from his coat pocket and opened it to reveal a blaze of diamonds. "It was Mother's first ring Father gave her. Eight rose-cut diamonds around a center stone. It was made to be seen by candlelight. She told me to find a woman deserving of it, and I have decided most emphatically that is you."

"It's a lovely piece, Archie."

"But I must say I haven't the faintest idea how you feel. You barely show any affection to me, Georgeanna, no sign of sentiment. Even here today, no tear of joy at my proposal."

"I do appreciate it all. This is all so sudden. I just need some time—"

"I daresay most ladies would not hesitate at such an offer." He snapped the case shut and secured it in his pocket. "I'm traveling to Saratoga Springs to consider a new gelding for purchase and will return in two weeks' time. I'd appreciate your answer upon my return."

"Certainly, Archie."

Mr. Burpee took my hand in his, raised it to his lips, and kissed it solemnly, then strode out, leaving the door open, and a stream of women came pouring in. They gathered around me, skirts rustling, in a cloud of violet and rose toilet waters.

"What did you answer?" Carry asked.

"Told him I'd think about it."

"Well, that's decisive," Hatty said.

I stepped behind the desk. "It is all so confusing."

"Frank Bacon will take to his bed when he hears," Mary said.

Carry jumped up and sat upon Father's desk. "I was appalled when he assumed Jemma was the maid."

"What do you *feel* about it all, Georgy?" Abby asked.

"Nothing, really. I suppose it's a flattering proposal."

Mother smoothed back my hair. "You take as long as you need, my dear."

I placed my palms on Father's blotter. "He offered a house of my choosing for my school."

Mary took my hand in hers. "Make sure it is him that you love, Georgy. This is forever. Perhaps inform Frank Bacon before you accept?"

"It's a fine offer," Abby said. "You must accept, of course. Father would want you to."

I turned to face her. "Don't say that, Abby."

"Someone must. You don't seem capable of any kind of emotion. I hope you're not waiting for Frank Bacon to leave his ladylove. That will never happen."

I hurried to the door. "Please, just leave me alone."

Abby followed. "You can have your school, Georgy. Don't be foolish and throw this away like you have every other chance."

"How infinitely cruel you can be, Abby." I left the room and swept up the stairs. "For once let me make up my own mind."

AFTER MR. BURPEE'S PROPOSAL, I needed to escape my sisters' prying looks, so Jemma and I kept our plans to visit what I had always called "Father's Beach," Rockaway Beach, on the southern shore of Long Island, Uncle Edward's favorite summertime spot.

Light rain fell as Jemma and I walked, heads down, alert for the misshapen bits of purple and white quahog shells that often washed up there, rinsed smooth by the pounding Atlantic. Perhaps knowing I had much to consider, Mother had been kind enough to send us off with her carriage and sandwiches wrapped in newsprint. We rode the Fulton Ferry to Brooklyn, and then made our long way to The Rockaways.

As we approached the beach my breath grew short. Perhaps I was not ready to return after all. I lifted my face to the light rain. "A soft," Father would have called it.

"Maybe we should turn back, Jemma. The sky is darkening."

"Could we stay a few moments more?" she asked. "The storm looks like it will hold off for the moment."

I breathed deep and the familiar scent of salt air filled my lungs.

Father.

Jemma hurried ahead, bent to pluck something from the sand, and turned. "Found my first piece!"

I came closer and examined the smooth, milky shell fragment, infused with purple. "Good one."

Jemma dropped it into the yellow silk drawstring bag she'd made for this purpose.

"My pa loved to walk the shore down in Maryland. Found pieces of old wood and dragged them home to make tables and chairs."

"Where is he now? You rarely speak of him."

"Died two years back. LeBaron and his boys got him strung up."

I stopped and turned. "Good Lord, Jemma, how cruel and barbaric. How can men do such a thing to another man?"

"Pa crossed them. But mostly on account of they felt like it."

"I'm so sorry. I had no intention of prying."

"No need to say sorry, Georgy. I've come to know that talking is healing."

"What was he like?"

Jemma looked to the sky and smiled. "Like the best day times ten. He didn't have much, but he'd give anybody whatever he had."

We walked on, the sweet lapping of the waves at the shore and the wild cry of gulls and terns the only sounds.

"You used to come here with your pa?" Jemma asked.

"It was our favorite stretch to walk. Now Mary brings her girls here with their sand pails and shovels."

I bent to pull a shell fragment and dropped it in Jemma's bag. How good to have a friend who enjoyed the simple hunt for nature's offerings.

"Must have been good times, being with your pa," she said.

"Made that ferry crossing with Father a hundred times and walked this beach searching for treasures with him, happy to discuss any little thing I fancied. We'd come upon every sort of treasure. A lady's perfume bottle. Pots and pans washed up from shipwrecks."

"This is where you found that pretty fan?"

"Oh, no. A Mrs. Winslow from Astoria, an acquaintance of Uncle Edward's actually, gifted it to Father and me, upon our safe retrieval of her son William, who'd swum out too far and was feared lost."

Jemma and I stopped at the water's edge, in the center of the half-moon bay. "Father and I found him just here, and revived him. He was graceful under pressure, my father. He set to work on the poor fellow immediately and I followed."

"Saved him?"

"Pressed a gallon of water out of the young man. But you have never seen a more grateful parent, and Mrs. Winslow presented Father and me with the fan, the sticks made of ivory, one of her most prized possessions, said to be once owned by a lady-in-waiting at Marie Antoinette's court."

"Is it worth a good deal of money?"

"To a collector, perhaps. But for me, it holds mostly sentimental value. It's all I have left of my father."

"Carry said you gave up coming here for a good reason. What's that?"

The rain fell harder and I gathered my cloak about me. "We'll be soaked, Jemma. We really should get back."

Jemma set one hand on my sleeve. "Weren't you were the one that said 'A person has to face things or you just get stuck'?"

I pulled my arm away. "I realize I may be infinitely better at giving advice than taking it, but I really think—"

"Maybe talk about Dr. Bacon, too? I can tell you feel something for him, but you can't show it. Maybe it's all because of what happened here. Have you shared it with your sisters?"

"It is too awful, Jemma. I can't discuss it with them."

"Can't keep it bottled up. How did he die?"

"I do wish we'd brought a watch. The last ferry back leaves at three o'clock."

Jemma stopped walking and stood, arms clasped behind her back.

I waved her along. "Are you coming?"

"Not until you talk about it."

I looked to the sky. "We'll be struck by lightning."

She shrugged.

"Fine. If you must know, he died aboard the Sound steamer *Lexington* on the night of January thirteenth, 1840. He was thirty-eight years old."

"And?"

"Father had traveled from Boston down to New York to visit Uncle Edward, who had just married, and Father was urged to stay on for a large family dinner about to be given in honor of the event. But Father insisted on getting back to Boston that night."

I bent and retrieved a piece of shell from the sand.

Jemma took it from my fingers and dropped it in her bag. "Go on."

"The night was a terrible one, the mercury at ten degrees below zero, the Sound filled with floating ice."

I stopped speaking, the image of it all so vivid in front of me. Jemma slipped her arm around my waist.

"The ship was well on its way and miles from shore when the alarm of fire was given. The boat was loaded with cotton bales, among which the fire had already made such headway that all hope of saving it was given up. Of the crew and one hundred and forty-three passengers, only four escaped, Father not among them. Whether he was burned or drowned God only knows."

"Your poor ma."

"Mother hid her sorrow from us. Just three months later, on the eighteenth day of April, 1840, our brother, Charles, was born, the son his father would have so rejoiced to see."

"Why did you have to stop coming out here after he died, Georgy?"

I looked out to sea. "I had Uncle Edward bring me out here, hoping to find Father and then became a bit preoccupied with the place. It was silly, I suppose."

"Not silly one bit."

"At first, I was so young, I thought Father would come back, wash up here, and I could save him like we did Willy Winslow. But as the years went on and I grew older, I just hoped for some sign of him or the steamer on which he died. I did find a bit of china with the *Lexington*'s green signature on it and slept with it under my pillow. I pressed Mother to help me contact the four survivors, but they remembered no one matching Father's description. Then, when I turned sixteen, Mother said I should stop coming out here. I snuck out anyway one winter day, on the January thirteenth anniversary of the accident, and as a result contracted scarlet fever. Mother forbade me from coming out after that and sent me to boarding school in Philadelphia."

"Did you miss home?"

"Terribly. They diagnosed me with severe nostalgia and prescribed vigorous exercise and a bland diet. At night, I would dream of Father and wondered if he had washed up out here with no one to find him. It haunts me still. What were the circumstances of his death? Was he alive when the ship sank? Did he try to save anyone? I miss him so terribly, Jemma. He was an infinitely kind man, so full of good humor, and no one understood me better. It's a knife to the breast every day that he's gone and I am to blame."

"For sure it wasn't your fault."

"But it was. That is the most terrible part of it."

I looked out to sea, the low clouds gathering over the white-capped swells.

"Go on."

"Uncle Edward urged Father to stay that night, but he insisted on coming home for my piano recital. Told his brother he wouldn't miss it. I had urged him to come for it. Begged, in fact."

"Can't blame you."

Hot tears filled my eyes. "What if I hadn't been such a spoiled girl and not urged him home for my own vanity? What if he had stayed that night in New York and made the trip under better circumstances? He would be with us still today. Mother would not have lost her one and only. We would all have our precious father."

Jemma pulled me close and I cried upon her wet shoulder.

"There," Jemma said and patted my back. "Doesn't that feel good?"

The rain pelted us as I convulsed against her. "I will never shake this terrible shame."

"I think you already have," Jemma said, as she held me close.

And for once I did not push someone away.

I WOKE THE FOLLOWING day a person renewed, with a freshened mind and newfound vigor. I slung my rucksack over my shoulder, and then gently lifted Father's fan from the mantel, the glass box smooth in my arms, and carried it out of the house and down Brevoort Place.

It was opening day of the Sanitary Fair and it seemed every person in New York City was squeezed into that great building at Fourteenth Street near Sixth Avenue. Schools closed and men shuttered their offices to promenade the stalls, where every conceivable item stood on grand display, resulting in a whirl of people, flags, and garlands, the scent of popping corn and taffy in the air.

The fair was divided into rooms: the Arms and Trophies Room, the Painting Gallery, and the Old Curiosity Shop, the glass cabinets there filled with taxidermied swans, Egyptian artifacts, a piece of the old cherry tree Washington cut down, and six hundred other oddities.

I held my glass case to my chest and pressed toward the Painting Gallery, through an immense throng of well-dressed visitors strolling the high-ceilinged rooms considering purchases. Everywhere the sweeping sound of silk could be heard as ladies brushed by one another and "The Star-Spangled Banner" swelled out from a great military band.

I made it to the gallery, by far the most prestigious room, the walls covered with donated old master paintings and shadowboxed war artifacts. I set the glass box upon the counter in front of a round little man who spoke with the trace of a German accent, my own face reflected in the lenses of his glasses.

"I wish to donate this to the cause."

He peered closer at the fan. "Is this—"

"Yes, once worn at the court of Marie Antoinette."

"How can I assign a value to this? It should be in a museum. How do I know it is yours to give?"

"Affixed with tape to the case bottom is the newspaper article about my father, Charles Woolsey, and how he saved a man's life. The fan was his reward from a grateful parent. He willed it to me, and it is now time for me to let it go."

"You must be very sad to relinquish it."

"Tremendously sad, sir. But a person has to face things or they just get stuck."

"This is *much* appreciated, Miss Woolsey."

I ran off, a weight lifted, and longed to stop and examine every room, but was late for my assignment, to sign copies of my literary creation, *Three Weeks at Gettysburg*, a chronicle of my time with Mother and the Sanitary Commission.

I rushed through the Great Hall, past the massive temple, lush with greenery and brightened by flowers and bearing inscriptions of the names of the battles they celebrated: *Gettysburg* in crimson flowers, *Antietam* in blue and white, *Roanoke* in yellow. I resisted the urge to linger there and breathe in the sweet scents, for it was as luxuriant as a tropical thicket, kept full to overflowing with sweet lilies and orchids, singing birds, and butterflies.

I patted my rucksack and felt a sheaf of papers there, copies of Mary's wildly popular new poem "Taps," which Mother had had printed on stationery in the patriotic color scheme of red and blue ink on white paper. Though Mary had published it anonymously and people assumed it was written by a male soldier dying in battle, those in our circle knew the true author and were proud of Mary.

I pulled in my skirt to keep it from being tread upon as I rushed by the Arms and Trophies Room, in which the central attraction of the fair stood—the relics and spoils of every battlefield. It was jammed to suffocation the whole day long with people eager to see swords, guns, and trophy flags from the four wars of American history, including the remnant of a flag borne at the last Battle of Bull Run.

I passed the stall, thronged with customers, where Mary and Jemma stood selling her bonnets. I cast my eye about the room in search of Frank Bacon. Would he attend the fair? Come to my book-signing table as Carry predicted? Freed somehow by my beach talk with Jemma, I longed to see him and share it all. How hard it is to see the truth when we are caught in the eye of the storm.

At last I made it to the Books and Autographs Room, out of breath, to find a line of autograph seekers snaking back from a table bearing a stack of my books to sign.

I sat behind the table, placed Mary's poems on display for a penny a sheet, and the first in line, a young woman dressed in silks, as if straight out of *Godey's Lady's Book,* handed me a book to sign.

"Please inscribe it *to Joanna.* I felt like I was there on the battlefield, reading your book, Miss Woolsey. And I will take a sheet of poetry, too. We lost my brother at Gettysburg and he had sent this very poem home to Mother before he died."

The line moved swiftly and soon my brother-in-law Reverend Robert Howland leaned over the table.

"I have come to ask a favor, Georgy. Mary listens to you. Can you convince her to slow her pace?"

I waved a patron behind Robert to the table and opened her book to sign. "I've tried, Robert. We all have."

"I believe, since you sisters contribute so much to the war effort, she feels she must work equally."

"But she's raising four girls. That's contribution enough."

He leaned closer. "I cannot tie her down, Georgy. She fainted yesterday, and even with the strongest smelling salts, we had trouble reviving her."

"Dr. Flynn says she is perfectly fine, but you have my word, Robert, once this is all over, we will force her to bed while her sisters take the children and you wait on her hand and foot. How does that sound?"

Robert hesitated, but took his leave and I signed many more books, with each one adding a dime for the Union cause.

I continued signing until, next in line, Frank Bacon stepped up to the table.

"Why, Frank Bacon." I could not suppress a wide smile.

He loomed over me in civilian clothes, somehow more attractive than ever from that angle, somewhat pale, a new sadness in his eyes. "I've come to purchase two copies."

I opened a book to the title page. "But Abby already sent you the book."

"Yes, I've read it and enjoyed it very much. Bethada and her aunt have requested copies. Would you sign them both?"

I opened one book to the title page. "You've been on my mind a great deal today, Frank. I've just had a most extraordinary epiphany. Could we meet somewhere to talk of it?"

"I'm afraid my time is limited. Bethada has my appointment book filled."

"Are you home on furlough?"

"A brief leave from the army. This war may never end. I'm back seeing patients for a time."

"Mostly one patient, I hear."

"Bethada's aunt has a complicated medical history. I saw your fan in the Painting Gallery. Are you auctioning it?"

"Yes, Frank. I think Father would be happy it's going to the cause."

The sadness in his eyes deepened.

I reached out one hand, which he disregarded.

"You look healthy, Frank. You've come a long way since Gettysburg."

"Good to see you as well, published author. What can't you do, Georgy? Now you're free to become a vagabond once more."

"I must admit my heart is still on the Pamunkey River."

My face grew hot as I recalled our inoculation on board the *Daniel Webster*. Did he see my red cheeks? How had I not realized then how deep my affections ran?

Frank attempted a smile. "That seems a million years past."

I signed the second book. "There's talk of an engagement for you and Bethada."

He looked off to the crowd. "Ah, the gossip mill."

"You've known Bethada quite a long time now. Your mother objects?"

He slid his hands into his pockets. "You do have an uncanny way of seeing the truth, Georgeanna Woolsey. But I cannot be a bachelor forever and she seems good as any."

"Well, that's a ringing declaration of affection."

"And you? I hear the good Mr. Burpee has been circling Brevoort Place in his Brewster wagon and perfect ponies."

"We need to speak privately, Frank. Can you come call at the house?"

The woman in line behind Frank craned her head around him. "Could you move your conversation along?"

Frank ran his fingers through his hair. "I'm very busy, Georgy. Half of New York City has the grippe. But you know I will discuss anything you like at any time."

"That is just it, Frank." I leaned in. "I must tell you about this incredible understanding I've come to and how terribly wrong I've—"

Bethada appeared at Frank's side and looped one arm through his. "Look at you, *tête-à-tête* over here—Georgy, the famous author."

She slid a book from the stack and considered the cover, head tilted. "Countless people—including true literary geniuses—have told me I should write a book, but I tell them I'm already so occupied with good works, there's little time to sit and write. Soon, Auntie and I are hosting War Secretary Stanton himself."

"Will he discuss Barnett Industries' continued profit from cotton?" I asked.

"Powerful people draw criticism." Bethada glanced back across the crowd. "Have you seen? Oysters are just thirty cents a dozen at the Knickerbocker Kitchen. And one can purchase tickets to vote between Grant and McClellan as to who is the best general. McClellan is in the lead, if you can believe it."

"Well, you must rush over, then," I said.

Bethada tossed the book back onto the table. "I do hate to cut things short, but Auntie's bad foot is acting up again and she must get home."

"Goodbye, Georgy," Frank said.

"Please wait, Frank. Robert's concerned about Mary. She's been terribly tired."

Frank turned back toward me. "Working too hard for the fair?"

"Yes. Mother had old Dr. Flynn examine her and he declared her sound."

"Could it be a fifth child?"

"Perhaps—"

Bethada tugged Frank's arm. "We must go, dear. Auntie is waiting."

I tried to smile. "Goodbye, Frank."

Bethada pulled Frank away and he turned back. "I'll do my best to get over and see Mary."

"She's in the millinery stall with Jemma."

Bethada led him off. I opened the next book to sign as Frank stepped away, and I watched him disappear, swallowed into a sea of black coats.

Jemma

✳

TOWARD THE END OF THE FIRST DAY, THE SANITARY FAIR GREW even more crowded as the gaslights turned on and every person in New York City crowded into the Great Hall, thick as bees. Seeing all those people there made me hope the North would win that terrible war and there'd be no more question of free or owned. I'd be together with Patience and Ma.

Georgy made sure I got the best stall for my bonnet selling. It held a waist-high counter on which we sat our ten wooden mannequin heads, each wearing one of my creations. After Miss Georgeanna and I had our good cry on the beach the day before, you've never seen such a change come over a person, her rushing about, happy as a clam at high water, a smile on her face, laughing now and then at the littlest things.

As I stood in my booth I caught my breath for a moment when I thought I saw Anne-May in the crowd, but I soon calmed myself, knowing she would never set foot in any event benefiting Northern troops.

Mary came over from her own booth, a bower of flowers, where she sold every kind of garden novelty—her white straw garden hats were the rage of the fair. She assisted me while tending all four of her girls, May—

ten, Bertha—five, Una—four, and baby Georgy—just two, in her arms. She looked pale and a bit glassy-eyed, but otherwise fully engaged in promoting my hats, as if that was the most important thing in the world. The bonnets sold fast and by five o'clock I'd made forty-five dollars for the treasury and only had one left, a child's size with pink calico roses.

When there came a lull in activity, Mary came to me. "You've sold almost all of them, Jemma. Outstanding."

She handed me an envelope. "Please accept this. I'd forgotten to give you the money from bonnets you sold at the church fair."

I peeked inside. "Ten dollars? That should go to the church."

"Keep it. You earned it and much more. You can put it to your lawyer fund to help your sister."

I circled her waist with one arm. "Thank you, Mary. Suits me to a dot." I felt her ribs through the back of her dress. "Perhaps you should rest. I'll look after the children."

"Later, Jemma." She leaned in and smiled. "Once we sell the last bonnet, I'll gladly take a lemonade."

I'd been looking over the crowd all day for Nathan, hoping we could stroll the fair and maybe see the botanical booth together. A little spark went through me when I finally spotted him, strolling through the crowd toward the exit, with a lady on his arm. I stood on my toes and tried to see his lady friend, dressed in plaid, what looked like taffeta. Sagging like a balloon leaking air, I watched as Nathan arranged her cashmere shawl around her shoulders.

"Please go and see the exhibits, Jemma," Mary said. "I'll take your booth. I need a break from my own."

"No, I'll stay," I said, watching the pair hurry away, heads together, in serious talk.

A frog-eyed lady, dressed all in creamy white, and her little daughter, in pink, wandered up to the stall.

Mary stepped to her. "Hello, Mrs. Caldecot. Good to see you out supporting the fair."

She nodded in Mary's direction, her gaze on the last bonnet, and she lifted it from the wooden mannequin head. "How much are you asking for this?"

Mary was all business. "Five dollars, ma'am."

Mrs. Caldecot placed it on the girl's head and tied the white ribbon. "Very smart."

She pulled her purse from her pocket and handed Mary a five-dollar gold coin. "Are the bonnets sent in from France?"

Mary accepted the coin and dropped it in our cash box.

I stepped forward. "No, I make them, ma'am."

She looked at me as if seeing me for the first time and her face grew paler. "*You* make them, your hands all over them?"

Mary smiled. "Jemma forms the bonnets over flowerpots, and then makes the flowers from scraps of fabric found all over. Puts things to good use."

The woman shoved her purse back into her pocket, pulled the bonnet from her daughter's head, and tossed it on the counter like she'd been stung. "Give me my money back this instant. You people are a plague."

I turned to Mary with a quizzical look.

Mary stepped toward the woman. "She objects to the purchase on account of your race, Jemma. Isn't that right, Mrs. Caldecot?"

"Who knows what kind of filth that darkie's brought to it. You return my money this instant or I will contact the fair authorities."

I handed the woman her coin. "Here, ma'am."

"Put it there." She nodded toward the counter.

I placed it on the counter and she snatched it up.

Mary handed baby Georgy to me, took the bonnet and placed it on her own Bertha's head and tied the ribbon under her chin. "She looks perfectly fine and healthy to me."

"You may allow that kind of trash to touch your child, but I love my daughter."

Mary stepped to her. "I must insist you deliver Jemma an apology."

"That's not necessary, Mary," I said. "Mrs. Caldecot just doesn't understand what they teach at church. God shows no partiality."

Mrs. Caldecot stood stock-still for a long second and then stepped away from the stall, calling back over her shoulder, "Go back to Liberia!"

Mary came to me all smiles. "Jemma, that was well done. You really put a cherry on it."

I shrugged. "Just how I feel."

Mary held on to the counter. "I'm so sorry, Jemma. This is no—" She slid to the floor, her skirt puddled around her.

"Mama!" Bertha called out, as May and Una came running and threw themselves upon their mother.

Baby in my arms, I dropped to my knees and felt for Mary's pulse with one hand.

"Get a doctor!" I called to anyone. "She's barely breathing."

Anne-May

I WALKED THE STREETS OF NEW YORK CITY MOST OF THE NIGHT. Around midnight, stuck in a sudden rainstorm, I dozed in the doorway of a girlie show. When I woke, I began walking again, chewing my fingernails to the quick. How would I afford Mr. Bigelow's services, not to mention train fare home when all I had was the cash I'd taken from the House of Industry? Worst of all, my snuff vial was near empty. My hands trembled. Clearly, I'd become dependent on it.

At first light I returned to Bigelow's National Detective Agency and found Mr. Bigelow at his desk eating an egg sandwich while reading the vulgar men's magazine *Trotter's Tales*.

I leaned closer and examined the page full of etchings of women less than fully clothed, many in athletic positions, one with a lampshade on her head.

Mr. Bigelow caught me looking. "Like what you see?"

I straightened. "Isn't it a bit early for that, Mr. Bigelow?"

He smiled an eggy grin and left the magazine open. "You hit some hard times all of a sudden?"

"If you must know, I was callously thrown out of my hotel last night by a hideous Yankee. But how could you tell?"

"You're wearin' the same dress you had on yesterday."

"Aren't you quite the detective."

"Look, you can get on your merry way, Miss Louisiana. I have too many jobs to count."

"Yes, you seem swamped. What have you found out about my job? I got into the Woolsey house at Brevoort Place. Found Jemma's bag, but no book. But I got into that house, better than I can say for you."

He leaned over his blotter and placed his considerable weight on his two forearms. "My sources say all the Woolsey sisters are working at the Sanitary Fair."

I sat down on the couch with no care of grace, my skirt billowing out around me. "I could have told you that. There are flyers on every telegraph pole for that wretched fair. Look, we need to pick up the pace of this investigation, since I can't afford to stay here much longer. If I'm to stay even one more night, I'll need a place to sleep."

"You can have the couch here. But that'll cost you, too."

"What more do you want?"

He shrugged. "Maybe those pretty hands of yours could be put to good use." He smiled.

"Touch you in a carnal way? I don't believe so, Mr. Bigelow." I stood and handed him the cash money from the envelope. "This should defray the cost."

He riffled through the bills. "There's barely fifty dollars here. You'll have to make up for it in other ways."

"You're not the type of man I ordinarily associate with, Mr. Bigelow."

"Is it poetry you Southern women want? *Love never dies—'tis as the sun, That for boundless ages, Ceaselessly its course has run. . . .* "

I stepped back and felt a sharp pain in my head, like wind on a bad tooth.

"What in the Sam Hill? Where did you learn that poem?"

"Right there in an advice column in *Trotter's Tales.* Author said, when put to memory and performed, that poem spreads a lady's legs faster than 'Open sesame.'"

I held back a sob. "But Jubal told me he wrote it."

"Whoever Jubal is, he's a big old liar." Detective Bigelow patted his lap. "Don't cry. Come sit here. How about a little kiss? That'll be a good start."

THERE WAS A TERRIBLY big and unruly crowd at the Yankee Sanitary Fair, hundreds of ill-mannered couples strutting around their grand hall in their fine clothes made from the cloth that slaves made possible.

Hypocrites.

Half of the bank accounts there had been fattened by trade with the South. I could barely look at the Union flag that hung from the rafters, swaying in the currents sent up from the crowds, taunting me. Had such a flag flown over my Harry as he died on the battlefield?

My head felt about to split open, listening to so many rude Northern tongues, and I longed for even the smallest pinch of snuff. I surveyed the paper map handed to me upon entering. How enormous that fair was. Printed across the map's top: OUR GOAL: TO RAISE $1,000,000 FOR THE CARE AND COMFORT OF U.S. ARMY TROOPS. And what of our Southern troops?

I ran one dirty finger down the list of volunteers at the booths, looking for the name Woolsey. I found a Mary Woolsey in the millinery booth and a Georgeanna Woolsey in the Author's Room. I was curious to see her. Perhaps Jemma was with one of them?

I wandered into a place called the Knickerbocker Kitchen, serving sweet, complimentary brandy cocktails, and drank three on an empty stomach and then toured the exhibits.

I stopped to take in one particularly repulsive one, the "Hairy Eagle," a taxidermied American bald eagle resting upon a globe and surmounted by a wreath made up of the hair of President Lincoln and twenty prominent senators. I turned, about to be sick to my stomach—was that the effect of the eagle or the brandy?—and went in search of the Author's Room.

I soon found it: there was a line gathering to speak with the author, and a hand-lettered sign taped to her table: GEORGEANNA WOOLSEY—THREE WEEKS AT GETTYSBURG. I stepped closer to examine the woman who'd taken my Jemma in. Slightly older than me, hair center-parted and neatly combed back into a gray silk snood. Nothing wrong with her looks that a little rouge couldn't help. I waited in line and after an eternity made it to the table.

She opened the book. "Would you like your name inscribed or a simple signature?"

The room spun; I was definitely feeling the effects of the brandy. "You were at Gettysburg?" I said. "How exciting. Knickerbocker Kitchen is serving free brandy cocktails, you know."

She signed the book, giving me a chance to examine her close up, her smug little smile and piercing gaze, tasteful little heirloom cameo at her throat.

"Just a signature, please," I said, and held on to the table.

She leaned in. "You are *drunk,* madam."

I squinted at her. "You are *right,* madam. Aren't you the high and mighty one?"

"I must ask you to step aside."

"On second thought, I don't want to read your book anyway, you aggressors bragging about all your good deeds."

Angry and feeling my liquor, I drifted off, to a room called Letters and Documents, where it seemed every vile creature in New York City gathered to gawk at a handful of yellowing sheets of stationery displayed about, many from the Revolutionary War.

I stepped up to one, set out next to a tintype of that arrogant General Grant, people crowded around it, excited over some words on a page. They'd set the letter up on a writing desk, the travel kind, with an ink bottle and the very quill pen Grant had used to write it. I edged closer and knocked the ink bottle over onto the letter, a great, black, satisfying splotch seeping into the page.

A man stepped back like he'd been kicked. "What have you done?"

I looked about. "It wasn't me."

The woman at the man's side leaned across him. "I saw you do it."

"Perhaps my sleeve caught it. I'm so terribly sorry."

A barrel-chested gentleman in a bowler hat wedged his way into our tight circle.

"Detective Todenhofer," he said. "What's the matter here?"

A man in a top hat pointed at me. "She defaced General Grant's letter with ink."

There was something familiar about the detective.

"Mrs. Watson, I believe? I met you at your lovely home in Maryland. With Detective Allan?"

It was the baby-man with the yellow curls who'd not said a word that day they came to arrest me. What a surprise to find his voice loud and deep.

Detective Todenhofer stepped to me. "You're under arrest."

He motioned to his lackey, who came and pulled my hands behind me, and none too gently.

"You can't be serious."

"We've been following you, here in New York. Concerned about your allegiances."

The detective manacled my hands behind my back and led me out through the Great Hall, like a common thief.

"My sleeve must have brushed that bottle," I explained as we walked. "Send a telegram to Mr. Jubal Smalls in Hollywood, Maryland. He will send bail money."

"Save it for the authorities at Castle Williams, ma'am."

THE STEAMER BUCKED THE WAVES, doing little for my inebriated state, as we sailed to the grim little island where the prison for Confederate soldiers stood, and it was all I could do not to retch up my brandy cocktails. Detective Todenhofer and I sat on deck for that mercifully quick ride, and we soon approached Castle Williams, an odd circular fortress, three stories of dark windows piercing the façade. Another big Union flag flew high above it, flapping furiously in the great wind.

"Sixteen hundred Rebel prisoners held here," Detective Todenhofer said.

Tears came to my eyes just thinking about all those brave Southern boys in there, boys like my Harry.

"You're good at evading the authorities. Took us a while to find you at Hotel Brevoort."

I kept mum, the sea spray dampening the last vestiges of my face powder.

Detective Todenhofer stood and looked out upon the fortress. "They call it the Cheesebox. On account of the round shape."

I kept my gaze straight ahead.

"You may not talk to me, but you better be straight with the U.S. Army or they could keep you here long as they want. You should see the prisoners, all Confederate boys. There's a measles outbreak now. You had measles?"

I shook my head. "No."

"Hate to see that pretty complexion of yours ruined by those spots. Three died from it already. Shame."

"I'm sure the conditions are deplorable."

"The guards shoot the rats for the prisoners in exchange for the jewelry they make. Otherwise, well, the rats make a dinner of the prisoners."

"Please, Detective Todenhofer. I'm quite unwell."

We reached a small dock and the ship rocked as we disembarked. Along the shore, rows of Union soldiers gathered, rifles at their sides, lined up facing the bay. A dirge played and upon the order of "Forward" given by an officer, a man bound by the hands ventured out of the fort. He came to the center of the group and knelt on a wooden box.

"Is that a coffin he's kneeling on?"

Todenhofer looked out over the little scene. "Executing a spy."

A shiver went through me.

"Caught giving stolen Union troop orders to Jeff Davis himself."

Upon an officer's command a whole line of them shot, and the man fell back onto the ground.

My knees shook after witnessing that barbarous act, and Detective Todenhofer took me inside the building, a wave of stench greeting us. We walked down a narrow stone passage, to the left a courtyard, onto which faced three stories of gated cells, and to my right, rows of cells. In each stood a tableau of human suffering more pitiable than the last. At the sound of our steps, emaciated men came and gripped the cell bars.

"Bless you, ma'am," came one Southern voice. "Water, please. We need water."

I stopped. "Where you from, soldier?"

"Baton Rouge, ma'am. Peter Clausen. Can you write my ma? Tell her I'm here?"

Todenhofer took my arm. "Move along, now."

I wrested my arm from his grasp. "My brother died in the service of the Confederacy and my heart bleeds for these men."

Detective Todenhofer ushered me to a room furnished only with one chair. I sat, and after an interminable wait, during which I was visited by one of Todenhofer's rats, two U.S. Army officers in deep blue uniform coats entered.

"Anne-May Wilson Watson?"

"I am. And in need of a cool drink. I think by law I am entitled—"

"Of New Orleans, Louisiana, now residing at Peeler Plantation, Hollywood, Maryland?"

I tried to smile, pretty as I could. "Yes, sir."

"Have you ever passed along U.S. Army secrets to the Confederates?"

"Certainly not."

"Our sources tell us you shared Union troop locations."

"Now, why would I do that? My husband lost his leg fighting for the Union, sirs. We operate a tobacco plantation, which supplies the U.S. Army. I have no time to run about secreting information in books. You simply have the wrong person."

"I didn't say anything about books, Mrs. Watson."

My belly turned upside down. "Well . . . it's all so confusing."

"Your husband, Major Watson, did he send you correspondence relating his location near the Phillipsburg railroad depot?"

"He wrote me many letters."

"Did you pass on this location?"

"Is there a lawyer in this hideous place?"

"Did you pass on the sighting of a U.S. Army ship known as the USS *Thomas Freeborn* from your home along the Patuxent River?"

"If you have evidence of my crimes, I'd like to see it. Not that the Yankees didn't deserve every bad thing that happened to them. My brother *died* at Northern hands, gentlemen. A good man who never hurt a person in his life, shot through his dear heart."

"You'll be held here until further notice."

I stood. "No. Please wait."

"The officer of the guard will accompany you to a cell."

"A cell? There must be some mistake. How can I fix this misunderstanding?"

"We know information is being funneled to someone high in the Confederacy. We're happy to set aside your transgressions if you could help us. Tell us who to watch in order to find those at fault higher up."

"I might be able to work with you all. Long as you can deliver something to me as well."

The two men exchanged looks.

"Deliver me my property, residing at number eight Brevoort Place in New York City—my runaway slave, name of Jemma."

Georgy

✴

NEW YORK CITY
APRIL 1864

JEMMA RUSHED TO ME IN THE BOOK-SIGNING STALL AND SET TWO
hands on the table. "It's Mary. Come quickly."

I stood. "Oh, Jemma—"

"She fainted dead away in our booth. Two doctors came from the
crowd in the Great Hall and they've called for an ambulance. Your mother
has Dr. Flynn on the way to Brevoort Place to meet us."

I gathered my cloak and left the line standing there. "Did you tell the
others? I'll send a messenger up to Tioronda for Eliza."

I arrived outside as the attendants loaded Mary by stretcher into an
ambulance. I clasped her hand. "We're here, my Mary."

She turned her face toward me. "Just a clumsy fall."

"You need to rest now."

I looked to her for an answer, but found she'd fallen back into the abyss.
Jemma and I stepped up onto the ambulance and knelt at either side of
Mary.

"You can't ride in there," the ambulance driver said.

"She's had a severe blow to the head and must have constant watch."

"Who made you a doctor?"

I held Jemma's hand across Mary's blanketed chest.

"We are U.S. Army nurses and must charge you to drive with care, for she is our most precious sister."

RAIN PELTED THE WINDOWS as Abby and I moved Mary's bed down to the library, just off the front parlor. Abby then went to stay with the girls at the rectory so Robert could be with Mary. Mother stayed with her most of the night as well, and Mother's old friend Dr. Flynn, a kind, lanky man with parchment-white hair and a reassuring Midwestern way, came periodically and did what he could. We sisters took turns relieving Robert and Mother in the sickroom. Pico sat watch outside Mary's door, rising with each person's exit as if waiting for news.

Just after dawn, Mother and Dr. Flynn came from the library and Carry hurried into the sickroom to take her turn with Mary.

I rushed to them. "Any improvement?"

Mother held Mary's pink camel hair shawl in her hands.

Dr. Flynn set his black bag upon the sofa and Margaret helped him into his greatcoat. "Mary is resting. We've done all we can for now."

Hot tears pricked my eyes. We could lose her, just like Father.

I stepped closer. "There must be more we can do, Doctor."

"Could be dropsy. Labored breathing. Very low pulse. I shall limit the narcotics we administer toward the end so she may speak her last words more clearly."

He walked toward the door and I followed.

"You will not limit her narcotics in order to extract some meaningless final pledge, sir. My sister will have every comfort."

"As the family wishes."

"And how can you speak of last words, Doctor? Are you giving *up*? There must be more we can do. Is she complaining of fever?"

"Yes, she is."

"Then it is *not* dropsy, Doctor, is it? You must give this diagnosis more careful consideration."

"I will return when I conclude my hospital rounds."

I paced the carpet. "Your hospital rounds? You will just allow our be-loved sister to die while you stroll your wards of malarial men?"

Mother took my hand and held it tight. "Get hold of yourself, Georgeanna."

Dr. Flynn took up his black bag. "Mary is stable for now. I will return in three hours."

I stepped to Mother's desk. "I'm afraid we will need to call Dr. Bacon here for another opinion."

"As you wish, Miss Woolsey."

Dr. Flynn took his leave, Mother returned to Mary, and I dashed off a note.

Dear Frank,

Please come at once to Brevoort Place. Mary has taken terribly ill. Dr. Flynn fears dropsy, but I am not at all confident in his diagno-sis. We await your reply.

> *Ever fondly,*
> *Georgy*

I called for Margaret and she came at once. "Deliver this note with the utmost urgency and care—all the way down Broadway, number seven-teen."

Margaret hurried off and Jane came to me and held me close. "Frank Bacon will know how to save Mary."

BUT THE HOURS PASSED and there was no sign of Frank Bacon. Jane stationed herself outside Mary's sickroom door and assaulted me as I emerged after changing Mary's linens.

"Where is Frank? Mary is dear to him."

Carry came to me, her face puffy and red-blotched from unending tears. "Why wouldn't he come?"

"Perhaps Margaret delivered to the wrong address?" Jane asked.

I sent a second note, more urgent, this time by a professional courier Mother had used to send Charley's enlistment papers.

Charley. He knew nothing of Mary's illness yet. He would be overwrought.

By noon Mary had worsened. If only Abigail could have been there, our anchor, to help us sort it all out, but she was watching the children at the rectory.

I entered the room to find the shades drawn, Mary asleep under the quilt, the sweet scent of opium in the air. Robert, in his shirtsleeves, knelt by Mary's bedside in prayer.

"Robert, please come take some tea."

"She is everything to me."

"Rest, now."

He looked up at me, eyes bloodshot. "You haven't slept, Georgy."

I ran one hand down his back. "You forget I'm used to this nursing life."

He stepped out, leaving me Mary all to myself. I sat next to her on the bed, her fresh pillowcase embroidered with morning glories, and held her hand. She lay there so pale and quiet, and not even the sound of a ticking clock broke the spell, since no one had thought to wind it. Each of her girls had sent along a favorite belonging for their mother; Una's gingham pony lay tucked into the top of her quilt.

I felt Mary's forehead—hot—then wrung water from a clean towel and laid it on her forehead.

Mary turned and looked up at me, glassy-eyed, her face swollen with inflammation. "You are so good, Georgy. Will the girls come?"

"The little ones mustn't visit until the fever is down."

"And Frank?" she asked.

"Any minute now. And Eliza is coming from Beacon at breakneck speed, she and Joe. And Moritz is bringing you pussy willows—and forsythia to force. And Jemma gave them a list of herbs and plants they can find this time of year, to bring down for medicines."

"A good deal of fuss."

I held her hand, so terribly hot, and my eyes filled with tears.

"How is the headache?" I dipped the towel in the water once again.

"I'm afraid it's worse, Georgy."

"Have you taken the biscuits as I directed?"

"I simply cannot. I'm sorry."

It was typhoid fever. No matter what Dr. Flynn said. How many times had I seen it in my patients on the ships? Abdominal pain. The terrible aches all over. Many of Robert's congregation had fallen to it and she'd had the early stages of it for weeks, no doubt, and just soldiered through. Why had I not acted then?

"Don't apologize, my Mary."

"I wish I'd done more in this life. You are all so accomplished."

"Quiet, now."

"Never nursed soldiers as you and the others have. Even Mother."

"You wrote so many lovely poems. What a great talent you have, to write so convincingly the spontaneous effusions of a dying soldier. That poem will outlast us all and has been a great comfort to so many. My book pales in comparison."

Mary smoothed her quilt. "Perhaps it's better if the world continues to believe a man wrote it."

"For now, Mary, perhaps. At the proper time we'll shout it to the world. Everyone will know the most talented Woolsey sister."

Mary held my hand tighter. "I asked Mother to write each sister a letter, to be read at a later time, but will you help me as well, Georgy? I wish to pen a letter to Mother and to each of my girls, to be read when they turn sixteen. That's the most tender age to hear a mother's advice, don't you agree?"

I smoothed back Mary's hair from her forehead.

She pointed toward the writing desk. "May could be the first married, being the eldest. Shall we start with her?"

"But there is no need, my Mary. You will be here—"

"Please let's not pretend, Georgy. Not you." Mary kept her gaze steady upon me. "I need this from you, sister."

"Then it shall be done, my love."

I barely stayed to the lines as I wrote, the tears hot down my face as my precious sister dictated a devoted mother's most loving counsel and hopes to her girls.

ONCE MARY FELL ASLEEP, I allowed Hatty her turn in the sickroom, and when I emerged into the front parlor, Jane pounced.

"Something must be wrong. Frank should have come by now. Why hasn't he?"

"I don't know, Jane."

Jane reached for her cloak. "I'll go down there and bring him back myself."

Jemma stepped forward. "Let me go. You stay here with Mary. I'll not return without Dr. Bacon."

Jemma

✴

THE SKIES OPENED AS I ARRIVED AT BETHADA'S AUNT'S HOUSE, all the way down on the tip of New York City, well after eight o'clock. As I stepped out of the carriage, even in the dark I could see that place was four times the size of the Woolseys' house on Brevoort Place.

I rang the bell, a white servant opened the door, and I stepped into the great hall, all parqueted floors and gaslights flickering on the walls. My heart beat wild in my chest, but once I saw Dr. Bacon's old doctor's bag on the front hall table I felt a gush of warmth down my arms.

Miss Bethada stepped into the hall, hands folded at her waist. "And what do you want?"

"Miss Georgy sent two messages. Her sister Mary is gravely ill and—"

"What has that to do with me?"

"She sent for Dr. Bacon to see if—"

"Dr. Bacon is tending to my aunt, and is not to be disturbed."

"If he could just come for a brief while—"

"He just returned from New Haven and needs to rest. Care from Dr. Flynn should be more than adequate."

"So, you *have* received Georgy's letters. How else would you know about Dr. Flynn?"

"And what if I have? Dr. Bacon is not well himself and cannot be at the beck and call of every person who requests assistance."

"Mary is his friend. How can you prevent word of her illness from reaching him?"

Bethada pushed me toward the door. "You go cure her with your colored medicine."

"Have mercy, Miss Bethada. Mary Woolsey has four little girls."

"I will not have your kind address me by my first name. Off with you, now."

Dr. Bacon stepped into the hallway behind Bethada. "How long has Mary been symptomatic?"

He turned down his shirtsleeves and the servant helped him into his black coat.

"Since yesterday at the fair, Dr. Bacon. Now she has a bad fever. Miss Georgy sent you word here, but heard nothing in return."

Dr. Bacon pulled his bag from the front table. "I've been away, but back long enough to have gotten word."

Bethada stepped to him. "Please stay, Frank."

"You withheld correspondence from me?"

Bethada tugged at his arm. "Don't go out. It's very late and the damp will hurt your chest."

Frank pulled his arm away.

Bethada gathered her shawl close. "Please don't be cross, Frank. I thought it best not to bother you. I'll come as well."

"You've done enough already, Bethada." Dr. Bacon took my arm. "Let us hurry, Jemma."

Georgy

NEW YORK CITY
APRIL 1864

J UST SHY OF NINE O'CLOCK DR. FLYNN STEPPED OUT OF THE library. "She is gone."

The world seemed to implode and I clung to Carry, and she to me, and I stroked her hair.

"This cannot be real, Georgy. That she who wrote so eloquently of death should join Father so young."

I stepped to Father's picture, lifted it from the wall, pulled the cool glass to my chest, and wept. How unfair it was we'd lost our Mary. Why had I not kept her away from that congregation? Forced her to rest? Suddenly the fair, Frank, Archie Burpee, none of it mattered. How trivial it all seemed.

Margaret crossed herself as she brought from the attic a paper box full of black muslin and crepe last used to mourn cousin Theodore Winthrop.

Dr. Flynn hurried to the front door and stepped into his galoshes. "Your mother will not leave Mary's side, despite repeated urging from Reverend Howland. Refusing a sedative, as well. Give her time. But do not allow the children in."

Once Mr. Sharpton, the undertaker, arrived, Jane and I brought Mother upstairs to rest, and she broke down several times on her way up the stairs.

"Those poor girls," she said over again. "To lose their dear mother."

Eliza arrived soon after, followed by Moritz, his arms full of dahlias. She embraced me tenderly and I lay my head on her smooth shoulder.

She dried her eyes. "Your Mary," she said. "Frank Bacon could do nothing?"

"He never came." I could barely breathe, an anvil on my chest.

"Poor Mary," Eliza said. "God could not have taken a more pure and tender soul."

Eliza stepped into the library to pay her last respects to Mary. Soon the little girls arrived, dressed in the closest thing they had to mourning colors, deep grays, and they sat about the front parlor, hands folded in their laps, looking very grown-up. I held Bertha on my knee and thought of the letter she would have to wait eleven years to read.

She rested her honest little head on my chest. "My mother was very tired and had to go home to God. Perhaps she will tell him she needs to come back here for us, Aunt Georgy?"

Before I could reply, the front door opened and Jemma entered, closing her umbrella, followed by a rain-soaked Frank Bacon.

Frank set his medical bag on the front table and shook the rain from his coat. "Where is Mary?"

I could not meet Frank's gaze.

Jemma hurried to my side. "What happened?"

Jane hurried in from the dining room, stepped to Frank, and struck him across the face with her hand.

I gasped. "Jane!"

She paced the carpet before him. "How could you stay away when she needed you so?"

Frank stood perfectly still.

I rose and handed Bertha to Jemma. "Mary left us over an hour ago, Frank. We finally got Mother to rest."

Frank sat at Mother's duck-footed table, staring at his hands.

Jane followed and stood over him, arms folded across her chest. "She loved you so and would have done anything for you. Where were you?"

Frank looked up at Jane, his slapped cheek scarlet. "I was where Mary asked me to be, in truth."

"You were at Bethada Barnett's house."

"I was not. I left for my uncle's house in New Rochelle last night, to see my mother about something urgent, and only just returned this evening."

"And what was so urgent?"

"In fact, it was at Mary's behest. But she pledged me to an oath of secrecy."

"If you'd been here you could've saved her," Jane said.

I stepped to Jane and took her hand in mine. "Mary had typhoid fever. You know as well as I, there was nothing to be done."

Jane and Jemma took the children into the dining room and Frank came to me. "I'm so terribly sorry I was not here for your Mary."

I wrapped my arms around him and drew him so close I felt the beat of his heart through his shirt, and breathed in his scent of bay rum soap and coffee.

"Don't leave me, Frank."

He returned my embrace and kissed my temple. "Never."

ONCE MARY PASSED, with heavy hearts we drew out our mourning fans and jet jewelry and set to work sewing black-edged handkerchiefs. Jane had funeral invitations printed and hand delivered to half of Manhattan, and printed copies of Mary's poem "Taps" for distribution at her service, the words eerily prescient of Mary's own death.

> Put out each earthly light
> It is God's shadow falls
> Along the darkening walls,
> Closing us round, when men say "it is night,"
> He draws so near it shuts the daylight out.

WE DID ANYTHING WE could to keep from thinking about our dear sister, set upon on a cooling board in the library, surrounded by one hundred candles. Mary's husband, Robert, prayed by her side for hours and seldom left the room.

Jemma was a valued friend to the whole family, always present, for she understood what we needed most was a simple hand with a needle project or an ear to hear about Mary, for she had loved our sister as well. Surely she was thinking of her own sister back in Maryland, for one person's loss often amplifies another's. Mary's death made me more determined than ever to reunite Jemma with Patience.

Jemma helped Nathan and Frank retrieve his things from Bethada's house, including his uniform, and he slept each night on the lumpy horse-hair sofa in the front parlor. Margaret delivered word to Mr. Burpee that I would not be marrying him and would be engaged to another, which he reportedly received with a marked lack of distress.

Frank Bacon was a tremendous comfort and I only wished Mary could have seen our reunion. What a pleasure it was to see Frank each morning, sitting taking his coffee in the dining room, sometimes hearing Mother's stories about Mary, his bedclothes folded military-style atop the piano.

One morning I entered the dining room to find him sitting alone at the table, a newly built fire burning in the fireplace. He stood as I entered. "Good morning, Georgy."

"I'm terribly sorry we have no better accommodations for you, Frank. Perhaps check in to Hotel Brevoort."

Frank had a fidgety air about him and looked behind me, toward the fireplace, more than once.

"What is it, Frank?"

"You are usually so observant. I hesitate to tell you."

I went to him and held his two hands. "Please tell me, Frank."

"Look above the mantel."

I turned and stepped to the fireplace, to find my fan, just as it had always been, encased in its old glass box, sitting upon the mantel, the fire-light adding a pinky glow to the pastoral scene depicted there on the silk.

"Oh, Frank. Father would be delighted."

Frank wrapped his arms around me and held me close. "I had to fight an Austrian dowager for it, but it was worth every cent."

Jemma

THE DAY OF MARY'S FUNERAL AND BURIAL AT GREEN-WOOD Cemetery out in Brooklyn, I did everything I could for the Woolseys, while trying to set a good example for the children and not cry myself, seeing Mary's girls and their brave way. I helped Hatty deck Mary's home, the rectory, and Brevoort Place with sheets of sheer black crepe, covering the windows, mirrors, and pictures, just like Ma and I did when Aunt Tandy Rose passed.

I sewed black mourning bonnets for Mrs. Woolsey and all the sisters, black trimmings for the older children's clothes, and a black ribbon for baby Georgy, who knew nothing of what happened to her brilliant ma. It was good to stay busy and keep my mind off of missing Miss Mary and of worrying about Anne-May maybe being close by. On my middle finger I wore the thimble Nathan gave me, and thoughts of him bubbled up now and then.

The funeral was the hardest for little Bertha—for she didn't want to say goodbye to her ma and ran after the hearse when they took the body to the graveyard. Then the poor child had to talk to every person in New York who came to the house to pay respects, so I had her help me make some mourning biscuits and cakes. When Nathan came by after the service and offered a hand of condolence to Bertha she shook it so serious and sweet and I caught a rare tear in his eye.

The day after the service everyone talked low and quiet and Mrs. Woolsey set her mourning clock to the sad hour Mary left us, which all Mary's daughters fixed on.

"If we set it forward, will she come back alive?" Bertha asked.

THE NEXT DAY, A LETTER arrived for me, addressed to Brevoort Place, in my sister Patience's hand. As soon as I found a moment alone, I tore it open, dried sunflower petals falling from the pages, and read.

> *Dear Jemma,*
>
> *Oh, how we long to see you!*
> *So much has happened since you and Sally*
> *took to the road.*
> *Am just hearing tragic news Miss Charlene*
> *yesterday lost Ambrosia on account of a bad indigo crop*
> *and has not paid the taxes. Mr. Smalls*
> *went from the mercantile, came and bought it.*
>
>

As always,
Your loving Patience
>

I sat and took it all in. Such a strange, short letter and no date at the top. Yes, it was Patience's handwriting for sure, but something about the way she wrote it didn't sound like her. I checked for any possible code. Did every other word make a secret sentence? No. I read it backward, with no success. No doubt Anne-May had made her write it to get me to come back down there, but it wasn't like Patience to miss a chance to code a letter.

I put the note aside and settled into bed as Georgy finished her nighttime toilette. Why would Patience write such a strange-sounding letter? And she'd added sunflower petals. As some kind of warning?

And then it hit me—I threw back the covers and snatched the letter from the bedside table. The first letter of every line? One of our early, old favorite codes we once used to hide our childish thoughts from Ma.

I ran one finger down the side of the body of the note and a chill ran through me as I read.

Do stay away.

ONE DAY NATHAN CAME to call on me at 8 Brevoort Place. I'd spent much of the day on the lookout for Anne-May, so it was nice to get out, though I knew I'd have to tell him it wouldn't work with us, since I saw him with another girl at the Sanitary Fair.

"Care to step out?" he asked.

"What for?" I asked.

"Brought some fish fry," he said, standing at the door with some good-smelling fish, the oil seeping a stain in the bag, skinny bread loaf under one arm.

Margaret, eyes big, handed me my cloak and motioned me all sorts of reminders about her *Rules of Proper Conduct* book we'd read together.

Nathan and I walked for a while, toward Broadway, past two pink wild pigs strolling by us on the sidewalk.

"This a date?" I asked.

"I suppose. If you like that kind of thing."

I pressed him away with two hands. "Need to keep a loaf of bread's distance between us when walking along a boulevard."

Nathan smiled. "As my brother says, 'Best thing about good manners is they're free.'"

I looked up at him and those green eyes.

"Didn't know you had a brother."

"We got separated when Dr. Gardener bought me. He joined the military soon as colored troops could sign up."

"How'd he find you?"

He shrugged. "Widow Gardener told him. Have a mind to sign up myself. They're stationed down at Point Lookout."

"You'd quit Dr. Bacon? He's getting back to the fight soon. Need you more than ever."

"Dr. Bacon'd understand if I left. Right now a man needs to fight for what's right."

We came to a jumble of iron folding chairs on the sidewalk. Nathan pulled out two, set them side by side, and we sat.

He opened his bag, letting out a cloud of good fish smell, and offered me some. "This isn't much of a date, I suppose."

I pulled out a piece of fish, the fry part hanging off. "This is impossibly good fish."

He smiled at me. "You have quite a vocabulary these days, Jemma."

We sat quiet for a while and just ate and watched every sort of person amble by.

He ripped a piece of bread off the loaf and handed it to me. "Want vinegar sauce?"

"No, thanks. Anne-May used to douse me with it after she was done with me. Can't stand the smell."

"Glad to see you having opinions."

"Here's another opinion. I think you have another girl." I leaned my head back and ate another piece of fish. "Saw you with a lady at the Sanitary Fair."

He kept his eyes on the bag.

I pulled the thimble from my pocket and set it on Nathan's knee. "So I thought I better bring this back."

Nathan kept at his fish, the thimble balancing there.

I wiped my fingers on the paper bag. "You two being so cozy and all."

Nathan looked up from his fish. "I liked you from the minute I first saw you in church, you know."

I squinted one eye at him. "You said you didn't remember me."

He waved a fly off the bag. "Of course I did. Remember your ma, too. Thought you and your sister were pretty as her."

"Remember my pa?"

He smiled. "He was big. I was somewhat scared of him, I'd say."

"I remembered you, too. Liked your eyes."

"Well then, you better keep this." He tucked the thimble back into my hand. "Means a person's engaged to be married, you know."

"May have heard that. Supposed to cut the silver part off the bottom for a wedding ring."

"Any opinion about that?"

I shrugged. "Surprised you never mentioned it. Plus, it's hard to be serious about a man who's got another woman on his arm."

"That lady you saw me with is my botany teacher. Mrs. Tompkins."

"How d'you know her?"

"Her father helped start Weeksville. And now she's the first black principal of a New York City school and teaches me nights. And nice as she is, she's married."

I brushed fish fry from my skirt and thought how happy I was Nathan was not, as Margaret would say, "otherwise engaged."

We finished the fish and Nathan crumpled up the bag.

"So next time we'll do a *serious* date. With napkins."

He unwrapped a peppermint and popped it in his mouth.

I smiled. "I guess. Got a feeling Anne-May wants me back in Maryland, though. Hard to step out on dates when I'm picking tobacco. I just feel her lurking around here."

He leaned closer. "I have some money saved up. Could make her an offer."

"You'd do that?"

"Of course I would."

"That's kind of you, but Anne-May'd never sell me. Besides, my ma and sister are still there. I can help get them out. Bring them up here."

"Let's ask Dr. Bacon to send somebody official down to get them. But promise you won't just up and go? As this war grinds folks down, they act crazy. No telling what'll happen if you go back there."

I slid the thimble in my pocket and just like that he kissed me full on the mouth. It was easy kissing him back, and he tasted of peppermint and chewing tobacco and impossibly good fish.

I sat back and breathed out, back of my hand to my mouth. "Why'd you do that?"

He smiled. "Just doing my best to make sure you stay."

I WAS STANDING IN the front parlor watching the street the next day, around noontime, replaying in my mind Nathan's awfully good kiss, when a knock came on the door and Margaret answered it. I sure knew that lady's voice right away and it was no surprise when you-know-who walked in that house.

"Who's calling?" Margaret asked.

"My name is Anne-May Wilson Watson of Louisiana and Hollywood, Maryland—Peeler Plantation, you may have heard of it."

As Anne-May stood on the stoop, my heart beat almost out of my chest and I looked for a place to hide.

"No, ma'am," Margaret said.

Then a man's voice came. "Mrs. Watson, here to regain her property."

"Perhaps come back next week, this house is—"

I tiptoed around so I could see through the crack in the door where it met the hinges and saw Anne-May standing with a fat little man, the chain of his pocket watch swaying as he talked.

"I'm Detective Karl Bigelow of the Bigelow Agency." He handed Margaret a card. "And these are Pinkerton detectives. We have a warrant for the arrest of one colored girl who goes by the name of Jemma. Mrs. Watson is here to make the identification."

Margaret glanced toward me. "There is no one here by that name."

Anne-May pushed by Margaret and the three men followed. "I demand to see the lady of the house."

Miss Jane and Georgy came into the front parlor.

"What's all this, Margaret?" Georgy asked.

"They want Jemma, ma'am," Margaret said in a trembling voice.

Anne-May stepped right up to Georgy. "She has broken the law and has to pay."

The white-bearded man stepped forward, packet of papers in hand.

"Samuel Cash, Pinkerton detective. We have orders to immediately apprehend and transport the person described to Maryland."

Georgy held out her hand. "May I see those papers?"

The Pinkerton handed her the papers and she read them.

I started breathing hard, frozen there.

Georgy handed back the papers. "But this says she's being held on charges of espionage."

Mother entered with Abby, the scarlet camel hair shawl Mary had given her around her shoulders.

"I thought I told you to leave and not come back," Abby said to Anne-May.

"She was in our *home*?" Mother asked. "What is happening here?"

"I am Anne-May Wilson Watson of Peeler Plantation in Hollywood, Maryland. These detectives are here in the name of the law to apprehend Jemma and take her back to Maryland to face the consequences."

Abby stepped to Anne-May. "I could tell you were an immoral liar, but thought you were just a thief going by an assumed name, not a godforsaken slaver."

Georgy joined Abby. "You were in my book line at the Sanitary Fair. How long have you been watching us?"

"Have we no privacy rights?" Carry asked. "You say you come here to uphold the law, but you've broken it by trespassing in our home under false pretenses."

Anne-May raised her chin. "Hiding law-breakers is punishable—"

I stepped out from my place behind the door. "I'm who she's looking for."

Georgy came and stood by my side.

Anne-May hurried toward me and reached out one hand.

"Jemma. My dear. When I heard the government was after you for spying I couldn't believe it." She inched closer. "Once they bring you back I will fight *hard* for you, Jemma. And when you're out of jail you can come home to Peeler and see your sister and ma. They're waiting for you. Every now and then I catch your ma looking up the road in a right wistful way."

"I didn't do any spying," I said. "That was you, Anne-May."

Mr. Bigelow stepped between us. "We'll get that all sorted out down in Maryland. But for now you best get your things."

I stood still and Georgy circled one arm around my shoulders.

"I've not been well without you." Anne-May held out her hands. "Look here. I've chewed my nails to the quick worrying about all this."

Mrs. Woolsey came to Anne-May and drew herself up tall. "This is a house in mourning, madam. I have lost a beloved child and will not lose another."

Anne-May surveyed her coolly. "Sorry for your loss, madam, but you'll just have to do without this one."

"This is a government matter, ma'am," the tall Pinkerton said.

Georgy stepped to her mother's side. "I am a U.S. Army nurse. Jemma has served her country as well. Surely I have some—"

The white-bearded one pulled handcuffs from his pocket. "Our orders are for immediate surrender." He turned to me. "Collect your personal effects."

"I will contact Mr. Lincoln personally," Mrs. Woolsey said. "Secretary Stanton, as well."

"You do that, ma'am," said Mr. Cash. "Meantime, we have our instructions."

As if in a dream, I started up the stairs.

Carry spoke to me, through the railing. "We'll fight this, Jemma."

Georgy followed me into the bedroom as I packed my carpetbag. "We have other options here."

I pulled from the armoire my black bombazine traveling dress I'd made. *Why had I not gone with Carter?*

"We shall appeal to Washington," she said, helping me unbutton my skirt. "Mother knows people."

I couldn't say much for fear of breaking down and wailing like an old steer.

"I'm leaving my nursing costume behind," I said. I slid my arms out of my jacket and slipped out of my shirtwaist.

That's when Georgy caught sight of my back all torn up like it was.

"Oh, Jemma," she said, sounding about to cry.

"It's fine, Georgy." I slid my black dress over my head.

"It is not *fine*. You cannot go back to that place."

"I can take care of myself."

Georgy took me by both hands. "Go out the window. I'll meet you in the back garden. We'll send Margaret for Judge Winthrop."

I turned back to my packing. "I'm not running, Georgy."

"I smell corruption here. Imagine, you accused of espionage."

"I'm not guilty. But it doesn't matter. They always win."

Once I finally got Georgy to button me up and came down the stairs to surrender myself, Mrs. Woolsey and all six sisters crowded about me and locked arms.

"It's time," I said. "Just let me go peaceable."

Anne-May called to me from the door. "Let's get this over and done, Jemma."

I stepped to the door and Jane grabbed me back, pulling me to her chest. "How can people be so cruel? Our country was founded on freedom."

The tall Pinkerton tugged me away from Jane, turned me around, and snapped the handcuffs on my wrists.

Georgy clasped my arm. "We'll fight this, Jemma."

I looked back to see the last of 8 Brevoort Place, the Woolsey women, good Pico at their feet, his little stub of a tail thumping on the floor, all awash in tears seeing me go.

"Miss Georgy," I called out. "Make sure and tell Nathan I would have stayed if I could."

Georgy

NEW YORK CITY
APRIL 1864

THE DAY AFTER THE PINKERTONS TOOK JEMMA BACK DOWN TO
Maryland, I sat at the dining room table with a fat stack of stationery, writing letters on Jemma's behalf. It was dark in the room, the window draped in black for Mary. Pico, still morose after his beloved mistress's death, lay upon the window seat, head resting on the sill, halfheartedly surveying the alley and street for cats.

I added one more black-edged letter to my already fat pile, appealing to every person of any prominence in Washington, begging help in overturning the espionage charge against Jemma.

Frank and Nathan bounded in, direct from spending a few days in New Jersey inoculating troops. Frank looked healthier than ever, a new light in his eyes. How good it was to see him each time now, with the still-fresh realization he was finally mine to love.

Frank removed his cap and Nathan followed. "Just received your letter saying they've taken Jemma. Came right away."

I stood and stepped to them. "My sisters and I have all sent letters and telegrams to anyone we know who can help. Mother has written as well and went to *The New York Times*, but they turned her away."

"Joe?"

"He's contacted Secretary Seward himself. I sent a telegram to Lincoln. No word yet."

"Busy running a war, I suppose," Nathan said.

"Any other state would be easier than Maryland," Frank said. "Lincoln won't rock the boat there, with them halfway out the door of the Union."

"Jemma's suffered so terribly down there, Frank. Jane and I came face-to-face with the overseer there and he is unspeakably cruel."

"Anne-May's from Louisiana," Nathan said. "They have a brutal way with their property. And I have a feeling Jemma won't go back to her old life easy."

Frank stepped to the window and surveyed the street as he scratched Pico's ear.

"What would you think about soliciting help from Bethada's aunt?"

Nathan and I exchanged a look of distaste. "Oh, Frank, no," I said.

"For all of her shortcomings, she's well connected."

The thought of the colorful Mrs. Barnett prompted a shudder. "It's a worthwhile idea, Frank, but you can imagine how awkward—"

"But what else do we do? If we simply wait for men of note to take up her cause it may never happen."

Then Nathan stood stock straight and gasped a sharp intake of air.

I touched his coat sleeve. "What is it, for goodness' sake?"

His face broke into a mile-wide smile. "How could I be so obtuse?"

"What's wrong?" Frank asked.

"Nothing wrong at all." He slapped his uniform cap on his head.

"Can you share your revelation, Nathan?" I asked. "We do need good news."

"I know exactly who we can call upon for help. Why didn't I think of it before?" He stepped to the door and turned back. "But we better go now. Things can go bad fast down at Peeler."

Jemma

I HUNG MY HEAD AS WE ARRIVED BY BOAT AT THE POINT LOOKout dock, where Jane, Georgy, and I'd come as U.S. Army nurses just the September before. The detectives led me off the boat, hands still bound, to a waiting carriage headed for the Leonardtown jail. Though Anne-May had begged to accompany us, they'd kept me overnight in New York and made Anne-May ride back from New York City by train, a small blessing. Least she wasn't talking at me the whole way back. I might have just begged those men to shoot me right there.

It was hard going back, after tasting freedom and then having it snatched away. I felt hollowed out, like I'd dropped a basket of blueberries and they'd rolled all over, too hard to chase them all down. At least they'd let me hold Pa's little bone cross in my hands for the trip. Felt good to have him there with me.

The detectives helped me up into the waiting carriage and we sat inside, close in there, them both facing me, and we started off with a lurch that sent them clutching the coach strap. They weren't big on talking, but I gabbed anyway, on account of the nerves.

"Used to be a nurse here," I said. "Saw my share of gangrene."

They just held their straps and looked out the window.

I had plenty of time on the way to look them up and down. The old one looked just like Rip Van Winkle, from the story I'd read Miss Tandy Rose six hundred times because it was short and she liked the dog. The not-so-old one resembled the picture of Captain Ahab from *Moby-Dick,* with his shaggy black hair and crazy eyes, shaking his fist at the sky.

Both were probably happy they'd be dumping me at Peeler soon.

Peeler. My breath came faster. Just the thought of slaving back there again for Anne-May made me want to jump from that carriage.

Her hickory switch. Sleeping at the foot of her bed.

I forced my mind back to Ma and Patience. Bad as it was coming back, my skin tingled all over at the thought of seeing them again. I'd get out of jail somehow and find some way to write to Georgy. She shook Mr. Lincoln's hand, after all.

Maybe he'd help.

We passed the contraband barracks of Point Lookout, a few former slaves coming and going, living in the protection of Mr. Lincoln, and I boiled with envy. Not that long ago I'd been helping others escape and now here I was, right back where I started. Anne-May always got her way.

Soon we turned down the road toward Peeler and passed Smalls and Sons, just a naked dress form in the big front window. It was warm for April, and Jubal Smalls's young ones played out front on his porch, pretty grown up since I'd seen them last, but still fat for such a skinny ma and pa.

"Wait," I said. "The jail's in Leonardtown. This is the wrong way." But neither one listened.

The wind picked up as we drove down Moneysunk Road. We passed the tobacco barn and LeBaron's shack, the smokehouse standing so smug and unapologetic, the rows of tobacco mounds in the fields, so stubbornly unchanged. I tried to force some gladness, a memory of good times with my kin or Celeste or Carter from somewhere but nothing good would come. I checked the fields for Ma, but not one soul stood out there.

As we pulled up around the drive to the house, wheels crunching on gravel, I told myself I wasn't really back, just stuck between there and my other life. It was still a pretty place but there was a sad way about it now, the crocuses in the garden beds trying to poke up through last year's chickweed. Someone had hung some dingy sheets out on the line to dry and they swayed a little in the breeze and the gutter over the door sagged and was rotted through, no Pa to fix it up.

Pa.

Anne-May met us at the courtyard, same place Delly and Charl and Celeste came down off that wagon so long ago.

Captain Ahab untied me and I kept Pa's bone cross in my hand. He helped me down from the carriage, his hand smooth on my wrist, since no calluses develop delivering fugitive slaves.

Anne-May came from the direction of the house. "About time you got here."

Rip Van Winkle winced at the sound of her voice.

She kicked a stone into the garden bed. "It's already noon and I've got nothing for supper."

"Why am I here, Anne-May?"

The detectives had Anne-May sign a paper and got off quick, rolling out in the carriage, and we went to the dining room. She'd made herself tea, a first to my recollection, and had folded into sloppy squares my old cut-down yellow calico dress and a white head rag and had laid them on the table, with a fresh hickory switch set next to them. I stared at that white rag, hating the thought of tying it on.

"Take that bonnet off, Jemma. And you're here because you were never going to jail. Just played that game to get you back here, so go ahead and change now."

"Right here?"

"Hurry up, don't have all day."

I removed my bonnet and unbuttoned my black dress down the back and stepped out of it, petticoats, too. Thought I'd be sick to my stomach as I stepped into my slave dress again and slipped the worn calico up over my shoulders. I took my little cross and tucked it into the dress pocket. Least I carried a bit of Pa with me.

Anne-May gathered my black silk dress and held it up by the shoulders.

"This'll do for my second best. You can start making this over, just a little tuck and a flounce at the hem, and I do believe it will suit me fine, the petticoats, too, long as you air it all out, so it doesn't smell like you."

I stood, fists balled at my sides. "Anything else?"

"Those are some nice boots you have on there. Too small for me, I suppose, unless we stretch them."

I stared at her, wondering what it would be like to switch her with that stick. She'd have LeBaron there in no time.

She handed me the head rag.

I tossed it back onto the table. "I'm not wearing this."

"You'll wear it and quick."

"Whip me till I'm blue, but I won't. I'm different now."

"Ruined, you mean?"

Anne-May looked me over for a long minute, and then turned and dismissed me with a wave.

"Quit your bellyaching and get yourself over to Miss Charlene's and fetch me some eggs. My chickens stopped laying. I'll have to get my own self ready to go to town."

We were quiet for a moment, listening to hoot owls out in the trees.

"Where's my ma?"

She waved toward the window. "Sable left ages ago."

Tears filled my eyes and I held the table to keep from falling. "Where to?"

"Lord knows, the way you coloreds disappear around here."

I stepped closer to her. "You must know."

"Honest to Pete, I do not. LeBaron even took the dogs out, went down to Point Lookout to check, and she's nowhere to be found."

"But you said Ma was waiting for me."

"Just told you all that to get you back without a fight. Jubal wants that book. Afraid you'll get us strung up."

I wiped my eyes with the back of my hand. "That book's hid for good."

Anne-May leaned over and reached for her switch.

"Do what you want to me, I won't tell you. You just want to pin it on me since I wrote it for you."

Anne-May sat back in her chair and played with her silver teaspoon, tarnished blue-black, I was happy to see. Not so easy taking care of a house all by yourself.

"Where's Patience?" I asked.

"You'll have to ask Miss Charlene about that. You get now, so you can be back in time to cook and clean the kitchen and start on that dress. I'm going into Hollywood right quick, but I'll be home and hungry soon, so no dawdlin'. And don't get any ideas about runnin' to that Point Lookout place. LeBaron's got his men patrolling that road now that Sable went off."

I stepped out of the dining room, peeped into the old kitchen, set off from the house, and thought about Sally and how that black stove seemed naked without her.

On the way to Ambrosia, I walked down to the shacks, Pa's door he made ajar. I'd only been gone a little under two years, but as I stepped in, it already looked much smaller than I remembered it, Pa's hoe still leaning by the hearth, Delly's old bed in the corner, dust an inch thick on everything.

I stepped to the table where it looked like Ma'd left Pa's plate and oyster shell at his place at the table, to remember him by. As I ran my finger down the smooth inside of the shell, the light caught something white by his plate, the little cross, the twin to the one he made me. I picked it up and pocketed it next to mine.

I hustled out back, past the empty hog pen, to our little cemetery, Sweet Clementine's, Celeste's, and Pa's graves lined up there. Little Kofi's fake one, too. The dirt in front of Pa's marker was sunk in, probably since he was buried with no box, and on his grave marker somebody'd set an old hammer. Ma? Just seeing his grave sunk in like that got me shaking with anger. How dare LeBaron steal our pa from us, such a good man, and Sweet Clementine and Celeste, too?

I took the twin to my bone cross and plunged it into the earth front of Pa's marker.

"Here you go, Pa," I said. "Thought you'd be happy to have yours back again." I stood and listened to the birds in the trees. "And just so you know, when you told me 'You don't know what you can do until you have to,' that was real true. I got out of here. Almost got Patience out, too. But we're not done. We'll get out, just like you wanted."

I rushed along the road to Ambrosia, set on getting Patience, and hoping she knew more about Ma. I'd get my sister out of that place that day if I had to kill somebody.

I passed the old gate to the sycamore where they hung Pa, barely able to look down that path, the old sunflower still tied there, just a gray, withered stalk now. Soon I saw Ambrosia, standing as it always had, that big old hulking place, dark in the trees.

I ran around the empty dog pen to the indigo shacks, and stepped into Patience's place, the whole thing cleaned out and left swept and neat, empty as the rest. I ran back to the kitchen door and stepped inside the kitchen, my wet palm on the screen door holding it back from slamming. I'd never been in that kitchen before and it was filthy dirty, with soiled napkins in a pile on the counter and, on top the icebox, a stack of dishes piled up ready to topple over.

"Who goes there?" A woman's voice came from somewhere deep in the house. "Harry, is that you?"

A shot rang out and hit the icebox and made those dishes clatter and I jumped straight up.

"It's just me, Miss Charlene," I called out with a shaky voice. "Jemma from Peeler."

"You get in here, you hear?"

"Don't shoot again and I'll come."

I followed the voice to a wide front parlor, the windows shuttered over what was probably a fine view of the river. My eyes adjusted to the dark to find Miss Charlene in her housedress, hair all loose down around her shoulders, white at the roots, sitting in a velvet easy chair, rifle across her lap. Smelled terrible in there, like the dirtiest necessary room.

"I thought you were Harry coming to borrow a saw," she said.

"Miss Anne-May's brother? He's been dead and gone two years now, Miss Charlene."

She took on a faraway look, fingers to her lips. "So he has. You know you're trespassin'."

"Just looking for my sister."

That's when I heard a dog growl and turned to see him crouched by the settee.

"He won't hurt you. Someone tried to poison him, so I keep him inside with me."

"Want me to let him out? Think he's been messing on the carpet."

"How's the house look to you, coming back here?"

"Same."

"Liar."

I picked up my skirt and stepped closer, mindful of the piles on the carpet.

Miss Charlene leaned forward in her chair. "We lost the house, you know. I have one week left before I'm forced to vacate."

"I'm sorry, ma'am."

"Jubal Smalls took it out from under us. Should have known when he tried to kiss me he had his eye on this place. Once the mealybugs fouled our indigo crop last year, we couldn't make the taxes. Killed my husband. Jubal came and took the deed from Mr. Weed's dying hand. Anne-May probably helped him, the viper."

I shifted in my boots and tried not to breathe in that stink as we both listened to the tick of the mantel clock.

"Know where my ma is?"

"Sable's been gone a while now."

Tears filled my eyes. "Where to?"

Charlene shrugged. "Heard rumors, but one never knows."

"Patience?"

Miss Charlene looked up to the ceiling. "You didn't see her?"

"Where's my sister, Miss Charlene?"

She reached out one skinny hand. "Can you stay and comb my hair?"

I stepped closer. "Patience. Where is she?"

Miss Charlene folded her fingers at her chest. "Had to give her up. Nothing I could do. Couldn't afford to pay Anne-May rent to use her anymore."

"Where *is* she?"

Miss Charlene laid both arms across her head and cried most piteously. "Don't *holler* at me. She's sold, for Lord's sake."

"To the speculator?"

"No. He said he can't get a sound price for her on account of her bein' crippled up."

I leaned over Charlene. "You don't tell me, so help me God—"

"Peeler overseer took her. Said he already taught her to dress game and clean his guns, so he might as well buy her."

I reached for the back of a chair, velvet warm under my shaking hand. "Anne-May sold Patience to LeBaron?"

"Just today. He swore up and down not to hurt her. Told me he only burned that *R* in her chest 'cause he had to. Runaways must be punished."

I lifted my skirt and ran out through the kitchen, Charlene calling after me, "Hated doin' it. She's like a daughter to me, sweet thing."

I RAN LIKE A PERSON on fire back to old Farmer Burns's gate, snuck down the road to LeBaron's shack, stayed quiet and set to watching. It looked the same as before, the shingles just more gray, the grass around it worn away to a patch of dirt. It was quiet out there, the only sounds the buzz of a horsefly circling my head and the way-far-off squeal of hogs down by the dock as the butchers did their slaughtering.

I snuck up closer, hid behind a tree, and all at once my heart started hammering when LeBaron came out on the little porch, shotgun in hand. He slid a shell in, then plopped himself down in that old bamboo chair of Anne-May's and set to polishing his gun with a cloth.

My breath caught in my throat as Patience came out of the shack, holding a maul by its long handle, fat metal head facing down, and set to riving a locust log. She stripped off her old sweater, leaving her bare-armed in her homespun dress, and I couldn't take my eyes off her chest, the shiny scar there, a fat *R* seared into her skin.

She drove her wedge into the heart of the log and then made her way down the length of it till she thwacked it clean in two, the wood popping and splintering as she went.

Just as she drew the maul up again, I came out from behind the tree.

"Patience," I called out, my voice echoing around the clearing.

She looked across the yard at me, set down the maul, and wiped her hands on her apron.

I reached out one hand. "Come here to me."

She looked over at LeBaron.

"Hold it right there." LeBaron picked up his gun from his lap. "Welcome back, Miss Jemma."

I waved Patience toward me, but she stood frozen like Lot's wife.

LeBaron raised his gun and looked down the sights at me. "Remember this place? That tree's where your old pappy died."

"Patience, walk to me," I said.

"Yes, sir, your pappy went quick. Not stubborn as a sticky drawer, like his girl."

I held out both hands. "You can do it, Patience."

"Maybe you didn't hear, but this is my property now." He nodded toward Patience. "Ink's still wet on the bill of sale. *One adult female Negro* is what it says. But you can substitute yourself if you like."

I stepped toward Patience, my boots quiet on the dirt.

LeBaron shot, and the bullet grazed the grass next to me.

"Come, Patience," I said.

"You and me go way back, Jemma. Ever seen me miss? Next time I won't. I'll tell Sheriff Whitman you died doing me grievous harm."

He reloaded his gun and looked again down the sights. "Matter of fact, it'd be fun to get you wounded, then finish you off slow."

I retreated toward the path. "I'll find Anne-May and tell her."

"Oh, you do that, Jemma." He set his shotgun back on his lap and returned to his polishing, and Patience picked up her maul and got back to her work.

"You'll regret this, LeBaron," I called back.

He stood and walked toward me. "What I tell you? Git."

I turned and stood my ground.

Quiet as the breeze, Patience stepped up behind him, holding that maul by the handle with two hands.

"I said, *git*. What you waiting for, Jemma?" LeBaron asked.

"For you to die," I said.

He turned at the last minute, maybe sensing someone there, and Patience swung that maul and hit him with the metal end in the back of the head.

LeBaron fell, twisting down onto the dirt in a puff of dust, and then settled, face-down. After that, things got real quiet. Even the hogs by the dock were silent.

I hurried to them and looked down on LeBaron, hair on the back of his head matted red-black with blood. I knelt and checked his wrist for a pulse and found only a faint beat. Then, with my boot tip, I tried to roll him over, half afraid he'd jump up and strangle us both.

"He dead?" Patience asked, her voice all watery-sounding.

"Not yet."

Patience threw down the maul with a thump.

"You got him good, Patience," I said, my legs still wobbly. "Always knew you were strong, but that was big."

She shivered, like somebody poured ice down her back. "We better hide him well to buy us some time."

Anne-May

WHEN I ARRIVED HOME FROM NEW YORK CITY, AFTER THE train ride from Hades, having to listen the whole way to Northerners argue about Abraham Lincoln's tubby little wife, Mary, and whether or not she had any genuine fashion sense, the answer to which was a flat no, I drove straight home to Peeler to ready myself to see Jubal at the store.

Just as I was reuniting with my cat, trying to get her to come out from under the sofa, the men arrived with Jemma, interrupting my tea. At least she'd come in a decent silk dress the Woolsey women had made up for her, their stitches well done, which I could seize as my own contraband.

I sent her off to Ambrosia to get eggs for dinner, made myself a fire in my bedroom fireplace, and freshened up best I could with no maid, powdering my face and underarms, taking charcoal to my roots, and curling my hair. My head pounding, and in dire need of snuff, I poured myself the last of the blackberry brandy and considered the disappointing offerings in my armoire.

I chose a pink silk dress Jubal had once admired, and tried with a bristle brush to scrub off the line of brown grime along the sleeves and neck. I took my diamond ring out from the safe and slid it back on my finger, put on my amethyst earbobs, and splashed some cologne down my front.

I drove myself to Smalls and Sons in the only buggy we had working, as it was, with two spokes broke out of one wheel. I lifted Jubal's hankie to my nose periodically to remind myself of his scent. Surely he'd rush to me and gather me in his arms. It had been nine months since I'd seen him. I would inquire about that poem he said he wrote and he'd have a suitable answer.

An apology, at least.

I approached the store and spied a handsome carriage out front, a liveried darkie brushing the horse's mane. I entered—announced by the jingle of bells above the door—and found Jubal behind his glass case, *tête-à-tête* with a woman customer, helping her with snuff, a second servant boy close by at attention. She was a delicate-looking young thing I knew from somewhere, with fresh-scrubbed skin and just a hint of rouge. What a pretty dress she wore, deep magenta wool, and the perfect hoop made her waist appear so small. The boy slid a mink cape about the woman's shoulders as she turned to leave.

She smiled and waved as he held the door open and she stepped out. "Until next time, Jubal."

Jubal waved to her and then began rearranging his snuff tins in the glass case. He barely glanced up as I approached. "So," he said, "the prodigal son returns."

"If that's a Bible reference, you know I don't understand those. They say Southern gentlemen greet their ladies with—"

He slammed his case shut. "Where've you *been*, Anne-May?"

"Got any snuff? I could use—"

"What has taken you so damn long?"

"Simmer down, now, Jubal. I told you where I was off to. Washington. And I sent you a letter from New York, for pity's sake."

"You better tell me you found Jemma."

"Well, I happen to have good news about that, for once. Got any Golden-Banded Oco? Feeling a bit peaky after that train ride."

"Where is she, Anne-May?"

"I found her after a great deal of effort. You wouldn't believe the terrible things the Yankees did, stole the money Reggie gave me—"

"Is she back?"

"Just now, courtesy of some fine Northern detectives. Got her sent back by the law."

"How?"

I eyed the snuff in the case. "Had to give them *something*."

"What have you done, Anne-May?"

"I just told them I'd been working with a group that may have accepted some information."

Jubal grabbed me by the shoulders and shook me, my ringlets bouncing against my face. "Are you insane?"

"They don't want *us*, Jubal. They want the big fish."

"You idiot, I'll have to go into hiding or have a spotter on the road. Last time they came, I had to hide from them like a dog, in my wife's armoire. I wondered why they stopped coming around. They wanted to get you to make their case."

"They assured me that everything will be fine once they have the person at the top. Then it will cool off."

"They don't have one bit of proof except that book, and if they *find* it they will take me to the Leonardtown jail and then *hang* me, Anne-May. You too."

I stepped to him and placed one hand on his chest. "I'm getting it, don't worry."

He pushed me away and I fell against a barrel. "You'd better or I'll tell them how you asked if I wanted those Yankee troop addresses, but I said no. And how you went on and sold them elsewhere. Sheriff Whitman will side with me."

"But it was all your idea, Jubal."

"You expect me to die for you? I have children."

"But you said you had feelings—"

He turned away and then back again, jabbing a finger at me. "Never said that."

"—that I would be your queen."

"Things *change*, Anne-May."

I held my palms to my stomach to hold back the bile. "You want me gone so you can take my house."

"No—though you can barely maintain it and Fergus missed the taxes this past quarter."

My head buzzed. I sat on a barrel and my skirt billowed and settled. "The poem. You didn't write it. That was all a lie. That woman in here just now . . ."

"No one—"

"I know her. Camille Tourand from Six Elms. You want her property, too. You have Charlene's. Soon mine. Then hers. Such a perfect plan."

Jubal reached for my hand and I pulled it away.

"You're tired, Anne-May. You go home and find that—"

"Enough about that stupid book, Jubal."

I walked out, those horrible little bells jangling. I stepped up into my old buggy and rode off toward Peeler Plantation, choking back the sobs, wind drying the tears on my face. I picked up speed until halfway home I let my hankie flutter in the breeze and then released it, not even watching where it went, lost to the dark night.

Georgy

POINT LOOKOUT, MARYLAND
APRIL 1864

FRANK, NATHAN, AND I ARRIVED AT POINT LOOKOUT BY TRANSPORT steamer, looking forward to seeking help on Jemma's behalf from the hospital staff and Nathan's brother.

Frank and I sat facing Nathan, our passage ensured by Mr. Olmsted himself, once I shared Nathan's plan and sought his help.

Nathan searched the shoreline through the steamer window. "My brother Joshua's commanding officer at Point Lookout is Colonel Draper. Perhaps we should request a meeting with him first?"

"Alonzo Draper?" Frank asked.

"You know him?" Nathan asked.

"Just by way of the newspapers. He's an abolitionist from Massachusetts. As a Union officer, he recruited a colored regiment—did great work smoking out Confederate sympathizers and they ended up taking over this whole place."

Frank had held my hand most of the trip, wearing his deep blue frock coat, his Colt firearm tucked in the sash at his waist.

Nathan had spent the voyage reading a botany journal. He looked handsome in his private's uniform, a blue sack coat and leather boots buffed to a dull shine. I longed to pry about his sentiment concerning

Jemma, but held back, for he seemed a private man. Certainly he cared about her deeply to risk his personal safety in such a devoted way.

We disembarked at Point Lookout wharf, which had changed much since my last time there, including the erection of makeshift pens holding Rebel soldiers, guarded by colored troops.

I led Frank and Nathan to the front office staff and they soon brought us to Colonel Draper, the new commander of the camp. He stood near the window, surveying his troops on the field outside.

Frank and Colonel Draper exchanged salutes.

"Captain Frank Bacon, Colonel. And may I present Miss Georgeanna Woolsey and my assistant, Nathan, whose brother, Joshua, serves in your ranks."

Nathan saluted. "Colonel Draper."

The colonel returned his salute. "Your brother's a good man."

Colonel Draper wore his uniform well, and his dark eyes shone deep in the folds of his face.

"I'm a great admirer, Colonel," I said, "of your support for workers in the New England shoemakers' strike and for your leadership of the colored troops."

"Thank you, Miss Woolsey. What can I do for you? Can't imagine what you'd want in this godforsaken place."

"I was stationed here as a U.S. Army nurse, just last year, in fact."

"A lot has changed. We've had a tremendous influx of Rebel prisoners. Guarded by the Thirty-sixth Colored Infantry Regiment. You've never seen finer troops. Ready to serve with distinction."

"We have a favor to ask," Frank said.

I stepped closer to Colonel Draper. "A friend of ours, a slave at nearby Peeler Plantation, had been living free in New York City with us. She was suddenly taken by federal order back here, reclaimed as property by Mrs. Anne-May Watson."

"And you come seeking my help?"

"We'd be most grateful," I said.

"I'm sorry. But I'm afraid that's not included in my purview. Besides, this being Maryland and a Union state, we have to tread a thin line."

"But we have come so far, Colonel," I said. "Please reconsider. She's a good person and has served the Union well."

"It's not my decision. Only in the narrowest circumstances do I have the power to overturn a federal order."

"We have no other recourse," Frank said.

"I wish things were different, believe me." Colonel Draper tossed his book onto the desk. "But if you hurry, you can catch the steamer back to New York."

Jemma

CHAPTER 57

PEELER PLANTATION, MARYLAND

APRIL 1864

WE DRAGGED LEBARON TO THE UNDERBRUSH BEHIND THE shack and then covered the trail of blood in the dirt best we could, sweeping pine boughs over our blood-smeared tracks.

"We should go to Anne-May," I said. "Maybe she'll hide us. I'm still her property after all. Worth nothing to her dead."

"I can't think straight, Jemma."

I pulled her close. "He have his way with you?"

"No. Told him I had the fever and he kept away. Last week it was the yaws."

"Smart girl."

Patience started to shake all over. "They'll see this blood and find him, Jemma. They'll come looking."

"We hide him good enough, they won't find him for a while. Meanwhile we gotta keep calm as we can. So, Miss Charlene told me Ma's gone. Is it true?"

"She left a long while ago."

Every part of me went limp. "Was hoping Charlene was making it up."

"One night Ma sent me a note she was waiting for me out by the road to Hollywood and ready for us to run together, but Miss Charlene kept me close all night and by the time I got out there Ma'd left. Heard they found somebody might have been Ma in the Big Stink. Too far gone to tell."

"They find bodies every week there."

Patience wiped her eyes with the hem of her apron. "She's gone, Jemma."

I squeezed her two hands. "I can't believe that, Patience. We'll find her. But right now we have to think. How do we leave quick with no money for train fares?"

"I know where Miss Charlene stashed some grocery money she forgot about."

Voices came, from deeper in the woods. Clem and the other patty-rollers.

I pulled her close and felt her heart banging against mine. "Meet me out on the road on the way to Hollywood. One hour."

I RACED BACK TO Peeler and found Anne-May in the dining room sitting at her big old table, staring into the fire, sleeves of her pink dress soiled along the edges, the light of the fire catching the purple of her earbobs.

She barely looked up at me. "Go poke that fire for me, Jemma."

"I need your assistance, Anne-May. Fast."

"*Assistance.* You've gotten so fancy in your speech since living with those wretched Yankee women. They're quite crass, you know, speaking their minds in public as they do. No wonder most of them are unmarried."

I checked the room for possible hiding spots in case Clem came for me. "LeBaron's been hurt."

She turned her face toward me. "Hurt how?"

I wiped my wet palms on my skirt. "Bad. And it won't be long before they find him."

She turned her gaze back to the fire. "You do it?"

"Had help. Patience."

"And now you need me."

"I'd say we need each other. Patience and I are going to try and find our ma and go somewhere we can be together and free. I'll tell you where that book is, but I want two things in return and I need them quick. First, I need your help leaving here with Patience. Second, I'll take those earbobs for my ma."

"You come back here all outspoken and demanding. I've never heard such a—"

"When Aunt Tandy Rose gave them to Ma, she said it didn't make up for losing a child. The day you had LeBaron snatch them back, it was like you took Toby all over again."

"Wasn't my fault you started that fire, playing the fool, stead of watchin' your little brother."

"I'm done taking the blame for what happened. You can tell me all day I'm stupid, but I'm not and it was an accident. I miss my brother every day. Patience doesn't remember this, but she kicked that lantern over. I tried to stop her from going back in to try and save him but she went anyway."

"You cost me two good pieces of property. That beam falling on Patience cut her value by half. You're lucky you at least pulled one of them out."

"How can you be so unfeeling? You know what it's like to lose a brother."

Anne-May looked to the fire, with what looked to be a tear in her eye, and stared at the flames for a good long minute.

I turned toward the door. "I'm leaving."

"Not until you tell me where the book's at."

I held out my hand. "The earbobs, Anne-May."

"You might never find your ma to give them to, you know."

Anne-May sat still so long I thought she'd had a spell, and then, slow as cold molasses, she took one earbob off and then the other and set them on the table. "Never did complement my complexion. Now, where's that book?"

I picked up the earbobs and slid them in my dress pocket. "You need to say how you'll help get us out—"

All at once, angry men's voices came from the courtyard.

I looked about the dining room. "They found LeBaron. I can hide in the pantry."

But before I could take one step, the courtyard door busted open and LeBaron's pattyroller friends, Clem at the head, hustled in, holding their little clubs and coiled whips, guns drawn.

Anne-May stood between me and Clem.

"Hand her over, Mrs. Watson," Clem said. "She's in a whole lotta trouble with the law for attacking LeBaron."

Anne-May raised her chin high. "How do you know what happened if he's dead?"

"He's pretty near dead, over by his place, head cracked bad. Awful clear who did it, that slave of his and this one, too. Got him with her log splitter."

"They're my property, Clem. I'm sorry about LeBaron, but she represents a considerable investment—"

"Take her." Clem waved his boys in and they grabbed me by each arm.

Anne-May came to stand near us. "Where you going with her?"

"Sorry about your investment, ma'am," Clem said. "But we're talkin' murder. And we figure what's good for their daddy out by the sycamore is good for them. Some women enjoy such a spectacle, but you best stay here, Mrs. Watson, refined and tenderhearted as you are."

I struggled as the men pulled me out into the courtyard, but they tied my hands and looped a fat rope around my neck so the one on horseback could jerk me along, burning my skin.

With a laugh, Clem called out to the man on the horse. "Christ, don't kill her before we get there, Jimmy.

"We brought the same log chain what got your pa," Clem said in my ear as we walked, his lips so close I could smell the whiskey on his breath.

My whole body went cold as we walked toward the path to Ambrosia. Just the thought of the spider tree sent my arms and legs to jelly, and I prayed Patience had not come to our meeting place after all.

Anne-May

NOT LONG AFTER THEY TOOK JEMMA, I WAS IN THE KITCHEN searching the pantry for the hundredth time when Euphemia swept in.

"Anne-May? You here?"

I stepped out of the pantry. "Hey, Pheme."

"Welcome back." She wore her same old black silk, a new ivory-colored knit wrap about her shoulders. She looked about the room. "This place needs a good cleaning. You can't live out of cans."

"Good to see you, too, sister. I'd make some beef Wellington, but all we have is rice and some old potatoes, and too much starch ruins the figure."

"Still looking for that book, aren't you?"

"Jemma still won't tell me where it is. Jubal's fit to be tied."

"Jemma's back?"

"Just today. Got her back from some Northern women hiding her in New York."

Euphemia looked down on me with a pained look. "How could you bring her back here, Anne-May?"

"Don't get on your high horse. I have a right to my property. But Clem and the boys just took her. Over to Burns Farm."

Euphemia gathered her wrap closer. "My God, Anne-May. What for?"

"She and her sister hurt LeBaron. Knocked him senseless, she said."

"Why didn't you say so? You have to *do* something."

"Relax, for pity's sake."

She paced the kitchen. "They'll kill her, just like Sweet Clementine. Celeste."

Euphemia turned and her wrap fell down off her shoulders, revealing a good deal of baby in her belly.

I grabbed hold of the counter. "Guess you had no trouble helping yourself to my husband, sister."

She looked out the window and smoothed one hand down her front. "It's Fergus's, if you're wondering."

"Figured it wasn't Sheriff Whitman's. Guess the sanctity of marriage means nothing anymore."

"I'm sorry, Anne-May."

I waved her away. "Truth is, I can't stand the sight of him."

She looked down at her swollen middle. "Wonder what Mama'll think."

"Bet it's a girl. They say girl babies rob you of your looks."

Euphemia gathered her wrap back up around her shoulders. "I'd go with you, but can't leave Fergus down at the shack too long. He's gotten so he can't move that well."

"Moved well enough to put that baby in your belly."

Euphemia colored and set one of Tandy Rose's Wedgwood plates in the sink. "You need to get over there fast and stop Clem and his boys. If nothing else, protect your property."

"How am I supposed to do that? There must be six of those patty-rollers."

"You've got a rifle. Show them who's boss. Plus, Jubal might be there. What if Jemma tells him where that book is and you're not there to hear it? He'll turn on you fast. Say it was only you that did it."

"S'pose you're right. Bein' with child's made you downright smarter, know that, Euphemia?"

Georgy

✳

POINT LOOKOUT, MARYLAND
APRIL 1864

COLONEL DRAPER WALKED NATHAN, FRANK, AND ME TOWARD the door.

"I'm sorry I couldn't be of more assistance," the colonel said. "Believe me, I'd like to help."

I turned. "Jemma was a former employee here, nursing soldiers with us. Does that make a difference?"

"Was she here in an official capacity?" the colonel asked.

"Well, no."

"But she fought at Gettysburg," Nathan said.

The colonel stopped and faced him. "Hold on. For the U.S. Army? How'd that happen?"

"A regiment came by Hagerstown and took her with them," Nathan said. "Major Ellis."

"Of the Connecticut Fourteenth?" the colonel asked. "Conscripted her?"

Nathan nodded. "Yes, sir."

"Why didn't you say so?" the colonel asked.

"I don't understand, Colonel," I said.

Nathan smiled. "That means she's official U.S. Army contraband, our property, and we have every right to reclaim her as such."

"Indeed." The colonel opened the door. "I'll send a rifle company with you. The three of you ready to ride?"

WE APPROACHED PEELER PLANTATION, Frank driving me in one of the camp's open four-seater surrey carriages. Nathan and his brother, Joshua, led his twenty blue-uniformed rifleman colleagues of the Thirty-sixth Regiment Colored Troops following us on horseback, in two exact lines. How good it had been to see Nathan reunited with his brother after so many years apart. Joshua was an only slightly smaller version of Nathan, with dark eyes and a similar forthright manner.

As we rode down the long drive to the plantation, I held the letter signed by Colonel Draper and the corners of it caught the breeze, his red sealing wax barely cooled.

A deep melancholy overtook me as we passed the outbuildings, tobacco fields, and barns where Jemma had been born into slavery and raised, her pa murdered.

We pulled into a gravel circular drive, and a tall woman opened the door and stood in the doorway, gathering her shawl about her.

"May I help you?" she asked.

"We're looking for Jemma. I believe she's just returned? I'm Georgeanna Woolsey and this is Captain Bacon and I have in my possession a document which demands her release."

"She's not here at the moment."

"I warn you, madam. It bears the signature of Colonel Draper of Point Lookout himself."

She stepped toward us with a worried air. "I'm Euphemia Wilson. Jemma's been taken, I'm afraid, by some ruffians with intent to do her great harm. My sister just left for there."

"Can you show us where they are?" Nathan asked.

She waved toward the woods. "Farmer Burns's old place, on the way to Ambrosia."

"I know it," Nathan said, and he, his brother, and the other riflemen turned and rode off in a spray of gravel.

Euphemia hurried out of the doorway, and for the first time since our conversation began I saw from her swollen belly she was due to deliver a child.

"I will accompany you," she said.

Frank handed her up into the carriage.

"Captain Watson can tend himself for a bit. But we must fly to get Jemma, sir, for I'm afraid we may already be too late."

Jemma

PEELER PLANTATION, MARYLAND
APRIL 1864

As clem and the pattyrollers dragged me down the overgrown path to old Mr. Burns's farm, we passed the dried sunflower on the gate, still shriveled up there, all the seeds dropped out of the middle. Someone once tried to tell us how dangerous that place was. If only I'd listened.

The horseman jerked me along by the rope, the blood sticky where it cut my neck. Soon LeBaron's shack came into view, the spider tree just beyond, and my whole body went cold. Jubal Smalls, already there, walked from the shack, silver cup in hand.

"Well, Miss Fancy returns. Seen what you've done to LeBaron."

Clem and his friends gathered around us, and I felt a hot sweat of relief all over, since Patience was not there.

"Just took his last earthly breath over there in his place. But not before he told us what you and your sister did. You didn't expect to get away with that, did you? Not how things work here, princess." He leaned in. "Where's that book?"

How natural they all went about their jobs, Clem hauling the log chain from LeBaron's shack, building up the same little stage they'd made for Pa.

"What book?" I asked.

Jubal shrugged. "You better start your praying, girl."

He took the chain from Clem and tossed it up and over a limb, looped the other end cold and heavy around my neck. Just what Pa felt, standing under this tree. A vision of him came to me, his arms tied tight behind his back just the same. Hot tears stung my eyes. All at once I missed Ma. Her quiet way and sweet smile. If she was alive somewhere, she'd cry for sure when they told her I went the same way as Pa.

Would Nathan miss me?

People from town started walking into the clearing, with that curious look folks get when they're new to a place. I recognized a few. The assistant postmaster. The butchers from the dock, one still in his shiny yellow apron. Two ladies from Leonardtown I'd seen in Smalls and Sons. At first I wondered why they were all the way out there and then the answer knocked the breath out of me.

They'd come for a hanging.

All at once, down the path came another horse, dragging someone behind, a whole group of men laughing and calling out as they followed. "Get up and walk, lazy."

"Patience." I started toward them but the chain held me back. I turned to Jubal. "Please, not her."

He sipped from his cup. "Word is, she killed a white man."

I felt weak all over. "Please. She can't walk."

"Where's the book, Jemma?"

The pattyrollers dragged Patience into the clearing, the rope tied around her middle, her dress dirt-smeared and worn through from scraping the ground.

"You'll let her go?" I asked.

Jubal crossed an X over his heart with his finger. "Gentleman's honor."

I thought for a long second as the men pulled Patience to the other side of the tree and brought another chain for her and tossed it over a branch. Clem rolled a barrel out to make a stage for her, too.

"Let her go, first. Then I'll tell."

Jubal adjusted the chain around my neck, casually as a man ties a tie. "You're playing on my last nerve, princess."

"You're lying. You won't let Patience go. Not with all these folks show-ing up for a show."

He smiled and leaned in close, Anne-May's favorite, bourbon, on his breath. "Guess that's the chance you take."

"You've always been a liar. Hope they find that book."

"Not a smart thing to say with a chain around your neck. But just to prove what a considerate man I am, you get to choose who goes first."

A blackness grew in my chest as more townsfolk gathered, greeting one another like any other day. You could feel the excitement in the crowd, like the time the circus came to Leonardtown, just before the lions came out.

He shrugged. "Fine, then, your sister'll go first."

Anne-May strode out of the woods and toward us into the clearing, holding her shotgun.

Jubal knocked back what was left in his cup. "Well, if it isn't the little dove hunter."

"What are you doing here, Jubal?" she asked.

Clem handed him a broom. He took it and then he turned again to Anne-May. "You coming to watch or not?"

"Hangin's not humane," Anne-May said. "Not this way. They'll just strangle."

"It's a two-for-one today, Anne-May, and folks've come for a show. But you have my permission to shoot either one if they dance too long. Some-times the skinny ones are too light to go fast."

He turned to me. "Not like that big old pa of yours. I heard the good Lord took him merciful quick. Didn't even have to pull on his feet."

Clem tightened the chain around Patience's neck and she cried out.

"I love you, Patience," I called over to her.

Patience looked down at the ground and then at me, eyes bright, too overcome to speak.

The pattyrollers moved away from Patience and me, just as they had from Pa before it happened, and joined the circle of onlookers.

Jubal cleared his throat. "You've come here to witness justice being done, folks. It's what a community does to cleanse itself of its shadowy elements. There's been grievous harm done to one of our own, LeBaron Caruthers, a good man who has served Hollywood well."

Jubal stepped toward Patience, who stood, chin high, arms tied behind her back, such a little thing, with that big chain around her neck.

"You wouldn't think this little girl could do grievous harm, but it just proves the power of evil in the colored soul."

Jubal grabbed the long end of the chain around Patience's neck and yanked. Patience gasped.

I looked to Anne-May. "Help us."

Jubal laughed. "She won't help you—only cares about herself. She's what's known as a *snuff* addict. Our little snuff addict has given up everything, including her self-respect. Isn't that right, Anne-May?"

Jubal stepped right behind Patience and with the end of his broomstick pushed her closer to the end of the stage and the crowd gasped as one.

"No, Anne-May won't help. Can't even keep a husband, let alone secrets."

He pushed Patience closer still to the edge.

I looked away—it was too hard to watch my sister die—and searched the faces in the crowd, some smiling, some excited, and saw a black face toward the back, looked like Nathan. I tried to call out, but the fear caught it in my throat.

Jubal started pushing Patience so only her toes were still on the stage.

"No, Anne-May can't help you," Jubal said. "She's in a bunch a trouble herself with the law, with that *book* a—"

And then, all at once, a gunshot rang out and the world stood still as Jubal fell to the ground, a perfect red hole blown through his snaky heart.

Georgy

EUPHEMIA DIRECTED US ALONG THE SAME ROAD JANE AND I had driven the Point Lookout ambulance down months before.

"It's just up here," she said. "I'm afraid they'll hang Jemma like they did her father. Hope we're not too late."

We came to the end of the road, disembarked, and followed her on foot down a path through the woods till we came upon an old barn and a clearing, a tremendous old sycamore standing over it all.

Jemma and her sister stood on crude wooden platforms, heavy chains about their necks, the other ends swung over the branches of the sycamore. Our New York City visitor Anne-May stood in the clearing, a shotgun in her hands, aimed at the little scene under the tree.

Frank drew his pistol as we approached the scene, just as Anne-May raised her gun to her shoulder, took aim, and shot the man next to Patience, the blast sending her backward. Joshua and his men in blue faced the crowd, their silver bayonets fixed, as Nathan ran to Jemma and unbound her, and Frank and I hurried to Patience.

The downed man called out, "Harriet!"

A woman from the crowd came to him, crying, "Jubal!"

Frank walked to him, knelt, and after a moment pronounced him dead.

Nathan's brother, Joshua, addressed the crowd: "Disperse immediately or be fired upon. Any survivors will be taken straightaway to Point Lookout Prison."

A few in the crowd threatened the rifle company with fists and harsh language but quickly drifted off into the woods. Once the crowd was dispersed, Joshua and his men surrounded the two platforms and helped the sisters make their way to a grassy spot.

Jemma reached for me with a trembling hand. "Georgy, you came."

After Jemma and Patience embraced, we helped them sit down and Frank tended their wounds best he could without his medical bag.

Euphemia stepped to both of the girls and I helped her kneel next to them in the grass. "I have some wonderful news for you two, but perhaps you need some time, before . . ."

The two sisters exchanged glances and held hands.

"Please, ma'am," Patience said. "We'd like to hear."

Euphemia looked down at her folded hands. "I've wanted to tell you for some time now, but the people I work with have strict rules."

"What is it?" I asked.

"I've recently had the good fortune to find out where your mother is and she sends a message. She wants you two home."

Anne-May

I WASN'T SCARED ALL THAT MUCH TO BE IN JAIL AT POINT LOOKOUT. It wasn't a real jail, just a white tent in a wire pen, guarded by some darkie soldiers. Fergus promised to arrange for a lawyer. Now that he was going to be a father, he was almost kind to me.

That first night there I heard the guards hollering and exclaiming about a great light in the sky and I walked out to see what the fuss was about.

"Something big's burst into flames up north," one said.

I watched the yellow glow against the dark sky. It was my house, of course. Could smell my beautiful place burn from all that way.

I rushed to the guard and called out, "That's my *home* burning. My cat's in there!" But he just walked away.

The next day, the colonel explained that the U.S. Army posthumously charged Jubal with spying and I was an accessory and, though not exempt from prosecution, I was released on bond.

Euphemia came to get me, and she drove me home in the carriage. "That was my house, wasn't it, burned last night?"

Euphemia nodded. "I was in the kitchen making myself a cup of tea. First clue I had that LeBaron's men were here, the tea in that cup started wobbling, from the horses' hooves pounding all around the house. Riding, those pattyrollers flashed across the windows, yelling about Jubal and how you chose black over white."

"Jubal's revenge, I guess." I felt nothing saying his name, like one of Fergus's empty snail shells.

"They torched the front parlor first, sent a gas bottle through the window there, and I watched Aunt Tandy Rose's portrait go up, orange flames licking the whole wall. I ran out to the kitchen, got a bucket of water, and threw it in, but it barely made a difference. Others got the far side of the house, lobbed another bottle into an upstairs window."

I held up one hand. "That's enough, Euphemia."

She turned to me, tears in her eyes. "I started up the stairs, but turned back, as the smoke was too bad. I ran out into the courtyard, coughing, as the men rode away. Ten minutes later, the upstairs caved in, and soon after the whole thing was a pile of charred ashes, smoking away, a few beams sticking up."

"Was Saint Joan in there?"

"Not sure, Anne-May. I tried to look for her, but it burned so fast."

"Thank you for trying, sister," I said, as I patted her free hand, and the horse trotted on toward home.

BATHING IN THE RIVER that afternoon, I left my hoop on the shore and waded in, the cool water cleansing. I looked up the hill, forgetting for one minute the house was gone, and watched the smoke drift in the wind from the embers. Then I dressed and made my way up to the kitchen, the only part of the house still standing, to fix myself some supper.

I stood near the stove, and considered Fergus's ring he'd given me so long before. I slid it off my finger and sent it around the handle of a wooden spoon and left it there for Euphemia. It was only right, if she was going to put up with that cross to bear.

I pawed through the boxes and cans I'd already been through, but there wasn't much food left but rice. I started water to boil and dug a tin cup into the pearly kernels and hit something hard. I dug my fingers in, touched leather, and pulled out that red Moroccan leather book.

I sat cross-legged on the floor and paged through it, thinking about Jubal and how he wanted my house so bad. Of course, Jemma'd hid the book where no one in this family'd ever go digging.

Walking through the charred remains of the house, I found some smoldering embers, set the book upon them, and they were only too happy to consume that book in flames, the smell of burning leather purifying somehow. How good to see it go up, the last evidence of my foolish actions for Jubal.

I took my bowl of cooked rice and a spoon to the whitewashed cabin down below, lit a fire best I could, cracked the door to let the smoke out, and ate my rice at the table there. As it grew dark I left my bowl on the table, climbed up to the loft, and stretched out on the bare mattress, the corn husks crackling under me.

All at once downstairs I heard spoon hit glass and my heart raced. Then came the softest sound of feet on wood approaching, and I felt a light body spring onto my chest.

It was my Joan, her taupe fur singed all over, rice on her cat breath. She walked around in a circle and set herself down on my chest, and proceeded to lick one paw.

The two of us waited together for night to come, looking out that four-paned, square window Harry'd made for Sally Smith all those months before, painted dove gray, the nails puttied well.

As the crescent moon sank in the sky, one star at its tip, I fell deep asleep, and dreamed of my beautiful brother.

Georgy

BREVOORT PLACE, NEW YORK CITY

JUNE 1864

I MARRIED FRANK BACON ON A THURSDAY EVENING AT BREVOORT Place. Frank's father, Reverend Leonard Bacon, performed the ceremony, with our cousin Theodore Dwight Woolsey, president of Yale College, assisting. Mother meant it should be as bright as plenty of June roses could make it and decorated with long garlands, and Carry and Hatty crammed every chair from the house into the front parlor. Mary's girls made flower crowns for all, and every family friend and acquaintance came, expecting strawberries and sponge cake, excepting dear Jemma, on important business with her sister.

Katharine Wormeley played "A Mighty Fortress Is Our God" as Pico sat next to her on the bench and howled along. Mary's daughters served as attendants, poised and ready to toss an abundance of rose petals onto the front parlor carpet.

Mary. Wouldn't their mother have cherished the flowers and everything so attractively arranged?

"Sing out," Mother called to Hatty. "When you sing, it's like praying twice."

"But I've forgotten the words," Hatty said.

"Just sing *watermelon* over and over again," Mother said. "No one will ever know the difference."

Abby and Jane felt the need to direct all activities, but it was a pleasant day regardless, and Abby exclaimed, "I think everyone is enjoying the wedding, even the bride herself."

Frank's parents even gifted us a key to a spacious town house in New Haven, with a whole floor to use for our nursing school.

Just as Reverend Bacon and I stood in the dining room set to emerge and face the walk down the aisle through the front parlor, Mother pressed a letter into my hands.

"I took this in dictation the night Mary left us," Mother said. "She wanted it opened on this day."

I read:

My dearest Georgy,

By now you have married Frank Bacon. I hope you don't mind too terribly much that I intervened on your behalf and told him that day at the Sanitary Fair how much you esteem him and the sentiment you felt for him was purely love and could not be mistaken for friendship of any kind and that you were only too proud to say it. He protested at first, since you are not the only stubborn one, sister, but he finally relented and promised to go immediately to yet again fetch his mother's ruby.

I swore him not to divulge my meddling, so please do not be cross with him for withholding this from you. He did so in the service of a friend and thanks to God he did, for the world nearly missed out on a couple that will change it.

Though I am far away I hope you will think of me now and then in your busy day and hold this letter close as a lasting token. And please keep a kind auntie's eye on my girls and remind them I am with them always in you and six other fine Woolsey women.

> *I will always be,*
> *Your Mary*

Wasn't it just like Mary to have sent Frank off on a mission for me, when she could have used his care so desperately?

I dried my eyes, slipped the letter into my prayer book, and we walked down the aisle, Reverend Bacon, Mary, and me.

Jemma

✳

BETHLEHEM, CONNECTICUT

JUNE 1864

I T SEEMED LIKE HALF THE TREES IN CONNECTICUT WERE WHITE with snow that spring day, with the dogwood trees in full bloom, swaying in the breeze, as Patience and I drove along in the fine carriage Georgy hired for us.

It was cold for June and we could barely stay in our skins as we rode into the little town of Bethlehem, driving past a couple of square buildings facing the town green, little gray puffs of smoke coming up from their chimneys, the Union flag swaying atop the town hall. That town made me smile inside—it was like some made-up place in a book where nothing bad ever happens. Patience and I couldn't stop smiling outside, too, since we'd heard that Maryland was about to officially end slavery. And though battles still raged, one especially bad one around Richmond, where Union attacks failed to dislodge General Lee, we were heartened by President Lincoln being nominated for a second term as president.

"Wouldn't Pa be glad to see us here," Patience said as she watched the scenery go by, like she barely believed it.

The coachman called "Whoa" to the horses and shouted "Bird Tavern" in front of a big yellow inn, up on a small rise. I opened the carriage door and breathed in the scent of June grass and honeysuckle and hope.

We gathered our wraps and I descended first and then helped Patience down the steps. I took her cold hand in mine, too struck by the moment to talk much.

"We go around to the back door?" I asked the coachman.

"Just go in that front door there, ma'am," he said with a little nod.

We made our way up the grassy hill and entered the tavern through the heavy door, into a vestibule and hallway, a bar lined with liquor bottles down the hall to the right, to the left a stone fireplace with a happy fire, the scent of pie crust and fowl in the air.

Down the hall came Ma, her eyes shining as she rushed to us.

"My girls," she said, hugging us both so hard, kissing us on our cheeks, first one, then the other, and then crying so bad we had to sit her down on a chair. They were happy tears, but all mixed up in there were tears for missing Pa and Celeste and little Toby.

Down the hall came another person.

I smiled ear to ear. "Delly."

A child trailed behind her, Kofi, our miracle baby, now high as my hip and carrying his Ma and Pa dolls, one in each arm. He was still a good smiler, from what I could tell of him hiding behind Delly's skirt.

"Remember Kofi?" Delly asked. "He's getting ready to go to school across the way." Kofi handed me the doll Patience had made in Pa's likeness. *Pa.*

Patience and I hugged and squeezed Delly, leaving her winded, as Ma came to us. "And you should see Charl in his frock coat, head of Mrs. Bellamy's horse barn over across the street."

"How did you all get here, Ma?" Patience asked. "They wouldn't tell us much."

"They're still helping folks, so it has to stay quiet for now. But old Widow Gardener and Miss Euphemia, with their people, they got Delly and Charl and the baby out first. It was them brought the knitted cap and blanket to the shack for the baby. They were talking to Delly on the sly since way back."

"We stayed at six places before we made it here, only traveling at night. Took us two months."

I turned to Ma. "So how'd you go?"

"Woolsey's friend Mrs. Gibbons worked with Euphemia for me. Left by boat down at Butcher's Dock. Late at night."

Ma held Patience tight and kissed the top of her head.

"I'd about lost my mind and started breaking things in the house, so Euphemia set me down and told me I should go, before LeBaron and his boys came after me. I waited long as I could for you, Patience, there in the woods, but had to finally go or be caught. Hardest thing I ever did, leaving you there."

"And Sally?" I asked.

"You remember Mag Palm? Sally said you met at Gettysburg—she helped Sally. Had her go down to Rock Creek to the mill and hide in the cog pit. When she finally made it up here you've never seen a happier woman, smiling at the stove, making her jelly, line out the door with people waitin' to buy it. Later, Mag wrote to Miss Euphemia at Peeler and told her Sally was safe."

"Where's Sally now?" I asked.

"We'll take you to her," Ma said.

The five of us walked, little Kofi holding my hand and Patience's, across the street and through the gate in the stone wall, then up the sloping lawn of the tall white Bellamy house.

We made our way by the house and past the big, quiet barns, through an overgrown apple orchard, to another stone wall. We stepped up and across the wooden stile and walked through the woods until little Kofi wanted to be carried and I picked him up and he rode on my hip.

"Almost there," Ma said.

We walked by a field of sunflower stalks on their way to blooming.

"What was it with so many sunflowers left around down at Peeler?" I asked.

Delly walked beside me. "Euphemia said that's an underground symbol, a sign of danger, so she and Widow Gardener would tie them anywhere we might find trouble on our route. Helped me and Charl make it down to Butcher's Dock without a hitch. Their folks picked us up there by boat."

Soon we saw a clearing up ahead, and as we neared, headstones came into view, like so many old teeth sticking up.

I let Kofi down to walk and held Patience's hand. Ma led us to a single stone, set away from the white graves, by the far edge of the woods, SALLY SMITH written there.

Ma pulled a wooden spoon from her pocket and set it on Sally's stone.

"She went peaceful. Had a fine room next to mine upstairs at the tavern, with a big window."

Delly set her spoon on the stone next to Ma's.

"You should have seen all of Bethlehem come for her breakfast at the tavern," Delly said. "Famous for her Freedom Jelly, 'made any way I please,' she said."

I whispered a little prayer over her, my granny.

We got quiet and started back to the woods on the path toward home and Patience nudged me. "Look who's here."

Nathan stood there across the way near the cemetery entrance, hat in hand.

Ma picked up Kofi. "You go on now. We'll meet you back."

Nathan and I walked toward each other and met halfway.

"How'd you get up here?" I asked.

"Horseback. To see you."

I got all shy all of a sudden and started back the way we came. "What's your plan?"

"Not sure. Been staying at the tavern a few days. My shot hand's not much better so I can't go back to much fighting *or* doctoring."

"Looks like the folks back in that big house could use a good doctor for those apple trees."

"Already talked to Mrs. Bellamy about maybe taking care of her grounds. She offered more pay than the army did."

We walked back along the forest path, old leaves crunching underfoot.

"Good to see your ma?" he asked.

I smiled up at him. "Best day ever."

"I've taken the name Gardener from good Dr. Gardener. Just to be polite, I wrote his widow and asked and she said yes."

I took up a stick and trailed it behind me in the leaves. "I took the name Strong. Patience did, too."

Nathan looked down at me, serious. "Jemma Strong." He smiled. "It suits you."

We walked back over the stile and across the meadow as the sun sank lower in the sky and the cows came back, lowing to one another in the wide barn.

"Would you ever take my name, Jemma Strong?"

I stepped along, kicking a single stone. "Jemma Strong Gardener. Has a ring to it, doesn't it, Mr. Gardener?"

I paused, chickadees singing in the meadow.

"Still getting used to being more than 'just Jemma,' though. Might need some time to think about it. Gardener will be with me forever after all."

I smiled wide as Nathan took my hand and walked me through the white gate and back toward Bird Tavern, finally free. And with everything in the world to look forward to.

Author's Note

..

IT HAS BEEN BITTERSWEET WRITING *SUNFLOWER SISTERS*, knowing it will be my last in the series about Caroline Ferriday's incredible family. I first discovered the Woolsey women in 2000 while researching Caroline's life in the archives she left at the Bellamy-Ferriday House and Garden in Bethlehem, Connecticut, which inspired my first novel, *Lilac Girls.*

Caroline cherished her Woolsey ancestry and carefully preserved the old family photos, memorabilia, and most important to this book, the Woolsey letters, which her great-aunt Eliza Woolsey Howland had so lovingly compiled.

It's hard to explain the feeling of holding the letters these women wrote over one hundred years ago. I came to recognize each sister's handwriting, and Mother Woolsey's as well, through reading their letters, filled with Civil War stories of the hospital ships, the Gettysburg battlefield, and everyday life in New York City. Sadly, many letters were destroyed in a warehouse fire, along with Mother Woolsey's household furnishings, including all of Charles Woolsey's letters from his military service, but thankfully hundreds survived. Many of the letters I have included here are reprinted verbatim, though some have been edited for length. The letter Mother Woolsey writes to the Confederate soldier Rauch's family was sent to me by a descendant of Private Rauch, and I have included it almost in its entirety.

For anyone interested in reading more of these letters, many have been beautifully reproduced in the book *My Heart Toward Home, Letters of a*

Family During the Civil War, written by Woolsey sisters Georgy and Eliza. It is a lovely companion book to *Sunflower Sisters.*

When I uncovered the fact that the sunflower was a sign of danger on the Underground Railroad, I knew I had the motif for the third book about Caroline Ferriday's family. The only other things I knew were that I wanted to tell the story from Caroline's great-aunt Georgeanna Woolsey's point of view, and from the points of view of an enslaved girl on a plantation and the mistress of that plantation.

Then I met Kathy Kane.

I was attending an event at the Bellamy-Ferriday House and Garden, and Kathy and I struck up a conversation. I told her I was starting to outline a novel about the Civil War, and Kathy shared a fascinating piece of her family history, about her great-great-grandparents, who had been enslaved on the Sotterley tobacco plantation in Maryland. Soon, Kathy sent me a wealth of information about her ancestors and assured me they would be my inspirational guides on my research journey. When my son, Michael, and I visited the former plantation, now a museum, it was incredibly moving to see Kathy's ancestors' names on the rosters of the enslaved at Sotterley, and it felt like the perfect place to set my story of Jemma and her fight for freedom.

Seeing Sotterley helped bring Jemma's world alive, and once I started writing her chapters, I chose to keep her voice relatively free from dialect. I found inspiration in the voice of Harriet A. Jacobs, whose memoir, *Incidents in the Life of a Slave Girl,* had a tremendous influence on my search to understand Jemma's life. In straightforward, beautiful prose, Harriet tells the story of her abuse at the hands of her slaveholders and how, in order to escape her abusers, she hid in a coffin-like garret, separated from her two children, for eight years. Since, in my novel, Jemma had access to books and was taught to read by Aunt Tandy Rose, I felt a similar voice was true to her character.

The scene where Jemma comes to New York City and is caught up in the Draft Riots is based on fact. During several days of rioting, the mostly Irish mob murdered eleven free black men and one child. I thought it important not to shy away from the truth of this horrific time, a reminder of how important it is to remember and confront our past and learn from it. Dr. James McCune Smith, whom Jemma meets at the orphan asylum, was the first black apothecary in New York City and the director of the asylum. He was also the first African American ever to hold a medical degree, graduating at the top of his class from the University of Glasgow.

Nathan Gardener's Brooklyn home, Weeksville, is based on the real place. In the 1860s, Weeksville had more than five hundred residents and was remarkable for the time, for it boasted its own churches, school, cemetery, old age home, and one of the first African American newspapers, *The Freedman's Torchlight.* It was the home of New York City's first Black principal, Sarah J. Tompkins Garnet, and during the New York Draft Riots of 1863, the community served as a refuge for many African Americans who fled the violence. After the completion of the Brooklyn Bridge and as New York City grew and expanded, Weeksville gradually became part of Crown Heights, and memory of the village was largely forgotten, but the Heritage Foundation has beautifully preserved a portion of the original town so visitors can still experience Weeksville today. You can learn more about it at weeksvillesociety.org.

Anne-May Watson is a fictitious character based on years of research about plantation mistresses of the day, and as I do with all my characters, I tried to make her flawed yet real. I made every effort to show the brutal reality of the cruelty inflicted by slave owners and wanted to show day-to-day life on a plantation as accurately as possible. I lived in Atlanta for eight years and spent much of that time visiting former plantations, now museums, and wove the history from that research into Peeler Plantation.

I patterned Anne-May's house on the main house at Sotterley, built in 1703, and it was helpful in bringing the world of a plantation mistress alive. The most moving thing about visiting Sotterley was seeing the Patuxent River from the front parlor windows and knowing that a slaver's ship, *Generous Jenny,* arrived on that very shore in 1720 and sold African captives from the deck of the ship anchored there. But what captivated me most stood down the hill from the main house: the renovated cabin once crowded with enslaved tobacco workers. It was chilling to think of them sleeping on corn-husk mattresses in that one-room house in winter, the small fireplace providing scant heat as the cold wind blew off the Maryland coast, while a handful of white owners slept on feather beds in the warm house above.

It's hard not to love the Woolsey women, strong and determined. As Jane Stuart Woolsey wrote in her book, *Hospital Days, Reminiscence of a Civil War Nurse,* "When the members of the Woolsey family gave up toys, they took up politics. Brought up by a mother who hated slavery, although her ancestors for generations had been Virginia slave-holders, they walked with her in the straight path of abolitionism."

One of seven children, Jane Eliza Newton Woolsey, the matriarch of the Woolsey family, was raised in her Scotch-Irish Presbyterian family until she lost her mother to disease at fourteen and went to live with her beloved Aunt Ricketts on a farm in Fairfax, Virginia. Living in a slaveholding family deeply affected Jane Eliza and inspired her to spend her life fighting slavery and supporting the famous abolitionist preachers of her time. The opening scene where the Woolsey women visit the slave market in Charleston, South Carolina, and meet an enslaved woman whose children are sold, is based on a true account found in Woolsey letters. For anyone visiting the mart today, now a museum and testament to the horrors of slavery, it is impossible not to be moved by the artifacts collected there.

Jane Eliza first met Charles William Woolsey, descended from a family with *Mayflower* lineage, when she passed him on the street on a trip to New York City, and it was love at first sight for both. They married and moved to Boston, had seven children, all girls, but then tragedy visited the happy family, as Mr. Woolsey died at sea while traveling home from New York City on the steamer *Lexington.* It was a dark time for the family and Mrs. Woolsey, pregnant with her eighth child, a son, moved her family to New York City to be near her husband's family, and they took up residence at 8 Brevoort Place, in what is today Greenwich Village.

All eight Woolsey children contributed a great deal to society at the time.

Abby, Jane, and Georgy were leaders in the evolution of the field of nursing and in the establishment of a system of professional training after the war. Abby sat on the boards of hospitals and charities for years and on the board of managers of Bellevue Training School of Nursing, which provided a model of nursing instruction. She wrote several hospital handbooks and supported women nurses for the rest of her life, and died in 1893 at sixty-five.

Jane Stuart Woolsey continued her nursing career after the Civil War ended and then taught at the Freedmen's Union Industrial School in Richmond, Virginia, working to help the formerly enslaved workers acquire sewing skills and literacy. She then wrote her memoir, *Hospital Days,* telling her story with great wit and honesty; it is another wonderful companion book to *Sunflower Sisters.* Toward the end of her life Jane suffered from rheumatic fever, and was cared for by her sister Abby until her death in 1891.

I chose to tell the Woolsey part of the story from the point of view of Georgeanna Muirson Woolsey because I fell in love with her straightforward, self-deprecating voice in her letters, and admired her great compassion and her accomplishments in the new field of nursing. She dealt with the multitudes of wounded with aplomb and adapted quickly to her army assignments both on the hospital ships and on land, all under the unrelenting abuse of U.S. Army doctors. In one letter in 1864, Georgy wrote,

> No one knows, who did not watch the thing from the beginning, how much opposition, how much ill-will, how much unfeeling want of thought these women nurses endured. Hardly a surgeon whom I can think of, received or treated them with even common courtesy . . . determined to make their lives so unbearable that they should be forced in self-defense to leave.

Georgy continued to nurse soldiers until the war's end when General Lee surrendered at the McLean House at Appomattox on April 9, 1865. On the last day of the war the Woolseys decorated 8 Brevoort Place inside and out with patriotic colors, a flag over the front door and colored lanterns on the balcony.

The Woolseys' elation and celebration was soon cut short when President Lincoln was shot on April 14, 1865, and died the following day.

Georgy on hearing the news ran to Carry's bedroom door and cried, "Let me in! Mr. Lincoln has been murdered!" Carry wrote the next day to Eliza, "We are all dumb with grief! What a moment for America!"

One doctor Georgy did end up getting along with was her longtime suitor and friend, Dr. Frank Bacon, whom she married in 1866. After the war, the couple moved to New Haven, where Dr. Bacon embarked on a distinguished career as a professor of surgery at the Yale Medical School, and Georgy and he helped found the Connecticut Training School for Nurses, her dream finally realized. She wrote a manual for nurses, *A Handbook of Nursing for Family and General Use,* and her book *Three Weeks at Gettysburg,* the account of her time at Gettysburg with her mother, continued to be widely read.

Georgy and Frank never had children, and Georgy threw her energy into the Connecticut Children's Aid Society, the Newington Hospital for Crippled Children, and Playridge, the retreat home for children she and Frank Bacon built in Woodmont, Connecticut. Georgy hung Frank's Civil War sword, a pistol, and two knives captured at the First Battle of Bull Run in the front hall of their redbrick home at 32 High Street in New Haven, and a shell that had been used to capture Tybee Island decorated the newel post. Georgy died in 1906. Although Frank Bacon lived until 1912, family members noted, "After Georgy's death, he lost interest in life and grew much older."

Mary Elizabeth Watts Woolsey Howland, "My Mary" to Georgy, died of a sudden illness in 1864. Mother of four daughters and devoted wife to Reverend Robert Howland, Mary was a talented painter and accomplished poet, though in her lifetime her literary gift was kept from the public because of her gender. In 1862, Mary wrote the poem "A Rainy Day at Camp" from the point of view of a soldier on his deathbed contemplating his mortality, which the Woolsey family privately printed and distributed. Newspapers soon picked up the poem and it became enormously popular with the troops, who sent copies home to their families, unaware it had been written by Mary. The Woolseys kept up the illusion, thinking it best to let the thousands of families believe a man had written the poem. Mary went on to write several more popular poems and died never having divulged her secret.

Eliza Newton Woolsey Howland, Georgy's best friend and younger sister by two years, and her nursing partner early in the war, spent the postwar years helping her husband, Joseph Howland, recover from wounds he'd received at the Battle of Gaines's Mill. They lived out their years at their Fishkill, New York, home, Tioronda, engaged in community philanthropy. Eliza took on the role of family historian, writing the *Woolsey Family Records*. She died in 1917 and Tioronda still stands in Fishkill today.

Harriet Roosevelt Woolsey, "Hatty," got married in 1869 to her cousin Dr. Hugh Lenox Hodge, a surgeon who taught at the University of Pennsylvania Medical School. The couple had two children, Hugh, who survived to adulthood, and Jane Eliza, who died at birth. Hatty died in 1878.

The youngest sister, Caroline Carson Woolsey, known as Carry, Caroline Ferriday's beloved grandmother, married Edward Mitchell and they had one child, Eliza Mitchell Ferriday. Carry met Edward, who became a highly respected lawyer after the war, through her sister Georgy, who had met Edward while he was working as a young supply administrator on board the hospital ships. He had taken ill and Georgy helped him recover and sent him home to New York City, where Carry picked up the relationship.

Carry not only worked in New York hospitals during the war, she dedicated herself to the children of the Colored Orphan Asylum, which was a casualty of the Draft Riots. Though all the children escaped death the night their home burned, they were displaced for months and the incident is a permanent stain on the mostly Irish mobs who looted and burned their home. Carry also supported the New York Orphan Asylum. Started in 1806 by a group of caring women, including Elizabeth Hamilton, wife of Alexander Hamilton, the New York asylum was first housed in a wood-frame home in Greenwich Village and was one of the first charities run by an all-female board and fully operated by women. It was moved to a new home in 1837, to what was then a bucolic, rural area considered far north of the city, what is now Seventy-third Street and Riverside Drive. Carry supported the asylum and its residents, referred to as "Carry's Bloomingdale orphans" in the Woolsey letters, until her death in 1914. The organization evolved to become Graham Windham, which continues to work at improving the lives of children in care today.

The Woolseys' only son, Charles William Woolsey, served with distinction during the Civil War. Though his letters home during this period were lost, we know he served as assistant to General Meade in the Army of the Potomac, and was wounded slightly at Gettysburg, which caused Georgy and Mrs. Woolsey to hurry to the battlefront there, fearing the worst, only to find Charley recovered and off with his regiment.

Charley was present when General Lee surrendered his Army of Northern Virginia to Ulysses S. Grant near Appomattox Court House in Virginia in 1865, which gave his family great pride. Charles married Arixene Southgate Smith in 1868 and moved to Asheville, North Carolina, later in life, due to health concerns. He had three children, but only his daughter Alice lived to adulthood. He died in 1907.

All the historical events in the Georgy chapters are drawn from the Woolsey family letters. Georgy's quest to become a nurse, her time with Eliza in Washington and on the hospital ships, and her experiences at Gettysburg and at the Sanitary Fair are all based on firsthand accounts.

I spent weeks at Gettysburg, tracing the steps of Mother Woolsey and Georgy, re-creating their three weeks there, when they first nursed soldiers at the train depot across from what would become Camp Letterman, the famous hospital where hundreds of Civil War soldiers, Confederate and U.S. Army, were tended. Glen Hayes of the Gettysburg Battlefield Preservation Association was invaluable in re-creating those steps. Today the GBPA is fighting to save a part of Camp Letterman General Hospital, and as of the writing of this book their Camp Letterman Committee has been fighting, with tremendous help from the public, for fifteen years to save the site from development. For more information, go to https://www.gbpa.org.

The Battle of Front Royal, where Harry Wilson is killed and Fergus Watson loses his leg, was also based on a real battle, which took place on May 23, 1862, when the Confederate First Maryland Infantry fought their fellow Marylanders, the Union First Regiment Maryland Volunteer Infantry. This is the only time in U.S. military history that two regiments of the same state and numerical designation have engaged each other in battle.

The Thirty-sixth U.S. Colored Infantry, which comes to rescue Jemma and Patience, was organized on February 8, 1864, under the command of Colonel Alonzo G. Draper. They served at Point Lookout guarding Confederate prisoners until they were sent into active duty, fighting at the Battle of Chaffin's Farm, the Battle of Fair Oaks, and others. The Thirty-sixth also fought at the Occupation of Richmond and helped the Union capture the Rebel capital of Richmond, Virginia, the most significant sign that the Confederacy was nearing its final days. Private James Daniel Gardner and Corporal Miles James, both of the Thirty-sixth, received the Medal of Honor, the United States of America's highest and most-prestigious personal military decoration, for acts of valor at the Battle of Chaffin's Farm.

I have included visits from a few historical figures of the time—President Abraham Lincoln, Secretary of War Edwin Stanton, Abigail Hopper Gibbons, Frederick Law Olmsted, and others—since I came upon them in the pages of the Woolseys' letters and they were part of their world. Georgy and Eliza did meet Lincoln at the Executive Mansion and Georgy did seek his help with securing chaplains for the troops and he granted that help. Henry Rauch, the young Confederate soldier from South Carolina, appears in the Woolsey letters as well, and died in the loving care of Mrs. Woolsey, in his brother's arms. The character Mag Palm, the woman who helps Sally Smith at Gettysburg, was based on a real person as well. Mag lived close to the Gettysburg battlefield, and after discovering her story while researching I fell in love with her strength and tenacity and thought she deserved to be remembered.

I stopped by the Bellamy-Ferriday Cemetery the first day I visited Caroline's house, back in 2000. Surrounded by Bellamy Land Trust land, it's a short walk from Caroline's house and is a typical place of rest for the time, bearing the graves of Bethlehem residents from the 1700s and beyond. Reverend Bellamy, who built Caroline's house, is buried there along with many other former inhabitants of Bethlehem. A woman named Sally Smith is buried there as well, but her grave is set apart from those of the white townspeople. My curiosity stirred, I searched for her story, but could not find a trace. The fact that even in death Sally was not included haunted me, and drove me to honor her life. Her headstone, origins lost to history, inspired the fictionalized Sally Smith.

Bird Tavern, which stands on a rise across the street from Caroline's house, was once a stop on the Underground Railroad. I knew the first time I saw the lovely old building on the Bethlehem village green that I would include it if I wrote a Civil War book one day. It seems the perfect place to end this trilogy, for Caroline Ferriday was a staunch supporter of civil rights. I think Caroline would be happy to know her abolitionist Woolsey ancestors' stories, and the stories of those they helped become free, are finally told.

Note on Sources

..

THERE ARE VARIOUS LETTERS AND POEMS FROM OR ADDRESSED to the Woolsey sisters throughout the novel, reprinted with permission from the Bellamy-Ferriday House & Garden Archives in Bethlehem, Connecticut, owned and operated by Connecticut Landmarks, unless otherwise noted.

Howland, Joseph. Letter to Eliza Woolsey Howland. July 21, 1861.

Howland, Mary Woolsey. Poem "A Rainy Day at Camp."

Howland, Eliza Woolsey. Letter to Joseph Howland. April 28, 1862.

Woolsey, Georgeanna. Letter to Jane Eliza Woolsey. June 28, 1862.

Woolsey, Abigail. Letter to Georgeanna Woolsey. July 11, 1862.

Woolsey, Jane. Letter to a friend. October 1862.

Woolsey, Jane Eliza. Letter to Reverend Rauch. From the private collection of Jene Klopp.

Crane, C. H. Letter to Surgeon Heger. September 26, 1863.

Woolsey, Eliza. Letter to Jane and Georgy. March 9, 1864.

Howland, Mary Woolsey. Poem "Taps."

Acknowledgments

..

I OWE SO MUCH TO THOSE WHO HELPED MAKE WRITING *SUNFLOWER Sisters* so rewarding: To my husband, Michael Kelly, who read every draft and so generously shared his deep Civil War wisdom and plot whispering. Thank you for sharing my dream of finishing Caroline Ferriday's family story, and for supporting everything I do with unflagging enthusiasm and love and for keeping us all so gloriously well fed. To my daughter Katherine, aka Kay, for sharing long walks and for imparting her supreme wit, worldly wisdom, and honest manuscript advice. To my daughter Mary Elizabeth, for her expert editorial suggestions, willingness to drop everything and read new chapters, and for working to create real change in the world, so long overdue. I couldn't have asked for two lovelier and more inspiring daughters. You're both there in the pages of this book, in the Woolsey sisters, more than you know. To my son, Michael, for his manuscript advice, book trailer skills, expert road-trip companionship, and, through his kindness and compassion, inspiring the character of Anne-May's brother, Harry Wilson. May we never stop traveling together. To my son-in law, Chase, for being a lovely addition to the family and for his superb scrambled eggs and for telling me about Moneysunk Road.

To Kara Cesare at Ballantine Bantam Dell, the most caring, talented editor a person could wish for, generous in every way, who first recognized Caroline Ferriday as a woman who needed to be remembered. Thank you for embracing the Woolsey women's stories with supreme care and grace and for so steadfastly having my back when I try new things. To all of "Team Sunflower" at Ballantine Bantam Dell for their seamless collaboration and boundless enthusiasm: Debbie Aroff, Barbara Bachman, Susan

Corcoran, Melanie DeNardo, Jennifer Hershey, Kim Hovey, Colleen Nuccio, Paolo Pepe, Kara Welsh, Gina Centrello, and Benjamin Dreyer and the whole copyediting team at Random House, to name a few. To my literary agent, Alexandra Machinist, who never ceases to amaze me with her unflagging support and spot-on advice, and who once upon a time plucked me from the slush pile, insisted these stories needed to be told, and made it happen. You are a brilliant force of nature.

To Kathy Kane, who shared the stories of her enslaved Kane ancestors and suggested I go to Sotterley Plantation and learn more about them. I'm so glad the universe brought us together that day. To Tiffany Smith, who so generously shared her struggles as a Black American today and read the manuscript, rough as it was at first. Thank you for your friendship and honesty. To Kathy Murray, who has helped me know there's nothing I can say to bridge the yawning gap between my experience and that of a Black woman, but that we can be allies to create real change.

To my sister Polly Simpkins, who models generosity and unconditional love, making the world a better place every day, and to her husband, Brad Simpkins, for his bottomless love and support. And to my sister Sally Hatcher, who first taught me that cats deserve to be loved as much as dogs and is still the best big sister. To my mother-in-law, Mariann, the strongest woman I know, and five sisters-in-law for their unending support and for bringing the whole clan to book events and showing me how important a loving, encouraging family can be. To my cousins Juanita Fowler, Patty Hill, Peggy Quinn, and Jane Huth, whose charming personas I drew upon to help create the Woolsey women and who have always served as proof that old-fashioned traits like honesty and loyalty never go out of style. To my cousin Wylie Savanas Quinn III who once served as organist and choirmaster at the Chapel of the Cross in Chapel Hill, North Carolina, whose suggestion to "Simply repeat the word *watermelon* if you forget the words to a song" was memorable advice.

To Glen Hayes of the Gettysburg Battlefield Preservation Association, who has been invaluable in keeping the military parts of this book accurate. Thank you for the countless time you spent reading the battle-focused chapters of *Sunflower Sisters,* offering corrections and suggestions, all out of kindness and a love for Civil War history. May you have great success in your quest to help preserve a piece of Camp Letterman at Gettysburg. More information about Glen's work can be found at https://www.gbpa .org. To Jene Klopp, who sent me a copy of the letter Mrs. Woolsey wrote to her great-great-grandfather Reverend Rauch, father of the young Confederate soldier from South Carolina whom Jane Eliza so tenderly cared for. I'm so moved each time I read it and it's one of my favorite stories connected with the book. I'm eternally grateful to you, Jene, for sharing such a meaningful family letter. I hope it offers people a better understanding of what it's like to offer kindness and mercy to those who happen to be fighting on opposite sides from us. To the Atlanta History Museum and its director, Kate Whitman, and to Joanna and Keith for giving me a behind-the-scenes tour of that incredible museum and opening the archives and sharing so many Civil War treasures to make the period come alive. A special thanks to Keith for playing his Civil War drum so authentically to the period it made me cry. To Heritage House in Madison, Georgia, for the incredible tour, where I learned that newly engaged Civil War–era ladies etched their names with their diamond rings on windowpanes to test whether or not their diamonds were real.

To the late, much-missed Alexander Neave, Caroline Ferriday's cousin, and his wife, Lynne, who so generously shared Caroline's family papers and photos and their memories of her. To Richard Furniss, who provided a fabulous tour of his antique gun collection. To the staff of Connecticut Landmarks, including the wonderful and tirelessly dedicated Peg Shimer, site administrator of the Bellamy-Ferriday House and Garden, and Jamie-Lynn Fontaine Connell, Robert Brock, and Jana Colacino, for taking such good care of Caroline's beloved home. To the brilliant and tireless Bellamy-Ferriday House and Garden tour guides: Gary P. Cicognani, Natalie De-Quarto, Muffy Barhydt, and Timothy Marcinek, and gardener Brett Bitner. Thank you for your hours of service and for making the house come alive so beautifully for visitors. Caroline and her ancestors would be proud. To the divine and immensely talented Betty Kelly Sargent, for her early encouragement and expertise, and who said, "All I need is a chapter," about *Lilac Girls*. Without her none of this would have come close to happening. To Susan Klein, freelance copyeditor extraordinaire, who brings a rough draft to heel like no other. To Elaine Hayes at the Fishkill Historical Society for her research help. To the St. Mary's County Historical Society's Peter LaPorte, Carol Moody, and Karen Wood for information about that fascinating county where my fictional Peeler Plantation stood.

To the wonderful independent booksellers and librarians everywhere who worked so hard to get this family's story into the hands of readers, including Fran Keilty at the Hickory Stick Bookstore in Washington Depot, Connecticut, for going the extra mile. To Madison Garner, Grace Hough, Morgan Burke, and Lauren Burke for being the best focus group ever. To Sophie Baker at Curtis Brown London for fifty incredible foreign editions of *Lilac Girls* and *Lost Roses*. To Shirl Knobloch and her husband for inviting me to their lovely Gettysburg home and for sharing her wonderful books along with her glorious period house and gardens. To Gary Parkes, my not-so-secret weapon, who keeps my social media up-to-date and fabulous. To the Old Bethlehem Historical Society, and Carol Ann Brown, keeper of Bethlehem's lovely past. To Mary Jane LaBoudy and the Old Bethlehem Burial Grounds Board for partnering with me to maintain the historic cemetery where Sally Smith and Reverend Bellamy rest. And to Stewart Rabinowitz for his friendship and for his hard work helping Caroline Ferriday's Land Trust thrive.

SUNFLOWER SISTERS

A Novel

MARTHA HALL KELLY

A BOOK CLUB

GUIDE

LETTER FROM
THE AUTHOR

Dear Readers,

It has been such a wild and wonderful journey writing *Lilac Girls* and *Lost Roses,* and finally being able to share *Sunflower Sisters* with you is a new treasured moment for me. Thank you for all the support you've shown along the way. Your outpouring of heartfelt messages and stories shared has been one of the best things about writing these books and I'm grateful for it every day.

Since that fated gray Mother's Day back in 2000 when I visited Caroline Ferriday's former home, now the Bellamy-Ferriday House and Garden, I knew I wanted to tell the world about her Woolsey ancestors eventually.

As I combed through Caroline's archives while researching *Lilac Girls,* it was hard not to be inspired by her great grandmother, Jane Eliza, and her eight accomplished children. I found hundreds of their letters to one another, beautifully boxed and preserved—along with photos, trinkets, and mementoes. Over time I read every one, each a work of art, written in their lovely penmanship, and a portrait of an incredible family emerged. Living with the Woolsey women and researching their lives, including their abolitionist, pro-Lincoln work, was a joy. They were principled and hardworking, but with a sense of humor about themselves, and I grew to feel like I knew each one of them and saw where Caroline drew her deep love of helping others. I wanted to write a story that showcased the depth of the Woolseys' devotion to one another and the gifts they gave our country, somehow lost to time.

Like *Lilac Girls* and *Lost Roses, Sunflower Sisters* tells that story through the eyes of three women, this time making their way through the American Civil War. It's a story still so remarkably relevant—of a country torn in half by the brutality of slavery, and how women find love and survive terrible hardship, even when posed with heartbreaking challenges and choices.

If *Sunflower Sisters* resonates with you, I hope you'll recommend it to your friends and fellow readers. Your support means the world to me.

All the best,
Martha

P.S. If you want to know more about *Lilac Girls, Lost Roses,* and *Sunflower Sisters,* please visit marthahallkelly.com, and by all means drop me a line there and tell me what you thought of the books. I'd love to hear from you!

QUESTIONS AND TOPICS
FOR DISCUSSION

1. Evaluate the treatment and role of women in the novel. Discuss the various types of power (or lack of) that Georgy, Jemma, and Anne-May experience. What provides, or denies, each of them access to forms of expression?

2. How might your interpretation of the book differ if the author had chosen to tell the story from a single point of view?

3. Jemma and her sister Patience communicate secretly through letters. What did you think about their story of survival and escaping the brutality of slavery under the cruel Anne-May? How did Jemma, Sable, and Joseph continue their relentless pursuit of self and freedom in the face of such a brutal system?

4. Have women's achievements in history been lost or overlooked? What do you think it takes to be a pioneer today?

5. Has your understanding of slavery been changed by reading *Sunflower Sisters*? What did you learn about it that you didn't know before? *Sunflower Sisters* takes the reader back to the roots of racism and a time of deep division in America. How has slavery left its mark in American life? To what extent has the wound been healed, if at all?

6. Are there ways in which Martha Hall Kelly's novel can help us see our own lives differently? How is this story relevant for us today?

7. The bonds of family—real or self-made—play an important role in the novel, inspiring and stymying the three characters at different points

along their journeys. How does each character view family? What about their traits and histories make them feel that way?

8.   All three women lost their fathers tragically; however, these losses draw Jemma and Georgy even closer to their families and force them to appreciate them more, whereas Anne-May never felt close to her sister and mother. How do you think tragedy shapes us? How do you think hardships shaped the several characters in the novel?

9.   The novel is set during the American Civil War, a turbulent time in history. What did you learn about this time period that you didn't know before? Was there something that surprised you about the role and treatment of women?

10.   Georgy and her family play a large role in society and yet each has an innate calling to help others. What do you think about the trajectory of Georgy's life and the choices she made?

11.   What did you think of Georgy's sisters and brother?

12.   Was it unfair Mary Woolsey never received recognition for her work? Should her family have broken with tradition and revealed her as the author or was it better to let people think the poems were written by a man?

13.   Anne-May was secretly working as a spy with Jubal. Were you surprised by anything in her storyline? What about her choices at the end?

14.   Sally Smith was not Jemma's blood relative, but in many ways she ended up feeling like one. Why do some unrelated relationships turn out stronger than blood ones?

15.   Sunflowers were used to indicate danger on the Underground Railroad. What is the effect of using something so bright and beautiful as a symbol like this?

16.   Martha Hall Kelly weaves real-life letters from the Woolsey sisters into the narrative, and while Georgy is based on the Ferriday family's ancestors, the character of Anne-May is fictional. What is the effect of weaving together history and fiction? Why do you think the author chose to include some of these letters verbatim?

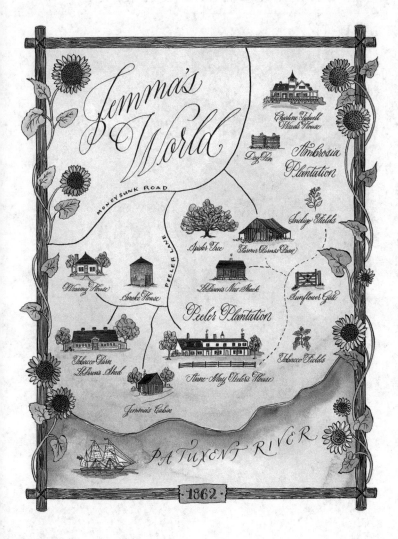

Jemma's World

Charlene Tidwell Weeds House

Ambrosia Plantation

Dog Pen

MONEYSUNK ROAD

PEELER LANE

Spider Tree

Farmer Burns Barn

Indigo Fields

Weaving House

Smoke House

St. Lawrence Men Shack

Sunflower Gate

Peeler Plantation

Tobacco Barn
St. Lawrence Shed

Anne-May Peeler's House

Tobacco Fields

Jemma's Cabin

PATUXENT RIVER

· 1862 ·

THE WOOLSEY FAMILY

*Jane Eliza Woolsey
(Mother)*

Mr. Woolsey

Abigail

Jane

Mary

Eliza

Georgy

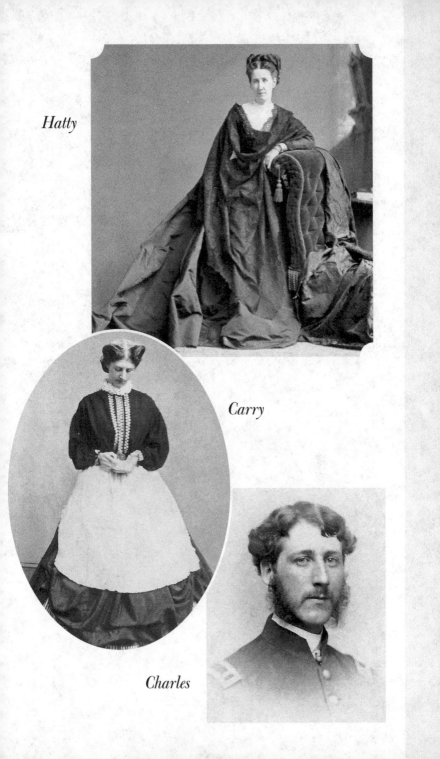

Hatty

Carry

Charles

PHOTO: © JEFFREY MOSIER PHOTOGRAPHY

MARTHA HALL KELLY is the *New York Times* bestselling author of *Lilac Girls, Lost Roses,* and *Sunflower Sisters.* She lives in Connecticut with her husband, Michael, and exceptional dog, Oliver, where she spends her days filling legal pads with scenes and trying to tell stories that will help make the world a better place. *Sunflower Sisters* is her third novel.

For photos of the Woolseys and more information behind the true story go to: marthahallkelly.com

Also find Martha on: Facebook.com/marthahallkelly

Twitter: @marthahallkelly

Instagram: @marthahallkelly1